The Last Laugh

The Last Laugh

Marie-Anne Taylor

VANTAGE PRESS
New York

FIRST EDITION

All rights reserved, including the right of
reproduction in whole or in part in any form.

Copyright © 1992 by Marie-Anne Taylor

Published by Vantage Press, Inc.
516 West 34th Street, New York, New York 10001

Manufactured in the United States of America
ISBN: 0-533-10110-7

Library of Congress Catalog Card No.: 91-91325

0 9 8 7 6 5 4 3 2 1

To Thompson Taylor, Emilie Taylor,
Joseph R. Proulx, and Rose St-Andre

Contents

One. Going On	1
Two. A Favor	9
Three. Alexandre	17
Four. Some Background	22
Five. Coming to America	27
Six. Meeting the Priest	30
Seven. A New Life	37
Eight. Settling Down	43
Nine. Memories	50
Ten. The Party	55
Eleven. Sorrowing Together	61
Twelve. Samuel	68
Thirteen. "Getting Along"	71
Fourteen. Simone	83
Fifteen. Simone's Sense of Humor	89
Sixteen. Family Talk	96
Seventeen. Discussion?	102
Eighteen. Togetherness	111
Nineteen. Isaac	120
Twenty. Going Home	124
Twenty-one. The Empty Nest	129
Twenty-two. The Parting of the Ways	134
Twenty-three. A Meeting of the Minds	144
Twenty-four. The Train Ride	147
Twenty-five. No School?	155
Twenty-six. Learning	163
Twenty-seven. New Friends	169
Twenty-eight. Years Later	176
Twenty-nine. Regrets	184
Thirty. The Meeting	190
Thirty-one. Falling in Love	197
Thirty-two. The Beatings	203
Thirty-three. Slow Recovery	213

Thirty-four. A New Life	221
Thirty-five. Alexandre and Philippe	225
Thirty-six. The Last Laugh	234

The Last Laugh

Chapter One
Going On

What do you say about an old man anyway? Do you speak about his experiences in life? Do you talk about his wrinkled skin or eyes that have become dim with time? Do we mention only the good things or dwell on the bad? No, I don't think so; then the whole thing becomes biased.

"Alexandre Boisvert." She spoke only to herself, as there was no one else sitting in the small office with her.

"Alexandre Boisvert." She repeated it again as though she were caressing the name.

Tears began to stream down her face, and she became annoyed with herself. She reached for a tissue that was in a box near to where she was sitting. She dabbed at her eyes and wiped her nose as though she were not even conscious of what she was doing. It was one of those unconscious movements that we learn in life and do without ever really being aware that we do them.

She sat at her typewriter with her hands poised, ready and willing to type when the inspiration came to her.

She was young, only thirty-four; but as you looked upon her, you quickly realized that her life had not been a bed of roses. She was not very tall, probably stood at about five feet, four inches tall, was very slender and had never weighed over one hundred and ten pounds in her entire life. I suppose it could be said that she was a wiry person. She was a beautiful woman and then again, she was not, not if you think of beauty as that of a movie star or that of an emaciated model. Her beauty was that of reality. She had very prominent cheekbones, almost as though she could be of Indian origin. Her hair was a dark chestnut color and shone all the time, as though it were polished. The most outstanding of all her features were her eyes, which even in her moments of sadness shone like the North Star itself.

The stories were told that even as a baby, if she smiled, the whole room would light up.

Harold had talked her into this. "Honey," he said to her last night as they were preparing for bed, "seeing that it is so difficult for you to talk about, it might help if you wrote it all down."

"Harold, you know that I am not a writer; I am a pianist."

"You will never know if you don't try."

She looked at her husband through the mirror on her dresser. *He is sort of handsome in his own way,* she thought. *Anyway, he suits me just fine.*

She smiled at this skinny, gangly, redheaded man with freckles all over his face, hands, and back. *He suits me just fine, and as long as I suit him, we're all set.*

He ducked as she threw her pillow at him. "You and your man's logic!" *He's never steered me wrong yet—I'll give it a try.*

There she sat, musing all by herself. *That is how I got into this. I guess I'd better get started. I've never written a book before. How do I go about it? Do I go about it chronologically or as I recall things? One life, one story, how trite and how corny it all sounds. I know that it's true, though. I really hope that I am doing the right thing, and that I do justice to Grand-père's life story.*

Well, there is one consolation in all of this. I am keeping a solemn promise that I made to Grand-père a long time ago. I wonder if that will be any consolation at all? I must go through with it, if only to keep my promise. What else can I do?

She sat in the simple little office that had once belonged to Grand-père and seemed oblivious to her surroundings. Everything seemed a big blur in her mind; nothing seemed to have any distinction at all. Everything was a big mass of confusion.

Is it all real, she thought, *or am I product of my own imagination? Is it fantasy?*

The afternoon was soft and pleasant. The sun made diamondlike sparkles wherever it landed. Genevieve was preoccupied as she watched the sunlight play its childish games, skipping to and fro over the snow-sparkled farmland.

"Alexandre Boisvert." Now she spoke the name reverently. "Alexandre Boisvert, who was he anyway?"

I think that I will write it as I remember it. Thus, having made her decision, she quickly placed a sheet of paper in the typewriter and began to type away.

"Alexandre Boisvert," she typed, "a Man." Sitting way back on her chair she looked at what she had typed. She nodded her head. *Yes, I like that.*

She gazed out the window. *What a difference in the weather compared to last week when we laid him to rest.* She had observed his wishes and not made a great big fuss over his last days or his departure from this earth.

"Was it only a week ago?" she asked herself. "It seems like a lifetime ago at least."

Alexandre was now ninety-two years of age, or as he was fond of saying, ninety-two years past.

He was fragile now, a shadow of his former self. His flesh hung upon him with the looseness of the elephant's skin. His eyes were sunken much deeper in his skull now and sometimes they appeared unaware of things, which was so unlike him. He was very unsteady on his feet, and even when he used his cane, he needed further assistance.

Genevieve had become worried because for the past several days he had not done anything but sit around or sleep, so she called his old and dear friend, Dr. Livernois.

"There is nothing we can do except to keep him comfortable. He is suffering the infirmities of old age."

"But . . . but, surely, there is something you can do?" Genevieve asked him.

Dr. Livernois looked intently into her eyes. "The ravages of time have taken their toll."

Genevieve moved her gaze from the doctor's eyes and hung her head down. She tried as best she could, but she could not stem the flow of tears. He took her hand in one of his bearlike paws and patted her hand as gently as he could. "My dear young lady, you must remember, he is not a child. He has lasted much longer than anyone could have hoped for. The plain fact is that his body has worn out.

"Genevieve," he said sternly, "in all the years I have known you, I have never seen you act weak. Why are you starting now? He needs you to be strong now more than ever."

"I'm sorry, Uncle Joseph. I can't picture my life without him. I know that I am being selfish. You and Anna love him as much as I do."

"Don't be too hard on yourself, my dear; we all feel the same way. Go and freshen yourself up, and I will visit with him for a while."

Genevieve walked over to where Anna, their rotund little housekeeper, was sitting and flung her arms around her, and the two women cried as though their hearts were broken, never to mend again.

Anna sat up and wiped her eyes and Genevieve's eyes and said, "What foolish women we are. What silly geese we are. We should be enjoying the time we *do* have left with him. There will be enough time for tears later on, eh?"

Genevieve smiled one of her thin smiles. "Yes, Anna, of course you are right."

Anna began to put her apron on and busy herself about. Genevieve looked up and said softly, "Anna."

Anna turned from the refrigerator where she was taking vegetables out to make some of her good homemade soup for Alexandre; this was all he ate in the evenings now.

"Yes." She waited impatiently, as she was the type of person that once she had made up her mind to do something, did it at once.

Genevieve hesitated for a moment. "I was wondering if I have ever told you how much you remind me of Grand-mère."

The older woman's eyes filled with tears once again, and she went over to Genevieve and gave her a resounding kiss on the cheek. "That is the nicest thing you have ever said to me."

"Anna," Genevieve said, "there is something that I want you to know."

Anna was really paying attention now. "And what is that?"

Genevieve's voice was faltering now. "This is your home, Anna, forever, as much as it is mine. We are a family, and as Grand-père always says, families stick together, right?"

Anna's voice was filled with emotion, and her "yes" was hardly audible.

Many years ago, Alexandre had given Anna the responsibility of the house and of the kitchen, and it was clearly her domain and no one ever interfered with her rule. Not that there was ever any need to.

Supper, as always, was served in the large dining room. Anna felt that the evening meal was family time, and she served everything very formally because she knew that it pleased the old man. They all sat around the dinner table. Grand-père was in his usual place at the head of the table. He was dressed, as was his custom at the dinner table, with a clean shirt, tie, and dinner jacket. He always insisted that everyone at his table dress for supper. It always irked him that people would dress up for strangers or to go out in public, but they would not do it for their loved ones.

It had taken both Dr. Livernois and Harold to get him dressed tonight. Harold had tried to tell him that it would not matter this once if he did not change for supper.

"Young man," he shook his finger in Harold's face, "I'll have you know that my granddaughter will never see me helpless or hopeless either."

Harold looked up and saw Dr. Livernois shaking his head at him, so he silently helped the old man. *Boy, this old buzzard's got the guts,* he thought. *He looks like he's going to die any moment!*

The old man fell across the bed and would have fallen to the floor if Harold had not caught him in his strong arms. "Let me rest for a moment, and I will be all right. Please leave me alone for a moment."

The two men looked at each other and silently left the room. When they got into the kitchen, Harold walked over to the clock and turned it back a half hour.

Harold looked at the two women and said, "We will let him rest a bit."

Genevieve began to panic. "Something is wrong!"

"Hush, Genevieve, hush. Allow him to preserve his dignity to the end."

Anna looked over at Genevieve. "In the twenty years that I have been here with you and your grandfather, we have never eaten late."

Dr. Livernois realized that Anna was having a nervous reaction rather than being worried about her supper. He went over to where she was standing and put his great big bear arms around her, and much to his surprise, she did not push him away.

After about half an hour, Harold went into the old man's room and helped him to the supper table. He was very shaky, both his legs and his arms. Harold was bearing all of the old man's weight and would have carried him if it had not been for the old man's pride.

Anna brought great big bowls of soup and homemade biscuits. She had made the vegetable soup that he loved so much.

"Ah!" He attempted one of his little bows toward Anna. "Another masterpiece. Did I smell apple pie before?"

Harold smiled and responded, "You surely did. A real beauty, too. I know because I had my hand slapped when I tried to get a piece before."

Everyone laughed except for Genevieve. The old man turned and looked at his granddaughter. "You are so quiet tonight. Is something the matter?"

"No, Grand-père, I think I am a little bit tired."

He was attempting to concentrate on eating his soup now. Dr. Livernois was watching his every move. He was trying to bring his soup to his mouth, but it was no use. Each bit that he picked up fell by the wayside. He was clearly upset.

"Grand-père," Genevieve said, "here, please let me help you?"

"Anna, I apologize to you, but tonight I am not hungry. Harold, if you will assist me to the parlor, I would like to speak to my granddaughter alone."

Harold was already on his feet. "Of course, I will be honored to assist you."

The journey into the living room was a long and tedious one, although it was only a few steps away. Harold was literally dragging the old man now.

Genevieve's heart was beating so fast and hard, she thought that it would burst through her rib cage and her flesh. "I can't do it!" she sobbed. "I can't handle it!" She wanted to get away, to run and pretend that all this wasn't happening to her. She knew, of course, that this moment had to come some day. She took a very deep breath and turned to face the doctor. "Is this it?" Her voice was quivering.

His voice was barely audible as he spoke. "Yes, I believe that it is."

Her lips were shaking and so were her hands. "Will it be bad? I mean, is it going to hurt him? Oh Lord, oh Lord, help me!"

Anna stood in the far corner of the room. She pulled up her apron and began to sob quietly on it. Her whole body shook.

The doctor walked over to Genevieve. "I believe that his heart will just stop quietly, like a car that has run out of gas. Can you handle it?"

"I will do it for his sake. Remember, a Boisvert can do anything that he sets his mind to! I, too, am a Boisvert!"

She walked over to the kitchen sink and threw some cold water on her face, squared her shoulders, and said, "I'm ready!"

When the two men reached the parlor and the old man was settled in his chair, he spoke faintly. "Harold, you will take care of her?"

Harold had a huge lump in his throat. "You didn't have to ask; I love her too!"

"Of course you do. I never doubted it for a moment! Does she know? Did Joseph tell her?"

Harold nodded his head. "Yes, she knows."

His voice was soft and raspy. "Tell me, how is she taking it?"

"She is totally devastated, but like you, she is putting on a big act."

"Come here, my boy, and kiss me good-bye, and please get Genevieve, for the time is short."

Harold went over and put his arms around this dear man that he had come to know and love, and he could not hold back his tears.

"Good-bye, my boy."

Harold could not speak. He turned and left the room quickly. As he entered the kitchen, Genevieve looked up at him and he nodded his head to her.

Before Genevieve went into her grandfather, Harold went to her and gave her a quick hug.

When Genevieve entered the living room, her grandfather was sitting so quietly and his eyes were closed. She thought, *I pray that I am not too late.* She stood quietly at the door of the room, looking all around as though she had never seen it before. She was weighing in her mind what she should do. She walked quietly over to where her grandfather was sitting and knelt beside him and gently placed her head on his lap. He showed the first sign of life since she had entered the room, and gently placed his hand upon her head.

"Did I frighten you?" She spoke in almost a whisper.

"No, you did not frighten me. You have pleased me very much." His voice was so faint that she had to use every bit of her concentration to understand what he was saying.

"How many times have we sat here like this?"

"I don't know. More times than I can count, that's for sure."

"Genevieve, please turn and look at me." She turned and looked him right in the eyes.

"You have been crying?"

"Yes." She hung her head.

"Don't cry for me. I am going to see your grand-mère and your maman and papa very soon, and you will have a good life with Harold and the baby."

"Grand-père, I am being selfish. I am crying for me!" Again the tears flowed from her eyes.

"Genevieve." His breathing was heavy and labored now. "You know that everything I have is yours. I have made it ironclad. You will take care of them for me? Anna and Joseph?"

"Yes, I promise you. Did you doubt it?"

"No, my darling girl, I never doubted it, but I wanted to hear it from your own mouth. You have never broken a promise to me yet. I want to thank you for the joy you have brought into my life. You made the years without Simone bearable for me. Now will you indulge me one last time?"

She was strangely calm. "Anything you want, I will do."

"Play something beautiful for me."

She stood up slowly and put her arms about him and gently kissed his timeworn cheek. She then proceeded to the piano that had long ago belonged to her mother and began to play his favorite by J. S. Bach, "Christe, du Lamm Gottes."

He closed his eyes as she played. When he had asked her to play, she had felt that she could not hit one right note, but now somehow she felt a strange calm. Even to her own ears, she had never played so well. *After all, she thought, it is the last gift for him!*

When she had finished, she once more walked over to him. His breathing was much more labored and he was gasping for air. He was trying to tell her something and she had to lean very close to hear him. He appeared cold and was shivering, so she wrapped her arms about him. She finally understood what he was telling her. "Don't waste your energy crying for me. Instead, do something good for someone." His whole body was shaking and his eyes were glazed. "Look! Look! Simone! Simone! . . ." he called out and then his head went limp on her chest.

"Grand-père," she whispered. "Grand-père." She knew that he could no longer respond. He was somewhere that she could not reach. She stood there cradling him in her arms. "Good-bye, old soldier. What is that old saying? Old soldiers never die, they just fade away."

Alexandre Boisvert died as he had lived; with dignity.

The plan to lay him to rest was very simple, but when they arrived at the church, there were over three hundred people there. Most of them Genevieve and Harold had never heard of. Each of them had a story to tell, too. Always a story of help or encouragement given by Alexandre Boisvert.

He always used to tell her as she was growing up that one person could really make a difference in this old world. He had proven it, too. Now she understood his last words: "Do something good for someone!"

Chapter Two
A Favor

Genevieve thought, *I really should be ashamed of myself, as I have not done any work on this book for weeks, but it has been on my mind almost constantly.* She had thought and wondered and pondered every possibility. *How can I do justice to someone as complex as Grand-père?*

Of course Harold's logic was, well, you will never know unless you try. So here she was again in the little office located toward the back part of the house. She looked around at her surroundings. "This really is a pleasant room, of sorts." The room was paneled in a light-colored knotty pine wood, which the old man had done himself. The floor was done in parquet-effect tile, which was a lighter color than the walls. Alexandre had wisely seen to it that the room was well lighted.

Genevieve decided that this was indeed a pleasant room. She had always loved her grandfather's huge rolltop desk, and it had not occurred to her that it was her desk now.

She put her head into her hands and started to cry. *My office! My desk! I hate the whole idea!* She wiped her teary face and gave herself a good shaking. *Where are all these tears coming from? I must get hold of myself. I know that the last thing Grand-père would want is for me to carry on like this. Also, I don't want to take a chance on hurting little Alex or little Simone by all this carrying on!* She smiled and patted her belly, which was just now beginning to spread into bloom.

She realized what Harold was up to. It was a good form of therapy for her. She would get it all out of her system and then concentrate on being a good wife and mother.

"Think of it this way, Doll Face. Even if nothing comes of it and it doesn't sell, we have some history for the children and grandchildren."

"Children!" she spoke up. "Children, like maybe plural or multiple?"

"You better believe it!" He grinned at her. "Grand-père told me one time that the reason he built such a big house was so that you could one day fill it with snotty-faced brats and stay out of trouble."

"Harold!" she said, pretending to be shocked. "You just made that up. Grand-père did not speak like that!"

"Face it, kiddo, when two guys get together, they speak a different language than when the ladies are present."

"Even Grand-père?"

"Even Grand-père," he said, and quietly left her to her own thoughts and ideas.

Strange, I did not think of it before, but there was a part of Grand-père that even I didn't know. I thought I knew everything there was to know about him! Was it only a few short weeks ago—that he had gone? She missed him so. No one seemed to understand.

She began to type rapidly now. She was thinking about an incident that had occurred a few weeks before he had gone home. *Why can't I write "died"? Because that is what really happened!*

Suppertime was over and the old man seemed refreshed and somewhat strengthened. The meal that night had been plain, but good and solid. All through his life Alexandre had loved a good homemade soup, and Anna delighted in making it for him. Tonight Anna had made some nice chicken and rice soup for him, and Genevieve had made him some whole wheat bread.

Years ago, he had always wanted soup before his meal, but now the soup was his meal. Genevieve was especially pleased when she noticed him eating tonight. He had eaten heartily, considering his frail condition. It was a big bowl of soup, in which Anna had put ginger because she felt that ginger had "healing properties." He had even eaten the whole slice of bread and butter, plus his cup of tea, and some bread pudding, too!

The old man had been jovial throughout the whole meal.

That's all he needs, thought Genevieve, *a few good meals in his belly to strengthen him up a bit.*

After they had finished eating, the old man turned to his granddaughter. "Shall we sit in the living room, my dear?"

"I should love that, Grand-père." Inside, she was so excited. He had not gone into the living room after supper for several weeks now. She knew that Anna would not mind if she did not help her clean up this once.

He struggled to get up from his chair, and although it broke Genevieve's heart not to help him, she sat silently by. Slowly he folded his napkin and placed it on the table. He placed his shaky arms on the arms of his chair and shakily pulled himself up to a standing position on his feeble and wobbly legs. He reached for his cane, steadied himself, straightened out his back as much as he was able to, and offered her his arm in the manner of a courtly gentleman.

Slowly and steadily they walked together, one a picture of youth and vitality, the other of fragility and age.

He had built the room, and it reflected him so well. The room showed forth warmth and the vitality of life, as he had once. He had designed the fireplace himself, and it was illuminated now by a glowing fire. The room was warm and cozy.

He escorted his granddaughter to the sofa and slowly and laboriously made his way to his big leather chair by the fire.

Genevieve watched his maneuvering with great interest. She noticed that he had a little color in his cheeks tonight, and it encouraged her as she had been quite concerned about him of late. Tonight she felt that she could relax a bit, so she let her body go limp and sank deep into the sofa's cushions. *My life,* she thought, *certainly has been unusual, to say the least. I can't imagine life without him. He was all the family I had until Harold.*

"Genevieve, are you sleeping?"

"No, Grand-père, just lost in thought for a moment."

"Aha!" he said jokingly. "I caught you daydreaming about that handsome husband of yours, eh?" And he started to chuckle.

"I cannot tell a lie," she said, smiling. "I've been caught in the act. What did you want, Grand-père?"

He was lost in thought for a moment, as he raised his hand to scratch his cheek. He cleared his throat and looked deeply into his granddaughter's eyes for a long moment.

She knew better than to try and rush him. It had been a little joke between them that he had only one speed. She thought back to the many times they had gone for a walk together and she would try to rush him, and his reply would always be, "Tell me, little girl, fifty years from now, who is going to know if Alexandre Boisvert took five minutes to walk around his property or five hours?"

Genevieve thought to herself, *I never came up with a right answer to that one!*

He cleared his throat again, and she knew that he was gathering his thoughts together. "Genevieve, I would like to ask a great favor of you."

"The answer is yes." She sat up straight on the sofa. "The answer very definitely is yes. Anything that you desire, I will do."

"Do not answer so quickly or so impulsively," he scolded her gently.

"Remember, you are no longer an impetuous child. While it makes me happy that you wish to be kind to me, you have no idea what it is that I require of you!"

She felt like a little girl again, and she gave him that special smile that made her eyes sparkle and dance. "You are right, of course. Pray, tell what is it that you desire of me?"

"Calm down." And as he smiled, the family resemblance between them was most obvious. If he could realize it, he would certainly know whom his granddaughter looked like.

"I will not ask you until Anna is here with us. While we are waiting, please play something lively for us, such as 'Tales of the Vienna Woods' by Strauss."

She got up and walked over to her piano and began to play for him. He had never in his lifetime heard anyone who could play like her. She had played all over the world, while he was yet able to travel. She claimed to be on a sabbatical, but he knew better. She had come home to be with him.

She interrupted his thoughts. "Hmmmm, Grand-père, do I sense a conspiracy going on? What are you two up to now? It must be a humdinger if you're bringing in the troops."

He looked at his granddaughter and laughed. "Has Anna revealed my little secret to you?"

"Calm down," she said, using his euphemism. "You know very well, Grand-père, that Anna is always on your side."

Just at that moment Anna came in and sat next to Genevieve. "Oh my, oh my." Jumping up as she spoke, she ran and removed her apron, her chubby little body jiggling as she scurried about. "I'd forget my head if it wasn't tied on!"

She was a very spry woman for her age, although no one knew just what her real age was. Alexandre felt that she had to be at least in her early seventies. No one knew for certain, though. She was what could be called a plain woman, or as they would say in the "olden days," a homely woman. She liked to dress in cotton house dresses, which she changed several times a day. She kept all of her dresses starched stiff. She kept herself looking neat. Her hair always had an unkempt look about it, almost as though a sudden wind followed her about. The possibility was that she spent so much time over the hot dishpan.

Anna never wore any makeup whatsoever, feeling that the good Lord had made her exactly as he wanted her to be and that was good enough for her. She never seemed to slow down, always running helter-skelter and darting to and fro. Of course, she wore "sensible shoes."

Genevieve looked at Anna's hands. She had often marveled at the short and stubby fingers and the dimples on each knuckle. Many years ago she and Grand-pèere had bought a mother's ring for Anna, and Anna, being very touched by the gesture, had told them, "I will never take it off." To Genevieve's knowledge, she never had, either. The ring sparkled in the light of the fireplace. The ring had Anna's birthstone and also Alexandre's and Genevieve's.

The old man turned to look at the two women. They were so different; each appeared to be lost in her own thoughts at the moment. The old man spoke a little more roughly than was his norm, almost as though he resented being ignored by the women.

"Are you both wool-gathering on me?"

Genevieve walked over to her grandfather and gave him a kiss on the cheek. "I love you." Alexandre could not be irritated any longer.

"And I love you, too, Anna." Anna's face flushed and she patted Genevieve's knee in an awkward show of affection.

"Now," he spoke, "let's get to the point." Anna and Genevieve sat quietly ready to listen. "I have spoken previously of this to Harold and also to Anna." He was looking only at Genevieve now.

"So," said Genevieve playfully, "I am the last to know?"

"Please, Genevieve, this is very important to me. You realize, of course, that I am a man of advanced age, and we must face the fact that my days are numbered now."

Genevieve became very angry. "If you are going to talk like that, I am going to leave this room."

Alexandre became equally angry and a little sarcastic. "Tell me, if you run away and refuse to face facts, will this make me any younger?"

Genevieve bit her tongue and kept her mouth shut, but her insides were shaking and her impulse was to run and hide.

"Many times we have sat here together and talked about the 'good old days,' so you both know much about me and my past. Many years ago when I married my beloved Simone, she and I had many dreams and ambitions, like all young people. We wanted to have and raise a family that would not have to go through all the bad times and hardships that we had to go through.

"We gave them so much and shielded them so much that, with the exception of your mother, we raised a bunch of brats. Your grand-mère and

I often spoke of how out of four children, we only raised one normal one. Laura, Laura, . . . " he whispered, "and her life, as you very well know, was snuffed out in a tragic accident." Tears flowed freely from the old man's eyes.

"No one knows how much I miss them, Simone and Laura. If I had not had you to care for"—he turned to Genevieve—"I might have done something foolish to myself a long time ago," he sighed.

Genevieve quickly arose and went and knelt by her grandfather and put her head on his lap. "Oh, Grand-père, I am so happy you did not do such a thing. Where would I be without you, and Anna, too!"

Anna nodded her head in quiet assent.

"A short time ago, I began to think that perhaps I would like to see those brats of mine, but the more I thought about it, I decided against it. My son Isaac (I pray that you ladies will excuse my language now) is nothing but a horse's ass, and Samuel is a worse horse's ass than Isaac. Now we come to Rachel, Rachel, our youngest child. There is really no way to describe Rachel except that she is a person I do not like very much!" He spoke in a tone of total disgust that Genevieve did not recognize as part of his nature.

"In spite of everything that has happened, I have kept track of them through various methods, and age has not improved any of them at all. So after this last report I received, I decided that I did not want to ever see any of them again. There is one thing that my heart longs for, and that is that I might be buried next to Simone in the little plot we bought many years ago in the little village cemetery. Do you remember, Genevieve? Your mama and papa are also laid to rest there."

"Yes, I remember; how could I ever forget?"

"Genevieve." He spoke gently as he patted her head and touched her hair in a manner of affection. "Don't ever forget, but don't let the old things stop you from living your life to the fullest. That would be such a terrible waste. Life is a precious gift and we must make the most of every moment. You see, my dear, although they may place me in a box and throw dirt over it, that does not mean that I am dead, because you," he smiled at her, "you are my continuity. You and that precious little one snuggled safely under your breast."

She shook her head and her eyes filled with tears. "I don't even want to think about it!"

"Listen to me, as I grow weary. I long ago made all the arrangements with the undertaker in town. Everything is paid in full, so you don't have to pay him a cent. He will keep the body in a place where it will be kept frozen until it is convenient for you to make the trip. All the paperwork is in order. Harold has worked long and hard on all these things so everything will go smoothly, and you will not have to worry your pretty head about details. There is a box in the safe with all the details necessary. My will and all the other papers that you might need are all there. Everything that I possess and own has been left to you and you alone. My will is airtight and cannot be broken; Harold and I saw to that!" he said rather smugly. "Now," he told her, "as I live and breathe there is one thing that I am sure of. The moment that Samuel, Rachel, and very possibly Isaac, too, find out that I have been alive all these years, they will come after you like a chicken hawk let loose in the henhouse! I have been in conference with Harold many, many times and he knows how to handle them." He chuckled. "I have always been one step ahead of them. You will take care of Anna?"

"Grand-père!" Her voice was angry now. "Anna is like my own mother to me. How dare you think that I would not care for her?" She sputtered, "Why, I don't know what I would do without her!"

"Easy, my girl," he laughed. "I have known all these years how much you cared for Anna, but she never fully believed it." All of a sudden his tone became very serious. "Will you honor my last request?"

Genevieve stood up to her full height, and fought to hold back the tears that were tearing at her. She felt betrayed by both of them; they were playing games and toying with her feelings. She turned and started to leave the room.

The old man called after her, "You did not answer me!"

She stood in the doorway, and now there was no stopping the tears. "Yes, damn you, yes!" And she ran out of the room as fast as she could. He had a puzzled look on his face now. "Why, in all the years that we have been together, and all the things that we have been through together, Genevieve has never spoken to me like that or walked out on me. I am shocked!"

Anna looked at him and told him, "The poor girl has been through a lot. She, too, is a person of honor. She learned that from you. Tonight you impugned that honor. I am sure Genevieve felt that you knew her well enough to know that she would do the right thing to the best of her ability as she always has. Tonight, you start out by tearing her world apart, then you treat her as an incompetent child. You and Harold, indeed! How about Genevieve? She is not a child to be babied and sheltered by you—it is time you realize her capabilities!"

Anna, too, would have walked out of the room, but she knew that he could not maneuver himself, so she stayed to lend him a hand.

His head was hanging down now, and she spoke his name. "Alexandre, Alexandre, are you all right?"

She noticed that his eyes were full of tears. "Anna," he said, "it is true that there is no fool like an old fool."

Chapter Three
Alexandre

"I've known so many people in my lifetime," he told Genevieve in a voice that seemed stronger than any he had used in months.

The day was one of those funny kind. The kind where you would like to wrap your arms completely around yourself and possibly take a long nap.

They were seated in the family room, which was Alexandre's favorite. He was enthroned in his favorite chair next to the fireplace, where the flames were dancing a dance that man could not comprehend even with his so-called wisdom.

He was dressed warmly. His trousers were made of corduroy and were a dark navy blue. His shirt was of light blue flannel, and his sweater dark blue; all helped to make his blue eyes seem even more blue than they actually were. His eyes had never grown colorless in his old age. They had clung fast to what was their due.

"You know, Genevieve," he said, sitting up as straight as he could. "You know what it is that I have been thinking about?"

Genevieve smiled at her grandfather indulgently. "No, Grand-père, I don't know what it is that you have been thinking about. Tell me."

He looked at his granddaughter intently for a moment or two. He liked what he saw. She had her dark hair tied back in what they call a ponytail. Her hair done in this manner tended to make her high cheekbones even more prominent. Her eyes were as dark as his were blue, and they sparkled as though they were rare and precious jewels.

She had on a red turtleneck sweater, and the reflection of it upon her face made her face bloom. *She has skin like her grandmother and doesn't need to use makeup at all,* he thought.

He was not fond of blue jeans and had not allowed her to wear them at the table, ever, but he admitted to himself that she was one of the few women that can wear them and still appear feminine. *Today she looks like a little girl again.*

He turned to look out the big sliding doors that opened up to the patio and noticed that it was snowing out. The flakes were the big fat kind that seemed to fall to the ground in their own sweet time. These flakes did not have a timetable so they sometimes floated in midair for a moment or two before falling to the ground.

Genevieve waited patiently for his thought processes to get moving again.

"Money." He spoke in a voice that was barely audible.

"What did you say?" she asked, coming out of some deep thoughts of her own.

"Money! I said money!" he replied in a tone of voice plainly betraying an annoyance that was so unlike his temperament so as to be out of character for him.

"Money? Do you want money?" she asked him.

"No! NO!" His annoyance reared forth again.

"For all these years, you ask me, Grand-père, why did we leave the United States and come to Canada? Now I tell you, the answer is Money."

"I don't understand," she said, obviously confused. "You have plenty of money."

"You must be still and allow me to continue. My strength fails me so quickly." His voice trailed off.

"Forgive me—" she began.

"Genevieve, you must be still, and remember that too many apologies are like too much sweetbread. Too much and they both get sour in the belly."

She smiled to herself. *He still thinks of me as a child.* Obviously bemused by it all, she settled herself into a more comfortable position. She was sitting Indian fashion, with her elbows on her knees holding her head up in a position of childlike concentration. She waited expectantly, every nerve concentrated, ready to spring forth like a racehorse given full rein.

"Money," he repeated softly. "Yes, money. You see, I have the money, but everyone else wanted to take it away from me. My son! My very own son. The eldest of all my children. He conspired to take everything away from us. Imagine! His own maman and papa! And from you, too, of course. Imagine that! My own son!

"Incidentally, I must tell you this. On my key chain there is a key for you to unlock my safety deposit box, which contains the key to the safe."

"But," she sputtered, taken totally by surprise, "we don't have a safe!"

"Genevieve, as a child there were many things I could not tell you. As you know, we have lived lives of secrecy, staying away from those leeches called children. Now allow me the courtesy to finish. In the cellar, I did not put in a root cellar. I," he said with pride, "put in a safe. Well hidden and well built, too, if I say so myself. The only one that knew about it was Anna and that only because if anything had happened to me before you were grown, she had sworn to be your guardian. In that safe are many treasures for you, such as your maman's jewelry, and also your grand-mère's.

"Genevieve," he spoke softly, "do your remember our trip out here?"

She nodded her head silently.

They both stared intently into the fire, each heart reliving moments that only that individual heart could remember.

Memories, she thought. *What makes a memory? Out of the mountain of life's experiences, why do we bring one thing to our recollection and not another? Some very simple item of joy or laughter comes to mind without effort and yet the sadnesses and solemnities cling like bloodsuckers and we are unable to shake them off.*

Grand-père had dozed off. She lost herself again in her own thoughts. *Here,* she thought, *is an old, old man.* Possibly, he was very unimpressive to others, but she could not imagine her world without him. She shuddered at the possibility. She knew that this possibility could become a reality at any given moment. A reality she forced herself not to think about. Was she prepared? *Heaven knows he certainly has tried to prepare me.*

She began to study him as though she had never seen him before or as though this might be the last time that she would see him. *He has such beautiful hair,* she thought, *even at his advanced age. . . . He still has a full head of hair. It is as white as the new-fallen snow. Every one of his hairs is curled, making little unexpected patterns that seem to be looking for a new adventure.*

I would imagine that Grand-mère was quite taken by his curly hair. I wonder if she ever ran her fingers idly through his hair? Inwardly, she began to giggle, like a teenager. She giggled the type of giggle that was only intended for one's own self. The picture of her grand-mère running her fingers through anyone's hair seemed so contrary to the Grand-mère she knew and loved.

Genevieve thought, *As serious and solemn as Grand-mère could be, she definitely had her own brand of humor.*

Genevieve remembered very well how Grand-mèere would send her to the store to buy copies of "Love Forever," and "Dear Heart." Love stories for the young and for the young at heart.

She remembered the time that her aunt caught her at the store buying those magazines and had marched Genevieve home to her grandmother's house. "Imagine that, Maman," her aunt spoke in that whiny voice. "Buying those magazines, of all things! I hope you punish her accordingly! That child needs to be taught a lesson. If I did not have an important meeting to go to, I would stay and see that she got what she deserved."

Blowing her mother a kiss in her general direction, she was gone. Aunt Rachel always had one committee or other which could not function without her illustrious presence. In all actuality they were nothing more than gossip gatherings.

The moment that Aunt Rachel left both women, the elderly one and the young one, looked at each other and broke into gales of laughter. Simone had her hands resting on her belly, and as she laughed her belly shook like a great big bowl of jelly. Her eyes filled with tears and so did Genevieve's, but neither could stop their laughing.

This was the scene that Alexandre walked into on a bright and sunny afternoon. He looked at these two that were his whole life. "I suspect that my girls have been up to something that did not please Rachel."

Grand-mère kept her love story magazines tucked under the cushion of her rocking chair. Putting them there made them readily accessible for her use, and it was a quick place to hide them should anyone happen on the scene. There she would sit, snug as a mother hen sitting upon her nest with her unhatched eggs beneath her, hands folded on her belly. She did not cluck but had about her an air of satisfaction because of her (so she thought) well-kept secret.

Genevieve had dearly loved her grandmother and could not believe that even after all these years she could still miss her so.

How well Genevieve could remember this beautiful lady who would tell her, "I was born very old, but I get younger every year!" This was always a mystery to Genevieve. "Grand-mère, it is impossible to be born old and grow younger year by year." Grand-mère would just smile at her and Genevieve concluded after a while that this must be some sort of family legend or something.

Grand-père's head began to bob about a bit, and a little snoring sound, barely audible, came forth from somewhere deep within him, almost as though he were too feeble to utter a full-fledged snore. His old hands were resting upon his breast as though he were ready for his burial.

I wish I were an artist, she thought. *I would paint him just as he is, and that would be a masterpiece, too.* He was a picture of life personified: his white head portraying the great snowcapped mountains; his tall stature an image of the mighty elm; and his strength that of the mustang who never loses his sense of adventure, nor his taste for freedom. His skin was brown-toned and had never lost its perpetual tan, giving his skin leatherlike tones. His wrinkled brow spoke out in boldness of the wisdom within.

His skin had loosened a lot and hung in folds over his spare frame, as though he were a young lad wearing his older brother's clothing. His cheekbones were the dominant feature of his face; he looked as though he were holding walnuts in them. The flesh hung loosely over his ears, exhausted from its lifelong endeavor. His dimples were as deep as the well waters, signs of youth clinging to the ancient.

He had fought a long and good battle, a terrific battle. He was the mighty warrior, the Roman centurion, and also the puppy dog sitting at the master's feet. His hands now belied their once powerful strength. Gentle as the breeze of summer they lay upon his breast, which was now sunken and shallow as a flag at half-mast. His arms, once rods of iron, were now willowy as fine lace. His legs, once solid oaks, had become softened just like the porridge that he ate so often lately, and served not much of a purpose anymore.

He seemed like an elder babe. His stomach and his thighs were almost nonexistent now, and his trousers hung from his hips as though they were on a coat hanger. His feet were large and seemed to belie the frailty of his body. He was a great ship that once had gone from harbor to harbor but now must remain in port.

Chapter Four
Some Background

Genevieve shook her whole body. *I really don't know what is the matter with me*, she thought. *I really must pull myself together.*

It was not like her at all to dwell upon the past. She realized that her face was wet with tears, as she had been reliving some of the moments of her past.

Everything is so real, as though it had just happened yesterday. You'd think after twenty years the memories wouldn't hurt as much. She walked over to one of the end tables and grabbed a tissue to wipe off her tear-stained face.

She had not been aware that her grandfather had been observing her until she turned to see if he was all right.

"Your memories are painful today, eh? I too have been indulging myself; perhaps it is good to do so after all these years. We have done so well these many years to put aside the past and to live each day as it came along. Your grand-mère, her, she believed strongly in doing this."

He smiled sweetly at his granddaughter. "We are both feeling a bit sentimental today. Oh, well, what better way is there to spend a cold winter day than beside an open fire? Come, let us indulge ourselves this once.

"When I returned to Canada with you, you were nothing but a mere child, and now you are a grown woman, making memories of your own. Sometimes I speak too quickly; for you it was not a return but it was for me. I was born here; perhaps I have told you this before?"

"Yes," she answered him, "I knew that you had gone to the United States as a young boy, but that is all I have known."

She could tell that his mental processes were hard at work, as he sat more comfortably and sank deeper into his chair. His concentration was absolute. She waited patiently until he could bring back to his memory the things he wanted to share with her.

"My papa," he said, betraying contempt in his voice, "was a very handsome man. People have told me that in the area where we lived there was not another man around that could equal him in looks. Some people even spoke of him as the 'pretty man.'"

Alexandre cleared his throat and took a sip of water. "He was tall and slender with wide shoulders and slim hips. His hair was dark and curly. You know the type, always had one of those naughty boy curls hanging down on his forehead. He worked hard at keeping it just right, too!

"He had that special charm and grace that had all the young girls falling over themselves for a smile or some other small attention he might choose to bestow upon them. All the girls wanted attention from him, and he thrived on it.

"His name was Philippe Magloire Boisvert. He was an only child and as far as his mother was concerned he could do no wrong! His father was a dark, somber man whose only interest in life was making money. Make it he did, too.

"My grandfather's name was Armand Jacques Boisvert. He did not approve of his son's philandering ways and totally disowned him in his will. This did not do any good though, for when he died, his widow left everything to her wayward son."

Genevieve was paying close attention to everything that her grandfather spoke. She literally hung upon his every word. "Is this where our money comes from?" she asked him.

The old man was plainly aggravated now. "Yes," he said, roughly. "But it was not because I wanted it, and don't forget, Miss, your grand-mère and I made our own fortune with our own hands."

Uh, oh, thought Genevieve. *I've obviously touched a delicate or sensitive chord. Methinks that I had better shut up and listen if I want to learn anything. Strange,* she mused, *I never heard him talk about his father before. Must be more there than meets the eye.*

"My maman," he continued on, "her, she was just the opposite. She was a very plain girl. Her name was Elisabeth Lorraine Langevin. She came from a very large family of poor means and she had to work very hard for most of her life, until I received the inheritance from my father's estate. Then I would not allow her to work, except doing the things she liked doing.

"One time . . ." he was speaking as though he were the only one there now. "One time my maman told me that when she was growing up she could never remember her parents ever saying a kind word to her or showing her any sign of affection either! Not one touch, not one hug, not one kiss! No display of affection was ever allowed in that home!

"Needless to say that when that handsome young man paid attention to her she fell at his feet, madly in love with him. She would have done anything in the world for him, which she did.

"When Maman found herself in the family way with me she was very frightened, of course. She went to Philippe and told him what had happened and he laughed at her, denying any responsibility! He even went so far as to pay several men to say that they had also slept with Maman.

"Elisabeth then had no other recourse than to go and tell her parents what had happened. Her father was livid with anger, and he removed his belt and gave her a good beating.

"His name was Allain Quilliaume Langevin. He was a boisterous and gregarious man with a red face. He liked his beer more than his wife or kids. One night he was sitting in the local beer hall, 'Le Chat,' talking with a man there, and they had a very interesting conversation.

" 'Hey, Allain, let me buy you a beer. I understand you are going to become a grandfather soon.'

" 'You shut up your damn mouth, Etienne, or I'll shut it for you!' He stood up and clenched his fist. He was one who loved to use his fists every chance he got.

" 'Calm down! Calm down for heaven sakes, I just wanted to know if it was true. Philippe Boisvert is going around all over the place collecting money on a bet he made here New Year's Eve.'

" 'What are you talking about, Etienne?' He was screaming at him now. 'Have you gone foolish? What does Philippe Boisvert's bet have to do with me?'

" 'Well, we were in here like I said on New Year's Eve, and you know how we Frenchmen are.'

" 'Get on with it!'

" 'Well, we started to talk about women, and Philippe said that he had slept with every young girl in town. He was really bragging up a storm, too. And someone piped up and said that he knew that Philippe had not slept with your daughter Elisabeth because, and I quote, "She is a good girl."

" 'Philippe stood there and hit himself on the head. "How did I miss that one?" Then he said to everyone in here, "Listen up everybody, I am going to let everyone here in on a bet."

" ' "What kind of bet? Yeah, Philippe, there you go with your big mouth again."

" ' "Look here, people, I'll tell you what I'm gonna do. I will not only sleep with Allain Langevin's daughter, I'll have her pregnant in three months!"

" 'I tell you, everyone took that bet!'

"Allain was sitting at the table clenching and unclenching his great big fists. No one had ever seen his face this red before. His teeth were clenched, too.

" 'Is that all?'

" 'No.' Everyone in the place was enjoying the situation. Allain did not know that the 'good people' of the bar had set Etienne up to get him riled up by promising him all the drinks he could handle in a week.

" 'Well,' Etienne said, looking at Allain, 'you are so upset now I don't think that I should tell you.'

"Allain was enraged and grabbed Etienne by the throat and would have squeezed the life out of him if several of the men had not held him back.

" 'Tell me or else you will also die.'

" 'Well,' he said, rubbing his throat, 'he said that not only would he get your daughter pregnant, but he would get away with it, too!'

"Allain let go of Etienne and shoved him across the room, and left the place in a boiling rage.

"Those were the days of the shotgun weddings. My mother's father found Philippe's father, and together they found Philippe. There was no way to hold Allain back; he filled Philippe's seat with buckshot. The result of all this was a wedding that never should have taken place.

"My mother was ecstatic, because she was sure that she would be such an excellent wife for Philippe and that he would soon see the error of his ways and become a model husband and that they would live happily ever after.

"Needless to say, my papa resented the marriage and had nothing to do with it. He continued on with his promiscuous ways, drinking and carousing and carrying on worse than ever. He liked having someone to wait on him hand and foot, which Maman obligingly did.

"When I was born he was nowhere in sight, and finally when they did find him he was in the bed of his mistress. My mother had given birth all alone in her little one-room cabin. Only two short years later my brother Napoleon was born and about one and one-half years later my brother Charles was born."

Genevieve looked at her grandfather, who was obviously overcome by his memories. "I did not know that you had brothers."

"They are long gone, long since.

"The first time my father ever saw me he called me 'The little bastard.'

That is all I ever remember him calling me. When I was little I did not know what it meant, but I did know one thing, and that was that I did not like to be called that! I hated that name and still do, and no person has ever gotten away with calling me that again!"

Chapter Five
Coming to America

"My brothers and I were all born in a little remote village in Canada. I have never revealed the name of this village to anyone with the exception, of course, of your grand-mère. I did not want anyone to know about my father. As far as I know, your grand-mère always respected my wishes concerning this matter.

"When I was about five years old and my brother Napoleon was about three years old and Charles, who was the baby, was about one and one-half years old, my father decided that he was going to take us all to the United States.

"My maman did not want to go at first, but Papa convinced her that this was going to be a new beginning for us all. He told her that he really wanted to change and that he wanted to be a family man and assume his responsibilities. He said that he did not want to be around his old friends because they might influence him to drink and run around, and these were the very things that he wanted out of his life.

"Maman, of course, was beside herself with joy, because this was the answer to all her prayers. Somehow, someway, this poor excuse for a man could always turn poor Maman's head.

"They hurriedly made their preparations to leave. Maman once told me that this short period was the happiest of her entire life.

"Papa had no money, so he devised the perfect plan to soften up his poor maman's heart, and that was by taking my brothers and me to see her. He got down on his knees and cried and begged her forgiveness for all the trouble he had caused her. He had us dressed in the worst clothes we owned, and had deliberately not fed us so that we would confess that we were hungry and thus melt his poor mother's heart. It worked like a charm and she gave him more money than he would have need of for a good long while!

"Never!" Alexandre said almost in a whisper, "never will I ever forget that time in my life! Never! The best thing I could ever say about my father is that he was a bum!

"Maman seemed so happy on the train. She played and laughed with us children in a way I had never seen her do before. She kept singing to us, 'We're going to Massachusetts.' My, how we laughed! None of us children could pronounce such a big word!

"Finally, when we arrived in Massachusetts after a long and very tedious journey, Papa told Maman, 'Elisabeth, you wait here with the children and I will go and see to the luggage.' He leaned over and gave Maman a little kiss on her cheek, and that was the last we ever saw of him!"

Genevieve gasped as she heard her grandfather speak these things.

"That is not all, my dear granddaughter."

"Please go on," she urged him. "That is, if it is not too painful for you."

"The truth is truth!" He started once again, as if he could not stop now that he had started.

"Later," he murmured, "we found out that he wanted to go to Massachusetts because his mistress had been deported for prostitution and other charges. Anyhow, due to some complication of the law which I have never comprehended, he could not get out of the country without his wife and children.

"Poor Maman, she waited and waited the whole day long there at the depot station. She was certain that it was all a mistake and that Philippe was returning for us.

"I can see it all now, as she stood there waiting for her knight in shining armor to return! How pathetic and how forlorn, that young woman with three babies, in a foreign country and not one penny to her name, either!" Tears were flowing freely from the old gentleman's eyes as he relived the horrors of the past. Genevieve too was overcome with emotion.

"Oh, Grand-père, all these years I was so selfish thinking what a terrible and horrible life I had to live and I never realized what you had been through!"

The old man seemed unaware of her presence. "We were a sorry sight, I tell you. While we had been waiting for Philippe to return, my brothers and I had been playing in the dusty streets. As dusk began to appear Maman's spirits seemed to fail her. I could see Maman's shoulders begin to sag, and she was aging before my eyes.

" 'Alexandre.' Maman's lips were trembling. This little small voice was so unlike her normal speech. 'Perhaps we should walk for a while. You take Napoleon's hand and I will carry Charles.'

" 'But Maman,' I protested, 'where are we going?'

"Maman screamed at me now, 'You be quiet! And for once in your life do as I tell you!'

"Somehow, even though I was little more than a baby myself, I could sense the fear in Maman's voice.

" '*Oui* Maman,' I said, and did everything that I could to keep the two boys quiet.

"I don't know for sure just how long it was that we walked, but in my childish mind it seemed like hours! I knew that Maman was praying, as I could see her lips moving in funny little motions. I had seen Maman pray so often, and one thing I knew for sure was that I'd better not disturb her when she was in prayer!

"Suddenly I looked up, and there before my very eyes was the most beautiful building that I had ever seen in my entire life. I stopped short and bent backwards so that I could see to the very top of the magnificent steeple.

"In my childish mind I felt that our problems were about to be solved. I was so overcome by that marvelous spectacle that I found it difficult even to speak. I turned to look at Maman, and in the dim moonlight I could see the tears glistening on her cheeks. The look upon her poor, tired face has been with me all my life.

"My poor dear Maman, here she was in the U.S.A., where she had never been before, not speaking any English. She was totally perplexed. Her three boys were cold, tired, and hungry. Where to turn?

"As I told you, I was only five years old, but I realized that the manly responsibilities of our little family hung upon my shoulders!

" '*Ne pluer pas, Maman* (do not cry, Mama). *Voici une eglise* (here is a church).' In my childish mind I thought where else to turn in your hour of need? Was this not the house of God?"

Chapter Six
Meeting the Priest

"I ran up the few stairs to the rectory, which is where the priest lives, and began to knock on the door as if my life depended on it. A very tall, slender and severe-looking woman came to the door. An imposing sight to a young man of such tender years. I was to find out later that she was the housekeeper.

" '*Oui?*' she asked. 'What do you want at this hour?'

"Maman in the meantime stood there trying to compose herself, and finally she replied in French, 'I am so sorry to disturb you, if only we could see Mr. *le curé* for just a moment. *S'il vous plait?* Please?'

"The housekeeper's voice was unnecessarily sharp. 'He is very busy, too busy to see you now. Come back tomorrow, perhaps he will see you then.'

"Maman was not a very big woman, barely five feet tall. Something sparked in her and she stood as tall as she could, her eyes with a peculiar gleam in them, and with all the authority she could muster, she said, 'We will wait!'

"Oh yes, I can picture it all as though it were today." He was smiling now. "Her eyes so fiery that they matched the black attire that she wore. Her long black skirt and her black coat, and her white blouse that covered her up to her neck. She did allow herself the luxury of a little lace around her collar. She was far from being stylish, believe me.

"We were not a pretty sight to behold. Our clothes were much mended and much the worse for wear. We were all dusty with tear-streaked faces.

"When the housekeeper heard Maman say that we would wait she appeared to become very agitated or nervous. '*Je ne sais pas,*' she said. '*Il mange son diner.*' (I don't know; he is eating his dinner.)

"My brothers and I were famished after such a long and tiring trip, and remember, we had not eaten all day long either! Just the mention or thought of food set both the babies crying in full force.

"All of a sudden, we could hear the sound of menacing, stomping footsteps coming nearer and nearer. I looked up and saw this short little man, perhaps about your height, come rushing to where we were standing.

"His fat face was beet red, and it was not too difficult to see that he was in a very bad mood, to say the least!

"He reminded me of a leprechaun. He stood on short, fat legs with his big fat belly sticking out. He put both hands on his hips and hollered out in a big loud voice, 'What, may I ask, is this terrible racket? Who has *les enfants* in my house and does not control them?'

" 'Pardon, Mr. *le curé*,' Maman began apologetically.

" 'PARDON!' he screamed. 'Pardon! You interrupt *mon diner* and all you can say is pardon!' The look he gave us was a look of utter contempt.

" 'What do you want here, where you do not belong? And at this hour, too!' Maman's lips were quivering now. 'And don't take all night to tell me either, my dinner becomes cold!'

"Maman mustered up all the courage at her disposal and said, 'Please, M'sieu *le curé*, due to circumstances beyond my control I am in desperate need of a place to stay tonight. Myself and my little boys, that is. I ask not for myself, but for my babies. You can see for yourself that they are weary and faint from hunger.'

" 'Madame,' he thundered, 'what is your name?'

" 'My name is Elisabeth Boisvert!' Maman was shaking so much it was difficult for her to speak, and her voice wavered as she tried. 'These,' she said with pride in her voice, 'these are my three sons, Alexandre, Napoleon, and Charles.'

" 'Madame Boisvert,' he sneered, 'pray tell me, does this appear to be a house of charity?' With his hands on his hips and his bald head glaring in the light and his nostrils flared, he appeared to us boys a fearsome giant.

" 'Do you really think that I pick up every stray off of the street, full of dirt and lice and only the good Lord knows what else, and put them in our beds? God himself only knows what else you are afflicted with!'

"Maman, tired and weary as she was, seemed to grow several inches in height at that moment. She drew upon the inner strength she did not know that she possessed.

" 'Monsieur *le curé*, forgive me; I have made a mistake. We do not need your help after all!'

"The priest just laughed vilely and ignored Maman's words. He turned to us boys and said, 'Boys, are you hungry?'

"In unison our reply was '*Oui! Oui! Oui!*'

" 'Come along then. *Vite! Vite!* (Hurry! Hurry!) I don't have all day!'

"Maman decided for our sakes that she must swallow her pride and allow us each to have a morsel of food, and then, strengthened, she would find a way out of our predicament.

"We all walked very quietly down the long somber hallway. This would be one time that we would not quibble about the food.

"Elisabeth's spirits were beginning to rise now and she thought that someday she would find a way to repay this kind though very gruff priest for his help.

"We walked through the formal dining room with its subdued floral wallpaper and solid mahogany woodwork, and on into the kitchen.

"When we reached the kitchen or cooking room the priest finally spoke. 'Ah, now, my boys, we shall see just how hungry you really are. We shall also see just how truthful Madame Boisvert is about her hungry boys!' He laughed maliciously.

"The priest walked over to the cupboard. All of our eyes were fastened upon his every move. The good smells in that kitchen had all of our stomachs growling, and our mouths were very definitely salivating!

"The priest had taken a great big platter from the cupboard, and now he walked very slowly and deliberately over to the stove. He began to fill the platter with some kind of delicious stew. It appeared to me to have the biggest hunks of meat in it that I had ever seen!

"Then he took some very large homemade biscuits and piled them on top of the stew. He put great big globs of butter on top of the biscuits until the butter was oozing out over the edges of the platter.

"I tell you that my brothers and I were completely spellbound. Their eyes were literally bulging out of their heads, and I assume that mine were also. My little brothers were ready to lunge forth at the food and forget all the manners they had been taught. As for myself, I had too much pride to let anyone see how I really felt.

"Maman had to hold the boys back, much as one would hold back a young mustang that had been put in harness for the first time.

"At this point Elisabeth had to admit to herself that the smell of food was making her feel rather faint and light-headed. She prayed silently to herself, 'Oh, thank you, dear God up in heaven, thank you for this kind, gruff man who would have compassion to feed three starving boys and their mother.'

"All this while the housekeeper stood silently by in stony silence. She was so still she appeared to not be breathing! She was so still she could have been a piece of marble standing there.

"The priest's movements seemed to be purposefully slowed down, each movement done in a precise and deliberate manner, as though he was enjoying seeing us half-crazed with hunger."

The old man turned to his granddaughter. "Genevieve, I have never told any of these things to anyone except for once, and that was to Simone before we were married."

Genevieve realized that since he had begun, he would have to tell it all, and she waited patiently for him to continue.

He took a long drink from his teacup and cleared his throat. She could see how difficult and how painful these memories were for him.

"'At last!' the priest turned toward us and said, 'the time has come.' He walked out of the kitchen through the back door, and was gone for several minutes. Then he returned with the biggest, meanest, and ugliest German Shepherd dog I have ever seen in my entire life!! I have never yet seen one to compare. He was black and white with a smattering of brown on him here and there. His ears were sharp and pointed and alert. It was very obvious that he did not like having us in his domain.

"The leash he was tied to was coiled around the priest's hand three or four times. That leash was handmade of interwoven strands of rawhide.

"The beast's eyes were darting to and fro among all of us. This was an animal to be respected!

"'Judas, my pretty, stay calm my baby. Soon now, very soon.' He was speaking to the animal as though it were his beloved.

"What a name for a dog—Judas! I have to admit it was a name that described him perfectly. It was easy enough to see that like his namesake he could be all sweetness and light one moment and the next moment be ready to devour you.

"Holding firmly to the strong leash, the priest walked over to the other side of the room and tied the leash securely to the foot of the old black cast-iron stove that stood there.

"Then, walking over to where we were standing, he put his face real low, coming down to our level, and he asked us, 'Boys, are you hungry? Are you really hungry? What I want to know is if you are really and truly hungry!'

"All three of us nodded our heads in a gesture of assent. 'I SAID,' he was screaming at us now, and his face was turning beet red, 'ARE YOU HUNGRY?'

"The two younger boys were rather frightened and they were hanging on to Maman for dear life, but I was too stubborn to show fear. I stretched myself as tall as it was possible for a five-year-old to stretch himself and said as politely as I could, '*Oui, M'sieu le curé*, we are all very hungry.'

" 'Boy,' he thundered out, 'tell me just how hungry you really are!'

" '*Très, très*! Very, very hungry!'

"The priest reached out and gave me a hard resounding backhander that sent me reeling to the floor. When I removed my hand from my cheek I had the full imprint of the priest's hand.

"The priest hollered at me, 'You are a fresh, insolent, and undisciplined brat! What is your name?'

" 'My name is Alexandre Boisvert, and these are my brothers, Napoleon and Charles.' I never flinched or batted an eye. I may have been young, but I was someone to contend with!

" 'You are a spoiled brat,' replied the priest as he applied a resounding slap to my other cheek. 'I only asked of you who *you* are!'

"I now had two matching red welts swelling on my face.

"The priest pointed his finger in my face and angrily hissed at me, 'You, you think that you are such a big man, the man of the family, but we shall see just what kind of a big man you are!' As he spoke to me his lips were curled in distaste.

"*M'sieu le curé* then walked over to the table where the big platter had been set. He placed it upon the floor and went over and began petting his dog. 'Come Judas.' He was grinning maliciously, 'Let us see who is more hungry, you or the boys.'

"He turned toward Maman. 'Madame Boisvert, are you a gambler? Tonight you cannot sing for your supper, but being kindly disposed toward you and your boys, I will make a deal with you.'

"Elisabeth tried to speak but the words stuck in her throat.

"The priest, obviously enjoying every moment, continued speaking. 'The odds, Madame, are in your favor. Three to one. Ha, ha, ha. Just to show you that my heart is in the right place, I will give your boys a ten-second head start. Ha, ha, ha, ha. Is this not fair of me? Being a fair-minded and righteous man, I will allow each boy one mouthful of food before I set Judas free. Ha, ha, ha.'

"It finally dawned on Elisabeth what he was up to and she tried to speak. 'But, but,' she sputtered.

"I, showing a maturity that belied my age, stepped bravely forth, once again trying to make myself appear taller than I was. My eyes were flashing and my lips were quivering. I looked the priest straight in the eye and said,

'*Non, merci beaucoup*, but Alexandre Boisvert and his family do not eat with the dogs.'

"The priest put his hands upon his hips, threw his head back, and began to laugh uproariously, so much so that tears ran down his cheeks. Then all of a sudden he stopped laughing and his eyes began flashing.

"In a mocking tone of voice, he repeated my tone of voice. '*Non, merci beaucoup*, but Alexandre Boisvert and his family do not eat with the dogs!'

"All of a sudden he stopped mocking and walked forward to where we stood and hissed at us. 'You will not move a muscle or even a hair until I tell you to, or Judas, at my command, will rip you apart. He will tear you to shreds like an old rag doll. He will make you non-existent.

"'Is that clear? Do you understand me? That goes for you too, Mrs. Garrand.' He spoke to the housekeeper, who was standing there very white-faced.

"The poor housekeeper was speechless and merely nodded her head in agreement.

"He then released the dog, all the time whispering words of endearment to him. The dog swiftly ran over to the dish of food and quickly made short work out of eating every morsel and licking the platter clean.

"Then the priest walked over to where the dog was and put the pot of stew that had been on the stove in front of the dog, including all of the biscuits. Once again the dog made short work of eating it all up with appropriate noises and grunts and groans. When the dog was finished, the pot shone as though it were brand new.

"The priest was making sure that there was nothing left for the woman and her sons!

"The priest was obviously enjoying every moment and he kept watching us. He gave the impression of being disappointed because we were not begging him.

"The 'good priest' then went and got a great big bowl of fresh milk and set that before his dog.

"No one moved a muscle!

"We boys were so hungry and thirsty that we were literally beside ourselves. We ran our tongues over our lips in a useless attempt to moisturize them.

"*M'sieu le curé* then retied the dog on his leash and brought him back outside.

"When he once again returned to the kitchen, Maman mustered up enough courage to ask him, 'Now are we free to leave?'

"The priest ignored her totally and walked over to where I was standing, pointing his finger maliciously in my face. He said to me very viciously, 'You have learned an important lesson tonight, boy, thanks to me. You see, boy,' he spat out, 'he who thinks he is too good to eat with the dogs, does not eat at all!'

"My anger was fully aroused against the priest. I spoke back to him in a loud voice, 'You do not eat out of the dog's dish. Your name is Father Renard, which means fox, but you are not a sly old fox. You, you are the devil himself!! I shall live long enough to see the devil himself walk on your grave!'

"My little lips were trembling as I finished my tirade.

"'Alexandre!' Maman realized that she had spawned a strong son in this her oldest child. She knew that in days to come she would have to depend on my strength and wisdom.

"*I have a five-year-old son that is going on fifty,* she thought."

Chapter Seven
A New Life

Genevieve had not mentioned anything to her grandfather about what he had told her concerning his voyage to America. She had felt that this was too private and personal to be discussed lightly. She knew him well enough to know that if he wanted to discuss the matter again he would do so in his own good time, not hers.

He had not said a word about the matter even though they had sat every afternoon in the living room by the fireside. He seemed content to stay just a short while as she played many of his favorite tunes and passages, and this seemed to relax him and soothe him.

About five days later as they sat once again in the very pleasant room, she had thought that he was asleep and was just about to doze off herself when she heard his voice.

"Genevieve." His voice was as soft as an April breeze. "Do you remember when I told you about that priest, Father Renard, and what he had done to my family, Maman and my two little brothers?"

"Yes," she said rather sharply, "what a terrible man! I tell you, Grand-père, if he were still alive, I would find him and give him what for!" She was very angry. "Imagine anyone doing such a thing to Grand-père! What kind of an animal was he anyhow?"

"Now, now, my dear." He was obviously trying to soothe her ruffled feathers. He was pleased to know that she loved him enough to want to defend him and his causes.

"When we left the rectory," he was once again lost in memories of his own, "Maman, Napoleon, Charles, and myself were very cold, hungry, and tired. Napoleon and Charles were crying at the top of their lungs, and as we walked along Maman's face was being washed with her silent tears. I myself could not cry because I felt that once I started to cry I should never stop again!

"We did not know which way to turn or which way to go. We had no idea of where we were or where we should go, either! You cannot understand the fear or the desolation that was in our hearts!" Tears were flowing freely down the old man's face now and he wiped his eyes with the backs of his hands.

"We stood out in the middle of the road, looking this way and that way. Where to turn? The boys were giving their voices a rest now, at least for the moment.

"The night was so dark and foreboding, everything was overcast and there was not a star to be seen in the sky. Even a sliver of the moon was nowhere to be found.

"We started to walk slowly and forlornly. Maman was carrying the baby and she had one of Napoleon's hands and I held on to the other.

"All of a sudden—we had taken a few steps—we heard the sound of a voice. 'Madame! Madame!' We children became frightened. Imagine a voice in the stillness and darkness of night!

"Maman told us to be quiet as she turned to see who was calling. It was Mrs. Garrand, the housekeeper from the rectory.

"Mrs. Garrand put her finger to her lips and indicated, Shh, shh. 'Please be quiet. If Père Renard knew that I was out here against his wishes, it would cost me my job! I must go back in there before he misses me.' She spoke hurriedly and in whispers. 'Go down to the end of the street, over there. See that big oak tree over there? Stay there and rest until I come for you. You must be quiet at all costs. I will come as quickly as I can. Oh, oh, I must go.' She was off like lightning. Her appearance had been so brief I wasn't sure if we had imagined it or not. . . ."

"Did you listen to her, Grand-père?"

"What else could we do?" he asked his granddaughter. "A poor abandoned woman and her three little boys! Not a cent in our pockets, either!

"We walked over to the great oak tree, and even though it was quite cool, we were grateful to be able to sit down. Maman also was happy to sit down as she had been carrying Charles in her arms for quite a while. We weren't seated for more than a moment or two when the boys fell asleep peacefully. 'Good!' Maman said. 'Now we will not have to worry about the boys being quiet.' Maman looked over at me and asked, 'Alexandre, are you all right?'

" 'Oh, *oui*, Maman, I am fine. How are you?'

" 'Alexandre, I do not want you to worry. Everything will be fine for us.'

" 'I am not worried, Maman.' We both knew that we were not telling the truth.

" 'Alexandre, I will not mind if you close your eyes and rest for a moment.'

" 'I don't need to, Maman; I am fine.' But I was young and could not help myself, and soon I too had my eyes closed and was resting.

"I do not know how long we waited. The next thing I knew Maman was waking me gently. 'Alexandre, Alexandre, make haste, we must go quickly. Hurry now.'

"I sat there for a moment and rubbed my eyes and saw Mrs. Garrand. She spoke to me, saying 'You are a big lad, you can walk,' and she picked Napoleon up as though he were a little rag doll and carried him.

" 'It is not far to go,' she told Maman. Meanwhile Napoleon had his little arms clasped tightly around her neck.

"We all walked silently until we arrived at an old brick building very much in disrepair, and Mrs. Garrand said, 'This is the place. There are five rooms here. I, being alone, only have use for three. In the meanwhile you and your boys may use the other two.'

"Maman began to cry and could not bring herself to stop until Mrs. Garrand said, 'Enough of that or you'll have all of us blubbering. Besides, I think that these boys have had enough tears for one day! Don't you? I think that you should take these boys and get them cleaned up. They look filthy and smell worse." She made a face.

" 'Yes,' Maman said. 'Oh yes.' And she took us all into the bathroom and gave us a good scrubbing.

"When we emerged we could smell the smell of a good homemade soup. Mrs. Garrand looked at Maman and said, 'It is not much and I had to add a lot of water so that we could share, but it is hot, and it is a lot better than an empty stomach, right?'

" 'You are right,' Maman said, 'and you are most kind. We accept your offer very gratefully.'

" 'C'mon,' said the lady, 'let's stop chitter chattering and eat.'

"Maman said, 'Yes boys, let us thank God for our food.' As Maman said this we bowed our heads and Maman said a brief prayer of thanks. All the while Mrs. Garrand watched us closely, and she turned to Maman and said, 'I cannot believe my eyes! Three starving boys; I would have thought that they would pounce at the food, but they waited for you to pray. I am amazed!'

"Maman just smiled that little smile of hers and said, 'My boys are not animals, and I try very hard to teach them.'

" 'Come, boys, let us eat.'

"I tell you, Genevieve, that soup that we were given that night was the best I've ever eaten. Maman made us eat slowly so that we would not get sick after not eating all day. Little Charles kept on saying, 'Mmmm, mmmm,' and clapping his little hands, and even Maman seemed to relax a little bit. As soon as we were done eating, little Charles fell asleep on Maman's lap. He was so tired.

"Napoleon had not taken his eyes off of Mrs. Garrand's face ever since she had picked him up and carried him. His big brown eyes were so solemn. He walked over to Mrs. Garrand and climbed up on her lap.

"Maman was very concerned as Mrs. Garrand had told her that she did not care much for children and that Maman should keep us out of her way.

"Mrs. Garrand just stared at Napoleon and he at her, and finally he took his little hand and started to caress her face. '*Tu es belle* (You are pretty). *Merci, merci!*'

"Mrs. Garrand's eyes began to mist over, even though she would never admit it, and she gave Napoleon a hug as if to indicate we were not so bad after all!

"Years later Mrs. Garrand told Maman that she had planned on sending us all upstairs to sleep in rooms that had not been cleaned in years, but after Napoleon had told her she was pretty she could not do it. Napoleon was the only one in her lifetime that had ever told her she was pretty!!

" 'We'd better get these gentlemen into bed as it is very late. Come, we will make a place on the living room floor for you and the boys.' Mrs. Garrand went over and took Napoleon by the hand and looked over at me and said, 'What are you waiting for? Shake a leg!!'

"She went into her bedroom and came back out carrying two great big homemade quilts, which were much the worse for wear, but we could not care less for we were all so tired. She also came out with an old threadbare nightgown for Maman to wear. I believe all of us fell to sleep that night the moment our heads hit the pillow.

"In the morning when Mrs. Garrand woke up, Maman had already been up for quite a while. She had a pot of coffee brewing and porridge was already being kept warm on the back of the stove.

"The apartment looked much worse in the daytime than it had at night. The walls had not been washed in many years and the floors gave the same appearance. *This could be a nice place if it were cleaned up,* Maman thought. *If this dear lady does not take offense, I will take it upon myself to do something about it.*

"As though sensing what Maman was thinking, Mrs. Garrand said, 'I do not like living like this, with all this clutter, but I have to work seven days a week and when I am home it seems that I am too tired to do what I want to do.' She heaved a great big sigh.

"Maman quickly went over and gave her a hug. 'You poor dear.'

"Napoleon had awakened and came out of the living room running as fast as he could. The very first thing that he did was run over and hug Mrs. Garrand. This brought forth a smile from her face.

"Maman told Mrs. Garrand, 'Last night I did not get the chance to thank you properly for what you are doing for me and my boys. You are an angel of mercy . . .'

"Before Maman could finish, Mrs. Garrand began to laugh uproariously. 'Me! An angel of mercy?' She looked at Maman with her squinty eyes. 'Believe me, Madame Boisvert, I expect to recover everything that I expend for you and your boys. I keep very accurate records!'

" 'Of course,' Maman said. 'I would not stay under any other conditions.'

" 'You can do what you want with the two rooms upstairs. Let me tell you that it will take a lot of work to get them cleaned up. I must run or M'sieu le curé will be eating his breakfast late, and he will not like it at all!'

"Maman worked that day as she had never worked in her life. My job was to keep the boys amused, and I worked hard at it, too!

"By the time Mrs. Garrand came home that night, no one would have dreamed that this was the same house she had left that morning. Maman had put us boys to bed so that the house would be quiet for her when she came home after a hard day's work. Maman had scrubbed and cleaned, and then she had a simple meal waiting for her when she got in.

"When Mrs. Garrand entered the house and saw what Maman had done she began to cry. 'I thought that I was in the wrong house,' she told Maman. 'I have never seen my little house look so nice.'

"Maman said, 'I fed the boys early and put them to bed. I waited to eat with you. I hope that is all right?'

" 'Of course it is. I must confess I looked forward to coming home with someone waiting for me.' As she spoke these words her face turned bright red.

"Maman spoke and said, 'May I ask a question of you?'

" 'Of course. What is it?' she asked.

" 'Well,' Maman said, 'my name is Elisabeth and I would like to know what yours is. If we are to be friends we should know each other's name.'

" 'My name is Jeannot.'

" 'Jeannot,' Maman said, as though she had never heard it before. 'Jeannot, yes it fits you, you are Jeannot.'

" 'Jeannot?' Maman spoke as though she were embarrassed.

" 'Yes,' Jeannot replied. 'What is it?'

"Maman said, 'I must find a job to support myself and my three boys. Do you have any idea where I could go or what I could do?'

" 'Elisabeth,' Jeannot said, 'I have been thinking perhaps we could work something out together, you and I.' Elisabeth's eyes opened wide. 'What do you mean?'

" 'Well.' Jeannot spoke contemplating every word. 'I have found that I like very much to come home to a house that is alive, and you have created miracles here, too. Would you consider staying in here as my companion? I don't have much and I am willing to share. Also, you are an excellent seamstress and perhaps I could get you some work doing sewing so that you might have a little money in your pocket, as I cannot afford to pay you.'

"Maman made an instant decision. She ran over to where Jeannot was sitting and said, 'Yes, yes! I accept! I accept!'

"Our problems were solved and Jeannot's problems were solved. She was no longer lonely. She would find special ways to find some treat or other for us, sometimes much to Maman's dismay.

"She stopped being Mrs. Garrand and became '*Ma Tante* Jeannot,' 'our very special aunt,' indeed! If it was not for her, I don't know what would have become of us. Even though we called her aunt, she really was more like a grandmother to us, and she watched over all of us like a mother hen does over her chicks.

"This, my dear granddaughter, is how we started our new life in America. Now this old man is tired and I must retire. Good night."

"Good night, Grand-père." She sat there in a world of her own, thinking over the things that he had told her.

Chapter Eight
Settling Down

Genevieve sat there in the little office, and her mind was racing in many directions at once. *If only I had paid more attention to Grand-père when he related all these things to me! Oh, dear, here I go again! Every time I sit in this office, I seem to have a pity party for myself. We . . . I have made a decision and that is that from now on this shall be known as Genevieve's office. So there! This is my office. This is my office!*

Tears were running down her face now and she could no longer control herself, and she began throwing everything in the office around. She swept everything off of the top of the desk with one sweep of her arm, she pulled open the desk drawers and dumped everything that was in them on the floor.

She tore down the drapes and everything that was hanging on the walls, and when she was done she threw herself down on top of the mess and lay there like a broken doll, and now she could not even cry!

Anna had come to the office to see what Genevieve would like for lunch, and when she viewed Genevieve in such a fit of rage she immediately called Harold at work. "Please, Harry, come home right away. I have never seen Genevieve like this, it is terrible. Please come home right away. Please, I beg you!"

"Anna! You've got to calm yourself down! Call Dr. Livernois and tell him to meet us at the house." Harold hung up the phone with a bang and ran out of his office as fast as his legs could carry him. "Home emergency!" he called out to his secretary as he was running out.

Harold tried hard to stay within the speed limits as he hurried home. He began to pray, "Dear God, please let Genevieve and the baby be all right." Even though he had a longer way to travel Harold pulled into the yard at the same time as the doctor.

"Harold," he boomed out, "what is this all about?"

"I don't know. All I know is that Anna called and she was terribly upset."

The older man towered above Harold in height but he put his arm around him in a gesture of camaraderie and said, "Come! Let's go see what is wrong with our girl!"

As they went through the door Harold said to Anna, "Where is she?"

"She is still in the office, crumpled up like an old rag doll." Anna began to sob with her face in her apron.

Harold ran to the office and, sure enough, there was Genevieve atop the pile of rubble on the floor. He thought Anna's description was true. Genevieve did look like an old crumpled rag doll.

Genevieve, apparently tired after her fit of rage, had fallen asleep, and Harold was not sure at first if she was asleep or if she had passed out.

"Genni, Genni!" He shook her softly. "Wake up!"

Genevieve sat up and looked at Harold in a bewildered manner, and as she sat there rubbing her eyes she said, "Harold? What are you doing home? Have I slept that long?"

"What is going on here, I would like to know? What has happened to the office?"

"Oh, Harry, I did it; it was me. I did it all myself!"

"But why? I don't understand why you would do such a thing? You have scared Anna half to death, not to mention Dr. Livernois and myself!" Harold's anger was flaring forth now.

"Harold, can't you understand? Life is not the same for me anymore. I mean without him! Nobody understands how I feel! NOBODY! Everywhere I look, everyone I see, all remind me of him!" She started to weep.

Genevieve would have thought that Harold would have comforted her and put his arms around her, but he did not.

If one knew Harold well enough, one would have seen his nostrils beginning to flare out in anger. "Forgive me, my dear," he said sarcastically, and he bowed before her. "You, of course, are the only one that misses him! All the rest of us, such as Anna, who has known him all her life, and myself, who has only known and loved him twenty years as has Dr. Livernois, we have no right to sorrow or grieve! That is the exclusive right of Miss Genevieve!"

Harold turned and walked out of the room, muttering to himself, "I am going to go and find Anna and the doctor so that we can all throw a tantrum!"

Genevieve sat there for a long, long time looking at the mess she had created. She was disgusted with herself. This behavior went against everything that she believed in.

"It's the old teapot syndrome," she said half aloud. "Grand-père warned me about it so many times. An ostrich is said to bury its head in the sand, but every once in a while he comes up for air. The person that lives in a teapot is all alone by himself. Living in a teapot is like living in a prison except that the sentence is self-imposed. Nothing matters to the prisoner in the teapot, for he has no room for anyone but himself! The sad part of it all is that once you get used to living in a teapot you become afraid to lift up the lid. The world passes by and all the teapot person sees is the inside of the teapot. Thus the world has passed by and you are still sitting there!

"What Grand-père was trying to tell me was that when I get hurt in some way or other I become very selfish and can only see my side of the thing. Harold is right; I am just a spoiled brat playing temper tantrum games."

Genevieve gave herself a mental shaking. *Grow up! Grow up! How can you be a mother if you can't even take care of yourself? I must make reparations with those I love. What can I do? I wonder if it is too late for me. I have never seen Harold as he was tonight. All the time I felt that I was being noble and devoting myself to Grand-père, I was neglecting all the people dear to me.*

I really thought that Harold liked working late at the office, but today I sensed that my idea about that was wrong. Grand-père tried many times to tell me that Harold should be the central part of my life, but I would not listen. I seem to get the idea that Harold is fed up with me.

Genevieve stood up slowly and turned to look at the mess she had created. *I made this mess; it is up to me to clean it up.* She began slowly picking up first one item and then another and finding a place for each. *This was so stupid of me. I could have redecorated any way I wanted to or rearranged everything for my convenience. Whatever prompted me to be so foolish?*

Genevieve worked for many hours to try and mend the damage that she had done. Even when she was finished things did not look the same. *I'll have to get some new draperies as these will not be able to be repaired.*

Genevieve looked at her watch and found that it was 2:30 A.M. She could hardly believe it! No one had bothered to come and see if she was all right or even thought to bring her something to eat or drink. *I guess I turned them all away from me!*

She began to feel the hunger pains rattling at her stomach and decided to go into the kitchen and look for something to eat or drink. She could not find even a remnant of supper. *Strange,* she thought, *Anna always sets aside a plate for me. Well, I guess I still know how to cook an egg for myself.* She cooked herself an egg and toast and poured herself some milk. She found that she could not eat and forced herself to drink the milk, "for the baby's sake."

When she came to the bedroom she found that Harold was fast asleep and she tried to be as quiet as possible so as not to awaken him, although deep down in her heart she wanted him to awaken and comfort her.

Genevieve lay awake for most of the night and finally in the early dawn hours fell into a deep and troubled sleep. This kind of sleep was not the kind that gave you rest, but rather the kind that you fell into because of exhaustion.

When she finally awakened she was disappointed to find that Harold had already left for work. *Well*, she sighed, *at least I can start mending fences with Anna*. Much to her dismay when she went downstairs Anna was nowhere to be found! She wandered around the big house rather aimlessly at first and then she decided, *I am not a quitter!* So she decided to work off all her feelings of frustration. *If that is how things are going to be, so be it!*

There was not much to be done, as Anna was a fastidious housekeeper, so she decided to work in her grandfather's room. *I wish I could always leave this room the way it is, but that would not bring him back.*

A shrine, she thought. *How he would have hated that idea. I suppose the thing to do would be to go through his clothes first. There must be someone somewhere that could use some good clothes. I'll let Harold go through them first and see if he wants something.*

She began going through all of the clothes in his closet and she checked everything over carefully as she did not want to give away anything that was not good. She smiled as she went through the pockets of his suit coats and sport jackets, for as she did, each one had a least a twenty dollar bill in it.

She remembered how he hated to be caught short without money in his pocket. *I wonder*, she thought, *if Anna would care to have this bedroom set*. Anna, being stubborn, had never allowed them to buy her a bedroom set. All she had were the odd pieces of furniture that she had when they had first become a little family together.

She noticed that the shades were down, casting a gloomy effect, so she went over and raised them up. She stood there for a moment or two looking out the window. The ground was covered with sparkling snow, crisp and clean and shiny. The trees appeared to have been frosted and were swaying gently so as not to disturb their shiny guests. *Just one single motion*, she thought, *and everything is changed from gloom and despair to light and beauty. How strange life is*. She smiled to herself.

As she began to empty the room of her grandfather's belongings and looked around, she began to think it would be the ideal place for Harold to put his office. *Why, we could even put in a private entrance for his legal clients to use and still have the privacy of our home.*

It seemed so long ago that they had talked about things. *I wonder if he still would want to be with me as he used to.*

We don't really have to worry about the money, and it would be nice to have him near. Somehow something had released the anger from within her and she felt that everything was going to work out for the best.

She felt the child kicking around in her womb, and this action brought a tender smile to her face. *You know, little one, we are going to be all right!*

She had made neat piles of underwear and socks and handkerchiefs and was starting to bring them into her bedroom when she heard a commotion in the kitchen. She went to the kitchen to see what was going on and saw Harold and Dr. Livernois, one on each side of Anna, who was on crutches!

"What happened?" Genevieve was so shocked and surprised, her voice was much louder than she intended it to be. "Anna, what has happened to you?"

Dr. Livernois spoke up, saying, "Let's get this young lady to bed and then we shall take the time to answer all of your questions."

The old doctor was so tender as he helped Anna to a chair.

Genevieve spoke up. "We will put Anna in the bedroom right off the kitchen," her voice trailed off. "Of course, Anna, if that is all right with you?"

Anna nodded her head in assent but did not speak.

Genevieve hurried about putting the kettle on for tea.

Harold noticed that when Genevieve had mentioned to Anna about the room she did not say "Grand-père's room off of the kitchen." This surprised him somewhat as he had thought that Genevieve would keep the room as a sort of shrine or something to that effect.

Imagine his further surprise when he entered the room and found that it was in the process of being cleared of all the old man's clothes. Harold, deep down in his heart, had hoped to turn the old man's room into an office for himself, but he had not dared to approach Genevieve on this matter for fear that she would fall apart.

"I did not know that we would need the room today," Genevieve spoke apologetically. "I think it is best to clear this room out as soon as possible."

Harold nodded quietly. "Yes, I think you are right."

"Harold, I think we had better hurry and put these things in the spare room for now and let Anna come in and rest. She looks so pale. Poor Anna!"

Harold and Genevieve worked together hand in hand as they used to do in times past. Soon they had the whole room cleared of the clutter and Genevieve was sweeping it clean. She hurried and turned down the bedcovers and watched as the two men gently brought Anna into the bedroom.

Genevieve went into Anna's room at the other end of the house and came quickly back with a nightgown and bathrobe. "Are these all right, Anna?"

Anna's complexion was very pale and she watched as Genevieve bustled about. "Now," said Genevieve, "you gentlemen will excuse us?"

The men quickly left the room so that Genevieve could help Anna undress and get more comfortable. Genevieve did not ask even one question, although she was dying to know what had happened to Anna.

Once Anna was comfortably settled, Genevieve went into the kitchen and made some tea and toast for Anna, and the men went in to see and visit with her.

Anna was embarrassed by all the attention, but it also pleased her to know that they were so concerned for her well-being, too. She had always been the mother hen, the strong one, and she had to admit that she did enjoy the fuss a little bit.

After Anna had finished eating, the doctor went into the kitchen and came back with a glass of water and some kind of medication for pain, which he had Anna take. Genevieve deduced that Anna must really be in a lot of pain, as she did not put up any fuss at all but did obediently what the doctor told her to do.

Anna soon fell asleep and the three of them went into the kitchen and sat at the kitchen table.

Genevieve could see that the men had been through a trying experience, so she hurriedly made coffee for all of them. Harold went over to help her carry the coffee and the plate of corn muffins she had baked earlier. When he got to the counter, he gave her a quick hug and patted her belly. "How's Junior doing?" As he did this he felt the baby kick for the first time. Harold started to laugh and so did Genevieve.

"Hey, Doc!" Harold boomed out. "Ya see that? The kid likes his name, Junior."

Genevieve laughed and said, "Hey, smarty, just suppose it's a little she?"

"Oh," Harold laughed, "no problem! If it's a she we'll call her Harriet."

The doctor looked at both of them with a deadpan expression. "What is wrong, may I ask, with a Joseph or a little Josephine?" They all laughed merrily.

"Now," asked Genevieve, "tell me, please, what happened to Anna?"

"Well," the doctor spoke up, "I had agreed to take Anna shopping this morning, early. We were to go to the mall, as she wanted to surprise you by being the first one to buy a present for the baby." He thought for a moment.

"We all felt that you had been through a very emotional time yesterday and decided that you should rest today. Harold had told us that you did not sleep all night. Early this morning Anna called me at home and said that she would walk down to the mailbox and meet me there. Harold had offered to give her a ride, but she said she would rather walk."

Harold then intervened. "Anna made my breakfast and then cleaned up and left to meet Doc. I was running a little late this morning, thank God, because when I got into my car and started down the road, there was Anna! She had slipped in the snow, and her leg was all twisted up under her. Just as I got out of my car to see what was wrong, Doc drove up and he put her leg in a splint and we carried her into the car and drove her to the hospital."

"I knew all the time that she had a compound fracture," said the doctor, "but as you know these things have to be set and we need X rays to do that. She really should have stayed in the hospital, but would not because she was afraid to worry you. This type of fracture is very painful, and she will have to be off of her feet for quite a while."

Genevieve looked over at the doctor and said, "Then we shall need you here to make sure that we take care of her properly. You can use the guest room if you like."

"I thought that you would never ask. I like, and thank you for your kind offer."

Chapter Nine
Memories

Genevieve did not often let her mind return to the days of the past. The memories could be very painful to her. Grand-père so often told her, "We must make the most of our lives each and every day. If we dwell on the past, we shall not have the time nor the energy to live for today."

He was a very wise man. What is the matter with me today? I really mean to say that he is a very wise man.

What do I really remember about Grand-mère? Oh, yes, I remember that in many ways she was very formal. She always wanted to be called Grand-mère instead of the more relaxed dialect form Memère, as so many of the French children called their grandparents.

Respect, she used to say. Respect in life is one of the most important things you will learn. Respect for yourself first, then you will have respect for others and for their property. The good God did not make people only for themselves, but to love, live, help, and to share together. You must remember as you go through your life that whatever you do always affects or touches the lives of others, too.

She was not a tall woman at all. Perhaps about five foot two, or even shorter. She appeared to be a most serious and severe person, on first appraisal. She had become rather heavyset as she grew into the years of her old age. Her complexion was remarkably unblemished and her rather chubby cheeks were dimpled and perpetually rosy. Her eyes of the palest blue were large and clear and seemingly could see into one's innermost soul. Many times she had known things that were untold to her for she had an intuitive perception given to those who have lived life to the utmost. Her hair never attained the snowy clarity of her husband's. And as long as she lived it contained streaks of the blond that once had been her possession. She (at least when Genevieve knew her) wore her hair neatly pulled back to the sides of her head, forming a bun or French twist, as it is sometimes called, at the back of her head.

She liked to sit with her hands folded on her somewhat large belly, and when something struck her funny and she would laugh, everything would jiggle like jelly. Her eyes would appear to contain the very lights of the stars themselves, at times.

She was not a weak little old lady, thought Genevieve fondly, almost rubbing her behind in remembrance of the past punishments. *She never let me get away with anything, that's for sure. She could reprimand and she could spank or punish when the occasion warranted it.*

Memories seemed to be flooding her mind one after another, like a tornado hitting suddenly and quickly.

When I was very young, Grand-père and Grand-mère's home was a wonderful place to visit. Mom and Dad took me there often.

Then one day a terrible tragedy happened. Tears began to flow involuntarily from her eyes. That terrible accident that killed both of them. One lousy drunk driver killing two innocent people and leaving one little girl orphaned. How well she remembered the terrible moment, being called out of her third grade classroom. She knew the moment they called her into the office that something terrible had happened.

Even though you are very young in age there is some kind of inner feeling or sense that tells you something is inherently wrong. Something wrong! What an understatement! "Not both of them!" she screamed out, and in the selfishness of youth, "Who will take care of me now?"

What a selfish little thing I was, she thought. *It really never dawned on me that Grand-mère and Grand-père had also suffered a terrible loss. A daughter and a son-in-law whom they considered a third son. Maybe all eight-year-olds are just as thoughtless and selfish as I was. I doubt it, though. There I go again, acting as though I had invented the vice of thoughtlessness and selfishness. Grand-père may be right, I am always the hardest on myself.*

Rationalize the situation, she told herself. *Okay, a cold wintry day, icy roads, and a drunken driver on the loose. A lethal combination in any book.*

The thing she remembered the most about the wake was the terrible scent of the flowers. The perfumes all running rampant through her nostrils, intermingled like some giant pot of overspiced multiple conglomeration of ethnic cooking.

She resented the fact that others were alive and her parents were gone and she was a stranger in the midst of her relatives, each one treating her as though she were fragile and ready to break. Soon enough they felt that her treatment should no longer be that of a special individual and she became a thing to be pitied, in their minds of toleration.

At the funeral there were many people that she had never seen and some she had never even heard of crying and patting her on the back or on the top of her head, really not aware that she was there but in a gesture of having something to do, to show the others that were watching. So, each in turn seemed to follow the leader. She did not want tears or pats, she wanted her Mom and Dad!

The snow continued on for three more days, the worst she'd ever seen. This did not limit the attendance. There were so many people there that the street had to be blocked off, as though this was a comfort to her.

The large cathedral was gruesome and forbidding, and the music was macabre in its intonations. Even if you didn't know the dear departed, the tone was somber enough to make even the hardest heart weep. Two caskets were slowly wheeled into the church and were placed in the position of honor side by side. The priest in his robes of black gave a eulogy, not of hope and anticipation, but of forboding. "They would have wanted it this way," he said. *Where does that leave me?* she thought. Many times her father had promised her that they would always be together. They were a team! A family!

She remembered the time she and her mom and dad were walking down the street, dressed in their Sunday best. "See," he told her, "notice all these people looking at Andrew L. Greenwood? They are all jealous," he said. "They are asking themselves, how does that old rascal rate, having the two most beautiful girls in the world in his family?" Mother actually blushed, she remembered.

As the funeral procession proceeded up to the top of the steep hill which overlooked the entire town, the undertakers had to stop two or three times to sand the road. When they reached their destination and the undertakers were dutifully opening all the car doors, her grandmother pulled her onto the safety of her lap and covered her over with her fur coat.

"We will stay here," she told the others.

"Are you sure?" her husband asked her.

"*Oui,*" she replied. "I am certain, you go. My place is here, to see that the living are taken care of."

They sat in the car holding onto each other quietly, and Genevieve held on to her grandmother for dear life.

"Grand-mère," she asked, "what are they doing?"

"They are just praying. Do not be concerned."

"Why do you not want me to hear the prayers?"

"I need you to be here with me," she told the child gently.

Each one of them was shivering in the cold, and they held one another even tighter. Somehow Genevieve felt that never again would life be the same for her, and it never was, either!

It seemed like an eternity before the others returned to the long black limousine. Right there in that car began a relationship between the child and the elderly woman that would never be replaced nor forgotten.

They could hear the voices now of those returning. Suddenly the car door burst open and a voice, very unpleasant in its tone, demanded, "Get off of your grand-mère's lap!"

This unpleasant voice came from a woman who was in her middle age and very thin. Her voice was as rasping and unpleasant as she desired it to be.

She startled the little girl and Genevieve jumped, frightened, and began to move off of her grandmother's lap, but her grandmother held her fast.

"Rachel," the old woman began, "it is not in your authority to decide who will sit on my lap or not!"

Rachel did not offer a reply but she gave Genevieve a look that brought to mind the old saying, "if looks could kill."

Her grandfather entered the car, looking as he always did, very dignified and proper. He reached over and took the little girl upon his own knees, needing a little tenderness and comforting himself, but not wanting anyone else to know it. He reached over and gave his wife's hand a gentle squeeze as though to reassure her. They had been through a lot together and always made it through and they would this time too.

He pulled the child a little more securely on his lap. Genevieve looked over at the aunt, and as always she felt guilty. She did not like her aunt, and deep down inside she felt that perhaps she should. Now in her heart she resented the fact that her aunt was alive and her mother was not.

I'm glad no one can read my thoughts, she thought to herself. *Mom was so good*, she thought, *and Aunt Rachel is such a stinker!* She let her eyes skim over her aunt. All of Rachel's clothes were very expensive. Her aunt truly felt for some reason that she deserved the best of everything at whatever cost others had to pay.

Ernest, sitting next to his wife, was a total opposite of his wife. He was very tall and was beginning to grow a paunch. For some reason Genevieve rather liked him. He was totally dominated by his wife in everything except when it came to the bottle, which was his mistress! He had often made Genevieve laugh when he would stick his neck way out like a goose, stick his rear way out, and walk around flapping his arms in his "barnyard strut."

She always liked it when he did this, for somehow the end result of it for her was always an ice cream cone.

Ernest had been blessed with a sense of humor that Rachel saw fit to squelch at every turn.

Chapter Ten
The Party

The ride home seemed to come to an end so quickly. Somehow there was a finality to things, no turning back now.

Genevieve could not understand why there had to be a party. Someone had said to her, "Not a party really, more like a gathering of the family and friends."

"As if that could make anyone feel better! I wish they'd all go away and leave us alone! Me and Grand-mère and Grand-père."

She really needed to be helped with all the "why"s and "wherefore"s of the situation. She had inherited the analytical mind of her father.

Grand-mère seemed to sense exactly what Genevieve was thinking and answered her thoughts before they could be formed into a question.

"We must feed the ones who have traveled a long distance, it is tradition."

"Who cares about tradition anyway?"

When they arrived at her grandparents' home Genevieve could not believe her eyes! The house was filled wall to wall with people. There was absolutely no place that one could be alone. Not one! There was even a waiting line to go into the bathroom.

That's all it is, she thought to herself, *a rotten, dirty party.*

She looked at the scene around her, and there they were, tons of people, drinking, laughing, smoking, and eating much more than they should, just taking advantage of the free meal. They felt that they had fulfilled their obligation by coming and that this time was their just reward or payment. They had done their duty toward the dear departed and now they deserved to be entertained. Talk about savages!

Even the so-called man of God was not feeling any pain, walking around with one drink after the other in his hand, telling off-color stories in French to anyone that would listen to him.

Genevieve had gone upstairs hoping to find a spot to be alone and had come upon a rather compromising situation. One of her aunts was lying down on the bed and this so-called man of God was running his hand up and down between her legs. Genevieve startled them as she entered the room, they were so deep in concentration. It was kind of funny in a way when he looked up and saw Genevieve standing there watching. He hemmed and hawed for a minute, and then said to her, "Your poor aunt hurt herself, and I was checking to see if we should call a doctor for her or not."

Her aunt Blanche at least had the decency to keep her mouth shut, until Genevieve said rather maliciously, "Dr. Secony is still downstairs; I will go and get him for you."

Only then did her aunt panic, much to Genevieve's delight. "No, no!" she tried to calm herself. "I am sure that it is nothing. Please, child, run and get me a cold cloth and I'll take some aspirin later."

Genevieve felt good inside because as young as she was she had done something mean to them. Even in her tenderness of years and her limited understanding of life, she knew within herself that what they were doing was not right or proper.

She dutifully brought a cold cloth to her aunt, who by now had properly pulled her clothes together. Genevieve, although sickened by her aunt's behavior, stood and listened to her dutifully as her aunt persuaded her that this was to be their little secret, and made Genevieve promise not to tell anyone about her little escapade.

Blanche stood there and looked at her niece in a very calculating manner. *This little girl is no dummy. I'd better do some fast talking*, she thought.

"Thank you for bringing this cloth to me; it was just what I needed. You are so thoughtful and kind." She smiled at the child affectionately. "I do appreciate it, you know. I guess I'd better watch my step and be a little more careful where I go from now on.

"We are all so terribly upset by this horrible tragedy." Her eyes began to be filled with moisture and she made a vague effort to dab at them thinking of course that she looked very pathetic.

"I want you to know, dear, sweet child, that if you ever need anything you come directly to me." All the while she spoke she was looking around making sure no one heard her make these promises that she had no intention of keeping. She patted Genevieve on the top of her head.

Genevieve almost choked listening to her aunt. Everyone that knew Blanche knew that she could not tolerate children in any way, shape, or form!

Her aunt spoke up rather loudly, "Do you hear me?"

Genevieve, more to silence her aunt than give credence to her words, said, "Yes, I hear you!"

"Well then," Blanche said, clearing her throat, "about that little matter that happened here"; and clearing her throat again, "you know about the fact that I hurt myself slightly. Can this be our little secret? You know how Grand-mère worries and also your uncle Samuel. Why, he is just a great big bundle of nerves. Now that's a good girl, you will promise me to keep our little secret?"

Genevieve hung her head down low as she felt ashamed and embarrassed for this woman who would go to such extremes to cover up her wrongdoings.

"Yes," she told her aunt. "Yes, I will keep your secret." She never told anyone either, even after she grew older.

"Come here, child, and give your favorite auntie a bit hug and a kiss." Genevieve went over and dutifully placed her unresponsive lips upon her aunt's cheek, and the action made her shudder involuntarily.

"I am so proud," Blanche cooed, "that I could speak to you like a big girl."

Genevieve thought to herself, *Now I know what it feels like to hug a rattlesnake! Brr!*

She ran to the bathroom. Thank God it was empty! "I'm going to be sick. Oh, dear God, don't let me be sick now." Before her thought was even finished she promptly emptied the contents of her stomach into the oval bowl. She was weakened by all the effort, and she pulled herself up with difficulty and leaned against the little sink. She unceremoniously splashed cold water on her face, trying to revive herself somewhat. She straightened herself up as best she could and decided to go back downstairs.

As she slowly descended the flight of stairs she caught full view of the activities that were taking place. "I guess you could call them festivities depending on your point of view."

Grand-mère was sitting by herself off to one side. Her face was solemn and serene. Genevieve believed that her grandmother's thoughts were the same as her own. *Why don't they all go away?*

Someone had brought Simone a plate of food, which she was not eating but rather rearranging, as though she were redesigning it.

Her grandfather's expression was that of total solemnity. She thought to herself, *They are the only ones that feel bad, except for me.*

Aunt Blanche was gazing adoringly into Uncle Samuel's eyes and hanging onto every word he uttered as though it were "Gospel."

Blanche was a very tiny woman and probably did not hit the scales at a full one hundred pounds. She had no shape or form that would visibly prove that she was a woman. If you looked at her from the rear, she looked like a young boy who had not yet attained the age of puberty. She always dressed in grays or blacks and kept her dresses long, almost down to her ankles. Her hair was always tied back into a bun at the back of her head. A perfect picture of piousness and religiosity, which she worked very hard to portray, too!

Her uncle Samuel was as rotund as his wife was slender. He was a very short man, which of course made him seem even heavier than he really was. In his own mind Samuel was a very "big man." He was (to himself at least) a very important man. He did literally run the little town. It was not because he was so powerful as much as the fact that no one else wanted the job. He was a selfish and greedy man in all areas of life, whether it was food, money, or extra-marital affairs. He was always on the lookout for ways to satisfy one or the other of his appetites. His sister's funeral was a good opportunity for him and he used every moment for his advantage, too!

As she stood there on the staircase, she then turned to the right, and there they were, her uncle Isaac and her aunt Susannah. She stared at them for a moment or two. *No wonder everyone calls them "Mr. and Mrs. five by five." No other description would fit them as well. Let's face it,* she thought, *they are fat! fat! fat!* Anyone who saw them would know that there was a competition going on as to whom could become the fattest or most physically unfit between them.

They were both so fat as to appear grotesque. Their whole ambition in life was the ingesting of food, as though they expected a famine at a moment's notice. How many double chins they possessed between them was anyone's guess. Each one of them had big rolls of loose fat that covered their knees when they sat down. They had no worldly possessions that mattered to them, except for their farm and for their ten children, who had complete freedom over the farm, coming and going as they would. Discipline was unheard of to them, and they had no respect for themselves or others either. Having a new addition to the family did not cause any more of a stir than when one of the cows calved.

As Genevieve observed all this she became even more despondent. *Why couldn't I have been in the car with Mom and Dad? Mom, Dad, why did you go without me? All of these people are a bunch of morons except for Grand-mère and Grand-père. Grand-mère says that I had to stay behind because God was not finished with me yet. I want to be with you!*

No one could understand the fears and horrors the young girl felt. After all, her whole life had been torn apart. "Thank God I have Grand-mère and Grand-père, or else I don't know what I would do.

"I wonder what will become of our little house, and all of Maman's beautiful clothes; and no one will take care of or love Daddy's books like he did. Oh my, I wonder if I'll still go to the same school!

"What will I do if everyone makes fun of me and feels sorry for me? Grand-mère and Grand-père are very old. What if they die too? I can't ever go to live with Uncle Samuel or Uncle Isaac, or Aunt Rachel either. Why didn't God take her instead of Mom, or even Aunt Blanche, that dirty pig!

"I have to get out of here; I can't take it anymore!" She tore her coat out of the hallway closet, put it on as quickly as she could, and ran for the door.

Her grandmother called out. But she could not bring herself to stop.

"Ma," Samuel said, "I told you that kid is nothing but trouble, but by golly I'll bring her back quick enough," and he started for his own coat.

The old man spoke up, "Let the child be."

Samuel reluctantly turned back. His mannerisms definitely showed his annoyance with the old man. But as he often thought, *The old fool still handles the purse strings.* So he obeyed.

Simone turned to her husband. "Alexandre, where do you think the child has gone?"

The old man thought for a moment. "I believe she had a need to get away and be by herself for a bit."

"But it is so cold out there."

"You must not worry; she will be back soon enough. If we were smart," he said, "we would have gone with her and also escaped from this farce. We should know better than to allow Rachel to take over something like this. Everything she does is just a big show. You can bet that she is going to pad all the expenses, too."

The old woman's sadness and weariness was very apparent. "What difference does it make?" she sighed heavily. "It will not bring Laura or Andrew back to us. Alexandre," she spoke in a half whisper, "how long is this going to last?"

"My dear," he said, "it is over now!" Thus speaking he walked over to his daughter Rachel and told her, "Maman and I are very tired, you will please bring this affair to an end."

Rachel looked into her father's eyes clearly showing she thought that he was an old fool. "Papa, I cannot tell our invited guests to leave, everything is still in full swing."

Raising himself to his full height and mustering all the authority at his disposal he said to her, "I personally do not care how you do it, but you have but five minutes to do it. Maman and I are weary and we wish to be alone. If I end this charade I will not be pleasant or diplomatic."

"But, but, Papa," she stammered.

"Five minutes, my dear, actually only four now. Let me tell you that if I have to clear this place you will carry the burden of all the expenses incurred here today."

"Damn you," she replied. "Damn you!"

The old gentleman bowed from the waist and said, "Thank you, my dear; you have reacted just as I knew you would."

Rachel reacted quickly. "May I have your attention please? Maman and Papa have suffered a great loss and you know that at their age it is so much more difficult to deal with things, so we are inviting you all to my brother Samuel's house."

Samuel did a complete turnabout when he heard what his sister had done. "That witch!" he muttered. "She is definitely going to get hers. I owe her one!"

He stood up and said very affably, "Yes, yes, you're all welcome to our home, isn't that right, Blanche? I don't know what we were thinking of, we should have, out of respect for our dear parents, made this get together at our house to begin with. Maman," he went over and kissed her cheek lightly, "and Papa, I apologize to you both."

Rachel's fury was burning deep within her. *That rotten so and so turned the whole situation around so that he gets all the credit.*

Samuel laughed to himself. "There's no one I'd rather get the best of than my dear little sister. She really thought that she had the best of me that time!"

Everyone was preparing to leave, but leave it to good old Isaac and Susannah—they were both worried about the food. Isaac had a disgusting mouthful of food, but still spoke up. "Hey, Sammy, are we bringing the food?"

Samuel actually disliked his brother, as he felt that Isaac was a source of embarrassment to him. "Ike," he replied, "the food is not mine to take." Samuel knew as he said this that his mother's reply would be, "Take it Samuel, what will I do with all that food?"

Chapter Eleven
Sorrowing Together

The house was quickly cleared in just a moment or two, and Simone and Alexandre looked at each other and both heaved sighs of relief.

He hugged his wife tenderly and said to her, "You are so exhausted, why don't you go lie down for a bit?"

She looked into her husband's eyes and said, "I cannot, as I am worried about Genevieve."

"You go and rest," he told his wife tenderly, "and I will go and look for the child."

"No!" She spoke in a tone he knew all too well, the one she used when she was determined to get her own way. "We will go together!"

She stood up and walked over to the closet and got their coats. Silently he held her coat for her, and quickly put on his own.

As they sat there in his large gray sedan he turned to his wife and asked her, "Where do you suppose the child would go on a cold day like this?"

She sat there deep in thought, then all of a sudden she smiled as though she had received a revelation. "I believe she has gone to the place where she knew happiness." She nodded her head, "Yes, that's it; drive to her home."

"Simone," he told her, "I myself made the house secure. I made sure that everything was locked securely and that no one would be able to enter in there!"

"Alexandre," she sighed, "I believe that I am right. She is there somewhere, and at any rate, what do we have to lose?"

When they arrived at the house, there was no sign of life to be found anywhere. They stood and called her name many times.

"I will check all the doors and windows again," he told his wife. Everything was securely bolted and he could find no signs of broken windows or forced entry. He shivered in the cold and told his wife, "You will catch your death of cold out here, we must return home."

The warmth of the car felt good to them, as each one sat there lost in their own thoughts, puzzling over the problem.

Alexandre broke the silence. "I don't want to call the police; imagine what Samuel will do to her?"

"No," Simone agreed. "We will do better to handle it ourselves."

Alexandre started the car up, and as he prepared to leave his wife said, "Let us sit here for a moment." She felt so weary, she leaned her head on Alexandre's shoulder, and prayed, "Dear God, help us, please help us, as we do not know where to turn."

Simone's eyes were darting to and fro over every piece of property, and then she saw, or perhaps she just thought she saw, a slight movement in the doghouse. *I must be dreaming things*, she thought to herself.

"Alexandre, did you take Genevieve's dog Tippie to the kennel for a few days?"

"Of course," he answered her discouragingly. "I took him there myself. I recall telling you that already."

"Wait here for me for a moment."

"Simone!" he called out. "Wait for me and I will come with you."

But his cry was to no avail as Simone was already on her way. Determination was one of her many strong qualities. He watched her as she slowly walked the several hundred yards to the doghouse, with the snow falling on her head and coat. The force of the wind had picked up greatly and the going was very difficult for her.

What a dreary and dismal day, he thought. *Everything appears to be in mourning as we are. There is a house that was filled with love and now it is nothing more than an empty shell. The place will never be the same again.*

Thank God it is snowing again, for all the old snow is dirty and stained. I wonder why, he thought, *Simone and I have raised such terrible children.* He smiled to himself. *Except for Laura, of course. She made it all worthwhile for us.*

We have been through so much together, Simone and I, but never anything as terrible as this. She had told him, "No one knows what it is like to lose a child that you have borne under your heart. It is like tearing a part of my inner being out of my insides, a part of me that can never be replaced. Oh, Alexandre, nothing has ever torn me apart like this. We will never be the same again! I try to tell myself to thank God that we did have her for all those years, but it really does not ease my heartache or the burden of my heart. Remember," she asked him, "how we longed for a daughter? When she was born we did both, laughed and cried, and then we laughed and cried again. We were so happy."

Alexandre was remembering how the first time he had held his little daughter in his arms she had curled her little fingers around his big finger and looked deep into his eyes as if to say, "I trust you." He had loved her from that moment on. She loved being with him and followed him all over the place whenever she could.

The last time he saw her, her eyes were glistening. "Guess what, Pa?"

"Must be something good." He smiled. "You are positively glowing."

She laughed. "Pa," she said, "I have a doctor's appointment tomorrow, and who knows, if it all works out as we planned, we may very well have a little Alexandre or Simone running around."

Now, he thought, *we will never have a little Simone or Alexandre around, nor do we have a Laura or Andrew around either!*

The force of the wind had picked up, and the old woman had great difficulty walking in the snow.

She prayed silently as she walked along, *What can I possibly say to this child who has been so badly hurt?*

As she drew nearer to the roughly built doghouse she could make out a little form in the interior. She got on her knees in the snow and looked into the opening. "Genevieve, thank the good Lord we found you." The child did not answer her. *Is she dead?* thought the old woman. Just then the child moved even further back into the recesses of the doghouse, although it would seem an impossibility to have done so.

The old woman could see that her granddaughter's lips were purple and quivering from the cold and her whole body was shaking as though she were a piece of machinery being operated by a high-powered motor. Her eyelids were filled with crystalline snow that had frozen there. Like her grandmother, she had not taken any hat or gloves.

"Come," said Simone. She put her arms out to the child, but the little girl would not be moved. "Genevieve, you will surely freeze out here. Please come."

The child gave no indication that she heard the words her grandmother spoke, and remained mute.

Genevieve looked out at her grandmother. She was quite a sight to behold, and under different circumstances she might have chuckled or even laughed about it.

The old woman said, "Genevieve, you know that I am an old lady and that I cannot possibly hold this position much longer. Your grandfather waits in the car for us. I wonder if this is what your Maman would have you do, or your Papa."

This is a low blow, thought the old woman, *but I have no other alternative.*

"Genevieve, I will go into the car now, where there is heat, as I am very cold; also I find that I am very hungry. We will wait five minutes for you, if you do not come then I will be forced to call the authorities."

Genevieve had been content to sit there and suffer, for whatever reason her young mind could fathom. But when her grandmother said, "the authorities," that meant only one thing! Uncle Samuel! That was one thing that she could not bear, and she would never live it down. Besides, a little heat and a little food sounded pretty good to her right now.

And, she thought to herself, *I don't have to talk to anyone if I don't want to, either.* She didn't know why she didn't want to talk to anyone, all she knew is that she didn't want to.

The elderly couple sat in the car silently and the time seemed an eternity. Neither one dared to look back, but somehow they knew that she was coming. The car door opened and Genevieve slowly entered.

Poor, poor child, thought the old man. *She is much too young to deal with such problems. But my wife and I, we have dealt with equally bad problems and made it through all right.*

The ride home was accomplished in total silence, each involved in a realm foreign to the other. Three reveries of sadness.

Genevieve had to admit that the warmth of the grandparents' home was very inviting and very superior to the doghouse she had been hiding in.

Genevieve had made up her mind that she would never again speak to anyone, so she totally ignored the conversation that her grandparents tried to engage her in.

"Genevieve," her grandmother said, "I would like you to take a nice warm bath."

Because it was in her nature to be an obedient child she went immediately to her bath, which her grandfather had drawn for her. Actually, it had never crossed her mind to disobey her grandparents.

She undressed herself and crawled into the warm tub and it felt so good to her. She had been chilled through to the bone, and she knew that this was exactly what she needed. She found herself wishing for some of her grandmother's good soup. She loved the tomato, macaroni, and rice soup that her grandmother made so well. She wanted some so badly that she actually thought she could smell it cooking.

She stayed in the tub for at least a half hour, until she heard a gentle tap on the door and heard her grandfather say gently, "Genevieve, come, our supper is waiting."

She admitted to herself that she was quite hungry. In her childish mind she felt guilty for being hungry. "Mom and Dad are dead and they'll never be able to eat anything again! How can I be hungry? I won't eat a thing, and they can't make me, either!"

"Ah, Genevieve, I take it you are much more comfortable now that you are warm again?" her grandmother said.

Genevieve ignored her grandmother's remark.

"Come, my dear," said her grandfather, "before this good soup your grandmother made especially for you gets cold."

Likewise she also ignored her grandfather's remark and sat there sulking on the rocking chair. Her grandmother placed three big bowls of soup on the table, and she and her husband sat down to eat. They bowed their heads in unison as he gave thanks for their many blessings.

They then began eating and talking to one another in quiet tones, almost as though they were unaware that she was there. In reality they were both beside themselves with anxiety for her.

The sounds and smells were too much for her to handle.

"I'll only take one bite," she promised herself.

Out of the corners of their eyes they saw her nearing the table, and neither one dared draw a breath lest she change her mind.

She could not resist a second mouthful and then a third. *After all,* she thought, *this is my favorite kind of soup.*

Her grandparents tried in vain to get her to speak, but she either would not or else could not.

They rose from the table but she just sat there staring at nothing in particular. She heard the sounds of their conversation as they did the dishes together. Under normal circumstances she loved helping her grandmother. Her grandmother would wrap one of her large aprons around her, and would allow her to make suds to her heart's content, but tonight she did not feel like it.

After the dishes had been done her grandmother took off her apron and hung it up.

"Tonight," she spoke quietly, "we have something very important to do."

Genevieve thought to herself, *Sure, the same old thing, important: pray. Who feels like praying when everything in life is gone?*

The custom at her grandparent's home (also a custom with her own parents) was to have supper, clean up, and then go down on your knees in prayer. It never mattered if someone came to the door or not, no one stirred.

If someone came to the door no one answered it, for the door was left unlocked. Folk could either come in and join in prayer time or come back later.

She was aware that both of her grandparents were kneeling, but she chose to ignore them.

"Genevieve!"—one little word spoken with a voice of authority and she quickly fell to her knees also.

Somehow they seemed to be praying twice as long as usual tonight. She became bored with it all and wished that it was over. *Good, they are rising to their feet. Good*, she thought.

Her grandmother went over and sat in her old rocking chair. This was the famed chair that she had rocked all of her babies in and also her grandchildren. Her husband also had a rocking chair that had been purchased at the same time for the same purpose.

Simone spoke to her granddaughter. "Come," she said to her, "and I will rock you." She spread open her arms and Genevieve literally ran into them. She climbed on her grandmother's lap and put both of her arms around her neck and settled her head on her bosom, hanging on for dear life as though the old woman would suddenly disappear from her sight.

She loved the smell of her grandmother, for she always smelled sweetly of lavender. The fragrance was gentle and not overpowering. Her breath always smelled of peppermint or rather of the "Canada" mints.

Her grandmother held her tightly, and for a time each felt secure. Suddenly her grandmother sat upright and spoke. "It occurs to me, Genevieve, that since you lost your maman and papa you have not shed one tear for your loss. Tonight we must take care of this matter. The same goes for you, Alexandre, you also have not shed a tear."

He looked at his wife silently and thought, *What is she up to now?*

"Genevieve," she said, "I want you to look at me." Slowly Genevieve raised her head and looked at her grandmother.

She said softly, "I want you to cry for the loss of your parents." Genevieve shook her head. She shook her head, meaning no, again and again.

Then her grandmother took both her hands and placed them gently but firmly on either side of her head. Genevieve could not help but look directly into her grandmother's faded blue eyes. The sadness reflected there made Genevieve want to turn away but she could not because of her grandmother's firm grip.

She looked directly into her grandmother's eyes, and she saw them fill with water. Her eyelashes became wet and sparkled as the teardrops found their way there. The teardrops became too many and they could not all stay upon her eyelids. Genevieve watched in a form of fascination as one large tear left its nest and formed a rivulet upon her grandmother's cheek. The next tear came from the opposite side and now both cheeks had pathways of teardrops. After the original start the tears flowed more freely and with complete abandon, one upon another, upon another. This was more than Genevieve could bear and the tears began to flow freely from her eyes until her face had the appearance of having been out in a rain shower.

At some undetermined point the old man had joined them. He was on his knees next to the rocking chair with his arms around both of them. His face was being bathed with his own tears; he was easing the sorrow within his own heart. All of a sudden Simone sat up straight in her chair. "Now, it is finished, and we must go on with our lives. God will sustain us through this as he has through all the other heartaches." She wiped both Genevieve's and Alexandre's faces, and then her own. She looked at her husband and reached for his hand. "Now, let us begin again!"

Chapter Twelve
Samuel

Who was Samuel David Boisvert? He was a man that never lived up to the meaning of his name. The name Samuel means "heir of promise," and David means "king of destiny."

His parents had thought hard and long to find just the right name for their son, and they truly felt that the name Samuel David was the ultimate.

He considered himself a brilliant man. He never really got off the ground. "Bad luck," he would mutter, or, "a lousy break."

His life was one of playing the big duck in a very small pond.

He never left the old hometown. He always stuck around, and he knew everything that was going on in the town. He always made sure that he was around either to glad-hand or to underhand, whatever suited the opportunity at that particular time. Of course, he always made sure that the scales were tipped in his favor.

He had neither the poise nor the stature of his father, rather, he resembled his mother's father, who had been known as "*Le Petit Coq*."

Samuel was a master craftsman. He turned any situation to his personal advantage or gain. He never did anything in his life that did not have an ulterior advantage for him in it.

He knew everyone in town: their weaknesses, their downfalls, and just how they might be useful to him. He knew everyone's coming ins and going outs; he knew it all: their associations, their debts, their liaisons or mistakes, and innermost secrets, and he did not fail to use this information for his personal advantage or gain.

It was rumored amongst the townsfolk that he held secret files on every family in town. No one had ever really seen them. The good people of the town felt that either his memory was phenomenal or else he really did keep secret records. One thing they all knew for sure was that nothing ever escaped his hawklike eyes.

He was known to have helped out hundreds of people, always with a big smile and a pat on the back and a "what are friends for?"

Yes, he helped out a good many in his day, but sooner or later they all had to pay the piper, so to speak. Maybe it might take ten years or even longer, but he never forgot that you "owed" him, and you always had to repay your debt to good old Samuel D. Boisvert. And believe me, you always paid with interest!

His stature was very short, probably about five foot seven or so, and he was quite portly, with a good-size paunch around his midsection. His neck was extremely thick and held up a head that would seem to belong to a much larger man's body.

His eyes were black and restless, constantly darting to and fro, seemingly taking everything in at once. His lips seemed to be sardonically smiling, almost as if he knew a secret that no one else knew. More than likely he did, too. His hair was almost totally gone except for the ridge middle-age men have around the base of their pates.

He had unusually small feet for a man and one would wonder if he ever saw them over his massive midsection.

He was very meticulous about himself, both in his personal hygiene and personal dress. He seemed to prefer double-breasted suits in black or grey pinstripes. His white shirts were starched very stiff. There was of course the ever present appropriate necktie.

On his tiny feet he wore imported Italian patent leather shoes. Some felt it was as if he wanted to frame his feet.

Even though he was well past fifty, he was still very vain, and he spent a lot of time in front of the mirror making certain that each of his nineteen or twenty hairs were perfectly in its proper place, combed straight back, and spread out as much as possible. It was a great source of mirth to many people. Never when he was around, of course. In spite of it all, he felt that all of his efforts gave him the appearance of having more hair than he really did have.

No one ever dared to laugh at him.

He had a fetish about dirt, and no one ever saw him with a speck of dirt upon his person. When he shook hands with a person, he would automatically wipe his hands on his jacket, and as soon as they left he would go and wash his hands right away. It was as though he felt that everyone was diseased or contaminated in some way.

If anyone had ever taken the time to observe him closely they would have seen the contempt and utter distaste in his eyes. His lips always held that thin smile and would turn white, and it appeared as though he might vomit. This was such a fleeting thing that no one seemed to take note of it.

He always looked as though he had just stepped out of the bathtub, and for some reason his flaws and imperfections were often unnoticed.

He had many of the teeth in his mouth filled with gold, and he loved to show them off and did so as often as he could get away with it. It always seemed as though if he parted his lips in a smile, it would be large enough to show off those gold teeth. When the sun was shining and he would smile that certain smile the gold on his teeth would reflect the sunlight and little rays would dart back and forth and back and forth again. He was acutely aware of this and he would pause to get just the right effect.

He was also the town's mayor. In fact, he was the youngest mayor the town had ever elected, and he had held the position ever since. He was at the ripe old age of twenty-three when first elected.

Some of those who were jealous of him claimed that he kept the job because no one else wanted it.

When he strolled down the street, the street would ring out with "Hi Sam"s, "Hello Sam"s, and so forth. If anyone ever said, "Hello, Mr. Mayor," he would pat them on the back and say, "Just call me Sam; I don't go for none of that fancy hullabaloo." He felt that his image was that of a good ole boy. He didn't want anyone to think that he was too smart as he felt it was to his advantage to just be "a good ole boy."

In his office things were very different. There he would tell his staff "we hafta observe the formalities here."

"Ya know, my staff drives me nuts." He would hit his head in dismay. "Protocol! Protocol! We gotta observe protocol. It doesn't mean a thing, but do me a favor will ya and in the office call me Mr. Mayor. O.K.? Sure do appreciate all your cooperation. I truly do.

"Hey, you know, we gotta keep the old sourpuss in the office happy ya know. She comes from England and they go for all that bull. Good old Mrs. Tromble, about as exciting as London Fog, but nobody can run an office like her. She truly believes that part of her job is to maintain protocol! Just like typing or keeping records. Good Lord, if she ever smiles her face will crack!"

Yup, Sam was a good ole boy all right, but underneath in his inner self it was a very different story altogether.

Chapter Thirteen
"Getting Along"

There was a special bond that grew between Simone and her granddaughter. The child was strong-willed and opinionated at times, but she was a good girl and brought much joy into Simone's and Alexandre's lives. She reminded both of them of her mother as she grew.

She loved being with Alexandre every chance she got and he sometimes indulged her a bit too much, as Simone would remind him every so often. Simone had to admit that she had also been known to indulge the child on an occasion or two.

Alexandre had bought Genevieve a bicycle, and she loved to ride it all over the little town. Simone worried some about her, but she also knew that the child needed room to grow and expand.

"It is not good that the child is so much with us old folk," she would say, and sometimes she and Genevieve would bake a big batch of cookies and bring them over to Isaac's house so she could be with young people. Young people there were, with ten different sized and aged children floating about.

When they came to the door Isaac would bellow in a loud voice, "Susannah, Susannah! Guess who's here?" Aunt Susannah, looking as though she had slept in her clothes, would come scrambling out of some other room, where she more than likely had been nursing one of the children. Isaac would grin from ear to ear and with a wide sweep of his hand clear a chair. "Sit down Maman, sit down, make yourself at home."

Simone would have to restrain herself as she always had a desire to get up and start some cleaning or dusting, but Susannah had put her in her place many years ago, saying, "Isaac and I like things the way they are." Instead, Susannah would plunk one of the kids on her lap. "Go and see Memere." Isaac would then call the rest of the children one by one, "Come and kiss your grandparents."

Simone loved each and every one of them, she had to admit, and so did Alexandre. One thing that can be said about Isaac and, yes, Susannah too, was that they were sincere, which is a lot more than could be said for the other members of the family.

Alexandre liked to visit with his son. He did not approve of his life-style, but they did have many lively conversations. One thing about Isaac, his family always came first in his life. It never bothered him to have a dirty, grubby child sitting on his lap, no matter who else was around. The child was the important thing.

Simone and Alexandre felt that they didn't have to live there and that the condition of house and children wasn't their concern.

Susannah as well as Isaac loved each and every one of the children, and all of the "kids" loved them back, too, not that they didn't sass or misbehave either.

Genevieve loved them both in spite of their bulk and life-style. Whenever she was at their home they made her a part of the family. "When Aunt Susannah or Uncle Isaac kiss or hug me," she told her grandmother, "I feel like they really do like me."

Grand-mère believed in "a well-balanced" meal, but Susannah would say, "The children want pizza and chips and root beer tonight," so that would become their meal. She was a great cook and made the best pizzas in the world. At least her family thought so. She gave the kids coffee if they wanted it, and many times the children would have cold pizza for breakfast if there was any left.

It was not unusual to see one or the other of the children, the younger ones at least, running around like the day they were born, stark naked. No one seemed to notice or pay much attention to the fact. "It's much easier to run and put them on the potty" was their brand of logic.

Both Isaac and Susannah were exceptionally light on their feet considering their bulk, and could be known to nab a child if the need ever arose. Isaac really loved his parents and did pay them the respect due them.

"I wonder if we would be so well liked if we closed the purse," Alexandre would say periodically.

Henry was the oldest of their children and Genevieve did not care for him very much, as he had attempted to touch her where he shouldn't a few times. She had told on him and now he kept a wide berth from her. He had a sulking kind of handsomeness. He always looked like a little boy pouting. He resented the fact that the next three children after him were all girls and he had to work alongside his father. The work was hard and he kept up with the ole man too.

Isaac would not allow his daughters to labor on the run down farm.

"This is man's work." So, Henry chopped wood, slopped the pigs, milked the cows and labored all about the farm at whatever task needed to be done. His big dream was to get off "this damn farm!"

Someday, he thought, *I'm going to be a businessman like my uncle Samuel.*

Simone often thought that Henry should have been Samuel's son, not that he looked like him, but he acted just like him and had the same set of values, too.

Genevieve's favorite of all her cousins was Nicole, who was only two months younger than she was. Nicole was the oldest girl in the family and a lot of the responsibility for the children rested on her young shoulders.

Nicole was old and serious for her age. She had long, mousy hair and hazel eyes. She never seemed to smile much and for some reason she would never make a decision about anything.

"What kind of ice cream would you like, Nicole?"

"I don't know."

On this particular night the three of them had a late start to go to Isaac's. When they got there it was close to the supper hour. When the children spotted their grandparents and Genevieve there was a stampede. They grabbed the cookies and yelled, "Ma! Look, cookies for us," and they all began to try and grab some at once.

Isaac called out, "There better be some for Ma and me, there's nothing better in this world than Ma's cookies."

Susannah called to Nicole, who was setting the table, "Put three more plates on."

Simone spoke up, saying, "We did not come to eat, we don't want to disturb your supper."

"Aw, come on, Ma," and all the kids started in, "Please! Please!"

Susannah said, "We have plenty, not fancy though, just spaghetti and meatballs."

Alexandre looked over at his wife to see what her reaction would be. She nodded her head and Alexandre said, "We accept with delight." So it was settled.

"Is there anything I can do to help?" Simone asked her granddaughter.

Nicole loved her grandmother. *She is always such a lady.* She did not think that her grandmother liked her very much though.

Simone had often wanted to take this girl to her bosom and hug her, but she always seemed to shy away.

"No thank you," Nicole said in her shy little way. Simone impulsively walked over to her granddaughter and gave her a big hug. Nicole was so surprised that she stood there with her mouth open. "You, uh, you hugged me."

"Yes, I did," Simone replied. "You are my granddaughter, why shouldn't I hug you?"

"Well," Nicole replied, "I never thought that you liked me."

Simone was taken aback. "Why my dear child, of course I like you, I also love you."

The child, overcome with emotion, put her arms tightly around her grandmother and hugged her for all she was worth. "I love you too, Grand-mère, I really do!"

Simone was overcome. The idea of the child thinking that she didn't like her, it was ridiculous!

Isaac was so pleased to see his daughter and mother in a hugging embrace. Isaac was a sincere man but he also liked money as much as Samuel did. His thought was, *Why didn't we think of it before? If we could get Nicole and the old lady together, like she is with Genevieve, that could be worth a few more bucks in our pockets.*

Susannah had told Isaac many years ago she would never ask his parents for a cent, and she never did, but Isaac hit them up every time he saw them. Susannah never had any qualms about spending the money once he got it. Alexandre did not know how much money his son owed him, but it was a sizeable amount.

The supper was a happy time. Simone just looked the other way as one or the other of the children served themselves spaghetti with their dirty hands. When the meal was over Susannah said to Nicole, "Get busy, girl. Don't think you are going to play your life away, you have work to do. Now get going!"

Isaac said, "Pa, could I see you alone for a minute?"

Simone and Alexandre looked at each other for a moment and Alexandre said, "Certainly," and off they went to the barn or some other quiet place.

Susannah was nursing the baby and Simone asked her, "Would you mind if I helped Nicole with the dishes? I feel so useless just sitting here and you are busy with the baby."

"Go ahead," Susannah said. "I declare that you are going to make a lazy thing out of her just like Genevieve is!"

Simone bit her tongue. She knew that her daughter-in-law resented the fact that she and Alexandre had gotten custody of Genevieve. She and Isaac had tried desperately to get her and of course her inheritance, but they were unsuccessful. Simone knew that Susannah felt that if anything ever happened to her or Alexandre they would get custody of the child. Samuel and Rachel both thought the same thing. *They will get a surprise,* thought Simone.

Simone went over and began helping her granddaughter with the dishes.

"You don't hafta help me, I do the dishes alone all the time."

"I know that I don't have to help you, I am helping you because I want to." Simone smiled at her granddaughter. "Besides, I want to get to know you better, and I found out throughout my lifetime that the best way to get to know another person is by doing the dishes together."

Nicole looked at her grandmother and gave her a smile of gratitude. *No one ever wants to help me,* she thought.

Simone looked at her granddaughter over and thought to herself, *This child could be attractive if she were taught a few things, like brushing her hair and teeth.*

"Nicole, on Saturday Genevieve and I are going to have our hair done and do some shopping and go out for lunch, you know, girl stuff. I was thinking perhaps you would like to join us, if your parents approve of course."

Just at that moment Isaac was coming in the door with his father and heard what his mother had said to Nicole. "Of course we approve, don't we Susannah? It will be good for Nicole to get away for a few hours." Isaac gave his wife a triumphant look that said, "At last a breakthrough, what we've been waiting for all along!"

Simone said, "That is all well and good, but does Nicole want to come with us?" She turned to Nicole and said to her, "You have not said if you'd like to join us or not."

Genevieve had heard the discussion and went over to Nicole and hugged her. "Nikki, please come. I guarantee that you will have a good time. Grand-mère is a lot of fun to be with, and maybe she'll take us to that Chinese restaurant where the waiters bow at you and make you feel like a queen."

Nicole smiled at Genevieve. She really liked her cousin and was not at all jealous of her as her parents felt she should be. That's not to say that she didn't wish she could be as attractive as her cousin or have her personality. Everyone seemed to like her. Her Dad said that everyone felt sorry for her more than liked her, because she was an orphan. *I never think of her as an orphan, though.*

"Grand-mère, could Nicole come over on Friday night and spend the night with me? Please? It would be a grand adventure for us."

Alexandre spoke up. "Since gentlemen are not allowed on this excursion, I tell you what I will do. If Grand-mère agrees, I will take you girls to the movies on Friday night."

All eyes in the house were fixed on Simone and she laughed heartily. "I am outnumbered, my answer is yes."

On the way home Simone asked Alexandre, "How much did it cost us for our humble spaghetti dinner?"

Alexandre cleared his throat and gave his wife a sidelong glance. Simone watched him carefully and said, "From the way you are acting, it must have been an expensive meal."

"That it was, that it was. You could never even guess how much he wanted."

"Five hundred dollars?"

Alexandre laughed. "I'm glad, my dear, that you still have your sense of humor. I feel that we should discuss this little matter later on when we are by ourselves."

Genevieve felt rejected, as she knew very well what Grand-père meant was "Let's not talk about this in front of her."

After they arrived home and were preparing to retire for the night Simone asked him point-blank what Isaac wanted.

"He wants one hundred thousand dollars for equipment to improve his house and farm. He says the kids are getting bigger and he wants to improve things, and he also thinks that he and Henry could make a good living if the farm was updated."

"Alexandre, these are the same things he has been telling you for years now, and he has always been too lazy to get off of his posterior and do anything!" Simone was clearly upset now.

Alexandre looked at his wife. "We have been foolish with Isaac, and yet I feel compassion for all the children. Isaac said that he is willing to forego any inheritance if we grant him this request."

"Of course he will, and we will make it legal this time. This is it, Alexandre; I am fed up! They think that we are old fools, using Nicole to get money from us. She is a nice little girl and I am sorry we have neglected her because her parents were leeches."

"Tomorrow we shall have a new will drawn up, eh?"

Alexandre looked keenly at his wife. "Are you trying to tell me something?"

"Yes," she whispered, "very soon now."

He put his arms around her. "What will I do without you?" His eyes filled with tears.

"You will continue on as always, you are a strong man, and you and Genevieve will do fine, and I'll be watching you from heaven."

They stood there with their arms around each other for a long while.

Simone spoke. "Tomorrow we will have papers drawn up for Isaac stating that he relinquished any claim to any inheritance he might have had. If he signs it he will get the money, if not then he will not get it, simple enough.

"Our plan for you and Genevieve is a good plan and it will work out if you do not let emotions get in your way."

After supper on Friday Alexandre and Genevieve picked Nicole up and they went to the movies together. He was totally unaware of what was playing as his mind was on Simone. They had known for a long time that she had a rare and incurable disease. He still could not bring himself to believe it, always believing that she would recover.

The girls had a good time together and stayed up half of the night giggling and talking, until Alexandre himself stood in the doorway and said one little word: "Enough!"

Not one further sound was heard from the room. Everyone overslept and Alexandre fixed breakfast so that "the women folk" could get going.

"I wonder if I'll recognize you ladies when you get back, or maybe you won't want to be seen with me, maybe I should go and get my hair styled too. That's it," he said. "Nicole, do you think that I would be attractive in a ponytail?" He teased them kindly and they all loved it.

The girls laughed, picturing in their minds their dignified grandfather in a ponytail.

Before the lady folk left he went to Simone and asked her, "Will you be all right?"

"Yes, please do not worry about me; I will be fine. You have work of your own to do, talking to Isaac. I wish I could be there to see his face when he finds out this is it."

"That, my dear, is not a nice sentiment," he laughed.

"No, it isn't, but sometimes I am not a nice person when people use us to their advantage."

"Be careful."

The girls ran up to their grandfather and gave him a kiss before leaving. "I also need a handshake," he said. Genevieve and Simone knew what he was up to, but Nicole did not and was astonished to find that as she shook hands with her grandfather he placed a twenty dollar bill in her hand.

"But, but, what is that for?"

Alexandre went over and shook hands with Genevieve and placed a twenty dollar bill in her hand also, and then he went over to Simone and repeated the same thing. "What is the rule, ladies?"

Genevieve said, "We must each spend this twenty dollar bill on ourselves, and also show you what we purchased and the cost."

"And," he prompted her, "if you don't spend it all on yourselves, what happens then?"

"Then," Genevieve said, "we forfeit the money and it returns to you."

"Absolutely correct. Absolutely correct."

"You mean," Nicole said in amazement, "this money is just for me and no one else?"

Alexandre smiled and told her, "Yes, it is, my dear."

As he looked at Nicole, he thought, *Simone and Genevieve have done wonders for her. Why, I hardly recognize her. Her hair has been washed and brushed until it shines, bringing out the natural highlights, and she has on some of Genevieve's clothes. She kept smiling this morning, and it gave her a totally different look. This girl,* he thought, *definitely has potential.*

Isaac was definitely not pleased with his parents' proposition. "Geez Pa, I never thought we'd need papers signed between us. I hafta talk to Susannah about this." He shook his head. "I always thought we had something special between us. I can't believe that you want me to sign papers! How about Sam and Rachel, did they sign papers with you?"

Alexandre was really getting exasperated with his son now. "This is between you and I and your mother, and what goes on with the other children is none of your business. Your mother and I have come to a decision, take it or leave it! Now, which will it be?"

"Can I have a coupla hours to think about it?" he asked, wiping his nose on his sleeve.

Alexandre thought to himself, *Oh how I would like to give him a backhander that would send him reeling across country.* He held himself at bay and turned to look at the scenery around him. *Scenery! Looks more like the town dump.* Isaac and Susannah took anything anyone gave them, no matter what it was or how junky it was either. The whole yard was filled with all kinds of junk, broken down cars, toys and all the trash that the pigs would not eat. All kinds of broken tools and farm equipment were lying around.

The sad part about it is that nobody gives a damn! What a waste of good land! The stench around there was almost unbearable. The land was wasted, there were dogs and cats all over the place. No one could even guess how many there were either.

Henry saw his grandfather looking around him and came over to where he was standing. "Hi, Grand-père."

Alexandre turned to look at his oldest grandson. "Why, hello, Henry."

Henry stood with his shoulders bent over. His posture made him appear much older than his sixteen years. He was kicking at something in the grass with his big work boot.

"Not exactly scenic America, is it?" he asked Alexandre.

"What do you mean?"

"What I mean is that it looks more like the city dump.

"Grand-père?"

"Yes?"

"You're not going to give them the money are you?"

"What do you mean? Why not?"

"Well, the old man and Maw, they're always talking about what big suckers you and Grand-mère are, and how Dad can talk you into anything."

Henry looked down at the ground, and Alexandre knew that he was trying to get his nerve up to ask him something.

Henry's eyes began to fill with tears. "Please! Please don't give them the money, I'm begging you." He wiped his eyes with his dirty hand.

Alexandre was puzzled. "But why not? Don't you want to see the farm improve?"

"Come on off of it. When did he ever improve anything before with the money you gave him? Never! Right? Never! If you give them the money I'll be stuck in this rotten hellhole for the rest of my life!"

"Don't you like it here?"

"I hate it here but I'm stuck! Tell me the truth; would you like to live here?"

He looked at the boy and said, "I get your point, I surely do. Well, Henry, you have spoken to me too late, but tell me something if you will."

"Yeah," he said morosely.

"What would you do with your life if it were left up to you?"

"I'd go to school and become a veterinarian and work with sick animals. . . ." His voice trailed off. "What's the use anyway?"

Alexandre ignored his remarks and asked him, "How are you doing in school?"

"What's the difference?"

"The difference is that I wish to know."

"What for?"

"If you'll be kind enough to answer my questions, I will tell you what I have in mind."

"I do real good in school. I have a B+ average."

"Could you do better, if you set your mind to it?"

"Yer damn right I could, but what's the use, nobody cares."

"I care," and he reached out and hugged his gangly grandson.

"Henry, can you keep a secret that will be just between you and me?"

"I'm not a baby, of course I can!" he replied indignantly.

"I tell you my proposition, I and your grandmother of course. I am going to set up a trust fund for you in your name for your education. There are two conditions on this: one is that no one must ever know about this, no one. I mean not your mother, not your father nor anyone else. The second condition is that you work hard. I will set it up so that all your school expenses are met, you will have a book and a clothing account. Should you not decide to further your education the trust fund will be donated to charity.

"If you further your education and stay out of trouble you can use the balance that is left to set yourself up in business. Agreed?"

Henry shook his grandfather's hand. "Agreed, sir, agreed! Thank you!"

All of a sudden Henry's mood shifted and Alexandre asked him, "What is it?"

"Well," he said, "I don't want to be like Dad, but there is one thing."

"What is it, boy? Speak up!"

"Well," he began slowly, "it's about my sister Nicole. She works her rear off around here and there is no way for her to get an education. She and I are just like slaves or workhorses around here, and I'm not kidding or feeling sorry for myself either. Could I share my trust fund with her?"

"Don't you worry your young head about that, your Grand-mère has seen to Nicole's education, but she must not know about it, nor your parents lest they try to void the trust funds and use them to their advantage."

Just then Isaac and Susannah came from the house. Isaac took one look at Henry and said, "Why are you standing there gawking, boy? Get to work," and looking at his father Isaac said, "I swear that boy gets lazier every day!"

Susannah looked at her father-in-law. "I want you to know that I do not approve of what you're doing to Isaac and me. If it were Samuel, he wouldn't have to sign any papers, I guarantee you that!"

Alexandre remembered Simone's words, "I am fed up," and he too was fed up. "*You* and Isaac have already received more than your share of any inheritance!"

Isaac began to panic, because he knew that his father spoke the truth. "Shut up, Susannah, before you screw everything up! Don't listen to her, Pa; she's late again and she always gets crabby when she's in the family way. I don't understand why we have to sign papers, but if it makes you happy, I'll do it. Let's go in the house and get it over with."

After Isaac had made a big deal about signing the papers he said, "How about it, Pa, wanna go fishing?"

"Not today," Alexandre said, and his shoulders were a little bent over. "I have things I must do."

Isaac was puzzled. Pa had never once refused to go fishing with him before. When his father had gone he looked at Susannah. "How many times I gotta tell you? Butt out when I'm dealing with the old man. Ya know, I think he's beginning to show his age."

Alexandre was just getting into the car when he spotted Henry waving to him as he fed the chickens. "Bye Grand-père!"

Alexandre motioned to the boy to come on over. Henry quickly ran over to the car and said, "What is it, Grand-père?"

"Get in. You and I are going for a ride."

"But, I still got chores to do."

"It will be all right. Come on, boy; we don't have all day."

Alexandre took the boy to his house and showed him some of his clothes. "Pick out a set of clothes and take a shower. We are going shopping."

"We are?" Now he was totally puzzled.

Alexandre sat in his living room reading the morning paper until his grandson was ready. Alexandre looked up and could not believe his eyes. The boy had become transformed. He really was a handsome kid. He had never seen the boy dressed up in anything but farm clothes before. The transformation was like a miracle.

They drove to a very expensive clothing store and Alexandre told him, "I buy a lot of my clothes here."

When they got inside the sales clerk came over and talked to Alexandre. "This is my grandson," the old man said with pride in his voice. "He is in need of clothes and a couple of sports coats and I would say about six pair of slacks. You know what I mean, set him up with a complete wardrobe; shoes, socks, handkerchiefs and so forth. I will pay for everything myself."

"Yes, Mr. Boisvert, I will oblige you in any way I can."

Alexandre said, "Let the boy pick and choose."

Henry just stood there with his mouth hanging open.

"I will be back in one hour."

Alexandre drove to a local car dealer's and asked him, "What kind of car are the young folk driving these days?"

He picked his grandson up in a brand new bright red convertible. "Henry, do you like this new car? I bought it while you were in the store. Do you like it?"

"It's beautiful," Henry said almost reverently while he ran his hands over the leather upholstery.

"Well," said Alexandre with relief, "I'm glad you like it because it's yours."

"What! What did you say?"

"I said it is yours. Meet me on Monday after school and we will go and pick up the registration."

"But why?"

"Let's just say that I am feeling generous today. Besides it is my money and I can spend it any way I want to! It pleases me today to spend it on you. By the way, the deal is that no one but you is to drive it and no one is to go in it without your permission. I believe you get what I mean."

"Yes, Grand-père, I do, and I will try to pay you back when I can."

"No, my boy, it is a gift and the only stipulations are the ones I made and that someday you do something nice for someone, too."

Alexandre later told Simone, "It was worth a million dollars to see the expressions on Isaac and Susannah's faces when I took the boy home!"

Simone looked at her husband indulgently and said, "Maybe we are going senile," and they both laughed at their little joke.

Simone wiped her eyes. "Just wait until Samuel and Rachel hear about it!"

Chapter Fourteen
Simone

Who was Simone Boisvert? She was definitely a woman of deep religious beliefs. She had named her sons after biblical figures, praying that they would grow up straight and honest. Perhaps she hoped that the fact of this naming would endow them with attributes above and beyond that of the average man. This desire of hers was never to materialize for her, but she never lost faith in it.

Alexandre had never concerned himself about what she would name the children. His philosophy was that she conceived, carried and birthed the children and going through all that entitled her at least to pick out the names. Not to forget the fact that she was concerned with most of the raising of the children. She felt that all the names were good and pleasant names and that was good enough for him, too.

Alexandre worked long and hard hours to support Simone and his family and "by golly" he felt she was worth all the time and effort.

She was a good woman, not at all like the frivolous women of today, who were always chitchatting or gossiping about unimportant matters. Giggling, he felt, was not for mature women. She was not what was known as sickening sweet, or bubbly, and she did not play the coy game either. When she opened her mouth to speak, she said something worth listening to.

She was a worker, that one, her well-worn hands were proof of that. To Alexandre, her hands were a thing of beauty, because they expressed the true meaning of love, not a love of just words, but a love of doing and working for those you love.

She loved him, of this there had never been any doubt in his mind, and he was still amazed that after spending all these years together the love had grown and not withered and died. He felt that she had put up with a lot from him, but it was in ignorance that he made mistakes, not from any other intent.

She had been through the tortures of hell as a young girl, but never spoke of these hard times. She always had compassion for others who were going through trying times, too.

Whenever Alexandre had tried to talk about her past she just pooh-poohed him and did not talk about it. "Will that change things?" she would ask, and of course the answer had to be "No."

Her favorite saying was taken from the Bible: "God will not try us above which we are capable of handling." She always claimed that the trials and tribulations we went through were for a good reason and we became stronger because of them.

"I have come this far in life because of *Le Bon Dieu* [God] and don't you forget it either!"

When Alexandre had first met her she was in the blossom of life and had a beauty the likes of which he had never seen before. Even then she was not an affected woman. She was never known to be blunt, but you always knew where you stood with her. When they were first married they had both tried the silent and long-suffering treatment but soon found out that did not solve much, and they soon rejected it and made a solemn promise to one another to always be truthful and that worked well for them.

Their wedding day was a solemn occasion for them as Simone had laid her mother to rest only two days before, but it was meaningful for both of them as they had never known the kind of love that they shared together before in their lives.

He had inherited "the Business" from his father, whom he hated with a vengeance, but he had to admit that it served him well. He and Simone had prospered the business and it was now worth at least several hundred times more than it had been worth when he had inherited it. They had worked side by side.

Anyone who did not know them would not believe that they were wealthy. They lived the simple life and that's the way they liked it, too.

Simone had never gone in for the nurse or baby-sitter idea; she felt God had entrusted these children to her and she was to bring them up. There was a nursery next to her office and the children stayed there with her.

Some of his business acquaintances did not like this idea, but Alexandre and Simone both felt, *Too bad*, because that's the way it was.

Simone handled all the creative aspects of the business and Alexandre handled all the business or money angles. "What do I know about hats anyhow? That is Simone's department."

No one ever put anything over on her either; no inferior materials or shoddy work got past her eagle eyes. She demanded the best and got it, too. The workers were paid top dollar and were loyal to Simone to a fault.

They had both loved the business world but were glad to sell out about four years ago. Simone had felt that it was time to sell. "Modern women are not concerned with hats any longer, they are too concerned trying to be equal with men." Somehow and for some reason she did not understand, not wearing hats made women feel free.

They had done some traveling, as much as they could with their responsibility to Genevieve. The three of them had enjoyed much together.

Simone had many delightful moments with her granddaughter, like the time she came home from school and said, "Guess what, Ma?"

Lord knows she had tried to stop Genevieve from calling her Ma, but she did it anyway. "What?"

"We had a special guest speaker today at school, and you know what?"

"No, miss, I don't know what until you tell me."

"Well, she was a lady who speaks to kids about what they wanna be when they grow up."

"Don't you mean want to be?"

"Oh, Ma!" she heaved a sigh. "Anyhow, this woman said that even at my age I am not too young to start planning what I should do with my life."

"She is right, of course."

"Ma," she said solemnly, "what do you think I should be when I grow up?"

"Well, first of all I would like you to be tender, kind and loving. . . ."

"No! That's not what I mean; I mean what occupation should I choose?"

"Well, what would you like to do with your life?"

"I don't know!" she said irritably. "You should know, you're the grown-up!"

"Yes, but it is your life. Think about it, what are your options?"

"Well . . . you and Grand-père always say that if I apply myself I can be whatever I want to be."

"That is true, Genevieve."

"I really like music, but nobody makes money playing the piano."

"Are you sure of that?"

"Well, I don't think so."

"Do you need more money in your life? Does making more money concern you, or does making people happy concern you more?"

"I like to see people happy."

Simone watched her young granddaughter so deep in thought, and could almost see the wheels turning around in her head.

"I've been thinking; you and Grand-père made a lot of money in your business, and you are both so good and kind and gentle, too. I love you both, but I don't want to be old-fashioned." She spoke so seriously that Simone had to smile. She was young and had a lot to learn yet, but she was really coming along and she would make it, too. Simone was sure of it.

"You know what Nicole wants to be?"

"No, I don't believe we ever discussed it."

"She told me that she wants to be a lawyer, and that every time she gets a penny or nickel or a dime that she has a special hiding place that nobody knows about but her and by the time she's old enough, she will have enough money saved to go to college."

"Your cousin is to be commended for attitude, but perhaps you should tell her that a far better place for her money would be in a bank."

"She can't do that 'cause if her old man and old lady found out about it they would steal her blind like always."

"What did you say?"

"I'm sorry, I meant if Uncle Isaac or Aunt Susannah ever found out about it they wouldn't like it. I don't want to be like Aunt Rachel either, because nobody likes her! I want people to like me. What does she do anyhow? I guess she's just a lady 'hahahaha' of leisure."

"What do you find so funny?"

"Well, calling Rachel a lady is funny."

"It is not nice to speak about people who are not here to defend themselves." Simone was becoming flustered.

"Well, Ma, do you think that she is a lady? I think she is obnoxious!"

"That," Simone spoke with authority now, "will be enough!"

Genevieve looked her grandmother straight in the eyes. "Tell me the truth, do you like her?"

"Young lady, don't be ridiculous; she is my daughter." But she did not answer the question posed to her.

Genevieve smiled to herself. *I knew she wouldn't answer me.*

"Then," she said, "there is Uncle Samuel, the biggest crook in town. Well, he made it to be the mayor, but I think he deserves the Academy Award. Wow, what a phony!"

She noticed a funny expression on Simone's face that she had never seen before. *Oh my,* she thought, *what an idiot I am. Here I am running her kids down in front of her.*

"Grand-mère? I'm sorry, I did not mean to hurt your feelings."

Simone went to her granddaughter and gave her a hug. "There is no apology necessary, little one. I must say that you are honest in your opinions and I'd rather see that than have you lie. One thing you must make sure is to be careful who and how you speak with your opinions, for you could cause a lot of hurt."

"By telling the truth? I thought that you read to me that the truth will make you free?"

"Yes, but some truths are not ours to tell. Tell me Genevieve, do you think that your uncle thinks of himself as a . . . let me see how you put it? Oh yes, now I remember. Do you think Samuel thinks of himself as a phony or Rachel thinks of herself as a lady of leisure?"

"Do you mean," she said in astonishment, "that Uncle Isaac and Aunt Susannah don't know that they are big globs of fat that make them look ugly, and they don't know that they are pigs living in a pigsty? They can't really believe that nice home stuff they tell everybody. I can't believe that they could be so dense. You mean he's not plain old lying when he tells us he lost weight or he's on a diet?"

Simone could not scold Genevieve for she and Alexandre had often spoken the very same things themselves. She sighed heavily and thought, *Thank God Rachel and Samuel are at least clean.*

"Nicole told me she is not going to be a baby-making machine like her mother, me neither. I think she looks so gross with her boob hanging out with a baby sucking on it all the time! Did you nurse your babies, Grand-mère?"

"I certainly did!"

"Did you walk around in front of everybody like Aunt Susannah does?"

Simone looked at her grandchild, too wise for her years. "No, it was a private thing between my babies and me."

"You know what I think?"

"No, I don't know what you think."

"I think Aunt Susannah likes to embarrass everybody walking around like that! I really do. One time she told me that her body was natural and that nature was beautiful. I had to try real hard not to laugh. That's not beauty, it's acting piggy, if you ask me."

"Did anyone ask you?"

"No, but I like to watch people and I've been watching her and if there is a man around, she makes sure that he sees her, and then she smiles that naughty obnoxious smile of hers! Why don't they at least wash up or get their teeth fixed?"

Genevieve sat quietly in the kitchen for about ten minutes deep in thought. All of a sudden she broke the silence. "Grand-mère?"

"What is it?"

"Can I ask you a question, one I've been thinking about for a long time, and you won't be angry with me?"

"Have I ever been angry with you?"

"Well, I don't know about angry, but I know for sure upset."

"You are in a strange mood today. Come sit on my lap and ask away."

Genevieve loved sitting on Simone's lap as these times brought them closer together. She looked deep into her grandmother's eyes and cleared her throat briefly. "You and Grand-père," she said, "are such wonderful, nice people."

"Thank you." Simone hugged her granddaughter closely. "You are not bad yourself."

"What I mean, Grand-mère, is how come your children are so different from you and Grand-père? I mean how come they're so weird, you know what I mean, selfish, and thinking they are better than everyone else?"

"Well," Simone replied thoughtfully, "what you say is true and I suppose if I knew the answer they wouldn't be like that. We created brats, as far as I can see."

"But Maman wasn't like that, was she?"

"*No*, she was not, somehow she was different than the others from the moment she was born and we knew it even then."

"I don't understand; I really don't," Genevieve said, puzzled. "I just don't understand how these things can be."

Simone looked at her granddaughter and said, "Neither do I. Sometimes I believe it is something inherited from our ancestors that makes us the way we are and of course if we do not work at improving ourselves, we stay as we are. Anyhow," she said philosophically, "it appears that Mother Nature gets the last laugh!"

Chapter Fifteen
Simone's Sense of Humor

The afternoon was a dark and cold one. Genevieve and her grandmother had both been feeling a little sad.

"Come here," her grandmother spoke, "and sit on my lap and we will rock for a while."

If the truth were known, the old woman got as much out of these rocking sessions as the child did. Simone also had a great need of love, and she did miss her daughter so.

Grandmother and child had both dozed off when suddenly the brightness of the light appeared and startled them both awake with a start. Evidently both had dozed off, comforted by each other in their moment of need.

"Genevieve!" The voice grated upon each one of Genevieve's nerves and she did not need to open her eyes to know who it was. Of course it was Aunt Rachel. She must have gone to a school for training in crystallized nastiness. Her aunt stood there in all of her self-imposed, or rather, "self-thought," perfection.

Her mink coat was calf-length, and her kid gloves were a perfect match. Every hair was, of course, in its perfect place, and sitting on the top of her head looking somewhat like a furry doughnut, the little mink hat. Her makeup was flawless, as though it had been applied by an artist.

She was dressed with all the things that go hand in hand with those who are affluent.

This woman, unlike her mother, gave the impression of being a woman tuned in only to her own situation. Money had not supplied her with graciousness, kindness, or tenderness, for these cannot be purchased with money, but rather with right living.

Waving her cigarette holder, which seemed to be at least a foot long, she seemed to have about a dozen poses that suited her fancy whenever she spoke. She used one of her favorites now. One hand on her right hip and the other arm extended holding her cigarette holder, she began her tirade. Head tilted to the right slightly, she wet her lips and seemingly looking nowhere in particular, said, "Genevieve! Genevieve! You naughty child, how many times do I have to tell you that you are too old to be sitting in your grandmother's lap?" Her words seemed to have no effect on the older woman, but Genevieve quietly removed herself from her grandmother's lap, and sat herself at the kitchen table where she would be out of the way.

She watched as her aunt walked over to where her grandmother sat and aimed her cheek in her mother's general direction and allowed her to place a slight peck on her cheek.

"Honestly, Maman! I just don't know about that girl! She is so scatterbrained! Imagine at her age parking herself on your lap like that!"

"Rachel," said the older woman with her voice of quiet authority, "leave the child alone." Her voice implied that she fully expected her wishes to be respected. And they were, too. Rachel would never do anything to jeopardize her inheritance.

"Come," said the older woman as she rose from her rocking chair. "Come, we will have some tea, and if I am not mistaken there must be something good to eat around here."

Genevieve sat quietly and ignored her aunt as much as she possibly could. *I wonder what she wants this time? She never comes just for a nice visit with Grand-mère. She only comes because she wants or needs something.*

Genevieve loved this spotless old-fashioned kitchen. It reflected her grandparents so well. They still had and used their old cast-iron stove, and it shone like the first day that it was bought. It shone so brightly that you could actually see your face in it!

The house had central heating in it, but it was very seldom used.

Grand-mère felt that *nothing cooks like my own stove*. Most of the furnishings were the original ones that they had bought after the "old man" built the place, many years ago.

The folk here had weathered many battles, and if the old house could talk, what tales it could tell!

It was obvious that each article had been chosen with love and care. Everything was strong and durable. Some of the children, like Isaac, thought that they were foolish to keep their old things, but Samuel felt that they should keep them, thus leaving an even larger inheritance for him to handle. After all he was the oldest.

The old folk had conceded on one point, though. They had allowed the children to gift them with an electric refrigerator, for which the old man received the bill a few days later. But he never said a word and quietly paid for it.

Simone had never allowed them to take away her old ice-box from the kitchen. She used it to store things in. It too appeared to be in new condition. It should too, as she spent so much time keeping all her things looking nice. Genevieve thought to herself, *As old as Grand-mère is, everything in her home is spotless, and she doesn't need any old maid like Aunt Rachel has, either!*

One item in particular always fascinated Genevieve. In one corner of the kitchen way back against the wall stood a huge metal cabinet. The top of this cabinet opened up and a big bag of flour was poured in on one side and a big bag of sugar on the other side. When Grand-mère needed either of these items she would jiggle a certain lever and as long as she jiggled the flour or sugar would flow down into the big bowl she would place under one of the chutes, all sifted and ready to be used. There was a counter on it, large enough to do your baking, or mixing, or even roll out a pie crust. Countless number of goodies had been made here and Genevieve had partaken of a good many of them herself.

There was also a large drawer under this, which was used to store many good things, such as raisins and walnuts and other nut meats, and it seemed that there must be at least a hundred different kinds of spices in there. Many of them she had grown and dried herself.

Below this drawer there were two doors, and shelves, which were used to store all the various paraphernalia used for cooking and baking.

Genevieve allowed her eyes the liberty to roam around the room. She loved every stick of furniture in this room. The kitchen set was dark and solid, as could be evidenced by its age. It had already withstood many of the scars of time. Of course, in the child's mind, as with all young folk, the idea of time was magnified.

It was certain that it had withstood all the antics of the Boisvert family. Now, it was standing firm upon all the attacks of the many grandchildren. Grand-mère would not allow anyone to abuse her furniture, and never failed to tell them to act like "little ladies and gentlemen," if you please.

"Maman, is there any cream around here?" Rachel spoke a little sharply. "Surely you of all people know that I always take real cream in my tea."

The older woman did not seem to take offense at the younger woman's tone. She started to rise and Genevieve spoke out a little louder than she had intended to, "I'll get it." And as she rose she tripped over her own feet and fell with a bang to the floor.

"Ouch! Ouch!" she exclaimed, rubbing her posterior. "Ouch!"

"Honestly, Maman!" Rachel spoke in exasperation. "You must do something about that child! She gets worse and worse every day. She is much too much for you to handle."

The older woman looked at her daughter and told her, "Rachel, you be quiet right now!"

"That child should be put in a boarding school somewhere. Maman, why don't you let me look around for a good school for the child?"

When Genevieve heard these last few words she had more than she could handle, and with tears flowing down her cheeks she ran sobbing out of the room.

"There, now you've done it! Why can't you let that poor child alone?"

"Oh, Maman, there you go again making a mountain out of a molehill! I only want what is best for you."

"What is best for me, Rachel, is that you tend to your own affairs and leave ours alone!" Thus saying the older woman began picking up the dirty dishes and brought them into the pantry to be washed. The younger woman made no pretense at all about helping her mother.

The older woman walked into her pantry, which stood off to the left side of her kitchen. This little room was perhaps her favorite of all in her large house. She felt comfortable there.

"I wonder," she said half out loud, "what our children would be like if we did not have two dimes to rub together?"

As she stood there washing her dishes she felt good doing something with her own two hands. She looked up at her ceiling and thought, *The six months is almost over, time to get the ceilings whitewashed once again. How I wish I could have my three children whitewashed and clean all the dirt and filth off of them and start them anew again. What's that old saying?* she thought. *Oh yes, if nickels were horses then beggars might ride.* She had a little smile playing upon her lips, amused by her own train of thoughts.

Yes, she thought, *we have been comfortable here.* Her eyes danced around. *I like my yellow kitchen and my sensible linoleum, too.*

I think that my selfish daughter needs to be taught a lesson or two!

She returned to the kitchen and sat at the table. She looked at her daughter intently and was about to speak when Rachel rudely interrupted her. "Before you speak, Maman, let me say something. All right? I'm sorry," and as she said this she patted her mother's hand. "I really am, Maman. I know what the child means to you, I just don't want you to overdo."

"Rachel," the mother said, "I have a wonderful surprise for you."

"Maman, I don't need a surprise." Her insides were shaking. *Has Maman seen the light and decided to give me the inheritance right now?*

"Rachel?"

"Yes, Maman?"

"Sometimes it takes me a long time to realize some things, but sooner or later I come to my senses about them."

Oh Lord, thought Rachel, *the old lady is going to go on and on and make a speech! Doesn't she realize that she is boring me to death? I guess I better put up with it so I don't aggravate her.*

The older woman sat quietly. She took a clean handkerchief out of her pocket and began slowly wiping off her glasses, one lens at a time.

Rachel was beside herself and ready to scream. *That woman is deliberately trying to drive me nuts.* She clenched her teeth and tried to remain calm.

The older woman knew very well the discomfort that she was causing her younger daughter, and was enjoying every moment of it, too.

Rachel thought to herself, *I do wish that Maman would stop wearing those old-fashioned aprons all the time, they make her look like an old house frau or something.*

"I have decided that you are right," the old woman said to her, with just the slightest hint of a smile playing on her lips.

"What about, Maman? What are you talking about?"

"Patience, my dear, patience! You know, of course, that Papa and I both came from very poor families?"

"Maman!" She did not try to hide the exasperation in her voice. "You have told me that story at least a thousand times!"

"So I have and you are right, of course." *Aha,* thought the old woman, *I'm getting under her skin more than I thought I could.*

"Well, Rachel, you will be very happy to know that Papa and I have finally decided to listen to you and take your advice." Thus saying she smiled and nodded her head with the attitude of someone who was quite pleased with herself.

Rachel was about ready to explode with curiosity. "Maman," her voice was beginning to shriek now and she tried to gain control of herself. "Tell me." Her voice was sickly sweet. "Is it a surprise?"

The older woman thought for a moment and then spoke. "Yes, yes! I think you will be surprised."

"Maman! You are deliberately drawing this out to drive me crazy."

Maman began to laugh. "My dear girl, you have never been known for your patience, have you?" The older woman was relishing each and every moment of her conversation with her daughter. *She deserves each and every moment, too!*

"Starting on Monday, your Papa, Genevieve, and I are turning over a new leaf in our lives! We have worked hard and long and now feel that it is about time that we take pleasure in all that we have earned, just like you have always told us! As soon as we can agree we are going to buy ourselves new cars. At first we were going to buy just one new car, but we have decided on buying two cars, one for each of us! I am so excited!"

"T–t–two cars?" Rachel sputtered. Her eyes were bulging and she appeared to choke.

"Oh yes." The older woman was trying with great difficulty not to laugh out loud. "I really am so excited. Oh, I know I've said it before. Papa and I were speaking and we decided that we are not getting any younger and it is time that we made all our dreams come true."

"Maman, I have never heard you speak like this before." Rachel was obviously much more upset than she wanted to admit, and she was trying very hard not to show her true feelings.

"Listen to this, my dear daughter; this is really the best part of all! Papa says that he has no interest in decorating, and that he is leaving it all up to us, that is, you and I."

"You and I?" Rachel mumbled half to herself.

"Yes, yes." Maman's eyes were shining now more than they had in many a day. Maman was obviously savoring every moment of her "surprise." "It will be a wonderful time for both of us. Just think about it, all those meetings with decorators and landscapers, choosing fabrics and all the rest of it."

Rachel sat there in stunned silence with her mouth hanging open. There had not been many times in her life that she had been speechless. This was one of them. Her mind was racing along at a hundred miles an hour. *What is going on with Maman? She never wants anything for herself. My God! What she wants to do is going to cost a fortune! Maybe she is going senile! I must go and talk to Sam.*

"Rachel! Are you already starting to plan? You are a hundred miles away. I still haven't told you the best part of all. Listen carefully now, Papa says that the sky is the limit!"

All of a sudden Rachel jumped up, almost knocking her chair over, and ran and got her own coat. "Maman, I have to go now, I'm running late," and, thus saying, she aimed a kiss in her mother's general direction and literally ran out of the room.

She ran so fast she ran right into her father's arms.

"Whoa! Little girl, did you get caught with your hand in the cookie jar?"

"Oh, Papa!" She was plainly irritated and she continued out the door, not leaving very quietly.

The old gent walked over to his wife, planted a gentle kiss on the top of her head, and asked her, "Tell me my dear, what have you been up to?"

As he was speaking these words Simone began to laugh and laugh and laugh as though she would never stop, and he joined in with her. "I was listening all the time," he said. "You were wonderful! You were wonderful!"

"Yes," she said, "yes, I was!" As she said it they looked into one another's eyes and promptly broke into gales of laughter. They laughed hard and long.

Somehow and for reasons of their own, it was their moment. How long they laughed and how long they stayed there it was their business.

Chapter Sixteen
Family Talk

When Rachel set her mind on something, the fur flew everywhere. She left her parents' home, as the saying goes, "like a house afire." She ran down the steps and into her white Cadillac as fast as she could go, and for once in her life was not concerned about the proper decorum. She actually "burned rubber" getting out of there.

She exceeded the speed limit all the way downtown. *I guess there is one good thing about having your brother the mayor of the town, as I can get away with a lot!*

She was right of course, because she was seen by a cruiser and nothing was done. Her name was on the "mayor's list" and one knew better than to touch anyone on the "mayor's list."

She arrived at the town hall, parked her car in a restricted zone and ran into the building. Running the whole length of the long marbled corridor she burst in on the mayor's secretary.

Mrs. Trombly was not accustomed to any situation where she did not have the upper hand, and today she looked especially severe. She had on her black polka-dotted dress. It had a big white collar on it and also white cuffs. Her hair as always was pulled back in a severe knot.

She was at her typewriter in deep concentration and was startled by all the commotion and clatter. Before she had a chance to say anything a vision clad in a fur coat ran past her into the mayor's private office.

"You can't go in there," she yelled out in her high-pitched voice. "The mayor is in conference!"

"Some conference indeed! For heaven's sake, Samuel," Rachel was screaming now, "when are you going to stop acting like a teenager?" As she spoke she pulled the young blonde off of Samuel's lap by pulling her hair with both hands. "Get outta here, you bimbo!"

The blonde raised her fists as though she were going to bop Rachel one, but Samuel grabbed both of her arms and shook her. "Didn't you hear what she said?" He threw twenty dollars at her and yelled, "Now, beat it!"

She screeched at him, "You're gonna get yours, Mr. Mayor!"

"Yeah, yeah, you scare me kid. Ha, ha, ha," he chortled, and wiped his hands on his rotund stomach. "Nice kid, you oughta see her in a bathing suit!"

"Samuel." Rachel was very perturbed with him now and threw her hands up in despair, then put one hand on her right hip and the other hand pointing in his face. "I give up! I give up! When are you ever going to grow up?"

Samuel slowly and deliberately put his hands upon his desk and pushed his chair back as far as his arms could push it and pulled his rotund body out of his chair.

His sister watched him as though fascinated by his every move. He walked over to where she stood, and as she was taller than him had to look up to meet her eyes. In a menacing tone of voice and with his eyes flashing, he reached out with his hands and grabbed her two cheeks, and as he was squeezing them tears were filling her eyes.

"Rachel! My business is my business!" He was squeezing even harder than before, so that her lips looked as though they were pouting, as he said, "Right? Come on, don't just stand there with your mouth open. It's obvious something's got your dander up. Let's go to that Chinese restaurant on the edge of town where we can have some privacy. I'm starving! If you wanna come with me, go fix your hair and hat, you look like you've been out on a drunk! While you're doing that I'll give the old lady a buzz."

He went over and pressed a button on his intercom. "Get me my home." His tone was that of authority. He sat back on his chair and chuckled to himself. *I finally found out how to handle that pest of a sister of mine. Who would have guessed that she was such a 'fraidy cat? Maybe I should paste her a good one. On second thought, I'd better not; she does come in handy some of the time.*

The buzz of the machine broke his reverie. "Yeah? Oh, hi, hon, got some bad news. I can't come home for dinner." He lowered his voice to a whisper. "It's Rachel; she's here reading me the riot act, and I gotta find out what's up. Can't talk now. We'll talk when I get home."

As Rachel came back into the room, he quickly hung up the phone. "Y'all set? I'm as hungry as a bear."

When they got outside, it had begun to snow. The snow was coming down at a good pace. It made the whole town look new and clean. It gave the old town a look of elegance, like a sparkling diamond. Even after just this short moment of standing there they were beginning to look like snowmen.

"Let's not stand here all night," Samuel said.

Rachel turned to look at her brother. "Do you think that we should just go home?"

"Look, my dear sister, you are the one who started all this. Now let's get it over with, for heaven's sake. We have to eat even if we run home." He grabbed his sister's arm. "Come on, we'll take my car."

He unlocked the door of his big black Cadillac and quickly got in and leaned over and unlocked the door on the passenger side.

Rachel quickly got in and gave her brother one of those looks that expressed her opinion without words.

The roads were definitely difficult to travel on, and they sat there in silence, each one absorbed in their own thoughts. Samuel was happy, as he felt that he had won a battle over his sister and had found a way to handle her, so to speak. Rachel was in a different frame of mind. *I owe him one! I'll see that he gets his yet!*

When they arrived at the Hun Yo restaurant they were treated like royalty. The owner himself came forward. He looked like the prototype of all other owners of these establishments: Black pants and a red jacket, quilted, with a mandarin collar.

"Good evening, Mr. Mayor. How are we tonight? Your table is ready for you." He turned to Rachel and said, "Good evening, Madam. Right this way please." He led them to a secluded booth where they were sure to have privacy. He pulled out the chair for Rachel, and she quickly sat down. Looking Rachel full in the eye, he gave her a very large smile and said, "Your waiter is James and he'll be right with you." He then bowed and left.

Rachel looked at Sam and she was not at all pleased. "You know that guy gives me the creeps; why did we have to come here anyway?"

"Rachel, damn it all, stop your complaining! You're getting a free meal and your problem solved too!"

Rachel sneered at her brother. "It's not my problem, brother dear; it is all our problem, mine, yours, and Isaac's, too!"

Samuel's ears perked up and he was all business now. "What are you talking about?"

"Let's order first." Rachel was enjoying the fact that she had the upper hand and wanted to relish the moment.

She could not believe her eyes as her brother ate his dinner. *You'd think he was a condemned man eating his last meal,* she thought. *Oh well, why should I care? I don't have to carry around all that blubber!*

Samuel looked intently at his sister and thought to himself, *She's stalled long enough, I gotta get her shaking.* He looked up from his Pu Pu platter and stared his sister straight in the eyes. "Okay, okay, enough dramatics for now, out with it. What is your problem that you can't solve?"

Rachel and Samuel's natures were so much alike that neither one of them gave an inch.

She wiped her mouth on her napkin and looked him square in the eye. "I told you before it is not my problem, it is our problem."

"Okay, okay," he used his favorite expression. "Spit it out, what is *our*," he sarcastically drew out the word, "problem."

"Today," she said, "I went over to see Maman and Papa, although Papa was not at home."

Samuel was obviously getting more irritable by the moment. "What'sa big deal about that? You visit them every time you want something."

"And of course you don't," Rachel answered like a shot out of a rifle. "Who's the one that talked Maman and Papa into buying him a new Cadillac for Christmas last year?"

"Okay, okay, let's call a truce. Just keep in mind, my dear sister, that you also received a Cadillac for Christmas! You know, it's not easy being the oldest. Whenever anyone can't handle anything, they come running to me!"

"Pity party over?" Rachel asked in a very saccharine voice.

Samuel thought to himself, *Someday, someday I'm gonna let that broad have it real good!*

"I went to see our parents, and it makes me so mad. I got to the house, and there she was, that big strap of a girl, sitting in Ma's lap, big as you please!"

"You're just as jealous of that kid as you were of Laura! Grow up! I certainly hope you didn't cause all this ruckus over that girl sitting on Ma's lap!"

"My God, Samuel," she was totally exasperated now, "can't you listen for one minute? Something is very wrong with Maman," she was speaking now in a monotone. "Yes, something is drastically wrong, I would say."

Samuel's ears perked up. "What'sa matter? She sick? Get a doctor, for Pete's sake!"

"Noooo!" She was carefully selecting each word now. "She's acting very, very strange. I've never known her to act this way before."

"Like what, like what?" Samuel was paying close attention now.

Rachel looked at her brother. "Come on, Samuel." She thought for a moment or two as she twirled her fork in her Chinese rice. "I don't know if I can explain it to you, but I really am worried."

Samuel looked at Rachel and thought, *Something really is up. Rachel is not acting at all like herself.* "Take your time, Rachie." *Geez, I haven't called her that since we were little kids.*

"Like I said, this afternoon I went up home and Maman was not acting like I've ever seen her act before."

"Whad'ya mean?" His impatient nature was coming through again.

"Well, I never saw Maman act this way before...." she trailed off.

"What way?" Samuel was screaming now. His face was beet red and his eyes looked as though they were going to bug out of his head.

"Well, give me a chance to tell you and please stop screaming at me. As I started to say, that little snip of a girl sitting there on Maman's lap, you know, that could very well be Ma's problem. That girl is too much for her!"

"Well, Maman asked me if I wanted a cup of tea and I said yes. Genevieve had stomped off to her room because she was upset that I told her that she was too big to be sitting on her grandmother's lap.

"Maman and I were sitting there side by side enjoying our tea when all of a sudden her eyes began to sparkle and she was like a little child that could not sit still.

"All of a sudden she said, 'I am not supposed to tell, but I cannot hold back any longer; I will burst if I don't tell someone.'

"I was very puzzled as this behavior is so unlike her. I asked her 'What is it, Maman?'

"Maman was even more excited than before. She sat up on the edge of her chair and said to me, 'Papa and I have been thinking about this a long time and have finally arrived at a decision.'

"Well, I could hardly wait to hear what she was about to say. Deep down inside I thought that maybe they had decided to give us our inheritances early. No such thing, though. Then she drops it on me!

" 'Papa and I have decided to follow your advice.'

"As you know, Maman and Papa have never once in my whole life taken my advice about anything. I was flabbergasted.

" 'We have ordered for ourselves two new cars. I think Papa's is a Rolls Royce and mine is a Lincoln Continental. Can't you see your Maman riding around like a grand lady with a chauffeur?' "

Samuel hit his head with the palm of his hand. "Tell me you're joking!"

Rachel was indignant now. "I wish I was joking! And that's not the half of it either!

"Now Maman stands up and starts tapping my shoulders. 'Listen, Rachel, listen to me. We are also going to do the whole house over from top to bottom, the grounds, and the whole shebang. Yes, yes, I must tell you this, we are going to put in a swimming pool, a tennis court, and also a few riding horses for the grandchildren.'

"Believe me, I was stunned. I was speechless.

"Maman began shaking me and saying, 'Rachel, you have not answered me.'

" 'What, Maman?' I asked.

" 'Well, my dear daughter, are you going to help me?'

"What could I say to her, Samuel? I stammered, 'Of course I'll help you, Maman.' Then I told her, 'I'm late for an appointment,' and I came here to see you."

"You did the right thing. Is that all?"

"No, it isn't. As I was leaving the house Maman yells out after me, 'Papa says we don't have to spare expenses either!' "

Samuel had lost all of his appetite now, and he had paled considerably. "Come on, let's get out of here. We better have a talk with our dear old brother Isaac."

Never were two people more upset than these two. For money they could get along and pull together.

Chapter Seventeen
Discussion?

The first thing Samuel did when they got into his car was grab his C.B. speaker and call his office to tell them where he was "gonna be in case of an emergency."

One thing about Samuel, he liked to feel important and could find a way to make himself important at the drop of a hat.

Rachel pulled her fur coat tighter about herself and shrugged her shoulders. She looked at her brother and with disdain in her voice said, "You and your toys. Are you ever going to grow up?"

"Shut up, Rachel; we have more important things on our minds tonight, and I don't wanna bicker with you. Besides, my dear sister, what's it to ya? I do as I please, when I please, and how I please, and the likes of you will never stop me. If you don't believe me, ask Blanche." He grinned maliciously. "Yeah, Blanche could tell you a thing or two about me, if she wanted to."

Rachel could be as malicious as he could. "Yes, brother dear, and while you're doing as you please, Blanche is also doing as she pleases."

"Damn you anyhow, Rachel, always gotta have the last word. What's Blanche up to now? You know you're gonna tell me sooner or later when it serves your purpose anyhow."

Rachel relaxed herself in the comfort of this luxurious automobile. She felt good. She had the upper hand right now with her brother and she relished every moment.

"Wel-l-l," he strung the word out, "at least I don't run Blanche around with a ring in her nose like you do your old man!"

Rachel just laughed and didn't answer for a moment and then she said, "I don't know if I can handle this tonight. He always makes every one of those dirty squirming brats come over and hug and kiss me. Ugh!"

"He does it on purpose to get your goat, haven't you figured that out yet?"

"Somehow, I think I would feel better kissing the pigs or hogs than all those brats. And kissing Susannah is even worse; she reeks of body odor, never brushes her teeth, and always looks like rag bag Annie!"

"Come on now, gettin yourself all riled up ain't gonna help anything. Tonight we all will need a clear head."

"Whatta you think, Sam? Think the old lady is going senile on us?"

"I was thinkin' along those lines, but right now I don't know, let's take one thing at a time, O.K.? Trust me, Rachel, things are gonna be all right." He patted her hand in a gesture of affection.

Rachel thought to herself, *Trust him! Why I'd sooner trust a trapped rattlesnake, or a bear protecting her cubs. I wouldn't trust Sam with my pet rat.*

She had seen Sam in action too many times. He had finagled Isaac, their parents, and even herself. *He didn't care who got in his way; he would get his results, and he didn't care how, either. I'd better think sharp tonight, and keep on my toes. Sam would like nothing better than to cheat me and Isaac out of our rightful inheritance. Oh yes, and Genevieve, too.*

Samuel broke into her thoughts, "We're almost there."

"Oh God . . . " Rachel began.

Samuel's temper flared up. "Look here, Rachel, don't start none of that crap, ya hear? We're gonna need Ike behind us, and don't you do nothin' to make him or Susannah mad. I mean it! Do ya hear me! I mean it, Rachel, don't you mess us up. You're gonna kiss and hug and pat until your lips and hands are sore. We hafta get to Isaac and the only way to do that is through his old lady and the kids, so tonight we are the dear auntie and uncle coming over for a family visit. Got that straight?"

"Where do you get off telling me what to do?"

"I'll tell you what to do and you'll do it all right, because you have as much a stake in this as I do."

"You know, Samuel, because I'm a lady, I won't tell you where you are a pain, but it's much lower than the neck."

"You! A lady? Who you tryna kid? Remember this is old Samuel and I've known you all of your life and I know all of your tricks too. C'mon, dear sister, it's Academy Awards time. Hey kid, you got a shower at home?" He began to laugh, which infuriated her all the more.

"Hey, Susannah, somebody's at the door." Isaac sat there in all his glory, and that consisted of an old torn flannel shirt, faded blue jeans with holes all over them, and of course worn and stained work boots. He was sitting in the parlor, or a room that could be called "parlor," if you were not fussy how you used the term.

"I'm nursing the baby; get it yourself." Susannah was sitting at the kitchen table with the part of her body hanging out of her dress that was familiar to everyone, but not particularly loved. Her dress looked older than she was and had not been washed in many a day. Her hair was greasy and stringy and she had it tied back with a rubber band.

Isaac slowly raised his bulk out of the easy chair, at least what was left of it, and muttered, "Who would be crazy enough to come out on a night like this anyway? Hey, Susannah! It's Sam and Rachel come to pay us a visit. Ain't that nice? We weren't expecting company, so you'll have to take us just the way we are. Come in; come in. Hey kids, come see who's here." All of a sudden a flurry of children appeared on the scene from every direction, and each one seemed more unkempt than the other.

Rachel hugged her brother. "How are you, Isaac?"

"Good, good, how's 'bout you, Sis?" Thus saying he patted her on the rear end as though she was one of the children. She wanted to belt him one, but Samuel was watching her every move.

"Hey, Suzy!" Samuel boomed out in what he thought was his most jovial voice, "you get better looking every time I see you. That the new baby? Cute as a button, isn't she Rachel?"

Susannah thought to herself, *This old blowhard is up to something.* "He," she said. "It's a boy."

"Oh yeah, sorry about that, but I mean it, he is cute as a button. Here's your chance, Rachel. Ya know, on the way up here Rachel was telling me how much she loves babies, but never gets to hold one." He turned to Susannah. "The poor woman is too shy to ask you, afraid to insult you, or hurt your feelings or something. Her exact words on the way over here were, 'I wonder if Susannah will let me hold the baby tonight.' Right, Rachel?"

Susannah got up off of her chair and plopped the baby in Rachel's lap unceremoniously. "She can hold him anytime she wants. Always thought that she didn't want to get her fancy duds dirty holding a kid."

The baby did not smell the best and Rachel was very uncomfortable sitting there with him on her lap. Samuel reached over and tickled the baby's tummy and made him laugh. "Whaddya call this one, Ike?"

"His name is Kenneth, but we call him Kenny."

"How many do you have now? I'm scatterbrained and lose track."

"We've got ten now, seven girls and three boys."

Samuel smiled at his brother and patted him on the back. "That's why Rachel and I don't have any children, Ike; you took all the good-looking ones."

Isaac beamed. Samuel was right about him, the way to his heart was through his kids and his wife.

Rachel almost choked getting the words out, but she asked, "Susannah, would you be kind enough to make us a cup of your good tea? I am chilled through to the bone and certainly could use something hot to drink."

"Good idea, Rachel," Isaac said. "I could use a little snack myself. Now, children, I want every one of you to come and greet your aunt and uncle." They all formed a line and kissed and hugged first one and then the other of their "eminent" relatives.

Rachel tried desperately not to show her distaste as they caressed her. The baby, for some strange reason or other, clung to her and would not go to anyone else. *That's all I need,* she thought.

Still, even in her warped mind she was like everyone else and she liked being accepted, even if it was only by a six month old snotty nosed brat.

Nicole entered the room and Samuel looked at her and whistled, "Look at that Rachel; a movie star just walked in."

Nicole began to blush and went over and kissed her uncle on the cheek, and as she did this Rachel took a moment to appraise herself of the situation. She had thought that Samuel was just throwing the bull as usual, but when she observed her niece she realized that a real transformation had taken place.

Nicole's hair had been cut and styled in the very height of fashion, which brought out her facial features to their best advantage. She even had on some nice clothes for a change, and everything about her seemed clean and shining. *Looks like they've buried the old, mousy Nicole and adopted this new creature. What an improvement, to say the least.*

Samuel looked up from his teacup and said, "Mighty good cup a tea Susannah, real good, hits the spot on a night like this."

Rachel murmured a demure, "Yes, it does."

Samuel cleared his throat and looked at Rachel as if to say, "It's now or never," then he looked at his brother and then his sister-in-law. He cleared his throat several times and then spoke.

"Look here, Ike old boy," Samuel cleared his throat again, "I don't want you to misunderstand or even to take this wrong, but is there somewhere quiet that we could have a serious talk, about something real important?"

Isaac's dander was already being aroused. "Whaddya mean?"

"Well, it's about the old man and old lady."

"Susannah," Isaac told his wife, "how about getting these wild Indians to bed? Huh?"

"Look," Susannah was plainly put out now, "if there's gonna be any talking going on I'm gonna sit right here. Whatever happens affects me and the kids as well as you! Besides, I'm not about to let this smooth-talking brother and sister of yours put anything over on you tonight as they've done in the past. No way!"

Samuel thought, *I'd like to punch out the couple rotten teeth she does have!* But instead he said, "She's right, ya know, gotta look out for number one. Right? Wish I had me a wife like that, always looking out for my best interests." *Why, you old so and so,* he thought.

"Nikki," Isaac bellowed, "get yourself over here."

"Yeah!" she hollered back.

"C'mere and take these kids and get them inta bed. Now!"

"Okay, okay. Can't even do my homework."

As all the kids scampered in various directions and the pandemonium began to die down, Isaac spoke up and said, "What's this all about, anyhow?"

Samuel looked intently at his brother for a long moment. "I told you, Ike, it's about the old man and Ma."

"What about 'em?" Isaac tipped his chair back and put both his hands behind his head and thought to himself, *I wonder if he knows what happened here last Saturday?* He looked at Susannah as if to say "watch what you say."

Susannah was thinking along the same lines. *I hope Isaac knows enough to keep his mouth shut and doesn't volunteer any information.* She tried to give him a warning look.

Samuel, always an observant person, noticed the looks that Isaac and Susannah had been exchanging and immediately set his guard up. *They're up to something. I don't know what, but my gut tells me these two are up to something. After all, I have gotten the best of Isaac all these years because I know him well enough to have that gut feeling when he's up to something.*

"Well," Samuel said, "I'm gonna let Rachel tell you what happened today when she went up to visit with Ma, then we'll talk about things. All right?"

Rachel was enjoying being the center of attention of her two brothers, as the times that this happened were few and far between indeed. She relished this moment and was determined to make it last as long as possible.

"Come on, Rachel," Samuel said irritably. "I'm getting older by the minute here. Heck, I wanna be able to walk outta here on my own. Get on with it."

"Well," Rachel retorted, "you want me to tell it right or not?"

Rachel got into the story of how she had visited their mother and what had happened. She told every detail and embellished a few also, to her own advantage. She had to make herself look good, didn't she?

Samuel had sat back on his chair and his eyes were fixed on Isaac and Susannah. He wanted to see each and every reaction, but none of the reactions were the ones that he expected. He puzzled these things back and forth in his mind as Rachel spoke. *They're upta something, I can smell it. If I didn't know better, I'd swear that they are amused by the whole thing and not surprised at all.*

"Well," Rachel was winding down now, "if we don't watch it there won't be any inheritance for any of us, and then what will we do? See what I mean, Ike?" said Samuel. "They're acting stranger and stranger every day. We gotta pull together on this one, cause we're all gonna lose out if we don't."

"Whaddya think we should do, Sam?"

Samuel thought to himself, *That son of a gun is making fun of me, but why?*

Susannah spoke up, "What do ya suppose he wants us to do? Why, Mr. Nice Guy here wants us to turn everything over to him. Isn't that right, Sam?"

Samuel cleared his throat. *She was a smart one all right. I better watch my step with her.* "Only in a manner of speaking," he said. "Well, do you all wanna wait till they spend it all and then decide to do something when it's all gone?"

"What should we do about it, it's their money ain't it? Seems fair to me that if a man earns the money he should be able to spend it as he sees fit."

Susannah gave Isaac a triumphant look. *He's gonna get the best of Samuel tonight, that's for sure. I waited a long time to see this. Talk about timing!* She grinned like the cat that swallowed the canary.

"Well," Samuel spoke again, "we're all concerned here and I think that the only thing left to do is to have them declared incompetent to handle their affairs, before it is too late."

Susannah gave Samuel a look of total disgust. "And you should be named the conservator?"

"Well," he grinned at her so that his gold teeth sparkled, "can I help it that I was born first and am the oldest son?"

"No," she spat out at him and as she did so some of her saliva found its way to Samuel's face, and he wiped it off with disgust. "But you sure can take advantage of that fact can't you?"

Isaac spoke up. "This bickering isn't gettin' us no place. What do you want from us, Sammy?"

"What we gotta do is start a petition that says they're not themselves anymore and prove it, but we gotta all agree and pull together."

Isaac let the front legs of his chair come to the floor with a bang. "Lemme get this straight; you want us all to testify against our own parents and have them declared incompetent and turn everything over to you." He scratched his head as though puzzled. "Not me, Sam, no sirree, not me!"

"You're a fool, Isaac, and ya know what, you've always been a fool and you're always gonna be too. And what's more, you'll be a poor fool too! I'll see ta that myself!"

Isaac looked at Susannah and they both began to laugh and laugh and couldn't stop.

Samuel was getting more and more angry.

Isaac's face turned bright red and the veins in his neck were sticking way out. "So," he said, "I'm a fool, am I? Don't know what I'm doing, do I? You just wait here a minute smart man and we'll see who's the dumbbell in this family!" And he stomped out of the room in his bare feet.

Susannah never said a word. She took both her hands and placed her ample bosoms on the table and never even had to lean over. Her expression was of sneering disdain toward both of them.

Samuel was getting impatient and began tapping his foot. *What can he be up to?*

Rachel did not seem to be registering any kind of emotion, but inwardly she was seething. *Samuel better not have messed this one up, because if he did he's really going to get it from me!*

Isaac returned to the messy kitchen and his look was one of total triumph; he was, in fact, exhilarated. Nicole and Henry had also come in with Isaac. Samuel and Rachel were all ears waiting to see just what was going on.

"Nicole," Isaac said, "tell your aunt and uncle where you went last weekend."

"Do you want me to start at the beginning?"

"Yeah, everything, and don't leave out one thing either."

"Well, last Friday Grand-mère and Grand-père came to visit us and Maman asked them to stay for supper, which they did. After supper Grand-mère came over and asked me if I wanted to go over to their house and go shopping with her and Genevieve the next day. You and Maman said yes, I could go, so I went home with them. The next day I went shopping with the two of them and Grand-mère took us all to the hairdresser, you know, the new one in town."

Rachel picked up on it right away and said, "Do you mean 'The Maison Blue'? That is a very exclusive place." Her eyes opened wide.

"Well, anyhow, Grand-mère told the hairdresser to make us all look beautiful and if she liked the work that the hairdressers did, they would each get a fifty dollar bonus! She gave the three hairdressers the tip plus the bill. It came to about, well, several hundred dollars, that's for sure.

"Next we all went to the Hun Yo restaurant. We took a cab to get there, and Grand-mère gave the cab driver a twenty-five dollar tip! I couldn't believe my eyes, but she did.

"When we got into the restaurant she told us, me and Genevieve, 'Today, the sky is the limit, you can have anything you want!'

"After the meal was over Grand-mère was laughing and said, 'Girls, what do you think, was Charlie a good waiter or not?'

"We both said he was a very good waiter.

"'Yes,' Grand-mère said, 'I believe that he is too, and a good worker deserves a good reward. Right?'

"We all laughed and said 'yes' and she left him a one hundred dollar tip!

"Well, we took a cab down to the Bon Marché store and even though we had the same driver as before she gave him another twenty-five dollar tip.

"Inside the store Grand-mère told the saleslady, 'I want these two girls outfitted from head to toe, and I mean everything from school clothes to play clothes and don't forget casual wear, sportswear and dressy either.'

"She came over to us and gave us each a kiss and said 'Get to, girls, and pick and choose at your hearts' content.'"

Isaac interrupted, "Nicole has at least several thousand dollars' worth of clothes upstairs. Want to go up and see the new bedroom set they bought her?"

"No thanks," Samuel said, and now it was his turn for the veins to seem ready to pop on his head.

Isaac turned to Rachel and Samuel. "Heard enough from Nicole?" They both nodded in agreement.

"Good," Isaac said, "now we can hear from Henry."

"Henry, too!" Rachel's voice surprised even her.

"Well," Henry said, "I can't tell everything because I promised Grand-père I wouldn't tell some of the things. He came and got me on Saturday and did the same thing for me that Grand-mère did for Nicole; he bought me a complete outfit of new clothes. Well," he paused, "while I was in the store being fitted for clothes, he left the store and was gone, oh, I guess it musta been a coupla hours. He picked me up in a brand new sports car, a real beauty too. When I climbed into the car he said, 'How do you like this car, Henry?'

"I said it was the most beautiful thing I had ever seen.

"He turned and looked at me and said, 'I'm so glad you said that, boy, because the car is yours.' I couldn't believe my ears, but he givita me all right. Wannasee it, it's right out the door."

Both Rachel and Samuel raced to the window, while Isaac and Susannah gleefully watched on.

"It's a beauty all right," said Samuel through his gritted teeth. "Anything else?"

"As a matter of fact, Sammy boy, there is. Yes, indeed there is. Take a gander at this," and he handed him his bank book, which showed a very recent deposit of one hundred thousand dollars.

Samuel's eyes literally bulged out of his head. "Where did you get that bundle?"

"I guess the old man thought I was too dumb for you and he gave me my share of my inheritance now."

Samuel looked at his brother. "I don't believe a word of it. You musta done some fast talking or something to get that amount."

Isaac laughed. "Whatsa matter, Sammy boy? You look like you seen a ghost. What it boils down to is this, my dear brother and sister; I got mine and you guys didn't get yours and you're mad. Now you gonna start some dirty work and you want me to do it for you. No siree, what I got is a heck of a lot more than you guys got. Right?" And he went into gales of laughter once again.

"Rachel," Samuel said, "let's get outta this dump!"

As Rachel and Samuel were leaving, Isaac couldn't resist one more barb and he called out the door, "Hey, Sammy, hey, Rachel! How much didya get?"

Rachel and Samuel could hear prolonged laughter as they got into their car to leave. Once they were in the car Samuel turned to Rachel. "Now are you gonna tell me what Blanche is up to or not?"

Rachel never uttered a word.

Chapter Eighteen
Togetherness

Anticipation is rather a large word, with an even larger meaning. Is it ever really possible to describe the total anticipation and dreams of youth? Do the dreams ever catch up with the anticipation? Or does the anticipation ever reach the dream? What causes dreams? Analysts have attempted for years to discern the causes and the effects of dreams upon a person. Just what does anticipation have to do with life anyhow? Does anticipation add to the enjoyment of life? Is anticipation blind to reality? Does anticipation build a wall or does it open doorways to otherwise inaccessible pathways? Is youth really wasted on the young? Are there some who subscribe to old age and yearn for infirmities and handicaps long before they are due them?

Why are some so happy and blissful in ignorance, or is ignorance indeed bliss, and why then is it that others never amass enough learning or understanding?

Genevieve loved the times that she and her grandmother spent alone, and the older woman many times would philosophize about life and terms, and the child would listen and observe and file away somewhere in her mental processes these things that she would use in her own life in the days to come.

The older woman seemed to come alive and become more vibrant at times like these. She actually seemed to revive and become more intense, or vibrant and youthful, as if the fire of her life was not ebbing out, but that there were still fires of life living within her.

Simone thought, *Not many young people would sit and listen to an old woman of seventy-two years, but the knowledge is there and the experience too. I may speak more slowly or hesitatingly, or take longer to say something than I did in years past, but there is one thing for sure, thank God, I still have my wits about me.*

Genevieve sat there looking intently at her grandmother. *Dear God, please don't let Grand-mère die; she looks so tired and old lately.*

Aloud, she said very formally, "Grand-mère, what is your hope and your anticipation? Just what is it you dream or hope? What does one really desire at seventy-two years of age?"

Simone looked over at Genevieve. She knew that a lot of things would hinge on her answer today. "My anticipations?" She laughed, and then paused and thought and she began to speak slowly. "I have had most of my desires fulfilled in my lifetime, and now my hopes are for you to grow up and become a fine woman, a strong woman, a woman who loves and fears God, a woman of honor and pride."

Simone eyed her granddaughter for a few moments and as she spoke the gentleness of her character came through as a ray of sunshine that had been hiding behind the overcast skies. "And you? *Ma petite*, come sit here on my lap and I will rock you, just as I did when you were a little slip of a girl no larger than a head of cabbage. Come," she coaxed her gently, "sit with me and share your dreams."

"Grand-mère, Aunt Rachel scolds me all the time for sitting on your lap. Perhaps she is right. I may be much too big to sit upon your lap anymore."

Simone's eyes were sparkling now. "Do you think, Mademoiselle Genevieve, that I lived seventy-two years and am not capable of knowing what I am able to do? Come," she sighed, "time at my age flows much too swiftly."

Genevieve went over and sat on her grandmother's lap, and Simone held her close against her and wrapped her crocheted shawl around both of them. She began to rock back and forth and to and fro in a rhythmic fashion, and the moment was one of contentment and tranquility.

"No one is too old for togetherness and love. Now speak, as I wait anxiously to hear what you have to say."

"Grand-mère, I have a confession to make to you," Genevieve spoke hesitantly and softly.

Simone hugged her even closer, if that was possible.

Grand-mère always smells nice, she thought. *She smells of lavender and peppermints.*

"I must confess to you that I am very selfish. I want to be rich and famous. I want to go to the best schools. I want to be a famous writer. I want a handsome husband, and a big car. I want beautiful children who will love no one else but me. I want tons and tons of money to spend as I like. I want to eat steak and roast beef every night, or whatever else that I like. I want to have flowers all over my house. I want to have a swimming pool in my backyard like the movie stars in Hollywood. I want to go out and dance all night with the handsomest boys. I want to be popular, and I want to be able to sing and you see," she began to sob, "I am a selfish person, and jealous too! All I can say is I want, I want, I want! And if I really told the truth, there is much, much more that I want."

The old woman tenderly wiped the tears from her granddaughter's eyes and cheeks and said, "Bon! It is good that you want much for you, because you shall work hard to achieve it. Don't you dare lose your dreams for you, or your anticipations either! When a person loses the vision he does not strive for higher things but becomes stagnant in his mediocrity, lazy and indolent, he is like the dog that returns to his own vomit. Remember that dreams and visions differ from greed. A person needs dreams and visions even when my age, otherwise we are merely taking up space on this planet. Understand what you want and why you want it; is it to make this world a better place? Some strive to get everything they can even if they really don't want it, just so someone else cannot have it. Your motives and intents are perhaps the most important part of what makes you!

"Do you understand, or am I merely rambling on? What you want the most is to be loved, *ma chère, oui?*"

She put the child's head on her shoulder and patted her back until the tears stopped flowing. When the child's body relaxed, Simone began singing to her in a soft voice that was meant for her alone. She sang all of the old French ditties that she could bring back to mind. They sat there until twilight was blossoming into full-fledged nightfall. How long they sat there could be anyone's guess; in any case, it was a treasured moment for both.

Genevieve felt loved and secure and protected, that wonderful feeling that all hope to achieve at some time or other in their lifetime. But, we all know that as the pendulum reaches the crest of its orbit it must once again return to its lower altitude in its arc of being a clock, then so must we come down sooner or later.

Alexandre came in and joined his "two girls," as he called them. "Is there no one hungry here except for me? My stomach tells me that it is long past the supper hour."

Genevieve ran over to her grandfather and gave him a big hug. The old man enjoyed the affection that he received from his young granddaughter.

"Oh, Grand-père, seeing it is so late could we call and have a pizza delivered for supper? That way Grand-mère won't have to cook or do dishes either."

"Genevieve," he said a little sternly, "take a moment and catch your breath and let us see what your grandmother has to say about this matter."

Simone, sitting there in the background, was shaking her head yes. Neither one of them would ever really deprive Genevieve of anything her heart desired as long as it would not be harmful to her well-being.

"Now," Alexandre told her, "you go into the other room and order that pizza and some salad, and of course we must have something to drink with it. Whatever you think tonight, miss, you choose and we'll eat. Run along now as I am really hungry."

Simone knew that Alexandre was getting Genevieve out of the room for a purpose, so that he could ask her a question. She knew what the question would be and she did not want to have to answer it, but she knew that she must.

Sooner or later "always" comes to haunt us, it is a form of reality that we cannot escape, no matter how we attempt to. For Simone tonight was sooner.

"Simone," Alexandre spoke tenderly, "you have not told the child?"

Simone put her head down and shook her head no. Alexandre went over to her and cupped her chin with his hand and raised her head so that her eyes met his. "It must be done, and soon, you realize that?"

"Yes, I realize it all too well, but in this matter I have become weak like jelly. I tried, really, Alexandre, I tried!"

He leaned over and kissed her lightly on the lips. "I will help you, we have faced many things together, we will face this also."

Genevieve came into the room like a thunderbolt and did not notice the tender moment between the two. "They'll be here in thirty minutes! Guess what kind I ordered? It's a combination pizza, but *no* anchovies and no olives either, but everything else is on it. I got a big one, okay, cause we are all starving."

Simone and Alexandre looked at one another and smiled at the vibrancy and exuberance of her youth. She seemed more vital and alive than ever before to Simone.

Genevieve stood and looked at them, and her eyes were sparkling. "You two are the best people in the whole world! Not just because of the pizza, but because of everything about you. I never want to be away from either one of you, never!" Then she ran over to each of them and gave them each a hug and kiss.

"Grand-mère, may I go and do my homework while we wait for the pizza?"

"Of course." She was off to another adventure of her youth, which no one escapes: homework.

"You know, Alexandre," Simone's voice seemed weak tonight, "before you came in, I was rocking Genevieve and we were sharing some things, and I may just be an old fool, but I pretended that it was Laura in my arms." Her eyes were misting now. "I am nothing but a sentimental old fool; it was so real, Laura and I. Even after all this time has passed, I miss her as much as the day she left."

"I know," he said tenderly. "I know."

"Did you get all your work accomplished?"

"Yes, I did all the shipping, jewelry and all. Anna has everything prepared as per your instructions."

"You will go through with it?"

"Yes, Beloved, because I love you, and because I loved Laura, and because I love the child."

"It is her only hope. To get away from all the things that go on in this family. Sad to say, isn't it? Alexandre, will you miss them? The other children?"

"I will miss them as much as I would a box full of vipers! It is settled, Simone, it is settled, rest assured."

The ringing of the doorbell startled them both back to the present moment. Alexandre went to the door and paid the young boy who had made the delivery. He gave him a twenty dollar tip, and the youth grinned from ear to ear. "Thanks mister, thanks a lot!"

Genevieve came running into the parlor. "Oh boy, the food is here. Let's go, I'm starving too." They all proceeded into the kitchen. Simone was so weak that she had to hold on to Alexandre very tightly. Genevieve did not notice anything, she was so absorbed by the pizza.

"Come and get it while it's hot," she laughed, "or cold, I guess, for the salad. I'll serve, okay?"

They ate quietly except for Genevieve, whose mouth was running steadily, telling them everything, every detail of her school day. "I gotta—"

"Do you mean 'have to,' Genevieve?" asked Alexandre.

"Yes, I do. I have to do a paper for a science project, and don't know what to do it on. What do you think I should do it on? Grand-mère, any ideas?"

"Pardon me, Genevieve, I had my mind on another matter."

"More important than my science project?"

"I'm afraid so, little one."

"Sounds ominous. Am I in the doghouse?"

"Are you finished eating yet?"

"Uh huh."

"I believe that means yes," said Alexandre. "Let us get into prayer now."

Alexandre and Genevieve knelt beside their chairs and Simone sat on her rocking chair and they prayed together. First Grand-père, then Simone and then Genevieve. She knew better than to rush it too, because if she did then they would begin all over again. It did not matter who came to the door when they were praying as no one rose for any man. The phone could ring from now to kingdom come, no one dared to interrupt their conversation to the heavenlies. Anyone coming to the house had several options. One was to turn around and come back later, the second was to sit and wait quietly so as not to disturb, and the third was to come in and join.

"Genevieve," Alexandre spoke very seriously now. "We must speak to you concerning a matter of great importance."

"Yes, Grand-père, I am listening."

Alexandre turned to Simone expectantly. *She looks so pale and tired,* he sighed. *We have made all kinds of plans, except for my heart, which is breaking moment by moment.*

Simone looked upon the child. *She has been through so much, how can I break her heart again?* She could feel Alexandre's penetrating gaze upon her even though she was not looking directly at him.

"Well, for Pete's sake somebody tell me what's going on, will ya?"

Simone opened her mouth to speak, but no sound came out. She deliberately cleared her throat and turned to Alexandre and said, "I can't."

"What is the matter? What is going on?"

Alexandre looked at Genevieve and said, "Your Grand-mère is going on a trip."

"What's the big deal?" Genevieve asked. "Grand-mère deserves to go on a trip and have a good time. Where are you going? I know why you're having such a hard time telling me, cause I can't go right?"

"Genevieve, I am indeed going on a trip and you are correct, where I am going you cannot come."

Genevieve felt something in the pit of her stomach that she could not describe.

"Is Grand-père going with you?"

"No, he is not."

"Then you must be going with Aunt Rachel! Ugh! Poor you!"

Alexandre had had enough of Genevieve. "Be still! Listen for a moment."

Simone looked into her granddaughter's eyes. "Do you trust your Grand-père and me?"

"You know I do. I trust you will all my heart!"

"Do you trust us enough to do what we ask of you without questioning us?"

"Yes, of course."

"Good, now I must ask can you keep a secret?"

"Grand-mère, haven't I always kept the secrets you told me?"

Simone heaved a big sigh. "Yes, you have, but I have never entrusted you with a secret like this one."

"Sounds like a life and death matter." Genevieve's insides were shaking, and her stomach was churning around like a hurricane or tornado was within her very being.

"Exactly," Simone told her, "exactly. It concerns my death and your life."

Genevieve's mouth hung open. "Wha–what did you say?"

"The time has come, my dear; the time has come."

"What are you saying to me?" she screamed. "You can't mean it! No! No! Not again!" She threw herself to the floor and pounded her fist and kicked her feet in the manner of a baby throwing a tantrum.

Simone and Alexandre looked at each other hopelessly, and let Genevieve give vent to her hurt, anger and frustrations as she needed to handle them.

Finally, Alexandre spoke her name harshly, "Genevieve, you will get up and conduct yourself in the manner of a young woman! Immediately!"

Genevieve ignored him for a few moments until Alexandre said, "Do you really think that this behavior will change anything? Believe me, if it would work I would get down there and kick away with you!"

Genevieve realized how foolish she was being. She arose and ran into her grandmother's arms. "I don't want you to die; I don't want you to die! Why? Why? It isn't fair! Why?"

Simone sat up very straight in her chair. "Tell me, are you crying for yourself, or are you crying for me?"

Genevieve looked puzzled. "I don't understand."

"Well," Simone spoke deliberately, "all my life I worked hard, I always to the best of my ability served God, looking forward to my homecoming, and my very own granddaughter wants to keep me from my reward."

"I didn't mean that; it's just, just, what will Grand-père and I do without you?"

"You know, my darling child," she pulled the child upon her lap even closer than before, "man or woman is never content while they are on this earth. They are just on a pilgrimage, and all the while they are here they are searching for something. Some think more possessions or money, others think the answer is more power or popularity, but none of it is real. The only reality is going home where we belong. We are just aliens here. We don't belong, it is like shoes that are too small and pinch the toes. This old world pulls us every which way that it can trying to keep us where we don't belong, but the day comes when we are released from this bondage.

"You have been taught the scriptures. Remember that 'to be absent from the body is to be present with the Lord'? In this life, Genevieve, we have to share and take turns; soon now it is my turn."

Genevieve held back her sobs. "How soon?"

"Maybe two weeks," Alexandre replied as he walked over and held them both in his arms.

Genevieve's eyes popped open. "Two weeks!"

Simone looked at her solemnly. "I thought that you would rather know than be surprised like you were about your mother and father."

"Yes, Grand-mère, you are right."

"There are some things that shall be required of you."

"Yes?"

"First of all, no one is to know about this except for us three. Agreed?"

"Agreed. Are you sure? Isn't there a doctor somewhere . . ." Her voice trailed off.

Simone shook her head. "No, we have tried all that already."

"Wasn't there some money left to me when Mom and Dad died?"

"Yes, a lot of money."

"I want you to use it all and see if you can be healed."

"You are a sweet, unselfish girl, but it is no use. Genevieve, when I was a very young girl, some terrible things happened to me that I have never been able to tell anyone about except for Alexandre. These things have taken their toll on my body and the situation cannot be reversed. The plain truth is that my body is worn out with age."

"What kind of things, Grand-mère?"

"I have instructed Alexandre to tell you someday when the right time comes, but I cannot talk about it. Now, I need a promise from you, that you will obey Grand-père without question when he tells you to do something in the next few weeks, no matter how strange it seems. I cannot tell you what these things are, but we have made special plans for you and Grand-père and no one else must know. Do you promise?"

Genevieve shook her head in assent, but Simone said, "That is not enough. I must hear the words."

"I promise."

"Thank you. Now I must retire, as I am weary, very weary. . . ."

Simone was in bed now, and she whispered, "Alexandre, will you miss me when I am gone?"

"No," he said gently, "I shall not miss you, for you will not be gone from me because I carry you always in my heart."

Chapter Nineteen
Isaac

His whole name was Isaac Solomon. His mother had felt that he would grow to live up to his names, Isaac meaning "a man of simple faith" and Solomon meaning "father of wisdom." He, like his brother, was sired from the same parents and their bodies, containing the identical genes, or so it would seem. Two brothers and yet as different as the night is from the day.

Isaac in his youth was much the handsomer of the two. He had inherited his father's height and his mother's blond hair that fell into curly locks. His handshake was firm and his smile seemed genuine and it was always there.

He was only a year younger than Samuel, and had lived in Samuel's shadow for such a long time that he disliked anything and everything that his brother stood for.

As Isaac grew older and fell into habits of procrastination, he lost much of his handsomeness, along with a lot of his hair, and now had a nonexistent waistline. His weight was massive but did not seem to bother him.

He married his childhood sweetheart when he was only eighteen and she was sixteen. Susannah at that time weighed about ninety pounds soaking wet, but now she was way over two hundred pounds.

Isaac weighed in the vicinity of three hundred pounds or better, but he would never reveal the true amount to anyone.

He was content with her and she with him, and that's the way it was in their opinion, take it or leave it. Already they had ten kids running around and who knows how many more to come.

All of the children had their friends hanging around and no one could ever count how many were around there at any given time. That suited them fine, plus a cow or two, and a couple of goats, a few chickens and of course the pigs. No one knew if Isaac really liked pigs or not. They believed that he kept pigs to upset Samuel, which it most certainly did.

The old farmhouse suited them fine, everyone was welcome there and everyone appeared to like it there.

He liked to be called Zack, but no one ever heard anyone call him that. He never had two nickels to rub together in his pocket and it never seemed to bother him much. After all Maman and Papa were always just a phone call or ten-minute drive away.

Susannah and Isaac worked together whenever they got the energy. They made their own sausage and head cheese. The kids had the responsibility of the garden, and one never really knew what the crop would be from year to year, not that anyone really cared.

They had their own fruit trees all around the property, which the children enjoyed a lot.

In contrast to his brother, Isaac's fingernails were dirty. He did not care about his clothes and always looked shabby and rumpled. His trousers were always holey and well worn.

The children followed him around and dogs and cats by the score, too. Animals had the run of the place. There was a legend around that if anyone did not want their dog and cat anymore they could drop them off at Isaac's place.

He and Susannah never turned away a hungry man or a hungry beast, either. All a person had to do was say he was going to have to put their dog or cat to sleep and a place would be found for the animal, and they stayed there as a permanent fixture on the farm.

Many a man out of work for whatever reason would come by the farm, and Isaac would always find some kind of work for him to do, and then send him home with more food than he could carry.

"The good Lord has given us more than we can use, or need," he'd say, "so we can share and still have plenty."

In his idleness Isaac loved to read and so obtained a smattering of knowledge in a good many fields. He read westerns and books on wildlife. He knew more about birds and fish and wild and tame animals than all of the good town folk put together.

He also read about trees and woodlands. He was a leader in the wildlife preservation field.

Isaac was not like his brother and would never consider being unfaithful to his Susannah. They were partners together for life. He would sometimes joke about the "for better or worse part."

Isaac loved his mother and father, but it was a selfish kind of love. He did not feel any remorse out of the fact that he played upon their sympathies for money, after all, "What are they gonna do with all their money, and besides that they like to see the kids have all they need. Hey, these children are part of them too, right?"

Isaac wasn't really bad, but then he wasn't really good either. He loved to tell tall tales, and of course he was always the hero of his little sagas. Depending on his mood or state of mind he would regale his audience with stories of how he performed plastic surgery, won in the Olympics, invented the filter for cigarettes, or played for the Philadelphia Philharmonic. His stories were so interesting and filled with details that could possibly be true, if you were listening carefully you could actually visualize these happenings as true fact.

Isaac didn't care if a child had a snotty nose or a wet diaper or a cold or any other of life's cares that we must all suffer. They were always welcome on his lap. Should a child wipe his nose on his sleeve or sneeze on him or cough open-mouthed, his reply would be, "Hell, I'm not going to the prom tonight, am I? What's more important, my child's feelings or this five-year-old shirt?"

Susannah shared Isaac's viewpoint for the most part, and this helped them to get along well. She was seen many times herself wiping a youngster's nose on her dress. The children were allowed to get as dirty as they pleased, and many happy smiles were seen on muddy faces. Isaac and Susannah always had the time to partake of some special mud cake or mud pie, made by little hands.

Whenever someone would complain about the children being dirty, Susannah's replay was always, "Thank God he made all my kids washable."

When the mood struck him, Isaac liked to tinker with the farm machinery, and many things were rendered useless after he had decided to repair them or to make them work better. He may not have been the world's worst carpenter but he came close.

They liked to take the kids swimming and on picnics. He took them fishing on occasion, but mostly this occupation was something he shared with his father.

Once a week like clockwork he would go and visit his mother. This was the one time in the week that he would put a razor to his face and change his clothing. He would always go by himself and this was the only time except for his fishing trips with his dad that he would go without his family.

Simone on her part would always make him a special lunch that they would partake of and enjoy together. She was disappointed in her second son, but her love for him held fast. He would always leave with his pockets lined a little more than they were when he arrived there.

Susannah on her part never minded that Isaac visited his mother without her; for one thing he seemed to get more money if she weren't around. Maybe it was her imagination but this is how it seemed to her.

Another fact was that Susannah was not extremely fond of her mother-in-law, as she felt that Simone was not as generous as she should be with them. She did not know their exact worth, but she knew it was plenty. Why she felt it was owed to her was anyone's guess.

Susannah felt that their were many things about her that Simone did not approve of or would like to change, and it was true, too. Simone had a hard time to accept Susannah's sloppiness and dirty house and children. Her own philosophy was that "cleanliness is next to godliness."

Simone had often felt that Susannah was a little responsible for Isaac's lackadaisical attitude about life and that she could be an incentive in his life for the better.

The strange part of it was that Susannah's people felt that Isaac was the one that deterred Susannah from being what she could be.

Simone often thought of how Isaac was before his marriage. He was what is called a fashion plate. Everything had to be just so: hair, clothes. How many times had she pressed his pants at the last moment, so that Susannah would not be offended.

They had obviously formed their own pattern of life and lived it the way they wanted to. They appeared to be content with their own philosophy of life. They formed it and never demanded that anyone else live in their way. They lived and let live.

The strange part of it all was that they did not feel different from others. They really felt that they lived in a nice house and were right up to par in their mode of living.

What could be said? They deserved each other and if they were happy what else did it matter about popular opinion? Were they really happy in their ignorance and bliss, or was it all a big act?

There's one thing for sure that no one could deny: Isaac and Susannah deserved one another.

Chapter Twenty
Going Home

The hospital did not differ from any other, for it was very antiseptic and clinical looking and interchangeable with any other small town hospital. The corridors were long and dreary. Why are hospitals so afraid of colors and brightness? Seems as though none of the architects who designed these places had ever seen a rainbow. For some unknown reason everything had to be muted and somber.

The two nurses walked down the long hallway to take over their shift. One was very young and even if you saw her from the rear, her hips were a testimony to her youth, for they swung as she walked almost in restless abandon. The older nurse, possibly in her late thirties, was much more reserved in her walking, almost as though she desired not to attract attention to herself.

They were walking quickly to get to their appointed tasks on time. The younger nurse looked at her supervisor and said, "I think Mrs. Boisvert is one of my patients today."

"I don't know; you'll have to check your schedule."

"She's such a living doll to have as a patient. Fantastic really! I wish all of my patients were like her."

"Me too."

Both were dressed in the nurse's traditional white and looked smart and crisp. Their soft sole shoes played in harmony as they walked along the long corridor.

When they arrived at room two-twenty, which was a private room, the older nurse tapped lightly on the door and waited for a moment.

The door was opened by a rather tall man with snow-capped white hair, which gave the appearance of being bleached. He was well dressed and very courteous. "Come in ladies."

His son Samuel was also there. He of course was dressed as always with his leering grin that showed his gold teeth off to their best advantage, if such a thing was a possibility. He spoke in quick hissing curt tones. "Are you girls taking good care of my mother? She is waiting for you."

Alexandre Boisvert had gone to sit beside his wife at her bedside and they seemed totally engrossed in each other's company.

"Good evening, Mrs. Boisvert. My name is Margie and this is my assistant Louise. Louise, this is Mr. and Mrs. Boisvert."

The old man with his ever-present old world courtliness took her hand gently in his and said, "I am most pleased to meet you, Louise."

Samuel, who had his eye on Louise and was perturbed that he had not been introduced first, stood up and spoke brusquely, "Allow me to introduce myself. I am Samuel Boisvert. I am the mayor of this town. Allow me to give you one of my cards, my dear."

As soon as he had finished making contact with her hand he unconsciously wiped both of his hands on his jacket. His handshake, unlike his father's, was limp and shallow. "Remember, I am a man of the people ready to be of service to you if the need should ever arise."

The older nurse, whose name was Margie, thought to herself, *Help! I'm going to be sick, here comes Samuel with his "Let me help you" pitch. I'd better set Louise straight on this one.*

Margie turned to the menfolk. "I must ask you gentlemen to leave for a moment."

Alexandre rose and told Simone, "I will go and take a little walk around; would you care for something? A little ice cream perhaps?"

Simone shook her head slightly. "No, thank you, I am not hungry. Alexandre, you will be back?"

"Of course, my dear," and smiling, "as soon as these bodyguards of yours let me back in."

"And me, Maman," Samuel said, "I gotta go. Big day ahead of me, political meetings don'tcha know." Then he leaned over the little hospital bed and kissed the time worn cheek of his mother, little realizing that it would be for the last time.

He immediately wiped his lips with his hand and then wiped his hand on his suit coat, in an unconscious manner.

"Samuel." She always said his name with a French accent; today she spoke in barely a whisper. "You . . ." She hesitated as if what she were about to say would be useless. "You . . . you be a good boy." It was a question more than a statement.

"Oh, *oui*, Maman," he said, laughing as though to him it was a big joke, but in Simone's eyes it was a very serious matter.

Alexandre stood by himself and smoked the big cigar he had just bought in the gift shop. He was not fond of smoking and didn't know why he bought it except that it gave him something to do. Somehow he was glad to have something to keep his mind occupied. He tried to remember when the last time was that he had smoked a cigar, but it had been such a long time that he forgot.

There was nothing to read of any consequence around, and at his age he had long since learned patience, so he waited to be told that he could return to be with his wife in her room.

He soon lost his fascination with the wad of rolled up tobacco and discarded it quickly. There was something about today, and he knew it. Things would never be the same again in his life. He wanted to play a game that would say that Simone would return to their home again.

The house was just a house without her, it was empty and bare. Devoid of her it became stagnant.

After what seemed to him an eternity Margie came in and he was so wrapped up in thought that he never even saw her coming. She tapped him gently on the shoulder. "You may come back in now, Mr. Boisvert."

He had been so wrapped up in his own thoughts that he did not realize what it was that she was saying at first.

"What . . . what did you say?"

"I said that your wife is ready to see you now."

He looked intently at the nurse. Was it only his imagination, or did Margie seem strange, more subdued and different somehow? He shook himself and thought, *You old fool, don't let your imagination run away with you.*

As quickly as he could, he walked to the room where his wife lay, softly tapped on the door, and heard her say, "*Entrez.*"

He walked over to where she lay, and she spoke in a semi-whisper, "Alexandre, is that you?"

At the first he did not think it too strange that she did not know him, as her eyes were closed.

She spoke using only French now. "Come," she said, "tonight, you and I shall hold hands together. Tonight, you and I will hold hands as we did in days of old. Do you remember when we were very young? Alexandre?"

He took her hand gently in his big hands. "Always," he said to her, "we will be lovers." He leaned over and said, "I cannot wait until you are home once again and at my side. I cannot wait until we are lying together in our own bed and I can hold you in my arms the whole night long."

"Alexandre, look at me, for it takes all of my strength to speak. Look at me. You know that these things cannot be so." Her eyes flooded over with tears now.

"Do not cry, Simone; it breaks my heart to see you cry." And his own eyes were filling up with teardrops.

Simone took a very deep breath. "I cannot go home with you anymore." She closed her eyes for a moment and when she opened them again he saw that they were becoming glassy. "I am being called to another home now."

He realized that she was in the final stages of life now. Margie came up to him and asked him, "Do you realize what is happening?" Alexandre shook his head for he could not speak.

"Simone, oh, Simone, if you go I want to die, too!"

She seemed to rally for a moment and though her breathing was very difficult, she scolded firmly. "Alexandre," her breathing was even more labored now, "it must not be so, you have so many things left to do, and responsibilities to keep. It is your duty. You are too proud of a man to neglect your responsibilities. You are honor bound. We made a solemn promise to one another, Alexandre, do not fail me now. All the years we have been together you have never failed me. Will you begin on my deathbed?"

"No, Simone, I will not fail, as you have never once failed me. I shall hate it without you, but I will carry on."

"Swear it to me, Alexandre; swear it to me here and now, that you will carry on with our plans."

"I swear it," he said, "by all that is good and holy!"

"Alexandre," she said with great difficulty, "I am counting on you."

"Yes, I know."

"Alexandre . . ." He could barely make it out. Her chest was heaving up and down and she was struggling for every breath. "Help me through this; hold me tightly."

He held her in his arms for a very long while, neither one of them spoke. He dared not move for fear lest he hurt her. Her breathing became even more labored, she opened her eyes briefly and started to say, "Alex . . ." She heaved a great sigh and went limp in his arms.

He knew then and there that Simone was somewhere other than with him, but still he held her, he did not move or speak. He wanted to hold her as long as he could, for he knew it was the last time.

The thought occurred to him that perhaps he should pray, but he could not. He knew that Simone had long ago made her peace with God.

Margie walked over to Alexandre. "Are you all right, Mr. Boisvert?"

He wanted to reach out and slap her for asking such a foolish question. *She is only trying to be nice.*

"Shall I call your family?"

"Yes," he said, "they must know."

He turned around and with shoulders stooped and bent over, he walked out of that hospital, never to return again.

Chapter Twenty-one
The Empty Nest

Alexandre went into his car and began to drive around aimlessly. Where he went or how long he was gone seemed immaterial to him now, and he drove down one dark road after another in sporadic fashion.

He arrived home as dawn was breaking. "I am thankful that Genevieve is over at Isaac's house and I do not have to worry about her for the moment.

"The children are probably furious with me for disappearing, but my grief is my own concern and no one else's!"

He stood at the door and put his key in the lock and even before he entered the premises it didn't seem like home anymore. He couldn't explain it, not even to himself. "A house is not a home," he said to no one in particular. Then, in an even louder voice, he hollered, "A house is not a home!"

He felt so strange, almost as though he had left his body and soul and was walking around in an empty shell, in a state of automation he was not really a part of, just an onlooker, as though he was an impartial onlooker, of sorts.

He walked around every area of the house almost as if he thought that she was hiding in a place that he had not yet discovered. "Emptiness! Nothing but emptiness!"

He went into the kitchen and made himself a cup of strong coffee, then he sat in his rocking chair for a brief moment, and his eyes wandered to the other rocking chair just a few feet away. He arose unconsciously and walked into "le salon," or living room.

The phone began to ring and ring and he made no effort to answer it; what could anyone have to tell him of consequence now?

He started to look over the records and selected one by a comedian that had been one of his and Simone's favorites. He found that he could not tolerate the music either and quickly turned the machine off.

He allowed his eyes to travel around the large room. He and Simone had always loved this room, after all, together they had seen to every detail, and everything reflected their tastes, and parts of their lives together.

The large overstuffed living room set in a beautiful wine-colored velvet had proved to be functional as well as beautiful. In the corner was the old-fashioned piano with the swivel stool that the children loved to twirl up and down but hated to sit and practice at.

How many times, he thought, *had I removed this rug and beat the dust out of it, and then turned it over so it would get worn evenly to please my wife?*

He smiled. "What logic she possessed."

"Alexandre," she had said, "we will purchase a rug with a little bit of every color in it so then it will match everything, and we will not have to change so often. Then we can use any color wallpaper or drapes that we like."

They had paid a lot of money for those days, but as she said it had lasted, and, he thought gruesomely, had even outlasted one of its owners. He remembered the surge of pride when he had placed it on the floor. She had always been careful and selective, and bought well, and her wisdom paid off.

He sat in one of the big overstuffed chairs and gave his eyes the freedom to roam around the room. His eyes lit upon the large fireplace. He realized that he was feeling chilly and went over and lit a fire. He went about it slowly and deliberately; he felt good to be doing something.

He went back to sit in his chair and he gazed deeply into the fire as though there were hidden secrets in there. He sat there for a long while before becoming conscious of where he was.

On the mantle above the fireplace were the various pictures that depicted his and Simone's life together: family pictures as the family grew; a picture of Laura when she graduated from college. *She was a beauty, that one*, he thought. *The only one to amount to anything, too. I wonder if Simone and Laura are together?*

There were several pictures of him and Simone on various anniversaries. Although they had not had a wedding picture, he still remembered every detail of that, "the happiest day of his life."

Over the mantle above the fireplace he and Simone had placed a huge picture of Jesus with his heart exposed because they believed that they could succeed only with God's help. The picture was so large that it was as wide as the fireplace and went from the top of the mantle to the ceiling. God was to have the place of honor in his household whether anyone else liked it nor not.

Alexandre thought how every night since he and Simone had married he and his wife and family knelt together in prayer. He had never been absolutely truthful with Simone on a few occasions; if it had been left to him he might have forgone the prayer time, but he always went through with it to please her.

He had to admit too that he had always felt invigorated and better afterwards. *Even tonight—no, I guess it was yesterday—we prayed together on our last night.* Simone had never forgotten the teachings of the good nun who had saved her life many years ago.

This room, he thought, *gives me the feel of her, us. It is a good room, a room that has been lived in and is still good for many more years of living.*

Life, he thought, *yes, what is life? Life is nothing more than a vapor that passes much too swiftly, an instant or a breath in the eternal scheme of things.*

He heaved a deep sigh and removed his spectacles and wiped them clean on a clean handkerchief, one of the two he always carried around with him. One to wipe your nose on and the other to clean your glasses with.

My mind is playing tricks on me now, he thought. The heat from the fireplace was beginning to warm him and the heat felt good to him.

He looked the fireplace over as though he had never seen it before and he felt a sense of pride that he had designed it himself and it was functional as well as beautiful. He had built it with his own two hands and he had been diligent in keeping it in good running order. He had always been diligent in keeping his home in good condition also.

He and his wife were proud people who had come from humble beginnings and they took good care of all their possessions.

Strange, he thought, *I have two sons and neither one of them is good for much. One is only good for making babies, and the other for throwing around the manure! 'I'm the mayor, I'm here to serve you.' It's enough to make a grown man sick!*

I wonder what the good people of this town would say if they knew that his own mother and father didn't vote for him.

At least he could sit and talk a bit with his son Isaac, that is, if you could find a place to sit among the clutter and debris. Or maybe if you didn't mind the noise and didn't mind kids and animals climbing all over you (who could really tell the difference?).

Isaac was all right though, in his own way; why he'd give away his own teeth if someone needed them more than he did. *I guess he and Susannah are happy in their own way; seems like all they do is eat and make babies.*

Isaac sounded like a buffoon and she like a hyena, but if they could stand each other who was Alexandre to complain? Simone used to tell him "they deserve each other." She would tell him firmly, "Leave them alone, they don't bother us! If they want to live like pigs, we'll buy them a trough. I didn't bring my son up to be a pig. We did not bring any of our children up to be what they are. They are the ones that have to live in the beds of their own making."

Sound logic, but he knew that it bothered her mother's heart perhaps even more than it bothered him.

The telephone kept on ringing and he didn't answer it because he didn't feel like it. Simple as that.

"Pa?" Alexandre had fallen asleep on his chair before the fire, which had almost died out now.

He opened his eyes and there stood Isaac, and he was crying like a baby. Alexandre stood up and put his arms about this big hulk of a man that he called son and both of them cried for a long time.

The phone once again was ringing in its loud, sonorous tone. Isaac wiped his eyes and nose on his shirt sleeve. "Want me to get that?"

"No!"

"Gee, Pa, it might be something important."

"What could be more important than what has already happened?"

"Well," Isaac said, clearing his throat, "I just thought it might be about arrangements or something like that."

Alexandre looked at his son and bluntly told him, "All of the arrangements were made a long time ago, so that no one need bother. Your mother was always very efficient. She picked everything out herself, so as to spare us. The phone call is either from Samuel or Rachel, and I am not ready for them yet."

"Pa," Isaac said hesitatingly, "I dunno what ta say."

"I know, Isaac; what is there that you can say to help my broken heart?"

"Did you eat yet, Pa?"

Alexandre suddenly remembered that he had not eaten since breakfast time yesterday morning, and he had to admit that he was feeling hunger pangs.

"Give me a moment to freshen up, Isaac, and we will go to the diner in Arey town and get some breakfast. It will be quiet there and your brother and sister will not find us for a while."

"Okay Pa."

Alexandre returned swiftly and Isaac noticed that he was freshly shaven and had changed his clothes.

"Let's go."

When they got outside he handed Isaac his car keys and they got into the car silently. Isaac was a good driver and drove the twelve miles efficiently and in control.

He thought, *Boy, the old man really has guts, here he is sitting as straight as a ramrod and inside his heart is broken. He's quite a guy all right, sure wish that I was more like him or like Maman.*

Isaac looked over at his father. "Pa, can I ask you a question?"

"Yes, you can."

"How come you don't wanna see Samuel or Rachel?"

"Well," he drawled out, "you see, son, it's like this. Rachel will want all of Maman's jewelry—wouldn't even have the decency to let us bury your mother in peace and quiet, and Samuel of course will think that he should have everything handed over to him, all my finances, that is.

"I have heard enough of 'I am the eldest, you know,' or 'I am the only living daughter you have,' " he mocked.

"Why do you think these things about them, Pa?"

Alexandre looked at his son quizzically. "Hasn't time proved me right again and again?"

"Whaddya mean?"

"Come on, Isaac." The old man was visibly irritated now. "You yourself know that it was only about three weeks ago that Samuel bargained with you to help declare that your mother and I were incompetent to handle our own affairs."

Isaac's mouth literally fell open. "Howdya hear about that?"

"I have my ways; yes, I have my ways. I also know that you refused to help him."

"I'm not afraid of him. Here we are, Pa."

They entered the busy diner and found an empty booth. They both ordered "the He-man Special." For the most part they ate in silence, until Alexandre said, "You know, Isaac, you may get the last laugh yet over your brother and not have to do a thing."

Alexandre knew at that moment which child would get the old homestead and everything in it. He almost laughed out loud as he thought of Isaac and Susannah in that house and Susannah wearing Simone's fur coat! *Just one thing, I will show Samuel and Rachel a thing or two.* He could actually envision their faces when they learned the truth.

Chapter Twenty-two
The Parting of the Ways

Alexandre would not allow any of them to make a circus out of the funeral. Simone would be laid to rest with dignity as she had lived!

He thought to himself, *First of all she had taught me to live, and now she has taught me how to die.*

He had avoided Samuel and Rachel for he could not handle their baloney at this time; it was difficult enough when he was in a good frame of mind.

He had spent the day alone with Isaac, they had eaten and gone fishing and eaten again. He had also taken Isaac out and bought him a new suit of clothes.

Finally he knew he had to face Genevieve. He was grateful that Susannah had taken over the task of telling the child. What could he say to her? "I just don't know."

When he arrived at Isaac's house, he was pleasantly surprised to see Susannah all dressed up and each child shiny clean. What a transformation had taken place, and he was not surprised when he heard that Genevieve and Nicole and Henry had taken over and accomplished this task.

He entered the door with trepidation, and Genevieve ran over and put her arms around him and cried as though she would never stop and Alexandre cried along with her. "Oh," she sobbed, "whatever will we do? Grand-père, Aunt Rachel says that now I have to go and live with her, because you cannot take care of me properly. I don't want to." Her tears flowed anew.

"Hush, child, don't you remember what you and Grand-mère talked about just a short time ago? Are you ready to go?"

"Yes," she replied, "I am as ready as I will ever be."

He wiped the tears off of her face and eyelids. "Come, my dear, we will be brave together. Our grief and sadness belong to us alone, it is a private thing."

They joined hands and walked out of the house together, and Isaac and his family followed behind.

"Pa," Isaac said, "will you be all right to drive?"

"Yes, I am fine. See you there."

"Grand-père? Am I a rotten person if I hate going to these things?"

"So do I," was his reply. And he thought, but did not say, *Especially this one*.

Alexandre thought that he was prepared for this, but he found out differently. He walked into the funeral home with his head held high and holding on to the child's hand very tightly. When he walked into the room where Simone lay, his breath was taken away. They had been to so many of these affairs together, but always someone else lay in the box. Not Simone! No, not Simone, and if he could have he would have taken her out of the confines of that three-by-six-foot box.

His whole body began to shake uncontrollably, and Genevieve tenderly wrapped her young arms around him and hugged him tightly. "It is not a bad thing to cry," she whispered, and she broke down and cried also.

Youth in her grief and age in his grief, somehow each feeling of grief was different and yet it was the same.

Alexandre had knelt to hold Genevieve in his arms and no one dared to interfere in their moment of sharing.

Isaac became concerned and said to Susannah, "I hope he is all right, what do you think?"

"Maybe," she replied, "he needs a little help to get up."

Samuel came up to Isaac, and the fury could be seen in his face. "Where the hell have you been hiding him?"

Isaac totally ignored his brother and walked away.

"Pa? You all right?" He helped his father onto his feet. He was surprised to find that this man that he had always considered a tower of strength was shaking uncontrollably.

"Sit down, Pa."

Alexandre, like a little child, sat on the chair and hung his head down low. "I wanted to be brave and strong for Genevieve's sake."

"You are, Pa; you are really!"

Susannah held Genevieve in her arms and pressed her head somewhere among her massive bosoms. "He is going to be all right, Genevieve; trust me. He is a fighter." She knew that Genevieve loved her grandfather more than anyone else on this earth, now that Simone was gone.

Henry had gone to get his grandfather a drink of water and as he came back with it Isaac took it and gave it to his father. "Here, Pa, drink this and catch your breath."

Samuel was boiling mad. "Look at that," he told Rachel. "He's sucking up to the old man so he can get everything. We hafta stop that lousy so and so or by the time he gets done with the old man there won't be anything left!"

"What can we do about it?" she asked him.

"I dunno yet, but one thing for sure I'm gonna get him somehow, mark my word!"

Alexandre lifted his eyes towards Samuel and Rachel and he could sense their displeasure with him and Isaac. He didn't care, he had gone beyond that point now and felt he would never return to that pivotal point again.

He stood up and held his hand out to Genevieve and said, "Come."

She took his hand in hers and thought, *Poor Grand-père, he really does love her so much, probably as much or even more than I do.*

Isaac took his father's arm to steady him as he was still shaking very badly, and he did not make any motion to refuse his son's help. Alexandre had not yet looked upon the coffin that bore his wife's remains, but had kept his eyes averted from that area.

They made quite a sight; the little girl, the big giant of a son and the husband in the middle with seemingly the weight of the world upon him. They approached the place where Simone lay, and as Alexandre looked into the coffin, every bit of his breath was released from him, and his knees began to buckle, and if it were not for Isaac holding him up, he would have collapsed for sure.

"Pa," Isaac whispered, "you want a chair?"

Alexandre shook his head no. He tried to straighten his posture as best he could and then allowed his eyes to rest upon his wife. She was dressed as she had wanted to be in the pale blue velvet dress he had bought her for their last anniversary. He remembered when he bought her the dress. He had chosen it because the blue in it was the exact match to the blue in her eyes. He had paid more for that dress than any dress she had ever owned before, and it was worth every penny.

He looked directly at Simone now; her eyes were closed and she looked so peaceful lying there that he began to regain strength. Her hands were folded upon her breast, and it seemed strange to him to see her idle, as she was always bustling about. Somehow something in her face seemed to give him the message that it was all right with her now, and he knew that she was at peace and it helped to console him.

For some strange reason, lying there like that, she reminded him of their first meeting. "She is so beautiful, she always was."

He remembered the promise that he had made to her concerning Genevieve and he renewed that promise to her again in words that were in thought, but not spoken.

He looked at Genevieve and she had tears streaming down her young cheeks and he bent over and put his arms about her little form and hugged her tightly to him. He once again looked at Simone. *I will keep my promise to you concerning the child, to the best of my ability. I swear it!*

All of a sudden there was the sound of screaming and yelling heard and Rachel came running forth screaming, "Maman, Maman, you can't leave me; I won't let you." Then she proceeded to act as though she were going to pull her mother's body out of the casket.

Samuel of course was the one attempting to restrain her and they were both being noticed by many people, which of course Alexandre knew was the whole purpose of this commotion.

Alexandre turned to Genevieve and told her, "Please go and sit with your aunt Susannah for a few minutes as I want to go and get some fresh air."

He turned to go out the door with Isaac close beside him. Once outside he spoke to Isaac and said, "You will please get your brother and sister for me."

Isaac looked at his father and could not remember ever seeing him this upset before.

"Yeah, Pa, I'll get them right away," and off he went into the funeral home.

Rachel sat on one of the seats looking very pathetic indeed with her black dress and veil that covered her face. She was speaking to a friend of hers and dabbing at her eyes every now and then with a handkerchief that was trimmed with black lace. "Yes," she was saying, "poor, dear Genevieve will be in my care now, where else can the poor dear go? Isaac has so many children, and Samuel is so busy with all his duties as mayor. You know that Papa is too old to care for such a young girl."

Isaac walked over to his sister. "Excuse me, but Pa wants to see you right *now*." And he emphasized the "now."

"Poor, poor dear, I must go. You will excuse me?"

Samuel was over in the corner doing some of his wheeling and dealing and was angry with Isaac for disturbing him.

"Sam, Pa wants you now!"

"Yeah, yeah, hold your horses, will ya?"

"Alls I know is that he said if you're not out there in two minutes he's comin' in to get ya!" and he turned and walked away.

Samuel followed his brother. "What da hell is going on? I tell you, Isaac, you get worse and worse every day."

Rachel had reached the veranda first. "You want to see me, Papa?"

"Yes, we shall wait for the others."

"Well, here I am," Samuel boomed out. "Whatsa matter?"

Alexandre stood up to his full height and let his eyes roam first to Samuel's face and then to Rachel's.

"You," he said to them, "will both be quiet and I will do the speaking. You," he said and began to shake again.

"Pa," Isaac said, "take it easy, will ya? It ain't worth you gettin' sick over."

"Isaac, you will please listen, too."

"Okay, Pa."

Alexandre took his index finger and shook it in Rachel's and Samuel's faces. "I have had it with both of you, and I will not allow you to make your mother's wake and funeral a circus and a mockery. I tell you tonight has been the straw that broke the camel's back and you will pay for it, believe me!" His voice was quivering now. "You will pay for it! Mark my words, both of you!"

"Aw, come on, Pa, you're just upset; things'll look different to you once all this is over with."

"Samuel, I am not just angry with things just now! I have been upset and angry with you and Rachel for years, but today, I have become fed up!"

"What's Isaac, a goody-two-shoes?"

"Isaac does not hurt anyone but himself, and besides that, we are talking about you and Rachel now.

"Don't either one of you say a word right now. You will listen to what I have to say and you will listen carefully and follow out my wishes to the letter! Understood? Remember the purse strings are completely in my hands now."

Alexandre's veins looked as though they were ready to pop and his face was beet red. "You will both of you conduct yourselves in the way that your mother taught you, no more stage plays or histrionics, no business deals, no lying. Samuel, you are not going to handle my affairs in any way, shape or manner. Ever! Do you understand? So stop manipulating.

"Rachel, you pull that ridiculous veil off of your face, and erase your crocodile tears. Shame on you, you couldn't even take a minute to visit your Maman in the hospital once in three weeks and you pull such an act! Furthermore neither one of you shall gain custody of Genevieve, nor her inheritance. Never! So don't make fools of yourselves by speaking such things."

Rachel and Samuel both stood there with their mouths open and watched as their father reentered the building.

Samuel scratched his head. "Well, I'll be damned. Isaac got to the old man, but it won't last for long. I'll guarantee that!"

"What can we do about it?"

"I dunno right now, but I don't think we oughta rile the old man up any more than he already is. C'mon, let's go and be the dutiful son and daughter."

Alexandre walked over to Susannah. "I have several favors to ask of you."

She looked at him intently. "Whatever I can do."

"Thank you. First of all, I would like to know if Genevieve could spend the night with you again? I feel that at this time it is better for her to be where there is more activity, and our house is so quiet."

She smiled at her father-in-law. "Of course, it is done. There is something else?"

"Yes, yes, there is. Would you be kind enough to let Isaac spend the next two nights with me? There are so many things I must go over with him and this is the only place where we will not be disturbed."

"Of course, it is the least that we can do."

"Susannah, I will see to it that you will not regret your kindness to me and Genevieve!"

"I do things for you and Genevieve because I love the both of you, not because I am looking for things."

"I know that, and I thank you."

Alexandre somehow got through the evening. Even years later when he pondered the situation, he could not explain how, but he did make it through.

Samuel and Rachel were on their best behavior and did everything in the way that they should. Samuel as the eldest invited everyone to his home for a light lunch. Blanche was not too thrilled by the idea, but she also acted the part of the dutiful wife.

Susannah declined the invitation, saying, "I must go home and get these children to bed." Inwardly she was happy to use the children as an excuse. She did not have a kindred spirit towards her sister-in-law, and did not enjoy even the thought of being in the same house with her for five minutes.

Alexandre looked at Isaac and said, "We will go for only a few minutes, as it would not be right to be rude to all these people."

"Whatever you think, Pa, is all right with me."

When the two men arrived at Samuel's house there was already many people around.

Samuel yelled out, "Somebody get a chair for my father!" Alexandre accepted the chair and sat down. It seemed that everyone in the place wanted to talk to him about some plan or other that they had for the future if only they had the finances to get started. Alexandre listened politely, not offering any money at all or any more conversation than he deemed necessary.

After about half an hour Isaac came over to his father and said to him, "How 'bout it, Pa, had enough?"

Alexandre nodded and Isaac helped him to his feet. When Samuel saw this he came running over. "You're not leavin', are you, Pa?"

"Yes, Samuel, I'm afraid so."

"Wait a sec until I tell Blanche and I'll take you home."

"There is no need, you have guests to entertain. Isaac will see me home as he has to go out anyhow."

Samuel was visibly upset by his father's declination of his offer, and it showed. *I'm gonna set that brother of mine straight, that's for sure. But I'd better not rock the boat now.*

He patted Isaac on the back. "Good boy, Ike, good boy, see to it that he gets some rest, will ya?"

Isaac and Alexandre were silent on the way home, each lost in his own thoughts. Isaac could not help but wonder what his father was up to. One thing he knew for sure was that the old man was up to something. *I haven't known him all these years not to realize that.*

They entered the house and Alexandre began to shiver. "It is cool in here tonight. Isaac, you start a fire and I'll start the coffee brewing."

Each set about their own task, once again lost in their own thoughts. Thoughts that belonged to each of them and could not be shared with anyone else.

"Let's take our coffee and sit by the fire, eh? I don't know what it is, but there is something about an open fire that conveys warmth and creates an atmosphere of contentment. I make a fire every day except on the extremely hot days. The fireplace has never failed to give me a feeling of well-being."

Isaac looked at his father intently for a long while. "Pa," he said very seriously.

"What is it, Isaac?"

"Pa," and he cleared his throat, "what are you up to?"

"Son," he now returned Isaac's look. "What are you saying?"

"Pa, look, I know that you're up to something. The way you're acting is not like you at all. Not to mention the way you are speaking. For instance you've never invited me over to spend the night with you before like this." He cleared his throat and paused, waiting for his father to shed some light on the situation.

"Well," Alexandre began, "we have never lost Maman before either."

"Look, Pa, I know better than to think that you are afraid of the dark and need someone to stay with you. You're upta somethin. I can feel it in my bones as you always say."

Alexandre smiled a wry smile. "You think that I am so transparent and you are so smart, do you?"

"Pa, I don't wanna offend you; that's just how I feel."

"Well, my smart son, are you willing to swear a vow to me that you will never repeat anything I should say to you tonight to anyone, not even Susannah?"

"Pa," he hesitated for a moment, "you know that Susannah and I have never had secrets from each other. I trust you, Pa, and if you ask me to keep your secrets I will do so."

Before his father could gather his thoughts together, Isaac said, "Pa, you're not gonna do something crazy, are you, with the kid?" He wet his lips with his tongue.

"I am appalled that you would even think such a thing about me. Isaac, you are right, I am up to something, as you put it, and as you have sworn to me that you will never betray my confidence, I will divulge my little plan to you."

"Plan? I'm confused, Pa."

"Isaac, your mother and I devised this plan several years ago should anything happen to either one of us. I am taking the child and leaving with her; we are going to a brand new life. All the arrangements have been made and everything has been set up. It has all been done legally, too!"

"B–b–but where are you going?"

"Where are we going? That, my son, is a good question, but I cannot give you the answer to it. Believe this: You nor anyone else will ever find us; everything, including transfer of monies and properties, has already taken place while your mother was yet alive."

"You mean we'll never see each other again?" he asked incredulously.

"You are right, Isaac. That is why I wanted these two days alone with you."

"Samuel and Rachel are gonna blow their tops."

"Your mother and I had reached the place where we no longer cared what they did or thought. Neither do I care now!"

Alexandre left the room and was gone for about five minutes or so and came back into the room with quite a few papers in his hands.

"I have some instructions for you to follow, and please listen carefully to them, as they must be followed to the letter.

"About a week after I am gone, you are to bring these papers to my attorney, George Sandler. You need not concern yourself as everything has been made ironclad.

"This paper here is your deed to this house and everything contained in it; it is all yours, including Maman's fur coat, which is to go to Susannah."

"B–b–but why me? How come I am getting the house?"

"Because your mother and I want it that way. That's why! Now these papers here are the trust funds that we started in each one of the children's names. They will receive the money either when they go to college or reach the age of twenty-one years.

"Oh, yes, that reminds me, you get this house and property only if you sign over your farm to Henry. He wants to be a veterinarian you know, and he really could do wonders over there. We have left him something to make renovations with. The money is his only if he finishes veterinarian school.

"Here are the transfer papers for the cars; one is to go to Susannah and the other to you.

"This paper here is the combination to the safe. In there are several boxes. Come and I will show you."

Isaac followed his father into the bedroom and watched as he uncovered a wall safe behind a portrait of Simone and himself.

"I didn't know that you had a safe!"

"You do now. Come and see if you can open it."

Isaac did as his father bid him and opened up the safe with no problem at all.

"See this box here?"

Isaac nodded his head.

"This is for your Nicole from her grandmother. Everything is clearly marked. All of the good jewelry has been sent on to our new home to be put away for Genevieve when she is old enough, both the jewelry from your Maman and from Laura, too."

"You did the right thing, Pa."

"I know that we did! Poor Genevieve has had such a terrible life so far that your mother and I felt that she should have a new beginning. Perhaps this will be better for her."

"Pa, look, I know that it's none of my business, but how about Samuel and Rachel? What do they get?"

"Rachel will receive a small yearly allowance of fifty thousand dollars, enough to keep her, but not in the life-style she has been accustomed to." He couldn't help himself and he chuckled aloud.

"Do you remember the little diner where we ate breakfast this morning?"

Isaac shook his head in puzzlement, wondering what that had to do with anything.

"Well," Alexandre said, "I bought it for your brother Samuel and from this day forward he receives no allowance except for twenty-five hundred dollars a year, and he will earn his living by the sweat of his brow." He threw back his head and laughed until he was weak.

Isaac joined him in laughter. "I love it! I really love it! Pa, does this mean that we will never see each other again?"

"I don't know, Isaac; I really don't know. Let's devise a code name, so that if the need arises I can get in touch with you. Ah," he said, "if you ever get a message that says 'laugh, clown, laugh,' you will know that it is from me."

"Laugh, clown, laugh?"

"Yes, that's it! Isaac, show the world what you can be. Forget Samuel and be you."

Chapter Twenty-three
A Meeting of the Minds

With an unexpected clamor of sound a voice seemed to boom out of nowhere, "Where's the old man? I haven't seen him for hours."

The man that spoke was a classic example of boorishness. He very obviously felt that he was God's gift to the world and that the world would stop functioning if he ever got off.

"Were you speaking to me?" He was a handsome youth, cocky and sure of himself. He was obviously feeling no pain and it was certainly to be assumed that his throat was not dry.

"Henry," obviously quite irritated with the youth, "did you hear your name called? Good Lord," he slapped his head in disgust, "nobody knows anything around here, but they're all hanging around for the free eats and drinks. What kind of place is this anyway?"

"You mean like you?" The youth spoke with obvious contempt for the older man.

With a motion that appeared like he was about to slap the youth, he said, "Don't you get smart with me!" But as he said this Samuel Boisvert began one of his quick and quiet appraisals of his nephew and held back. *He might just be useful to me in some way*, he thought. *Maybe I'd better take it a little easy on the boy.*

He put on what he thought was his most jovial smile and said, "Hell, boy, we've had enough unhappiness for one day, what with your grandmother passing away and all. I guess we all have a right to be a little bit on edge, eh? Come on over here and your old uncle will pour you a drink."

Henry cocked his head to one side, and as he did so a lock of his hair fell forward, giving him the appearance of a naughty little boy with his hand caught in the cookie jar.

The boy had had enough to drink that his words were already beginning to slur. His sneer was very obvious. "What you looking for Sam? You know darn well I'm only sixteen, and if the old man caught me drinking, he'd have my hide."

Even at his young age Henry stood several inches taller than his portly uncle. Henry had a smile of bemusement upon his lips as he observed the older man.

Jeez, he thought, *the old fool has about thirty hairs on his head and tries to spread them out. Who does he think he's fooling, anyhow?*

"Hey, boy, you just remember who the mayor around here is. Anyhow, I'll take care of any hassle from your old man. Remember, I've been one step ahead of him all of our lives!"

"Hey, Mr. Mayor, sir, that's not how I've heard it." He spoke in a very crude manner.

The boy had been cut out of the same cloth as his uncle. He thought to himself, *Well, I guess I won't aggravate the old cuss any further. Besides, I really could use a drink.*

"Well, sir, I guess my brothers and I all tell our stories differently, too. We all see things in a different light. Right?" *That ought to smooth the old guy's feathers for him. The old goat! I almost choked on that 'sir' bit.*

The older man seemed appeased. "You're right; you're right, my boy. We are family and we all have to stick together in these trying times. Here, while no one else is around let's have some of my old man's brandy."

The youth, sensing what the older man was up to, put the glass slowly up to his lips and started to fake that he was choking.

"Easy, my boy; this is a real man's drink." He chuckled, obviously having accomplished what he had intended.

You rotten old so and so, thought Henry. *I would really like to tell him off. Better not though, he might be useful to me yet.*

Both of them were deep in their own thoughts for a moment until Sam spoke up and said, "Tell me, have you see your grandfather at all?"

The young man seemed to be taken aback for a moment. "No . . . no, sir, I haven't seen him at all since we first came back from church this morning."

"Well, that sure is strange," said Sam. "All he told me is that he wanted to take Genevieve for a ride because she was so upset."

This kid is starting to get on my nerves, and besides that, he's boring me to death! The way he's slugging down that booze, this certainly was not his first drink! Well, the time is not totally wasted; I found out his weakness.

"Go and get your aunt for me." The older man was clearly using his voice of authority now.

The boy picked up on it immediately. "Why should I? I'm not your slave."

"You'd better do as I say, and do it right away, too, or you might be sorry. Go ahead or else!"

"Or else what? You old bat."

"Or else, you young idiot, I'll tell your father I caught you in here drinking my old man's booze."

The boy stood as straight as he could under the circumstances. "You rotten bum! I should have known that you couldn't even pretend to be nice for even two minutes! Don't worry you creep, you're gonna get yours yet." And he began to laugh uncontrollably.

Heaven forbid! That stupid brat is going to cause a scene.

Just then Henry appeared in the doorway. He was trying desperately to stand straight, but was somewhat unsuccessful. He had to reach out and steady himself on the door casing.

"Hey! Uncle Mayor, sir." His words were becoming more and more slurred now. "Does the name Donna Neals mean anything to you? Ha! Gotcha!" He once again started to laugh, and staggered away.

I never saw him speechless before, I bet his jaw fell to the floor, thought Henry.

He laughed hard and long, so much in fact that he had to hold himself up by leaning against the wall. He laughed until tears flowed down his young cheeks.

And this is how his mother found the lad, and thinking that his poor heart was broken, she cuddled him against her bosom in an attempt to comfort him. After all the poor boy had just lost his grandmother.

Uncle Samuel was not as amused as his nephew was. *Just what can he possibly know about Donna? Maybe he just pulled that name at random. No, that little brat isn't that bright.* He paced the floor nervously back and forth and back and forth again. He was beginning to perspire, a condition he hated because he had no control over it.

Chapter Twenty-four
The Train Ride

There they were, the elderly man, white-haired, clean-shaven, rugged and tan, giving the appearance (if it wasn't for the lack of a beard) of a sea captain out of his realm. His appearance belied his true lifelong occupation. It was quite apparent that he was a man of confidence and used to giving orders.

Now for the first time in his life he was overwhelmed with the responsibilities that lay ahead of him. His wife had dropped everything in his lap. *God rest her soul*, he thought. He heaved a great big sigh. *Am I able?* he thought.

She (his dear wife) had always felt that he was capable of doing everything and anything and had always expected him to do the impossible. *Perhaps it was a good thing for me*, he thought, *because it was only because of her help that I did become a success.* This was not because of her bossiness but because of her confidence in his abilities.

He turned his head slightly and peered down at the lithe figure of the young girl beside him. A mere child, confused, heartbroken. In reality she would soon be approaching the blossoming of young womanhood. Right now she was more boyish, perhaps pixieish would be a more apt description, in her appearance. *Soon*, he thought, *she will become a woman much like her grandmother and mother were.* He could see them in her even now.

She reminded him so much of the young woman that he had made his bride, and of another young woman who had been his daughter and the mother of this waif. Not really a waif perhaps, but truly an orphan.

Her hair was chestnut in color with sparkling reddish golden highlights, not actually curly but wavy enough to frame her face almost into a cameo effect. Her eyes, very dark and very bright, seemed to have hidden generators of light behind them. She was the type of child that immediately illuminated a room merely by entering into it. Her smile revealed very bright and well taken care of teeth, and this minor action of smiling had turned many a head in her direction, even at her unadvanced age.

She was very neat about herself, a quality that he approved of greatly and admired in one so young.

"Genevieve," he said softly, and as she turned he saw her eyes slowly filling with tears, glistening upon her eyelids and slowly overflowing upon her cheeks, making their downward trip, careful not to form a pattern but each tear with a uniqueness of its own making on its downward trek.

"Oh, Grand-père," she said, with a small trace of sobbing in her voice and a barely noticeable quiver in her tone, "are you really sure that we are doing the right thing?"

"*Oui, cherie*," he replied. "It is not for you to worry your pretty little head about, eh." He smiled and drew her a little closer to him and said to her, "Everything is, how do you young people say, oh yes, pretty cool."

In spite of his levity her tears continued to flow freely. *Poor child*, he thought, *maybe it will help her to let some of her hurt flow out through her tears*.

"Oh, Grand-père," she said, "first Mom and Dad are killed in a terrible automobile accident and now Grand-mère is gone, too. Except for you there is no one else in this whole wide world that cares about me."

"*Cherie*," he said, with all of the courage that he could muster up, "remember, we have one another and that is enough!"

She turned toward the old man and stood up on tiptoes and kissed him ever so gently on the cheek. "You sound just like Grand-mère," she told him through her tears.

"Genevieve," he said, with a tinge of pride in his voice, "I am seventy-two years past and this is the nicest compliment that has ever been said to me. You give me honor and respect. Merci, I thank you, little one. Now, let us go on board and find our seats where we can lean back and rest as much as we can. This journey is a long and tedious one and we will need all of our strength."

They found their seats without much effort and both tried to relax, each in his own fashion.

He put his head back on the seat and gave the appearance that he might be going to sleep. Actually, he had not traveled by train for a good many years and his stomach was feeling the effects of it; either that, he thought, or the excitement of the past few days was taking effect upon his nervous system.

His mind seemed to be going along at a crazy pace, and he could not slow down his thought processes. *Life*, he thought, *what is it all about? What is it for? Have I accomplished anything? Is there any reason to go on with it?*

He slanted his head so that he could get a glimpse of his granddaughter and he knew the reason for his life to go on. She was the reason; without him she had no other person to care.

He had made a sacred promise to his wife before she died that he would care for this slip of a girl. He was a man who never backed down on his word, and he had committed himself and would do the best he could.

He knew at this moment, if he had not realized it before, that there was no turning back. He had always looked forward and was not about to turn around now.

As his mind wandered he smiled to himself; actually, he was laughing in the interior depths of his being.

Those fools, he thought, *those damn fools, if only they knew the real truth. I've always been a good poker player. If only I could see the expressions on their stupid faces. Oh, well, we have a whole month to get things settled.*

Again he chuckled to himself. *I still wish I could be there to see a few faces when they discover us gone. What is done is done!*

His mind began to race again, and he felt that his thoughts were racing about as fast as the train traveled. *It is good that the child is resting*, he thought. *She has been through so much in her young lifetime.*

In reality she was not asleep, her mind also was hyperactive and she could not calm her thoughts nor her fears. She gave the impression of resting so that her grandfather would not be concerned so much with her, so that he might rest.

She felt very uncomfortable in the clothes that she was wearing. *How can boys be comfortable in clothes like these?* she thought. Although she had not been told anything about the charade that they were playing, she knew there was a reason that her hair was tucked very carefully into her cap. Her grandfather had gone somewhere and bought them both second-hand clothing. She knew enough about clothing to realize that fact. He wanted them to travel most inconspicuously. In his realism he had bought her a necktie replete with a spot on it. So complete was his deception that he even saw to it that she had dirt under her fingernails, much to her dismay. "No boy your age," he told her, "has spotless fingernails."

He had shaved in the rest room of a little diner they had stopped at for breakfast. He looked so different to her as he had worn a beard for as long as she had known him.

"You and I," he had told her, "we are going on an adventure, we are going to play a game together. Will you trust me?"

She looked at him solemnly and said, "Yes." somehow she sensed that her whole future life depended on the outcome of this so-called "game."

"While we are on our trip," he told her, "you and I must be careful at all times to speak only in French."

"Why?" she asked him, her curiosity being aroused by this.

"When the time is right, I will tell you everything. Until then I pray that you will respect my wishes."

"*Oui*," she said. After all, he had never let her down before. She knew him to always be a man of his word as far as she was concerned.

"Soon I promise that you shall understand. Your Grand-mère and I had made all these arrangements together before she died; if I had gone before her, she would be with you now with these very same plans. Everything will be fine, you are not to worry your pretty little head."

Her mind would not stay still. *How can I possibly remember everything that I have to do?* She sighed a sigh of the weary in spirit. *On this trip my name is Eugene Trahan. When we arrive at our destination I am Genevieve. Let me see, when we disembark from the train I am to go directly to the ladies room at the depot and change all of my clothes, clean the dirt from my fingernails, make sure my hair is combed in a feminine manner, discard all these boyish clothes (that won't be hard for me to do! Boys can keep their old clothes!), and meet Grand-père as soon as possible.*

He also will be undergoing changes; change of hair-style, he will be dressed in a business suit rather than those old clothes he has on now.

We will have a car waiting for us and we shall proceed on to our new life. I wonder what our new life will be like, she thought. *Where will we be? One thing for sure, I'll soon find out, won't I? Well one good thing is it can't be worse than our old lives.*

I can't believe that Grand-mère has been gone eight whole days already. Grand-père says that she has gone home up in heaven and that she is all better now. He said that she is happy being there with Mom and Dad. All I know for sure is that I miss her like crazy and I want her back here with us, just like it used to be. Stupid me, here I am crying again. I hope nobody saw me; then they'll know for sure that I'm not a boy, because boys aren't supposed to cry. I miss her so much. She would want me to stay with Grand-père. Oh dear, what if he dies too, then what will I do? What will become of me? Tears were now much in abundance upon her cheeks, a lonely lost child paired with a lonely lost man.

Heartache and loneliness so often go hand in hand, one close on the heels of the other, but when it is shared the burden becomes lighter. The old man reached over and took her hand in a gesture of reassurance; it not only helped her, but by that simple gesture of looking beyond himself he began to heal also.

The clackety-clack of the train became more rhythmic as they relaxed and soon each did restlessly fall asleep, for a short time.

A town is a town is a town and on and on it goes, one begins where the other leaves off, and the motif becomes repetitive in its explanation. This was employed by a great poet in his description of the rose.

What is it that would make one town differ from another? Are there blueprints in the great beyond that would pick out an area here and one there, and thus one becomes the prototype for the other?

What philosophy is there? Are the good folk trying to convert the bad folk, or is it vice versa and the bad folk are trying to corrupt the good folk? Why is a town always composed of a mixture of the moral along with the immoral? Those who are law abiding and trustworthy having to live beside the criminal element. Those whose lives are lived in truth and those who are total procrastinators. Those who labor, toil and sweat, and those who are content to sit back and live, and grow fat off of the labors of others.

Then we find those who are not absolutely black with sin and also those who are not pure white with goodness, or as they might put it, merely on the grey side, if there be such a thing. We cannot forget the vultures who turn every situation to their own advantage, whose greed forms great tentacles of self-indulgences. There are also others who suffer from the obesity of the misuse of others' goods rather than the overuse of food, always adding to their portliness of acquisition.

We find many who are lean of brain and do not yearn for knowledge of learning of any kind, nor for the enrichment of their soul, but are totally content in their existence of non-knowledge. They are willing to leave to their progeny an inheritance of ignorance and not necessarily bliss. Pity the poor man (and he forms a great majority) who has handicapped himself in ignorance, content to let life deal to him a crippling blow.

There are many who tolerate the ignorance that runs rampant within themselves, but refuse to accept it in others.

Each town has its own form of government, which more than likely serves those who are at the head of it rather than the people who really need the help and assistance, the ones who really believe all those campaign promises as though they were gospel truths.

Most of our towns could be interchanged one with the other without any noticeable difference. The wide main street with its smattering of stores and small diners. The cop on the beat, for the most part ignored, a man of small powers, with no more respect than that given to the lowly ant.

A few barbershops and so-called houses of beauty, where all the gossip of the day can be interchanged and compared, but most of all revised and embellished for emphasis and self-importance.

Scattered about, a few houses of worship, some so elegant they appear out of place in the humble town and some so humble they seemingly belong, but normally are frowned upon for their lack of ostentation.

Always, always the town character, shabby, looking for a handout, panhandling so that he might indulge in the favorite pastime of his own self-indulgence, tolerated because he is the only color or divergence in this otherwise drab little parcel of land called "town."

The old man's face spread to a slow smile. *I certainly won't miss that town much. Perhaps where I am heading won't be much better, but at least we will be away from all the old memories and hurts.*

She was smart, my woman. How she hated it when he called her his woman. "I am not your woman; I am your wife. Your woman is one that you pay for an hour's pleasure, but your wife is the one you spend your life with." He loved to tease her in so many ways. She knew of course that it was a game they played together. He would tease her and she would pretend to be angry with him. Actually she loved every moment of it, as she craved for attention in her own way, not demanding it, but desirous of it, as one would crave for food after fasting for many days.

The parting had been so hard for him. For some unknown reason he had always felt that he would go first. *One just never knows*, he thought.

Now here I am, an old man with the awesome responsibility of raising a child by himself. I never even brought up my own children, he thought. *I just abided by her wishes as they always made good sense to me. Dear God up in heaven help me, help us both.*

Half turning, he gazed lovingly upon the child. *So much like her mother,* he thought. What a terrible tragedy that had brought the two of them alone, in a train heading for a place known only to himself and the old woman. This slip of a girl had been the only child of his daughter Laura-Anne, named after both of her grandmothers because neither he nor his wife would give in. She was like a child out of heaven, cherubic and angelic, as far as he was concerned anyway. Out of four children he always told his wife, "She is the only one that is normal."

Poor little girl, he thought about his granddaughter, *first of all the tragic accident that took the lives of both of her parents and now the loss of the*

Grand-mère that had really taken her mother's place in her life. All she had was him, and by golly he was a fighter and was not out for the count yet.

Evening was beginning to draw near and he heard the porter going through the cars announcing that the dining car was now open. He decided to awaken the child so that she could have something to eat. They were traveling as poor folk, so he had packed them a lunch, keeping up the image, so to speak.

"I don't think that I can eat, Grand-père," she said. "My stomach isn't feeling good."

"You stop that thinking," he told her rather sharply. "You are my flesh and blood, and we are strong people in times of tragedy and sadness! Now sit up here and eat as we will need all of our strength to begin our new lives. I have for you something very special that you have wanted for a long, long time but due to circumstances were unable to have thus far."

"Do you really mean something very special?" she asked.

"Is that not what I said?" he answered almost in a teasing manner, which was unusual for him.

"Please, Grand-père, tell me what the surprise is, please!"

"No, I cannot do that, for don't you see if I told you then it would not be a surprise, eh?" He patted her arm gently. "Let us eat."

Silently she ate the sandwich he offered her, and together they drank the thermos of coffee that he had brought along, she from the cup and he directly from the thermos itself.

At last, at long last, the long trip was over, and they could disembark from the train. Genevieve rubbed her posterior. "I feel like part of me stayed behind on the miserable old train." She was all alone in the ladies room at the depot, and had swiftly changed into her girlish clothing, and had freed her hair and brushed it until it shone, just as her Grand-mère had taught her to do. *I must not keep Grand-père waiting,* she thought. *I wonder what is to happen now?*

Her grandfather was quietly waiting for her beside the door. "Come, we would not want to keep these good people waiting," he said.

"Who are they?" she asked him.

His only reply was, "You shall soon see."

He took her hand as they walked along, and finally they saw two people in the distance. Her grandfather put up his hand in greeting. One of them was a rather seedy man of some nondescript age. In reality he was only forty-five years old, but had many years of hard living under his belt.

The other was a rather short, rather plump woman inclined to be overly jovial, or so thought Genevieve.

Her grandfather ran up to the woman, perhaps about fifty-eight or -nine years old, and put his arms around her and gave her a great big bear hug. They were both laughing and crying at the same time, then her grandfather began shaking the other man's hand and patting him on the back.

Oh, no, thought Genevieve, *Grand-père has a girlfriend. I just know I am going to hate it here.*

Genevieve shook herself from her memories and turned toward her grandfather and thought that he was still asleep. She realized that she had been locked in some faraway memories just as he had been.

"We are wool-gathering today," he spoke very tenderly. "I have been thinking," he said softly, "about memories. What makes a memory? Out of all the mountains of life experiences why do we bring to our recollections certain things and not the others? Some simple item that brought joy or laughter comes into our minds without effort or concentration, and yet the sadness and solemnities cling like bloodsuckers, and we are unable to shake them off." He stopped and dozed off again.

She shuddered involuntarily at the possibility; inwardly she knew that the possibility could very soon become a reality. A reality she dared not think about.

Was she prepared if the reality came about? *Am I prepared?* she thought. *Heaven knows that he has tried to prepare me.*

She began to study him in a depth of extreme concentration, as though she felt that this might be the last chance she would have to do so.

He has beautiful hair, she thought, *fresh and shiny as the new fallen snow. Even at his age, he has a full head of hair.* Every hair was curled gently and formed its own pattern of ups and downs that seemed so much a part of his nature.

I wonder, she thought, *if Grand-mère ever ran her fingers through his hair?* Inwardly she giggled like a little girl as the thought seemed so ludicrous to her. The thought of her grandmother running her fingers idly through anyone's hair was really funny as Genevieve brought to her mind the portrait that she had inwardly created of her grandmother.

Chapter Twenty-five
No School?

The day was exceptionally beautiful, the kind of day that seemed to touch the very essence of man's soul. The sun was shining brightly, causing that special kind of glow that reassures us that all is well with the world.

Alexandre had awakened early this morning; he did not want to miss a single moment! After all at his age each moment was very precious.

The sun had awakened him just at daybreak. He had been in a very deep sleep and had felt something warm upon his cheek. He awoke delighted. "The good Lord, he has given me another day.

"I always have liked the warmth of the sun. It always renews and invigorates me. It makes my bones feel good and makes my face want to smile."

This was the kind of day that he and Simone enjoyed together so much. "Oh yes," he sighed, "the kind of a day where we could forget all of our troubles and concentrate upon ourselves!

"I wish I could relive just one of those wonderful days again," he sighed. "What is it that I always tell Genevieve? Oh yes, all the time that you spend living in the past, you lose for today."

He looked up to the sky. "Simone, Simone! If you only knew, the passing days without you do not get any better, they get harder and harder as time goes on.

"I never realized just how much I depended on you until you were taken away from me. I pray every day that I will do what is right for the child. If you were here today all three of us would pack up and go somewhere very beautiful and private, and be together. You would pack us some of your good food and off we would go into the wild blue yonder.

"When I awoke this morning I thought that Genevieve and I would do the very same thing, but the poor child had been looking so peaked lately, I thought I would let her rest.

"Here I am acting the old fool. How many times have I heard you say that if nickels were wishes beggars might ride?"

The man shook himself as if to say, "Get a hold of yourself," and began to walk slowly until he came to one of his favorite spots on his property.

He stood there on a little rise that overlooked the fifteen or so acres of property. He called this place "The Meadow," but when the locals spoke of it, they called it "The Meddah."

There he stood alone, communing with nature. The little mound could have been the royal chamber of his domain. There he stood, tall, slender, and very handsome. His shoulders were squared back, head held erect, as he overlooked his domain. Both hands were in his pockets, elbows tilted back.

His eyes appeared to be gazing in an upward direction, they were overlooking the meadow.

I wish I were an artist, he thought. *No use, though; no artist, no matter how talented, could do this spot justice.*

His gaze was fixed on the left-hand part of the land where the green, green land seemed to intermarry with the very deep blue sky. All around, the meadow area was surrounded with all sorts of evergreen trees. There were tall ones, short ones and medium-sized ones. Some were very tall and slender, and others had much more of a girth about them. Every here and there were some other kind of tree, such as a mighty oak, many maple varieties; alders were in abundance also.

Strange, he thought, *the whole midsection of the meadow was inexplicably bare, with no growth there, as if something or someone were keeping the area bare, sort of a breathing space for nature.* The wild grasses that covered the land appeared as a green carpet, and the growth of five or six inches was moving to an unheard melody in the sunlight.

Every tree, separate from the other, seemed to be moving in a syncopation unheard by any man. As a matter of fact, if one looked closely enough, he would realize that every leaf, every bristle, was moving with its own separate melodic influence.

Just from this particular spot, he could overlook five counties, so he was told. Way beyond the line of trees there was another meadow of about five acres, where he kept his horses. He had not planned on horses but his granddaughter loved them so!

"Maybe I am just an old fool, but she has had so much heartache in her young life!"

From where he stood, the meadow seemed to slope downward, but it was so slight that the land gave the appearance of being level no matter which side you were standing on.

Land is a good thing, he thought almost aloud. *It gives one a feeling of continuity. Someday it will all belong to Genevieve as her grandmother and I planned.*

The man turned very slowly, allowing his gaze to concentrate on other aspects of the property, such as the wall of ledges on his left-hand side. They always appeared to him to form a table for the mountains that formed the backdrop of the property so beautifully.

He was so taken by the beauty of it all that a half smile formed on his thin lips, and he stood up straighter and a little taller, so as not to break the symmetry of it all.

At this moment he felt as complete as a man could feel with his lot in life.

He half turned his body once again, looking toward the southern portion of his property. Over here is where the house stood. It could not be defined as grandiose or even pretentious, but it was totally liveable. *Good enough to meet all of our needs, that's for sure. I suppose that one could call it a sort of colonial dwelling.* It was all white except for the shutters, which were bright red, Genevieve's favorite color.

The housekeeper had planted many, many flowers around and it made the house appear much more homelike than it would have without them.

I would suppose that I should not call Anna the housekeeper, as she really is family of sorts, being my cousin and all. I must admit that I don't know what we would do without her.

He began to observe the many cloud patterns overhead and he became so involved with it that he did not realize at first that Anna was calling him and gesturing frantically.

He thought, *Perhaps we have an unexpected guest or something.*

He turned and waved to her to let her know that he saw her and would be coming in.

She just kept up her frenetic movements, and as he watched her he could not help but smile. She was a short little thing, only five feet tall, and Mother Nature had ungraciously given her legs that were unusually short even for a person of her height.

When she ran, as she was now doing, she ran with little short steps much like those of a three- or four-year-old child. She carried too much weight for a person of her stature. As she ran everything on her body jiggled and wiggled, especially her jowls.

She would have made a humorous sight to the elderly gentleman if he had not realized that she was greatly upset.

What could have upset her so? he thought as he started toward her.

"Anna, what is it? What has happened?"

She was desperately trying to catch her breath. "It's . . . it's Genevieve, it's Genevieve!" She was gasping for breath.

Fear gripped the old man, and, never being known to raise his voice, he now did so. "The child," he yelled, "is she hurt?"

"*Non, non!* But there is something wrong with her." And she began to cry.

"There, there now," he said soothingly, as he helplessly patted her round shoulders.

Why, he thought to himself, *she loves the child as much as I do; I must try to remember that.*

"You must calm down and tell me what is wrong." He handed her his ever-present handkerchief, which she grabbed unceremoniously and used to blow her nose. The noise that she made caused Alexandre to shudder, as she sounded like the fatted goose.

"Oh, Alexandre, it is Genevieve! I have never seen her act in this way before!" And she began to cry all over again.

Alexandre realized that the only thing that he could do was wait for her to compose herself.

"She," sob, "she told me to shut up," and she began to speak in French as fast as she could. "*Je ne comprends pas, pourquoi elle me parle comme ca?*"

Alexandre could feel the anger creeping upon him. He was always known to be a very calm and rational man, but this he found inexcusable. The idea! How dare his granddaughter speak in this manner to this dear lady who had devoted her life to care for them.

He could not remember any time that he had been angry with his dear Genevieve, but this was certainly it.

He turned abruptly from where they were standing and began walking toward the house at a very rapid stride. His whole being gave the portrait of total determination.

He entered the house and began to call out, "Genevieve! Genevieve! Where are you?" There was no answer to his call, which incensed him all the more.

He entered into her bedroom without knocking, which was something he had never done before, as he had always afforded her the courtesy of treating her like a lady.

Genevieve was in her room quietly lying on her bed. Her room looked more like a boy's room than that of a young girl. She was very much the tomboy. Her room reflected as much of the old man as it did the young girl. Alexandre always felt that as she grew older she would reflect more femininity.

Fourteen is very young, he thought. *When I was fourteen, I was earning my own living and supporting Maman too! Enough of this, I must take care of the business at hand.*

As he stood there in her room, he could not help but think, *How unlike this gentle child to act in such a way. What could have provoked her?*

"Mademoiselle Genevieve! Are you not aware that I am speaking to you?"

There was no reply or even a sign of movement from the area of the bed.

"Now," he said rather sharply, "you are adding rudeness to this matter. Now," he continued in his sharp manner, "you will turn yourself around so that we can get this matter settled!"

Again, no response. The old man had to control himself, as his impulse was to grab the girl forcibly and turn her around himself.

Composing himself a little and taking a deep breath, he spoke in a much gentler manner. "Come, child, let's work this out together."

As he stood there quietly pondering what he should do next, he heard a barely discernible little sob.

When he heard the sound his heart melted within him and he quickly walked over to the bed. He sat on the edge and took her into his arms and held her tightly as though she would evaporate on the spot.

When he did this she began to cry as though her poor young heart would break and never mend again.

It was a portrait that any artist would have died to be able to reproduce on canvas. This was a special kind of love expressed between the man and the child. There was almost a holiness about it. All they had was each other.

There they sat together much as they had done once before, only then, he thought, *Simone was with us*.

He decided to allow her to cry it out. He could feel the wetness upon his shirt when the tears stopped, and she was shaking and sobbing. Only then did he sit her up and quietly begin to wipe the moisture from her tear-washed face.

His actions were so tender that one would have thought that her face was being washed by a very gentle breeze.

He smiled at her tenderly. "Genevieve," he spoke softly now, "did we not make a solemn agreement a long time ago that we were partners?"

She sat there in her blue pajamas. *Poor child*, he thought, *she really is heartbroken. What could have caused so much distress in her little life?*

She looked at her grandfather and nodded her head slowly up and down.

"Partners," he said to her gently, "must trust each other or else they have no business being partners. Do you understand what I am saying? Either we are partners or else we are not. Which is it to be?"

She threw herself into her grandfather's arms and began to cry all over again. He held her close once more.

"Now," he told her, "you must tell me, as I am fast losing patience, and I cannot take all this suspense."

"You don't know." She cried all the more. "You don't know."

"Tell me, my dear, for at my age there is not much I have not seen or heard."

"Oh, Grand-père." She sobbed a great big sob. "I'm dying."

The old man's heart leaped in his breast. "Wh–what are you trying to tell me?"

Her voice was high-pitched now. "Can't you hear me?" She almost screamed it out. "I tell you, I'm dying, I'm dying!"

Again her body shook with sobs, and she pulled him even closer to her and fell into his arms a totally wrecked speck of a girl.

Just then there was a knock on the door. "Who is it?" His voice showed his irritability.

"It is Anna!" Then hesitatingly, "The school bus is here."

The old man hollered out, "You tell Mr. Locke that there will be no school for Miss Genevieve today. Thank you."

"Very well." The voice was muffled through the thick wood of the door. As Anna walked away her heart was heavy and concern was written all over her face. "I pray that I did not get that dear child in any great trouble. I guess that I was so surprised at her speaking to me like that. I wish I could draw her out more. I know that she is hesitant to love too much because she might get hurt again. Oh well, maybe in time. I think I will cook us all a special meal. That turkey I bought the other day will be just the thing!"

She was the type of person who had to keep herself busy at all times. This was how she worked off her nervous energy.

"Have you seen a doctor, Miss?"

She sat up a little straighter on her bed and shook her head slowly in a negative manner.

"Then," he said, "I demand to know who it is that has told you that you are dying?"

"No–no–one," she said falteringly.

His eyes were flashing now. "You mean to tell me that you have decided all by yourself that you are dying!"

She sat there a pathetic sight indeed, and shook her head yes.

The young face was teary and blotched, her hair was only obeying its own whims and fancy and its style was helter-skelter.

She really believes that she is dying, he thought to himself. *But why?*

"Start from the beginning," he tried to speak soothingly and calmly now. "What makes you think that you are going to die?"

She took several deep breaths, as though to calm herself. "It all started a long time ago. . . ." she said, and her voice began to trail off.

"Yes," he said. "Please continue, as I cannot stand all this suspense."

"About a year ago, I began having awful, awful pains in my stomach."

"Why didn't you come to me then?" he asked her.

"Well . . . the pains came and went, they were not there all of the time, but sometimes the pains were so bad I couldn't even move. Then the pains would go away for a long time and I was all better; then the bad pains would start again."

"You poor baby," he murmured. "Is there any more?"

"Yes," she told him. "Yesterday the pains came back, worse than ever before."

He felt ashamed of himself now as both he and Anna had remarked yesterday how "peaked" the child looked.

"You remember," she looked at him, "last night I went to bed early?"

"Yes, I remember."

"Well, I came to bed, but the pains would not stop no matter what I did. Then I remembered what Grand-mère used to say, that God will never leave you nor forsake you. So I prayed for God to help me."

"Then what happened?"

"I guess I fell asleep for a while. Real late in the night, long after everyone was asleep, I woke up feeling very sick, like I was going to throw up or something. When I tried to get out of bed, the room was spinning around and I fell to the floor and could not get up for quite a while."

Her whole body began to shudder as though she were reliving the whole ordeal over again. He reached out and patted her hand. "Go on."

"When I finally got up off the floor, I went into the bathroom, and I was bleeding real bad."

"Where were you bleeding? Was your nose bleeding?"

Her face turned a bright red. "I cannot tell you."

The old man's face also turned a beet red. "Genevieve! I insist that you tell me at once so that this matter will be cleared up!"

"I tried to clean up the blood, but the more I tried to clean it up, the more blood came!"

"Where!?" the old man demanded.

She bent her head so that he could not see her face. "Down there, in my private parts."

The old man heaved a great sigh of relief and he smiled at his granddaughter.

"You are making fun of me," she said resentfully. "I know that I should never have told you, and now I'm sorry that I did. Leave me alone."

"Look at me," he told her. She did not respond to him, so he took her chin gently in his hand and turned her face towards his.

"I only smiled when I realized that you were not going to die and I was so relieved. Forgive me if I have been insensitive."

"How do you know if I am going to die or not? You're not a doctor either!"

"Genevieve, do you trust me?"

"Yes, I do."

"Have I ever lied to you?"

She shook her head at him, indicating no.

"Then listen to me, and listen very carefully. You are not going to die. What has happened to you is that you have become a young lady. I am not going to try to explain the facts to you, but I will get someone who has the proper knowledge to explain it all to you. Now firstly, I am going to call Dr. Livernois to come and examine you and make sure that everything is in order with you. You will cooperate, will you not?"

She shook her head yes. "Do you really mean it?" she asked. "I'm not going to die?"

"Yes, my darling granddaughter, you are destined to live to a ripe old age. Now," he spoke sternly. "We have another bit of business."

"I know; I must apologize to Ma Tante Anna."

"You are right; you are right indeed. I will not tolerate such behavior again, no matter what the situation. Is that clear?"

Chapter Twenty-six
Learning

Alexandre walked out of his granddaughter's room and headed for the large kitchen on the eastern side of the house. He and Simone both loved to see the sun rise in the mornings.

Anna was standing there cooking something that smelled delightful.

"I see that it is getting close to lunchtime," he said.

Anna turned from where she was cooking and said, "Genevieve, is she all right?"

"Yes, the emergency was not as bad as we thought. The poor child." He shook his head.

Anna looked almost comical standing there with a big spoon in her hand. "What do you mean, poor child?"

"It seems that our girl thought that she was going to die."

Anna's heart began to pound within her breast. "Our girl!" "Our girl." This is what he said. It was the first time he had used the term "our."

She began stirring the soup with vigor. "Now why would the child think such a thing?"

"It is because of the stupidity of an old man. Tell me, what is the number for Dr. Livernois?"

"It is right before you on the chart that you yourself put up there. Is Genevieve sick?"

He shook his head no as he dialed the number. "Dr. Livernois? . . . Thank God I caught you at home. This is Alexandre Boisvert. Is it possible for you to come out here today? I have an emergency of sorts. . . . I really appreciate this. We'll be looking for you; plan on having your lunch with us."

He hung up the phone with a sort of a clang.

"I thought that you told me that the child is not ill." Anna was almost whining now.

"I assure you that she is well. Today Genevieve has become a young lady. May I ask a favor of you?"

"Of course, you can ask anything of me and I will do it if I can; what can I do?"

"The child, she is a mess, and I do not think that a young lady wants her Grand-père at a time like this, or else I would do it. I do not want you to feel that I ask you to do all the dirty work."

"You make me so angry when you speak like that," she spoke sharply now. "I will go to the child. It is only a woman that can understand what another woman is going through anyway." Her attitude implied, "so there."

Anna was always happy to be needed, and she trotted off to Genevieve's room feeling needed and in the midst of things.

She rapped softly on the bedroom door and heard a very soft and faint "come in."

Genevieve looked so pathetic sitting there in the middle of her great big bed. Anna walked over to the bed and sat down quietly, all the while her eyes never left the young girl's face.

Without any hesitation whatsoever Genevieve threw herself into the older woman's arms and began to cry. The tears in her eyes flowed swiftly, making rivulets upon her young cheeks. "I'm sorry; oh, I'm so sorry. I should never have spoken to you like that."

Anna's eyes were also misting up, but she did not want to show it. She was a very private person.

"Correct," she told Genevieve. "You should not talk to me like that, nor should you talk to anyone else like that either. Humph!"

Genevieve looked at the older woman. "I love you."

Anna was taken completely by surprise. "Wha–wha–what did you say?"

"I said," and she spoke up louder than before, "I said I love you."

The woman put her chubby arms about Genevieve and she began to cry out loud. Then she took out her handkerchief and began to dab at her deep brown eyes and said, "I never thought that I would hear you say that to me."

"Why not?"

"Well, you had such a wonderful Maman and such a lovely Grand-mère, I never thought that you could love an old biddie like me. I am just an old farm girl."

Genevieve looked at Anna severely and told her, "Now you stop that. Why Grand-père and you are the two people that I love most on this earth, and don't you forget it either!"

Anna sat there with the child for a long time, cradling her and holding her to her bosom. At that moment a bond of love was forged between the woman and child and it was to endure.

"Come now, we must not dawdle. You must get yourself cleaned up before the doctor gets here. He should be here at any moment now."

"Did Grand-père tell you about what happened?" Genevieve asked, still not moving off the bed.

"Yes, he did," said Anna, trying to be more stern than she really was. "He did and you see what happens when you keep secrets from us? You cause yourself much trouble and many heartaches. I pray that you will not do this again!"

After Genevieve was all cleaned up and ready to see the doctor, Anna left the room and closed the door. A short moment later the door opened slightly.

"Genevieve," she spoke in a voice that seemed foreign for her.
"Yes?"
She cleared her throat. "I love you, too!"
Just then the doctor came in to see "Mademoiselle Genevieve."

Both ladies had their worlds shaken that day, and neither one would ever forget it. Real love often escapes even the most gentle of spirits, like the twinkling stars overhead that lose their luster in the morning.

Dr. Livernois was a large man who took you by shock when he entered a room. He was a loud and boisterous man, but he never could be classified as obnoxious. No doubt about it, though, you always knew when he was around.

His feet were so large that his shoes had to be specially made, his hands were so large that they looked like great big hams, yet everyone in town spoke of his gentle touch.

His smile was real and genuine. It was said of him that if everyone that owed him money paid him all at once he would be a millionaire. Sad to say he barely made ends meet, but in his own way he was content.

He was so different from Alexandre, but there was something about him that appealed to Alexandre and they became great friends and great competitors in the game of chess. They were seen many a time riding together in the early morning. He was not hesitant to inform Alexandre if someone had a real need. So together they were known as the "Good Samaritans." Neither one ever hesitated to perform an act of benevolence.

"There's nothing wrong with the girl," he boomed as he entered the kitchen where Alexandre was sitting. "Nature will take her course and have her own way. Nothing we can do about it either."

Anna came to the table and brought two big mugs of steaming coffee, which the men gratefully accepted. She busied herself about the kitchen silently. She always kept her distance from the doctor. He was forever asking her to marry him and she could never figure out if he was teasing her or not.

They would have made a comical couple indeed, as she only reached his elbow. He was well over six feet tall, and she barely five feet tall. She was as round and jellylike as he was tall and muscular.

On his part the good doctor was not fooling; he would have married Anna in a moment had she agreed. He felt that because of one bad experience she hated all men.

"Anna," he spoke with authority, "come here and join us as we need to speak to you concerning Genevieve."

When Anna heard this she did not hesitate for even a moment. She poured herself a mug of coffee also and came over to the table and sat next to Alexandre, as always keeping her distance from the doctor.

"What is it? What is wrong?" she sat there wiping her hands on her apron.

"Don't fret so!" His voice boomed out even when he did not want or expect it to. "I didn't want to be so blunt, sometimes I think I scare her."

He tried to keep his voice under control now, and as he did, his voice tended to squeak.

"What we need, my dear Anna, is a woman to teach her the facts of life. Only another woman can understand what she is going through. Would you do this for us?"

Anna got herself all tensed up and began wringing her hands even more than before. "Please do not ask such a thing from me, as I am so confused myself. All my Maman ever did to the girls in my family was to scare us with many old wives' tales."

Alexandre turned to the doctor and asked him, "What are we to do then?"

"Don't fret." Again his voice boomed louder than he wanted it to. "If you are agreeable, I feel that I have the perfect solution.

"I know a young minister right here in town, and he has a lovely wife and three nice kids, too. If you are agreeable perhaps we can solve your problem and help them a bit, too."

Alexandre appeared a little flustered now. "What do we need a minister for when we have our own priest?"

The doctor threw his head back and began to laugh until tears ran down his cheeks.

Alexandre was plainly irritated now. "I fail to see what is so funny!"

The doctor was trying to stop his laughing now. "Oh yes, Alexandre, I can see it all now. Poor little Genevieve sitting there as quiet as a mouse while old stone face, *Le Pere Marchand*, tells her the facts of life." He began laughing all over again.

"I agree with you on that point. Please continue."

The doctor turned and looked directly into Alexandre's eyes and asked him point-blank, "Are you ready to listen?" Then he cleared his throat several times. "As I said before there is a young minister in town, he is here trying to start a new church. So far things have not gone well for him. He is a hard worker and takes any job offered to him, but they are few and far between. Their young daughter has just 'become a young lady' and I tell you, it was beautiful to see."

"What makes you think that they would help us?" Alexandre's ears had perked up.

"Well," the doctor drawled out as he slumped down in his chair and crossed one of his long legs over the top of the knee of the other, "it's like this; I have been telling you for a long time that you need young people around here for Genevieve to associate with. These folk also need someone for their children to associate with. They have three children, a boy, Harold, sixteen, and a thirteen-year-old girl named Karie-May, and a boy of about six or seven called Zachariah. They're good kids.

"They live in a, yes, literally a shack in the downtown area. He has been trying to fix the place up, but with no work and with no material it is a slow and difficult process indeed."

"Doctor," Alexandre spoke thoughtfully, weighing every word, "how can we help them? With money?"

"No! No! They are much too proud to just accept money. Didn't you tell me that you are looking for a reliable handyman around here, and a kid to come in on Saturdays?"

"Yes, I did," said Alexandre. "Can you arrange this for us?" he asked.

The doctor inclined his head and told him, "I will speak to Stephanie about speaking to Genevieve, but the rest is up to you."

Dr. Livernois turned toward Anna and asked her, "Do I have the liberty of inviting them over for one of your good suppers?"

She did not speak but nodded her head in assent.

"Heaven knows they could all do with a good meal under their belts!"

"Speaking of meals," Anna said abruptly, "we have soup and hot biscuits waiting for us; what are we waiting for? Someone go get Genevieve. Alexandre, you must go and buy some groceries if we are having company. Let's eat. I have a lot of work to do! Hurry!"

Chapter Twenty-seven
New Friends

As you approached the house you could actually smell celebration in the air. Anna had really outdone herself.

Alexandre had gone to the market and bought the groceries, all that he could find. Anna had also given him a list, at least as long as his arm, of other things that they absolutely must have.

Alexandre took it all in his stride. He did not mind the extravagance, and they certainly were not hurting for money. He thought to himself, *We have more money than I can ever use in one lifetime, or Genevieve or her children to come, either.*

He chuckled to himself. *That's what comes from marrying the right woman. The good Lord knows that I was not smart enough to make all that money.* Again he chuckled to himself. *Imagine,* he thought, *that little woman and her needle and thread, and all we have given away, and we still have so much. I know, Simone, if you were here you would say "God is so good to us."*

The market was not crowded and he enjoyed looking for "bargains." It was an old habit that he could not get rid of.

When he arrived back at the house he had to make several trips back and forth with all the groceries he had purchased.

Anna was waiting very impatiently for him. "Did you get everything I told you to get?"

"Yes, Madam," and he bowed to her with his hand across his stomach. "Yes Madam, you know that your every wish is my command."

"Very well then, I command you to get busy and peel the turnips and to stop fooling around. Get busy sir, just as this young lady is busy. Now!"

"*Oui, oui, mon Capitaine,*" and he saluted her smartly.

"You won't act so smart if our company gets here and we are not prepared for them. Now, we all have work to do."

Genevieve looked up at her grandfather and said, "What do you think of the cake I made?"

"I think that it is lovely, it will be the perfect dessert for our guests."

The guests arrived exactly on time, and they proved to be as delightful as the doctor had made them out to be. The father was tall and lanky with very red hair that had been imparted to all of his children. He did not look like Alexandre's mental picture of what a minister should look like at all.

His wife was a dainty, petite and very pleasant blonde. The daughter, whose name was Karie, could only be described as a sweet girl, considering that she was a teenager. The youngest child was about seven years old and immediately touched Alexandre's heart.

For some reason that Alexandre could not name he reminded him of his own little brother who had died at the age of three in the flu epidemic, along with the baby Charles, over seventy years ago.

Alexandre looked at the lad with the badly deformed legs and thought, *Surely something must be able to be done for this lad.*

Everyone was uncomfortable at first, rather strained really. Anna knew that with a good meal in the belly things would improve. "Come, come, let's go and eat and we can observe the formalities later. Heaven only knows that they all look like they can use a good meal."

The tall red-headed man spoke up, saying, "My name is Harold and this is my wife Stephanie, my son Junior, my daughter Karie-May, and Zachariah."

Alexandre went up to Stephanie and offered her his arm. "Allow me to escort you into the dining room."

She smiled at him and graciously accepted the arm he offered her, and they looked elegant walking into the dining room, as if they were at a formal ball.

Stephanie was happy to have his arm to lean on as she and Harold had not eaten in several days. They had not told anyone that they had no food but had kept on trusting in the Lord and as always, thought Stephanie, *He has come through!* She had told the children to eat slowly and she and Harold knew enough to do the same.

Stephanie thought she was about to pass out when she saw all the good food on the table, and she found it very difficult to stifle the impulse to gulp food down.

Harold had picked up his younger son Zachariah in his arms to carry him into the dining room. He busied himself looking around. "Look, Dad! They have a piano! Please may I go in and see it, oh, please?"

"Perhaps after supper, son."

They sat at the table and no one spoke a word until they had bowed their heads and prayed, then Alexandre looked at Zachariah. "So, you like the piano, do you?"

"Yes, sir, I do."

"Perhaps," Alexandre said, "when we finish dining you would be kind enough to play us a little tune?"

Zachariah's little face became so sad. "I can't, because I don't know how to play."

"Genevieve plays beautifully," he said with pride. "Would you like her to play for you afterwards?"

He turned and looked at Genevieve. "Wow! Would you play for me? Really?"

Genevieve hated it when her grandfather made her do things like this, but she would never refuse him. "Of course I will, if Grand-père will sing while I play." She smiled and thought to herself, *Gotcha!*

Alexandre looked this family over with his keen eye and liked what he saw. "You are a minister?"

"Yes, I am. My family and I have come here to do what we call pioneer work."

"Pioneer work. I have never heard of such a thing."

"Well," Harold cleared his throat, "all that really means is that we are trying to start a new church in the area."

"But isn't everyone around here Catholic?"

Harold laughed. "It certainly seems that way."

Alexandre found himself liking this man and his family, but he was curious. "May I ask you a question?"

"Yes, you can."

The children were eating everything in sight and it thrilled Anna that all of her labor had not been in vain.

Harold Junior had been looking at Genevieve and he thought, *She is positively beautiful, and she may not know it yet, but someday I'm gonna marry that girl!*

Alexandre looked thoughtful for a moment, almost as if he dared not ask the question that he had in his mind. "Why do you want to take people away from the religion they have known all their lives and change them?"

"That is an excellent question, Mr. Boisvert, but the thing is, we are not trying to change anyone from their religion; we are trying to get them into a personal knowledge and into a personal walk with the Lord Jesus Christ."

"I have a favor to ask of you."

"If I am able, I will do to the best of my ability."

"I thought that your being a minister might bring you into contact with more people than I meet, being retired and all, and I need help around here."

Alexandre was being slow and deliberate in his speaking as he was watching the reactions of all of them. He noticed that Junior had almost fallen out of his seat when he heard his words.

Zachariah spoke up bluntly. "Dad and Junior are looking for a job, right, Dad?"

The elder Harold's face turned redder than his hair as he blushed. He did not know what to say.

Alexandre picked up on Zachariah's statement and asked, "What kind of work are you gentlemen interested in?"

Harold Junior spoke up quickly. "Anything, anything we can get, sir, anything at all, that is. Me and my Dad are good workers!"

"Well, let me tell you what I need. First of all I need an overseer, you know, to look after the whole place, mending fences and so forth, someone to manage the other workers. I want to get a couple of cows and some chickens and ducks and maybe even a few turkeys. Not for commercial purposes but for our own use. I also want to get a few more horses for riding as I promised my granddaughter that I would get her a horse of her very own. I am getting along in years and cannot do as much as I used to do in years past.

"We will also need someone to help Anna at times, with the heavy work and canning and whatever else that women do."

Stephanie looked at Genevieve. "I think that perhaps we should go and have our discussion now. Karie-May, you stay and help with the dishes like a good girl."

Stephanie looked at Alexandre and asked, "May we be excused?"

"Yes, most certainly."

"You gentlemen can carry on with your talk about business."

Alexandre looked at the three menfolk and said, "The job does not pay a large sum, but your rent is free and your lights and heat also, plus a telephone and a small allowance for long distance calls."

"Rent?" Harold said in disbelief.

"How foolish I am. Come, I will show you the place, that is, if you think that you would care to?"

"Definitely. I certainly would."

"If you like it, you can bring your wife out here later."

Alexandre went over and picked little Zachariah up into his arms and carried him over to the piano. "Play away old man, to your heart's content."

The little house had five rooms in it and a bath and a half; everything had been done to make it liveable. "It has never been lived in," Alexandre told him, "and it is a shame to let it go to waste."

Tears began to roll down Harold's cheeks, and he began to sniffle. Alexandre turned and looked at Junior and found him in the same state.

"Have I done or said something wrong, perhaps to offend you?"

Harold shook his head and tried to speak. "Mr. Boisvert, when the call came that you wanted someone to talk to your granddaughter, my wife and I were just about to turn back in desperation. Until tonight Stephanie and I have not really had anything to eat for two days. All we had for the children was some old potatoes that we cut the rot out of. The grocer would not trust us for one cent.

"We decided to wait until tomorrow to leave, because we felt that we would travel better if we had a meal tonight. We have been living out of doors, and it is getting into cold weather now, too. The only clothes we have are those we have on our backs. We have not slept in a bed for over three months now, and I cannot remember the last time we had a bath except for going into the lake. I don't know what to say, I am overwhelmed!"

Alexandre walked over to the cupboard, opened a drawer and took out some keys, and handed them to Harold. "Tonight," he said, "you shall all sleep in beds. Tomorrow we shall get better acquainted and I will show you around and show you all your duties. It will be so good for Genevieve to have some young people around here."

Stephanie was sitting in the living room chatting with Anna while Genevieve played the piano for Karie and Zachariah.

"Play something else, please? Please! It's so beautiful. Pulease?"

Harold Junior came bounding in. "Guess what, Ma? We got a new home, and we all have jobs."

"Me, too?" Zachariah spoke up. "Me, too?"

Alexandre quickly spoke up and pretended to be gruff. "Yes, young man, you too have a job. Perhaps it is the most difficult of all!"

Zachariah stared wide-eyed. "Will I get paid?"

"Zach . . ." Harold Senior began.

"Yes, you will get paid, but only if you earn it!"

"What is it? What do I have to do?"

"You," Alexandre spoke gruffly, "you must take piano lessons from me! I am a hard taskmaster, too!"

Genevieve had a smile on her face and shook her head in agreement with her grandfather.

"Well," said Zachariah, "I thought if one took piano lessons, he had to pay the teacher."

"Not always. I want to sharpen up my skills, and besides, that is not all you will have to do either!"

"What else do I gotta do?"

"Well, let me tell you! You will have to escort me and help me when Anna gives me a list as long as my arm to purchase. I can no longer do it alone, I need help! Well," Alexandre looked into the young boy's face, "will you help me or not?"

"I will; I will!"

"We have a gentlemen's agreement. Let us shake hands on it to seal the bargain."

Zachariah, with all the seriousness of a much older man, struck a bargain that day that he upheld for the rest of his short life.

These two families had formed a bond that would endure the sands of time. They all worked above and beyond the call of duty for this man who had dealt with them so kindly.

Junior watched over Genevieve like a mother hen. All of them had a special bond with Zachariah, and his happiest moments were beside the old gentleman at the piano.

"Listen, Ma; listen, Anna; I can make such pretty sounds, too." When he became too weak to be brought to the big house, Alexandre, with tears in his eyes and a heavy heart, bought him an instrument of his own.

One day as he and Alexandre were together he asked him, "Grandpère, do you think that there is music in heaven?"

Alexandre, all choked up, answered, "I believe that there is the most beautiful music that ears will ever hear in heaven."

"Do you think that Jesus will let me play music for him?"

"I think that you will be the leader of the band."

When the time came for the end of his life he asked for Alexandre. "Will you play the piano for me? Cause I won't be scared if I hear beautiful music."

Alexandre sat and played for the several days that it took for his little life to ebb away. He played mostly songs of joy that the youth loved so much.

When he saw his little friend laid in his coffin the old man cried unashamedly. Harold and Stephanie both put their arms around him in comfort.

Alexandre looked at both. "Can I play for him at the wake and the funeral?"

"We wanted to ask you, but we felt that it was an imposition."

"I want to do it."

It turned out to be his swan song as he lost all interest in playing the piano after that, even though he always loved to hear Genevieve play.

Chapter Twenty-eight
Years Later

The elderly gentleman sat quietly in the parlor, an old sweater vainly attempting to keep him warm. Just a glance would show that the garment was a failure. The old man seemed to be shivering, and the cold that shook him was not the one that is normal.

This was a coldness from deep within. His hands resting upon his cane made one think of the rings in a tree that tell the story of the tree's very life. Gnarled and twisted, it is certain that they had many a tale to tell. One could see by his appearance that at one time he had turned many a girlish head in his direction. His eyes were the most interesting aspect of the timeworn old face. They gave forth the appearance of being able to look within the very soul; the acute depth and penetration was beyond a logical description.

He was peering deeply into the old fireplace, but not really seeing the flames licking at the wood burning within. His thoughts were beyond the realm of the commonplace activity, his head hung to one side almost as if it took more strength than he possessed to keep it erect, as he once had so much pride in doing. If one were to enter the room, it would be thought that he was asleep. For a very long time not one movement could be observed, and if it were not for those eyes, one would perhaps have considered him expired.

"Are you sleeping, Grand-père?" All of a sudden the old man and the old granite face broke into a smile that could have been created only in heaven. The voice was that of Genevieve, now a young woman perhaps in her mid-twenties. Neat and attractive, well poised and of an erect stature that seemed unusual in this day and age. Although roughly attired in the ever so popular blue jeans, she gave forth the appearance of elegance. Her hair was of a chestnut color, such as that which is the normal coloring of the royal Morgan horses. Her eyes sparkled as though the gleam had been permanently set within them or perhaps someone had dared to pilfer one of the stars. They were of such a dark color that often she had been told that they were black. She really was not that tall, perhaps five foot four or so, but her poise gave her the appearance of being much taller than she really was. With only one glance, the observation was that here is a woman that is satisfied with herself totally, and that she, being satisfied with herself, was comfortable with herself and thus was very adept at accepting others as they were, and being satisfied with them.

"No," he said weakly, "I am not asleep; I am just an old man indulging himself with all my memories of the past." He reached forth and patted her hand with as much strength as he could muster and she bent herself forward and planted a tender kiss on his forehead, and gave him a soft pat on his right shoulder.

He did not respond as much as he normally would have, his thoughts were beyond the simple everyday scene of grandfather and beloved granddaughter. His thoughts were of the story of his life.

"Now tell me," she said, somehow feeling that this would not be one of their ordinary conversations, "what does a gentleman have to think about on a beautiful day such as this, sitting beside his hearth, with all the comforts of a great English mansion?"

He sensed the light tone of her voice. Haltingly he began to speak. "Always it was not so for me. I was born in Canada, and my mother took my brothers and me to the United States when I was just a boy."

A feeling of foreboding shook her, and quietly she kneeled beside his chair. "Grand-père," she said, "never once have you told me why we came here to this farm. You would always tell me not to think about the past, and to live our lives the best we knew how. Now I am a grown woman, and I would like to know."

"Today," he said, as he stared intently into her eyes, "I will tell you all that you want to know."

Involuntarily, she began to shiver and a terrible feeling of foreboding or tragedy came upon her and the same feeling of coldness came upon her that had lain upon the old man.

"Perhaps while I collect my thoughts you will bring me a glass of water to wet my throat a bit."

"Anything you desire," she said, "I will do for you." One knew as she spoke that these were not words spoken idly. She moved silently and swiftly to meet his needs. When she left the room he seemed to slump back into old age. His concentration was such that he was startled when she returned once again into the room.

"I apologize." She spoke tenderly. "I did not mean to startle you." He raised his hand in a gesture to convey the needlessness of her apology. She looked upon his face and saw that tears were flowing freely upon his worn and tired old cheeks. "Tell me, what is it? Are you in pain?" she asked with a concern of rarity.

"Yes, my little one, I am in deep pain, but not the type that you think; I am in pain that comes from deep within the soul." She silently sat upon the floor and leaned her head most gently upon his knee.

The moments passed and she thought that perhaps he had fallen once more into one of the deep sleeps that seem to accompany the aged. Slowly and haltingly he began to speak. "I miss so many things that I once held dear. Today, I would even like to see that rogue of a son of mine, Samuel. I don't suppose he's changed much. . . ." His voice trailed on, and she was tempted to question him, but her natural instinct toward this man was to remain silent and let him continue at his own pace, so she relaxed herself totally. She glanced up and saw that he had fallen asleep for a bit.

Poor Grand-père, she thought, *he certainly has given up so much for me. I really never thought that he would miss those vague characters that made up our whole family. Perhaps for his birthday next month, I should try and see if I can get in touch with some of them.* "What do I really remember about my background?" she wondered half-aloud. A smile played softly upon her lips in remembrance of some vague memory.

"Ah, I have forsaken you for a bit, but I did not forget what I said to you. Soon I will be ninety-two years; for anybody that is a long time. The bible tells the story of many that lived much longer, but for me ninety-two years accomplished is a long time. It is time enough to live, to laugh, and to die." He smiled. "You must forgive an old man who rambles on and adds his philosophy along with his tale, but, my dear, such are the ways of an old man."

She began to laugh gently. "I will remember that thought when I too become somewhat advanced in years."

Genevieve looked about her, not really seeing her surroundings, but in a sense they were such a part of her totality that she could not avoid being aware of them. *This is his room*, she thought, *so much reflecting him as he is or, rather, what he was.* Sturdy, yes, dependable, relaxing, comfortable, the room allowed one to be oneself. The room was square in shape, all of the walls were paneled in knotty pine, the floors were solid, of a strong oak; strewn about in a casual manner were several braided rugs of orange and brown tones. The fireplace was a magnificent work of art that had been designed and built by the old man himself.

He had personally overseen each detail of its structure. The fireplace encompassed one whole wall of the room. It was constructed of brick, some in a horizontal position and some in a vertical position, all patterned in the beauty of absolute, simple geometrical design. On the outer portions of this, designs were formed of various sizes and sorts of multicolored fieldstone. A floor space possibly as large as the average room was set in front of the fireplace, all laid in with fieldstone. The furnishings were more in the realm of comfort than of beauty. Sturdy sofas and chairs with leather upholstery were strewn about in an atmosphere of comfort and relaxation.

On the walls were a few tapestries with a horsey type of motif, some watercolors done by Genevieve herself, and her high school graduation picture, which the old man had so proudly hung there.

Over the fireplace hung a magnificent painting of the old man, which showed him in the light of strength and of power; the kind of power that shows through a self-made man, a man who was satisfied with the accomplishments of his days here on the earth. This was not a formal portrait, but one that showed him as he truly was, a man like any other man and yet unlike any other, as he was of special design.

The overall appraisal of this room would be "a place where there is a lack of clutter." *How like him*, she thought, *he never filled his mind with the clutter or garbage of the day, which ran so rampant in this day and age.*

She was especially fond of the large sliding doors that opened up into their backyard. Each season, as it came forth into birth and later on into fruition, showed forth in its best wardrobe, its shining eminence or shabby degradation, without any restraint.

I hope that I will be able to live here all of my life, she thought, *for truly without any doubt this is my home.*

The room had become somewhat chilly, and Genevieve stood up and walked over to the fireplace and put a couple more logs on the fire. When she turned to look at her grandfather she saw that his cheeks were wet with tears. She realized that he had many painful memories of his own, buried deep down inside of him, in a place where not many had been invited to share, a refuge of his own making.

Strange, she thought to herself, *all of these years I looked upon this man as just merely Grand-père, not really a person, but someone put on this earth to be content to be Grand-père. Now I find that he is a person in his own right, not just one of my possessions. He has memories and dreams that have not contained me in them. Hopes, plans, desires and ambitions, all of which, I have no part in.*

"Grand-père," she said tenderly, "I love you," and very tenderly she wiped his tear-ridden cheeks.

"You do not have to tell me that, my little one; all of your actions tell me every day."

"I wanted to tell you," she said almost shyly, like a young schoolgirl. "Grand-père, there is something I wish to tell you."

"Are you getting sentimental on me, Miss?" he asked, showing some of his old spark, and a very definite twinkle in his eyes.

"Is this not the day that we set apart to be sentimental and even maudlin if we desire?"

"You are right, of course; forgive an old man's very poor joke."

"Grand-père," she said, scolding him gently, "are you not the one who always says that too many apologies are like too much sweetbread?"

The old man laughed. "I have lived too long; my very own words are coming back to haunt me."

The warmth of the extra logs on the fire was filling the room, forming a cozy background for reminiscing or just lazily lounging around.

Genevieve sat in a very pensive mood for a few moments. "I was thinking about Mom and Dad," she said.

The old man turned and inclined his head toward her, as though he were afraid to miss one of her words or perhaps miss some of the context of her statement.

"I find it so strange, Grand-père, that there were two people that lived upon the face of this earth, fell in love, married and had a child, that child being me, and what do I know about them? My parents are total strangers to me.

"I do remember a few vague things about them, like how Mom was so pretty, and how she always smelled so good. Dad was a serious person and I feel that he was a well-educated man. What do you know about your parents, little girl? Oh, I know all about my parents: Mom smelled good and Dad read a lot."

The old man said to her, "I am afraid that you are allowing yourself to feel sorry for yourself."

"You are right," she answered him. "I should be ashamed of myself."

"To want or wish for something that cannot be," he said, "is nothing to be ashamed of, it is just useless to do so."

"You, my dear grandfather, as usual, are right."

"I understand what you are going through. Many times I wished for my life to be different, too. I wanted a father like all the other boys. I dreamed many times that my father would come running back to us and tell us that he was sorry, and buy Maman some beautiful clothes and give me all the ice cream that I could eat, but it was a useless dream that wasted time.

"I think that I will rest for a little bit," he told her. "I am afraid that the old bones are somewhat weary." He chuckled. "I know that you will excuse me for a bit."

"Of course, Grand-père," she replied. "Shall I help you?"

"I believe that I can manage," he told her, in his somewhat weary voice, "but your company would be appreciated."

Genevieve was careful not to be too helpful. She realized that he was afraid to fall, if left on his own. She wanted to leave his pride intact as long as it was possible.

He stood up very carefully and slowly, leaning heavily upon his cane. When he had gained a degree of steadiness, he offered her his arm, which she promptly took, and this helped to steady him a little more.

It was only a very short distance to his bedroom but it seemed to take forever to get there.

The old man was working very hard to keep himself going, and when finally he made it to the bed, he sat wearily and heaved a long sigh of relief.

"Can I get you anything?" she asked him, much as one would speak to a child that one was indulging.

"No, but I would like you to sit with me if you have the time."

"Of course, you know that I will."

She turned and walked to the corner of the room and picked up a chair, and when she turned, he was already in a deep sleep.

"I wonder," she sighed, "if I should leave and let him sleep. I think I'll stay, as I told him that I would."

I wonder why I feel so tired and worn out today. She began rubbing her stomach gently. *I can hardly wait to tell Grand-père the good news, but I promised Harold I would wait until he returned from his conferences, and then we would tell Grand-père together.*

S'funny, she thought, *even ministers have business meetings. I never thought of religion being a business. Oh well, I have other things to think about.* But her mind kept rambling on in pell-mell fashion. *I wonder if it is allowable to preach when you're pregnant. Harold,* she giggled to herself. *I still think it is a funny name. I wonder what he would say if I told him that? Oh dear, suppose we have a son and he wants to name him Harold, what then? One thing I know for sure, my daughter will never be named Genevieve!*

What a funny mood we both are in today, I wonder why?

Even if I didn't know Grand-père, she thought, *this room would definitely be a portrait of him.* It was simply furnished, in all aspects a bed chamber, with a large old-fashioned bed, with no bedspread ever upon it. He liked the old-fashioned homemade quilts. Everything was sturdy, as though once he had furnished it he did not want to be bothered to do it again. He told her many times to do things properly the first time, as repetition was time-consuming and often futile. If something was to be done and was done right, there was no need to think that you could do it better the second time around.

She had often teased him, asking him if he had measured and marked off the exact spot where his hair brush and comb were placed, for she had never found any variance in their position.

Alexandre was lying upon his big bed, covered with an old quilt which still had much use left in it, perhaps even more use than was left in the old man himself. His old hands were folded and resting upon his feeble breast as though he were in position for his interment.

Genevieve shuddered involuntarily. *I wish that I were an artist,* she thought. *I wish I could paint him exactly as he was. I mean is!*

He was the picture of life personified: his white head portraying the great snow-capped mountains, the very peak itself; his tall stature an image of the mighty elm; and his strength that of the mustang that never loses its sense of adventure or its taste for freedom. His skin was brown-toned, never losing its perpetual tan, giving his skin leathery tones. His wrinkled brow spoke out in boldness, acknowledging the wisdom deep within. His skin had loosened a lot and hung loosely upon his wiry frame as though he were a young boy wearing his elder brother's garments. His cheeks were, perhaps, his most prominent features, looking as though he were carrying walnuts or acorns in them. The flesh hung tiredly over his ears, as though exhausted from its lifelong endeavors. His dimples were as deep as well waters, a sign of youth clinging yet upon the ancient.

He had fought a long battle. Put up a good fight, too! He was the mighty warrior! The mighty centurion! He was also the big puppy dog sitting contentedly at the master's feet. His hands did not belie the fact of their once powerful strength. Gently as the breeze of the summer they lay upon his breast, now shrunken and shallow as a flag flown at half-mast. His arms, once rods of iron, were now willowy as lace, and his legs, once solid as oaks, had become softened and did not serve him for much purpose any longer. He had become softened much in the same manner as the porridge that he ate so often lately.

He was a contradiction of himself, an elder babe, so to speak. His stomach and his thighs were almost nonexistent now, and his neatly pressed trousers hung from his hips as though his hips were coat hangers. His feet were large and almost seemed to belie the frailty of his body; great ships which had once carried him through the pathways of life. The voyage from port to port seemed now almost an absurdity of contradiction.

Chapter Twenty-nine
Regrets

She turned and looked towards his dresser, and there in the most prominent place of all was a photograph of Grand-mère just after her first son was born. Her face was all aglow with the joy of living. Her dress was a dark brown color, and the collar of it went right up to her chin. The collar was trimmed with a row of small ecru-colored lace, and of course her sleeves were long, right down to her wrists. The colors blended perfectly with her own natural coloring and seemed to bring out the golden highlights in her hair. The eyes were of the type of blue that is seen in a hot summer sky, pale yet explicitly prominent, the kind of day where the clouds move rather swiftly, so as not to dim the horizon. She had very prominent cheekbones, and her nose was not a striking part of her face, not overly large nor too small, just a nose that blended in perfect harmony with all the other features of her face. The same could be said of her chin, nothing unusual, it just belonged. Her hair was soft, framing her face almost in a cloud of tender expression. Dimples decorated her cheeks, giving a clue to the humor therein contained.

Yes, she told herself, *I can understand why Grand-père could fall in love with her. They definitely made a good pair.*

Genevieve had been so deep in thought that when the old man spoke to her she jumped, thinking he was still asleep.

"Wh–what did you say?" she asked him.

"I simply said you are woolgathering again; I did not intend to startle you so."

"I know you didn't. I was looking at the picture of Grand-mère and thinking that I could really understand how you could fall in love with her."

"Did I ever tell you how I met your grandmother?"

"No," she answered with a smile upon her lips, "is this the time?"

"If you would like to hear, I will tell you, but I do not want to bore you with the rambling on of a very old man."

"Grand-père, you have never been boring to me; why should things change now?"

He gently patted her hand and said, "You are much too kind and indulgent to me."

"Never," she replied, "can I equal what you have done for me."

"Today," he smiled that thin smile of his, "we are forming a mutual admiration society."

"I love it," she told him with a big smile on her face. "Let's keep the membership to just you and me."

"A closed society," he replied.

"Absolutely," she replied, "you and I blood brothers!" And they both laughed at their secret joke.

Just then the housekeeper, Anna, came in with a tray containing tea and cookies. She had not changed much over the years, and still tended to be rather portly, and just as Genevieve had observed when meeting her for the first time, she tended to be overly jovial.

"Tea time, tea time." She actually sang it out in her rather high-pitched voice. "Tea time."

"Madame La Barge," he answered her in a voice of exasperation. "Our ears are in fine condition, and we are capable of hearing you the first time! I will take my tea, as will my granddaughter, in the parlor. I am not that feeble yet."

Anna turned and walked away with the tray and headed for the parlor. Her pretense of being annoyed was an act for the old man's benefit.

Genevieve knew that Anna loved her grandfather deeply and that there was nothing that she wouldn't do for him. They had always had a relationship of seemingly being annoyed with one another, but in all truth they respected one another, and probably would not know what to do without one another. Her grandfather had long ago made Genevieve promise to take care of Anna if anything ever happened to him. He had always maintained a respectful, cordial and polite relationship with Anna.

"Something is funny, Miss," said Anna. She recognized this tone from her growing up days, the days when all girls giggle unceremoniously at everything. "Please enlighten us so we may laugh also."

"I have taken you by surprise, ladies. It is good to know that I am not totally over the hill yet," said Alexandre, obviously relishing the moment. "Come, come Anna," he deliberately drew out the name, "let us give thanks together and drink this tea before it gets cold."

Genevieve and Anna bowed their heads slowly, as they were stunned by his use of her name. The old man saw their reactions and relished his little joke all the more. He could not wait for his grandson (Genevieve's husband) to come home, as he felt he had a good one to tell him.

While the old man had always spoken in formal tones to his housekeeper, she was far from being their servant; she was a total member of the family in all ways, and he personally saw to it that she lacked nothing.

"I have been doing much reminiscing today, for some reason, and so has Genevieve. I know that my mental wanderings are due to my advanced years, but for my granddaughter there must be another reason; perhaps she is pregnant, eh?"

Genevieve's mouth flew open in disbelief. *How could he know such a thing? We have told no one except for the doctor.*

The old man looked at his housekeeper with one of his triumphant looks. "Genevieve is not as good at keeping secrets as she thinks she is." He laughed till tears rolled down his cheeks.

"You notice, Anna," he was using that familiar tone once again, "my granddaughter does not offer denials."

"No, and I shall not deceive you. What you say is true. I cannot understand how you have found out, as we have told no one."

"You see, my dear," he told her lovingly, "how the experience of being aged is very useful. A lifetime of observation and living make for a keen insight into human nature. Besides that I know you so well."

"Grand-père, I have never been able to keep a secret from you yet. Harold will be so disappointed, as we had planned to tell you together."

"I know that you and Harold will do a better job of raising your child than I did with my children."

"Oh, Grand-père, you are much too hard on yourself," she told him.

"Am I really?" he asked, but not really asking her, speaking mostly to himself. "Am I really?" he repeated softly. "When your grand-mère and I had our children we decided that our children would not have to suffer and toil like we had to do. Our life was one struggle after another. We decided that we would never discipline our children and that we would give them anything in our power to give them."

"You and Grand-mère sure never hesitated to discipline me," she said, almost with the attitude of a petulant child.

"That is because by then we had learned the error of our ways." He told her this with more than a tinge of sadness in his quavering old voice.

Hesitatingly, with unaccustomed hesitancy in his voice, the old man began to speak. As he spoke Genevieve realized that he was really not present with her, he was in another time and place, one that she had never been part of.

"When I was a young man, I used to dream about doing something special for my Maman. She had been through so much for me and had suffered so many tragedies. When she was a young girl, Maman had a sister that she loved above all the others in her family. Her name was Olivia. When Olivia was born Maman had the complete responsibility of caring for her baby sister. This was the only person who had ever loved Maman until we children came along. Through the years they stayed in touch with one another through correspondence. Maman could not read or write, and neither could Ma Tante (Aunt) Olivia, but they made certain that their children learned to.

"Unbeknownst to Maman, I found some extra work and saved the money, then I made reservations on the train and took Maman to see her sister. By then they had not seen one another for almost twenty years.

"I had never seen Maman so excited before, nor did I ever see her that excited again. We had not told Olivia that we were coming, as we wanted to surprise her, and we did!

"She was standing outside, hanging clothes on an old worn-out clothesline, and it appeared that there must have been about twenty children about. She was a heavyset woman, but not overly so. Anna here is very much like her Maman was."

"What did you say?" asked Genevieve.

"Am I speaking so softly that you cannot hear me?" he asked her.

"But, but," she managed to sputter out, "that means that you and Anna are cousins." *That explains a lot*, she thought.

Seemingly annoyed, he replied, "Elementary, my dear, if two sisters have children these offspring are therefore cousins."

It never occurred to me, she thought. *That then is the answer.*

"Shall I continue on?" he asked, using a tone of formality with her.

"Oh please, yes, yes," she replied, anxious lest she offend him and that he might not continue on. Genevieve realized that she was ravenous, not for food but for the knowledge of her ancestry.

"Maman stood in the hot summer sun, totally speechless. I saw her mouth move, but no words or sounds came out. We were sweaty and dusty from our long journey, and not a pretty sight at all to behold.

" 'You stay here, Maman,' I told her, and I walked over to the lady hanging clothes. 'Excuse me, but are you Olivia La Barge?'

" '*Oui*,' she replied hesitantly. 'I am, but what concerns you about that?'

"I was somewhat taken aback by her attitude, and I thought to myself, *What if she does not want us here?*

"I tried to speak again but my voice failed me, but lo and behold just at that moment Maman spoke up, 'Olivia?'

"The lady at the clothesline turned quickly and looked up, and then, I swear to you that it was in one leap, she hung on Maman's neck.

" 'Elisabeth! Elisabeth!' She made the sign of the cross upon herself. 'Is it really you? I must pinch myself, for I think I must be dreaming! Oh, Elisabeth! Elisabeth, this is the miracle that we have prayed for all these years! Dear God up in heaven. Thank you, thank you!' By now both ladies' cheeks were wet with many tears.

"Ah yes," he said, only half-aloud, "I remember it well. Indeed I remember it so well.

"I stood there off to the side watching the scene before me. All of a sudden children began to appear from everywhere, all yelling and hollering, 'Who is this? Who is this?'

"Maman and Aunt Olivia stood there with their arms around each other, smiling through their tears on that hot sunny afternoon.

" 'Be quiet, all of you,' replied my aunt. To my amazement all of a sudden there was a complete and total silence amongst all the grubby faces.

"My aunt stood up to her full height and said proudly, while still clinging to Maman, 'This is my sister!' The pride of it all was so evident in her voice. 'This is my sister Elisabeth. Come around, children, quickly, quickly now, come and meet your aunt.'

"Then as Maman and I stood there we went through the formality of the introductions. 'This one here, he is my oldest; his name is Michel. Michel, this is your aunt Elisabeth from the United States. Give your aunt a great big kiss and hug. This here is my daughter Nicole. She is now ten years of age. Nicole, this is your aunt Elisabeth from the United States. Give your aunt a great big hug and kiss.' Before she could continue on in her singsong fashion a boy of about nine years of age came up to his aunt and quickly gave her a hug and kiss and shook hands with me.

" 'My name is Francois,' he said with a big smile, 'but I prefer to be called Frank or Frankie.'

"His mother gave him a slap across his mouth. 'Boy, you are to wait until I introduce you. You are getting too big for your britches.'

" 'I'm sorry, Maman,' he told her, but he never lost the hint of a smile that played upon his lips, nor the gleam in his eyes.

"He walked over to me and told me, 'Maman carries on so, you know, making a big issue out of nothing. You are my cousin, so what am I supposed to do? I've never seen you before and I probably won't ever see you again, and Maman wants us to love one another.' Then he walked away whistling a vague tune, hands in pockets, obviously not overcome with the presence of the honored guests.

"I smiled to myself as I heard the monotone introductions, without any variations at all in the tone or the wording. 'This is Eugene and Eugenia, the twins,' etc. 'This is Paul. This is Antoine. This is Monique. And this here is Zeraphine, and this is Elisabeth and this is Anna *le bébé*.' "

Chapter Thirty
The Meeting

The old man seemed to be unaware of anyone around him, but rather, was lost in a time and place that no one but he was aware of.

A vague smile played around his lips as his mind was absorbed with things long ago accomplished. His attitude betrayed a contentment with things as they had happened. No one but himself could be the judge.

"I am as much married to your grandmother today as I ever was, death could not change that fact in my life." His voice was subdued as though he was speaking to himself more than to anyone else.

He allowed his mind to rove the distance of time. "Ah, yes, I remember it well, as though it all happened yesterday. I supposed one could say that it did happen yesterday, at least it was my yesterday."

He looked at his granddaughter. "An old man rambles on, they say it is one of the benefits of age to be able to ramble on and on if one should so desire. Am I boring you?"

"No, Grand-père, not at all. I have always had an inquisitive mind as to my background. Please go on."

Alexandre smiled indulgently at his granddaughter. "Forgive me for saying so, but your mind had always been inquisitive in a good many areas."

"That's a low blow, Grand-père, even if it is true," she laughed.

"Maman and Ma Tante Olivia were totally involved with one another trying to catch up on all the news, and of course Maman spent a lot of time getting to know her nieces and nephews, and I was left to fend for myself a lot.

"Early one morning I decided to go for a walk and see the surrounding countryside, which was a novelty to me, since going to the United States had made me a city boy. At least all my cousins thought so, and I enjoyed the reputation, although if the truth were known I was not at all involved with city life.

"I had not been aware that there was another building that Uncle Jacques had built a few hundred yards behind the barn. It was a fairly small building, only had four rooms in it, yet it was solid. Somehow it seemed to fit the personality of the uncle who built it, very commodious but not at all showy.

"I observed smoke flowing out of the chimney, and for some reason I decided to walk past this little house, as I was curious as to who lived there."

"Aha!" Genevieve spoke up. "Now we know where my curiosity comes from."

Alexandre smiled at her. "I pray that all the other qualities you inherited from this old man are more constructive than that one is. On the other hand, if I had not been 'curious' I would never have met your grand-mère.

"As I was walking around the building, all of a sudden a little old lady (at least I thought she was old. I later found out that she was not as old as I had originally thought she was) came running out towards me and started hugging me and yelling, 'Papa, I knew you would come! I knew it! Simone, Simone, come quickly, my papa is here, he is come to get me.'

"The sun was just beginning to rise, and I felt I could see the place where the darkness left and the line of light began. I was puzzled and tried to reason with this little lady, but she was certain I had come to get her.

" 'I am sorry,' I told her, 'but I am not your Papa. My name is Alexandre Boisvert and I am very pleased to make your acquaintance.'

"The poor little lady began to cry and cry, and I watched helplessly as the tears rolled down her little face. 'No,' I repeated, 'I am not your papa, but I wish I could be the papa of a lovely lady like you.'

"Of course, by then I realized that this lady had emotional problems. I began to pat her on the back, trying to console her.

"Suddenly, she smiled at me and said, 'Do you mean it that you would like to be my papa?'

" 'Yes,' I said, 'because you are a lovely person and if you want to pretend that I am your papa, it is all right with me.'

" 'Oh, yes, I will do it. You really don't look at all like my papa anyway.'

"Just then two ladies stepped out of the little house. One of them was dressed in the garment of a nun, and the other was a young woman, not very tall and slender. Her face portrayed a maturity that belied her age. She had the bluest eyes that I had ever seen and her hair looked like spun gold, and as she walked into the sunlight the rays of the sun hit her hair in such a manner that her hair sparkled.

"I found myself thinking even at that moment, *I am going to marry that girl!* This was a strange thought, as I had not even contemplated marriage before as I had felt that my lot in life was to take care of Maman.

"Then, I heard her speak, and my legs turned to jelly and my insides were shaking, and I felt like an awkward dolt.

" 'Please excuse Maman; she does not realize sometimes what she is doing.'

" 'Don't say that; don't say that or I'll pull your hair again. This nice man says that I can call him papa if'n I want to, so there.' And she stuck her tongue out at the younger woman.

"I could tell that the young lady was obviously embarrassed by her mother's goings on, so I said, 'Yes I did, but you must be good and not harm anyone.'

"The lady dressed as a nun spoke up and said, 'Please forgive our poor manners. I am sister Yvonne, and this dear lady is Imogene Archambeault and her daughter, Simone. I believe that you must be Olivia and Raymond's guest?'

" 'Yes.' I bowed courteously and said, 'My name is Alexandre Boisvert and I am their nephew. I have come with my maman to visit her sister and her family.'

" 'Alexandre Boisvert,' she repeated. 'I like it, and it fits you, you are definitely an Alexandre. Tell me, Alexandre Boisvert, have you eaten your breakfast yet?'

" 'No, Madame, I have not.'

" 'Then,' she spoke very distinctly, 'will you kindly do us the honor of eating with us?'

" 'I accept gratefully.'

"I held the door open for the ladies as they all went into the little house. I suddenly became very conscious of the fact that I had not shaved yet that morning.

" 'I hope that you ladies will forgive the fact that I have not shaved yet, but I arose early and did not want to wake the others, so I left quietly. I really did not expect to meet three lovely ladies and be invited to eat with them.'

"Imogene spoke up. 'Four, you mean four, don't you? Four lovely ladies.'

"Just at that moment another lady appeared seemingly out of nowhere. She was an impressive sight to behold. Every part of her was spotless and she wore a white cap on her head that was starched stiff. She had on high buckled shoes that shone so that you could see your resemblance in them.

" 'So,' she eyed me with obvious disdain, 'You finally found your way clear to come and see your old grandmother, but did not have enough respect for me to bother to shave!'

" 'Grandmother?' I was obviously in a state of shock. 'Grandmother?' I repeated it again.

" 'Are you not only unkempt but also stupid and cannot understand a simple word like "grandmother"? Boy,' she spoke in disgust, 'grandmother means that I am your mother's mother.'

"I was sweating, as the old saying goes, like a pig. I could feel the rivulets of moisture running down my torso and legs. My hands were sweaty and wet.

" 'Don't just stand there with your mouth open, boy, come and help me to my chair.'

"I literally tripped over my own feet trying to help her.

" 'Clumsy, too,' she spoke harshly.

"What a crew we were sitting in the little kitchen at the handmade little table. The elderly lady thought that she was Queen Victoria, never lifting a finger to help the others. Indeed, she was tall and regal-looking.

"The other lady, with the emotional problems, dressed in a clean little house dress with variegated flowers all over it, she kept on saying, 'I hate eggs, I'm gonna spit them out.' There was the nun Yvonne, sort of chubby and dressed in her robe, which showed her office, and finally, there sat Simone. She had on a blue blouse which brought out the color of her eyes, making them seem even bluer than they were.

"Despite all the oddities of the group things went fairly well.

"Simone spoke to her mother. 'Come on, Maman, eat your eggs; they're very good today.'

" 'No! I won't. I'm gonna spit them at you!'

" 'Oh, oh,' I said, 'now we cannot play our little game.'

" 'What's that you say?' She walked up to where I was sitting and looked me square in the eye. 'What you mean you, eh?' She was very upset now.

"Everyone looked at me, wondering what I was going to do next. I took Imogene's little hand in my larger one and said, 'Well, my Maman told me to play only with nice people, but if you are going to spit at Simone, that's not nice is it?'

"Imogene shook her head no and looked at me quizzically. I cleared my throat, knowing a lot hinged on how I handled this situation and that everyone was watching me and listening to my every move.

" 'I won't spit at Simone anymore, I won't, I really won't.'

" 'Well,' I said slowly, 'I need more than that; I need a promise that you'll never do it again. Will you promise that to me?'

" 'Ya, ya, I promise, I promise.'

" 'Very good, now we can be friends, okay?'

" 'I like you, you are a nice man. I like him, Simone, yup, I like him.'

" 'Good, because I like you, too.'

" 'Hey, Papa, watch me, I'm gonna eat all my eggs.'

" 'You make me proud of you.'

"Imogene's face beamed like that of child on Christmas morning.

"Yvonne rose and told Imogene, 'I am going for a walk, as I missed my early walk. Would you like to go with me and I will read to you?'

"Imogene looked at me. 'Papa, may I go with Yvonne for a walk, please?'

" 'Yes, if Simone says that it is all right, because it is up to her.'

"Simone smiled and shook her head yes, and Imogene grabbed Yvonne's hand and off they went on an adventure of their own making.

"Simone could feel herself blushing in my presence, and could not understand it. *I am acting like a fool, like a little schoolgirl. What would a handsome man from a large city want with a little country girl with a sick Maman, anyhow? He is only being polite.*

"We had both forgotten that the elderly woman was still in the room with us until her loud voice said harshly, 'Young man, has not that wayward daughter of mine taught you any manners at all?'

"I could not figure out what I had done wrong and turned to her and said, 'Madame?'

" 'Do you not have enough manners to help your grandmother out of her chair?'

" 'Of course,' I answered her, and walked over to where she sat and put my arm out to her, which she accepted, and I helped her to her feet.

" 'You are the spitting image of that bum that you call father; are you a bum, too?'

"Simone watched me carefully and she could see that the skin under my shirt collar was getting redder and redder. *She better not push him too far,* she thought to herself, *for he won't stand for it.*

"I stretched my frame to its full potential of height and looked at her glaringly. 'No, Madame, I am not a bum; are you?'

"The older woman retorted, 'Young man, how dare you speak to me in that manner?'

"I said, 'Madame, I dare! And,' I told her, 'as to my father, perhaps you are correct, perhaps he is a bum! Perhaps he had a mother like you!'

"The old woman stretched her hand back and hit me across the face as hard as she could. I took the brunt of the blow across my nose, which began to bleed profusely. Simone quickly grabbed a dish towel and put it across my nose.

"The old woman watched the scenario that she had created and walked out of the door, going to her daughter's house to play on their sympathy.

"I was very conscious of Simone standing so close to me and the nearness of her. My nose was still bleeding and Simone stood even closer to apply pressure to it.

" 'Does it hurt very much?'

" 'No,' I replied. 'It is my pride that hurts.'

"Simone said, 'I'd better get to those dishes before they all get back and wonder what we have all been up to.'

" 'Allow me to wash the dishes for you?'

" 'Do you think that is a good idea, seeing your nose has not stopped bleeding yet?'

" 'It is just about done now. Strange, isn't it? An hour ago I didn't know that I even had a grandmother and now here I am nursing my bruises.'

"Simone looked at me and I really did look comical with my swollen nose and blood smeared all over my face, and she started to laugh. I rose up and went over to the mirror over the sink and looked at myself, and when I saw what I looked like I joined Simone in her laughter.

" 'Sit down,' she ordered me. 'Let me wash your face off.'

"She took a clean washcloth and put some warm water and soap on it and walked over to where I was sitting, and she began to wash my face off. I was a goner and from that moment on I tried to always oblige her wishes.

"Simone looked at me as if for the first time. 'Thank you,' she said softly.

" 'Why are you thanking me?'

"She looked at me as if to say, 'Dare I tell him?' She said in a voice so soft that I could hardly hear her, 'Because you have made me laugh, and I cannot remember the last time I laughed like that.'

" 'Me, too,' I said to her. 'I cannot remember the last time or if there was any time ever that I felt this happy.'

"I reached over and took her hand in mine and lightly put my lips upon it.

"Tears welled up in her eyes.

"I stood up and put my arms around her shoulders. 'Please forgive me, I did not mean to make you cry.'

"I held her close to me for a long moment and a craving that had long haunted her was fulfilled. All she had ever wanted was someone that would show her kindness or gentleness, and I had done both. She felt as though she could stay here in my arms forever.

"I could feel my heart beating a mile a minute and once again my legs felt wobbly, and my hands were sweating. 'We'd better do the dishes.'

"We busied ourselves about the business that must be done, chatting away like two magpies about anything and everything we could think about. 'Do you work in the States?' she asked me.

" 'Yes, I do. I am a singer in several of the churches in our city.'

" 'Really!' she exclaimed. 'A singer? Would you sing something for me?'

" 'Well,' I spoke, 'I will if you really want me to.' In my heart she was my queen and I would do anything that she commanded.

"I stood up as straight as I could and took a deep breath and began to sing 'The Lord's Prayer.' Never had any man sung so beautifully as I did at that moment.

"Simone had never heard anything so beautiful, and she was totally engrossed in the moment.

"Yvonne and Imogene entered the house quietly and both of them stood also totally enthralled. Neither one of them wanted to destroy the moment, but as is usually the case someone did.

" 'What is this terrible loud noise that I hear grating on my ears? Who can be so thoughtless as to cause such a ruckus?'

" 'You guessed it, Madame; it is I.'

" 'Yes,' she said curtly, 'it is you!' And thus saying, she swept by me as though I were not there and went to her room and slammed the door.

" 'Perhaps,' I said, 'I should be going. Thank you ladies one and all.' I saluted them and left as quickly and quietly as I had first appeared in their lives.

"Simone was downcast and she thought to herself, *I shall never see him again!*"

Chapter Thirty-one
Falling in Love

Simone watched out of the window as Alexandre walked into the woods, whistling as he went. His hands were in his pockets, and his head was held high and erect, almost as though he were saying, "Come on, world."

He saw a great black snake making itself warm lying on a large rock, as though it were king of all it saw. "I certainly will not disturb you, big boy." Alexandre made immediate distance between himself and the reptile.

All his thoughts were centered on Simone. *I wonder if she likes me? Why did I go out without shaving?* This was something no one had known him to do.

I wonder, he thought again to himself, *what she would have done if I kissed her like I wanted to?* He had never kissed a girl in a boy and girl relationship in his entire life and was not sure he even knew how.

We have so much in common. We are both bound by responsibilities that we have never asked for. Yet he knew that she was as honorable as he was and that they would both take care of their responsibilities.

I wonder, he mused, *just what did happen to Simone's maman? Poor little lady! Something really terrible must have happened to her.* Simone mentioned while we were doing the dishes something about "Maman's accident."

I wish that I could go back to that little house and get Simone and have both of us run off somewhere together and forget that there is "duty and responsibility" in this old world. He shrugged his shoulders and started to walk again.

Alexandre came to a pine grove and the fragrance was a sweet aroma to his nostrils. He threw himself down clumsily and nestled his body even deeper into the fallen needles. The sky was bluer than he had ever seen it before and he lay there lazily trying to identify various forms as they floated gently by.

The birds were singing over his head and the melody was sweet and variegated. He felt that he had found an oasis, a world where he was the only participant, and probably for the first time in his life he felt at ease with his surroundings and with himself.

"I must bring Simone here."

He made decisions lying there that day, decisions that only a man can make. *First of all, I must think of myself as a man from now on and not as a boy as I have always done!*

He knew without a doubt that his life would never be the same again. Simone had come into his life to fill that void of emptiness and loneliness. He believed that they were made for each other, and he was willing to accept her responsibilities as well as his own. He was determined.

All of a sudden he stood up and brushed himself off and started back towards the little house where Simone lived with the three women. He had made decisions and now he felt anxious to follow through on them.

Simone had watched Alexandre until he was out of sight, and then a strange sadness seemed to fill her. She felt as though everything had turned dark and she felt more alone than she had ever felt before.

I must get myself out of this dark mood and busy myself about. She tried valiantly but somehow she could not overcome the feeling.

She was hanging laundry slowly and deliberately when she looked up and there he was! Simone did not know whether to laugh or to cry as her eyes beheld him. Alexandre smiled broadly and held out his arms and she quickly dropped the laundry and ran as fast as her legs would carry her. Alexandre was running too, his long legs covering more ground than Simone's short ones, until at last they came together, both breathless.

"Simone, I must be with you! I don't understand what has happened to us, but I know that the time I spent here this morning with you has been the happiest time in my entire life."

She looked into his eyes, and she could see them shining and she knew that her eyes were shining, too. "Oh, Alexandre, I have never felt like this before either."

He hugged her tight and they stood there for a long, long time unaware that they were being observed by three pairs of eyes through the window of the house.

"Simone," he said tenderly, "I only have a very short time here and I want to spend every moment I can being with you."

"Yes," she said, "that is what I want, too."

She caressed his face gently. "Your poor eye is all black. Your grand-mère is very strong. Let's walk to the brook and put some cool water on it."

He took her hand and they walked the few hundred feet to the little brook looking into each other's eyes and smiling broadly at one another.

She gently bathed his eye with the cool water and he could feel some of the feverishness leaving for a bit.

"What are you going to tell your Maman about your eye and nose?"

He laughed. "I am going to tell her that you hit me because I tried to kiss you!"

She looked at him. "You wouldn't do that, would you?"

"That all depends," he said, "on if you hit me when I kiss you or not."

He leaned over and kissed her gently on the lips and she stepped up on her tiptoes and kissed him gently on the lips also, catching him by surprise. But he was not as surprised as she was in doing it.

"Let's go back," he said huskily. "I must go and get cleaned up and then I will be back and we will spend the day together. Is that agreeable to you?"

"Oh, yes, I will be waiting for you."

He gave her a quick hug, turned and waved and was on his way.

From that moment on they were inseparable. He rose early in the morning and walked over to the little house and worked side by side with Simone; if she was cooking, he was cooking, if she was cleaning house, he was cleaning house, and on and on it went. Neither one of them wanted the time to end.

Even Grand-mère took a liking to Alexandre. He would act silly for them and he loved having all the attention from all four of the ladies. Grand-mère even joined in when they were singing "Toutes en roun."

Alexandre sang "Frère Jacques" or "Au Claire de la Lune" or sometimes even the old favorites like "La Cantiniere" or "Alouette." Grand-mère would laugh as long and as hard as the rest of them.

Grand-mère even cooked some of her "specialties" for him, some ragout and a special chocolate mocha cake that her own grandmother taught her to make. She even gave Simone the recipes.

One lazy, hot afternoon Grand-mère was sitting on the porch and called Alexandre to her. "Alexandre."

"Oui," he replied.

"You are in love with little Simone?"

"Does it show that much, Grand-mère?"

"Yes. She is a good girl, Alexandre; don't take advantage of her."

His temper flared. "I would never do such a thing!"

"You are thinking marriage then?"

"Yes, but I don't know how or when. As soon as I can earn enough money to support a wife."

"I wish I had money. I would give it to you. But I do not have any money."

Alexandre's heart was deeply touched and he leaned over and kissed her cheek, and she gave him a lovely smile.

"I wish that my sons were like you," she shrugged her shoulders. "Anyway, I have something to give you."

Alexandre was totally surprised. "Me? You have something for me?" *What in the world can it be?* he thought.

She took a clean handkerchief out of her pocket and slowly untied the knot she had made in the corner of it and she took out the most beautiful ring that he had ever seen, and placed it in the palm of his hand.

He took the ring in his fingers and looked at it.

"It is very valuable. When you find someone like Simone, you don't take chances on losing her. It is for your betrothal."

"B–b–but, Grand-mère," he stuttered, "you have daughters and granddaughters, why are you giving this ring to me?"

"Young man!" Somehow it never took much for her to be irritated with Alexandre. He reminded her so much of herself in many of his ways. "I will decide who I shall give my things to!"

"You are right, of course, Madame. I am truly overwhelmed and I thank you from the bottom of my heart."

"Come here and give your old grandmother a kiss now."

Alexandre really was overwhelmed with this gift, and he could hardly wait to present it to Simone.

Alexandre sat back on his chair on the porch next to his grandmother. He liked the look and the smell of her. *She looks exactly the way a grandmother should,* he thought. He took the ring in his fingers and looked it over carefully.

"You know, Grand-mère, it should be something special that we do together when I give her the ring."

"Simone will be happy to be your wife."

"Do you really think so?" he asked somberly.

"Yes, I do, or I would not say so."

"Grand-mère, if she'll have me we will name the first baby after you," he said laughingly.

"Young man!" She tried to sound stern. "If you ever dare to name your child Adelaide, I will take my ring back." She joined in the laughter.

Just at the moment Simone came out to the porch and asked if she could join them.

"Of course you can."

Simone also sat down on one of the old rocking chairs that they kept out there and asked, "What have you been up to, or is it a big secret?"

Alexandre and his grandmother looked at one another and both spoke at the same moment: "It is a big secret."

Simone was happy to see that they were getting along so well now as she had been concerned about their relationship. She could see that they admired each other and it made her feel good.

Grand-mère stood up and said, "I am a little weary, I think I shall go in the house for a bit."

Bless her soul, she is giving us a few moments alone, thought Alexandre.

"Let's go for a little walk, Simone." Alexandre felt in his pocket as he did not want to lose the ring. He took her by the hand and they began to walk in contentment.

Simone was leaning against the old elm tree, and Alexandre put his hands on her shoulders. "Simone." His voice was deep and husky now. "I will be leaving for home in three days."

"I know," she whispered, and her eyes began to fill with tears.

Alexandre took his handkerchief out of his pocket and gently wiped her eyes.

"Simone, look at me; there is something I must tell you, and I am not quite sure I know how."

"What is it?"

"Simone, I love you." He was a nervous wreck.

Simone never blinked but kept on looking into Alexandre's eyes. "Don't say it if you don't mean it."

"I mean it; I mean it—I love you!" his voice was louder now.

She started to cry softly.

"I prayed, Simone, that you could love me, too. Have I made a mistake?"

"No."

"Then for God's sake tell me so that I will know."

Her voice was barely audible now. "I don't know how to say it! I have never said these words to anyone before."

"Neither have I, but I found it easy when it came to telling you. If you'll have me, I want you for my wife."

"Oh, Alexandre, you don't understand, it is an impossible situation. I can never marry you, it would not be right."

"Simone," he spoke up, "whatever are you talking about? I am confused." He put his hand behind the nape of her neck, causing her hair to come undone and hang upon her shoulders. He bent down and kissed her fully on her lips and she did not try to push him away.

"I was right; you do care about me! Now what is all this nonsense about things being impossible?"

"Alexandre, I cannot tell you because I cannot talk about it even yet. Go and talk to your grandmother and she will explain things to you."

"Simone, look at this," and he pulled the ring out of his pocket. "Grand-mère gave it to me this afternoon so that I could ask you to be my wife. This ring belonged to my great grandmother and it is very valuable."

The rays of the sun made highlights on the ring and it danced and sparkled.

Simone had never seen anything so beautiful in all of her life.

"I love you." He could barely make out what she had said.

"What did you say?"

"I said I love you!"

"Say it again."

"I love you."

"I love you, too," and then louder, "I love you, too!" And then he shouted it; "I love Simone!"

"Alexandre, after you talk to your grandmother, if you still want me, I will marry you."

"No matter what, I want you for my wife! I don't know when or where or how, but we will be man and wife, Simone. I swear it!"

Chapter Thirty-two
The Beatings

Genevieve's thoughts turned to her grandmother, or Grand-mère, as she preferred to be called. *It's strange,* she thought, *that after all these years I can still miss her so much. Imagine how poor Grand-père feels after all the years that they spent together. Who was Grand-mère really?* she asked herself, *and how would I portray her?*

Oh yes, she definitely was a woman of very strong and deep-rooted religious beliefs. All of her children received a biblical name in some form or other. She had a sincere hope or desire that through these names they might be especially blessed and endowed with above average attributes of intelligence and other moral character which were so important to her. Of course this was her own personal desire which never came to fruition. In her humble opinion none of the children ever amounted to much.

Her husband, being an indulgent man as far as she was concerned, allowed her to name the children by whatever name that she felt comfortable with. As long as the name sounded pleasant. "After all," he reasoned, "she did all the bearing and the birthing and also raising. She could do the naming."

During these first years of their marriage Alexandre spent many weeks at a time away from home trying to eke out a living for her and also for his children. He always swore that his offspring would not have the existence that he had as a boy. His Simone would never have to take in laundry and work out as a maid. He always considered what his mother had to do slave work.

"By golly," the old man often had told Genevieve, "she was worth it all. She was not like most young women of her day, who were only interested in 'chitchatting' or giggling; isn't that what the youngsters of today call it? I could never stand a woman who was overly bubbly or unnecessarily coy. When Simone spoke and said something, it was always worth listening to!"

She was a worker, too, that one, all one had to do was look at her hands and the proof was there. To Alexandre this was more beautiful than the best manicured hands around. These hands were proof to him of a faithful woman who worked as hard as he did out of mutual love and admiration, one for the other. A woman who not only had a deep compassion for love, but a woman who did for those she loved. She loved him, of this he had always been certain. There had never been any doubt in his mind. He didn't know why or how he managed to get himself such a woman but he certainly was thankful that he had been blessed in this manner. Sometimes it amazed him to realize how much she had put up with from him in their lifetime.

She'd had a very tough life as a young girl, but whenever anyone brought that subject up she would just pooh-pooh the subject away, and never wanted to talk about it. She would always say that the good Lord would never test us above what we are capable of withstanding. Many times this dear lady had been through hell, so to speak, but never, as she always claimed, without the help of *Le Bon Dieu*.

She made it through. She was an overcomer, a survivor. Her father was an alcoholic, a little mouse of a man. He stood only about five feet four inches tall and was the possessor of blond, curly hair. His name was Marcelle Louis Archambeault. A great big name for a little man. He spawned only daughters and he blamed his wife for this. Out of the four daughters only one lived past the age of seven. Needless to say the local "Canuch" loved to tease the *petit coq*, the "little rooster," because it bothered him so much. All it took was one or two drinks to set him off. Sometimes one of his friends, such as Bernard or Gerard, would say to him, "Hey, *Petit Coq*, we just saw a 'real' man go into your house. Now maybe your wife will see the difference, eh?"

Anyone who knew Imogene Archambeault knew that she was not the type of woman to have men in her house, but his so-called friends thought that this was a big joke. Marcelle had a very poor self-image and had no confidence at all in himself, so he would leave the tavern in a fit of flying rage and run into his house and literally turn everything inside out and proceed to beat both his wife and daughter. Both were known to walk around town with many cuts and bruises over the years. Simone made a promise to herself and swore that she would never again in her lifetime be afraid of any man.

Until the day that she died Simone could never understand why her mother put up with this poor excuse for a man. Many, many times when she was just a little slip of a girl and her father was drinking, she would beg her mother, "Maman, let's go far, far away from here, just you and I."

Her mother would cradle her in her arms and say, "*Pauvre, Simone, c'est impossible. Impossible!*"

Her mother would always say the same thing. Simone knew the routine by heart. As far as Simone knew, they had no other living relatives except for her father. Marcelle's jealousy was so intense that of course he never brought any friends home with him either.

She had to admit, even though it might be somewhat grudgingly, that when he wasn't on the bottle he sometimes acted almost decent. In these times he would bring home his wages and they might have a halfway decent meal, and might also eat regularly for as long as his "sabbatical" lasted. In those times her mother tried as best as she could to buy things and fix up their one-room shack. Sometimes in his sober times he would take Simone and her mother for walks and he would explain many things about nature to them. Needless to say these moments, thought few and far between, were savored by both mother and daughter.

But sooner or later his mistress, the bottle, would beckon him and he ran to be with her. Their home once again would become a den of hell and fury.

Imogene's greatest desire was for her daughter, Simone, to learn to read and cipher, as it was called in those days. So she made arrangements for Simone to attend school. Mother and daughter were so excited and Imogene went over and over her daughter's one and only dress, making sure there were no rips or tears in it. She told her daughter more than once, "You must brush and brush your hair and make it shine. We don't want anyone to think that we are not as good as they are, eh?"

Imogene had discussed this coming event with Marcelle and it appeared that he was not going to be difficult or pose any objections, that is, at first, until one night he was in the tavern discussing this coming event of schooling for his young daughter.

As was their habit in the tavern, the men began to tease him. "Hey, *Petit Coq*," they told him, "your daughter is going to be smarter than you, eh? Just think, when you want to know something you can go and ask Simone, and maybe being the good girl that she is she will give you the good answer." As could well be imagined this brought forth peals of laughter from the men and caused Marcelle to fly into a rage.

The more Marcelle's mind dwelled on the circumstances the more enraged he became; the more inadequate he felt, too. "The nerve of that slip of a girl, thinking she is better than her Maman or, worse yet, thinking she is better than her own Papa. I can't read or cipher but my food is good enough for her to fill her belly on.

"Imagine that ungrateful wife of mine filling that girl's head with these crazy ideas. Simone's head is already too swollen for her own good. I'll fix them once and for all! Make a fool out of me, would they?"

On and on he carried it until all good sense was removed from him. He went home all right, when he had become so drunken he could hardly walk. He went home in the wee small hours of the morning when mother and daughter were fast asleep.

He struck like a wild animal, catching them unawares. He began his work of destruction blindly, striking blow after blow while cursing them over and over again.

The screaming of the two was to no avail as he struck them again and again and again until they both were nothing but a mess of bloody pulp. They were both bruised and swollen beyond recognition. "School!" he screamed. "School! I'll teach you that there will be no school. No more school!" he raged on. "There will be no more talk of school in this house. School is done for in this house." He then passed out cold on the floor of the old one-room shack.

He woke up the next day and began cursing. "Imogene, where is my breakfast," he hollered. "You are no good for anything." When he heard no response he rose up and saw the result of his handiwork. Both wife and daughter were unrecognizable. He sobered mighty quick then. He never even took the time to see if they were alive or not, his only thought was to save his own skin. He truly believed that he had killed them both.

He didn't leave in glory like the fighting rooster, but more like the dirty skunk who lurks in the darkness, tail between his legs.

Many times Simone thanked "*Le Bon Dieu*" (God) for the good nun who was the teacher in the one-room schoolhouse. The good nun had walked a good three miles to see why Simone had not attended school on the first day. *She seemed most anxious to go to school, I can't understand why she did not come.* As she approached the little run-down shack, she couldn't help thinking, *In spite of her poverty Mrs. Archambeault keeps everything immaculate.*

Maybe, she thought, *I could get someone to donate a little paint and come and help the dear soul paint this little shack. I believe that it would encourage her.*

As she approached the cabin she saw that the door was ajar and pushed on it and then she was witness to the gruesome sight. She thought both mother and child were dead. There was blood everywhere. She began to get sick to her stomach and became very faint. As her knees began to buckle under her she prayed, "*Oh mon Dieu,* God help me!"

She checked both mother and daughter over and over. "What can I do?" Just then she noticed an empty pot sitting on a shelf. She grabbed it and quickly ran to the well and filled it with cold water. She tore her petticoat into pieces and began to wash them slowly and very gently. She went from one to the other washing the dried blood off them. Then she began to drizzle the cold well water over them. She tried to remove their blood-soaked clothing. She drizzled more water upon their faces until Mrs. Archambeault began to moan, and try to move, but she could not. The nun then took another piece of her petticoat and let fresh water drip over the lady's mouth and tongue.

The nun began to cry. "Thank you, thank you, *bon Dieu*. And the child, let her be alive also." She bathed the child again and again, getting fresh water as needed. She found a bottle of brandy that had been discarded as empty; it only had a drop or two left in it. She added a little water to the brandy and with much patience forced it between the lips of the child.

The child began to choke violently, this action causing her frail little body to warm itself, and she began to breathe.

The nun then began to search around the little room and found some articles of clothing and made them beds right where they lay, as they were hurt too badly to be moved. She made certain they were both warm, and she knelt and prayed by their side. *Dear God*, she prayed, *I know that you are a good God. I place them in your care.*

She then set out on foot to get some assistance. She had to walk quite a way before she came to the nearest neighbor's home.

She tapped on the door and a heavyset woman came to the door very much annoyed. "Sister, I have nothing to give to charity, so please be gone. I have enough to do already and I am late with all my chores today."

The nun, mustering up all the courage at her command, spoke somewhat hesitatingly. "Please, madame, I did indeed come for charitable purposes, but it is not as you think. It is not for myself, it is for Madame Archambeault and her child."

The woman put her hands on her hips and replied, "Don't tell me; let me guess." She was obviously out of sorts. In a churlish voice she said, "That no-good son of a snake husband of hers has beaten them up again."

"*Oui, oui,*" said the nun, "and this time he has really outdone himself. I believe that they are both dying. Please madame, I beg of you, please help me. I am at my wits' end. They are both lying on the floor, no blankets, not a morsel of food to be found anywhere, and there is blood all over the place."

All of a sudden the woman came alive. "Jacques! Jacques!" she called out and the tone of her voice showed that something was up. A tall slender man with a head of black hair that was beginning to grey at the temples came out of the big barn. "*Vite!* Hurry! Hurry!" She told him to prepare the horse and the buggy and keep an eye on the children. "There is an emergency at the Archambeault home."

She beckoned to the nun. "Come, come," she said. "As you say, every moment is most important. What is your name?"

"Uh, uh, Seour Yvonne du Sacre Coeur."

"Hurry up, Yvonne; if things are as you say time is important and each moment is important."

The nun was so taken aback by her use of her given name and not her title that she stood motionless for a second or two. "Are you coming or not, Yvonne?"

All the time the woman was speaking she had been hustling about. "Marie, you get me some blankets, the ones in the old trunk upstairs. Henri, get me some towels, quickly now, all of you. Maude, you get some food items together." All this time she herself was gathering together various items, such as iodine and other things.

"Let us make haste, Yvonne; why does your mouth hang open?" Together they ran to the horse and wagon. The poor nun had never had such a ride in her life. Even the horse seemed to sense that something was amiss.

They disembarked from the buggy and entered the little shack. They both felt weak and very faint when they viewed the scene.

The older woman, Olivia, thought to herself, *She may be a nun, but she is very young. I must be strong enough for the both of us.* The stench in the heat of the midday sun was unbearable. Both their stomachs were churning and turning about. The older woman felt very weak. As she turned to look at the young nun she knew that she also felt the same way.

"Quickly, Yvonne, open the window and the door. Then take the wagon and go and get Jacques. Tell him to put the feather bed down on the wagon. Make haste!"

The older woman busied herself about. She decided not to wash away the evidence of the blood from the little room. She quickly went out to the well and drew some cold water. She took the whole bucket and poured half on the woman and the other half on the child.

The woman came to for a moment. Her eyes were glazed, not seeing, and she tried to mutter something. "S–Si–Sim—" and she passed out again. Olivia began to wipe her dry with one of the towels and she removed her blood-soaked clothes as gently as she could. She spread out one of the blankets she had brought in a corner of the room after she had cleaned away the debris. As gently as she could she moved the woman to the blanket and wrapped her snugly. As gentle as she tried to be the woman screamed and cried out in pain. She continued to alternate between screaming and passing out. Olivia then proceeded to cleanse the young girl much in the same manner.

"The names that I would like to call that man would not be printable," she muttered. "I would like to do the same to him as he has done. Torture would be too good for him. I'd better not see him again!"

She had begun to feel better once she had busied herself with the two injured persons. More than likely because she was not thinking of herself.

"What is taking that husband of mine so long to get here?" she muttered. "It's not like him at all."

She took her little bundle of "medications" and the clean rags that she had brought along and began going over the two. The iodine caused some movement in the patients as she tried gently to apply it.

It is better to apply this iodine, she thought, *to help get rid of any possible infection there might be.*

Imogene's head was cut in the back in several places. One of the cuts was about six inches long; she had several more of differing sizes. Her whole face was a complete mess and she was totally unrecognizable. Anyone who did not know her would have sworn that she was a black woman. Where there should have been eyes there were narrow slits. She had a jagged cut that ran from within her hairline, going across her cheek diagonally, through the corner of her mouth, which was torn right to the middle of her chin. Blood was coming out of the corners of her mouth. Olivia knew that there was much more wrong with Imogene, but not being a doctor she could not tell what.

The child had almost identical wounds, although she did not have the massive gash on her cheek.

All of a sudden Olivia heard the sounds of the wagon returning.

"Thank God, thank God!" she yelled, and tears started to roll down her cheeks. She stood up and looked out and found that there were two wagons approaching. Jacques had thought to go and find Doctor Bernier.

Jacques and the doctor came running into the little shack. Olivia began to cry in great sobbing breaths. Jacques, that big hulk of a man who never said much and whose hands felt like cement, went over to his wife and gently comforted her.

The doctor meanwhile had taken his little black bag and opened it.

"Woman," he spoke in a harsh voice, "if you are done with your hysterics I need your help. Both of you. It is a good thing that you arrived when you did," he told her. His voice was much calmer now.

"It was not me," said Olivia. "It was that young nun, Yvonne. She is the one that is to be praised. By the way," she asked, "where is Yvonne?"

Jacques answered, "I asked her to stay with the children, as I did not know how long we would be here."

"It looks like he beat them with a stick of firewood besides his fists!" said the doctor. "Look here, Olivia, I have found signs of life, but to tell you the truth I don't know if either one of them will live. Imogene has both arms and legs broken, beside ribs, fingers and toes. I believe that she also has a broken back." He shook his head sadly. "I have never seen anyone injured so badly, and I don't know of anyone that has lived with a broken back. Even the lumberjacks don't inflict this kind of bodily harm to themselves in all of their brawls."

"Doctor, what are we going to do?" asked Olivia.

"I don't know," said the doctor. "What can we do except to pray?"

"Rest assured that Yvonne is doing that, and I believe she also has the children praying, too."

"One thing is for sure," he said, "they cannot be left alone. This poses a problem as my wife and I already have six patients at home to take care of. We have no more room anywhere in the house."

"I don't see what your problem is," Olivia answered him. "We have a big house and plenty of food. Of course they will come home with us."

The doctor turned and looked at Olivia right in her eyes and just stared at her for what seemed a long time. "I believe you could do it," he said. "I hope that you fully understand what you are saying. This is going to take months of tender loving care if they are to survive."

"Jacques, we must act quickly and steadily. We will place them in the wagon as carefully as possible."

"We have a featherbed in the wagon."

"Good! Good. Let us hurry before the darkness is upon us." The doctor began giving orders. "Jacques! Break the legs off of that table, we are going to use it as a stretcher."

Jacques quickly went to the little makeshift table and found that it had no legs on it.

"Olivia," the doctor said, "you come and hold the child's head steady so that it does not roll back."

Thus saying, in the most gentle manner that was within him, he picked up the child as though she were a feather and carried her while Olivia held her head in a steady position.

While the doctor walked back into the little shack Olivia busied herself making sure the child was covered.

The two men working in unison took the table top, which was really just an old board, and laid it upon the floor next to Imogene.

"We must be very careful to move her so as to inflict no more harm to her body than has already been done. We must tie her upon this board. Now, what can we use to tie her with?"

"We can use my suspenders," volunteered Jacques.

"Very good," said the doctor, "very good."

Jacques removed his suspenders so quickly it was almost inapparent. The gentleness that these men used in putting the woman upon the board was of an unusual kind. Both men were deeply moved by what had been done to these two. With extreme care and caution they carried her over to the wagon and laid her gently beside her daughter.

"I will follow you," said Doctor Bernier.

Olivia rode in the back of the wagon between the two patients. *I know that it doesn't do them any good*, she told herself, *but it reassures me.*

Jacques drove as he had never driven before, very slowly, attempting to avoid the biggest ruts and holes. It seemed like an eternity before they arrived at the old farmhouse.

Never had the old weather-beaten house looked so good to Olivia. Never had she appreciated Jacques more than at this moment.

As they arrived in the yard the children all came running out. Their cries of distress were multiple and varied. Olivia never had been so joyous at seeing them all well and happy.

The doctor came from his wagon. "We must hurry," he said, "for our work has just begun. All the broken bones must be set and there are so many of them that I am sure that it will take most of the night. We will need all of the lamps that you have for light."

Olivia was so grateful as she entered her home. Yvonne had finished all the chores she had left behind. Her nose breathed in the aroma of a good stew cooking. The table was all set; the children were all clean.

Yvonne asked the doctor, "Is it all right, doctor, if we eat first?"

"Yes," he answered, "but we must be quick about it."

Jacques went out and carried the little girl into the house and placed her upon the bed that belonged to one of his daughters.

Yvonne and Olivia were bustling about putting the food on the big old table: pitchers of milk, fresh baked bread, and plates full of the good stew Yvonne had made.

"Yvonne," Olivia spoke up, "I told the doctor that I felt you would be willing to stay here and help me nurse these two. Is that all right with you?"

Yvonne shook her head signifying her assent.

"We will put you in the room with little Simone, and I myself will take care of Imogene. Agreed?" The nun did not speak and once again nodded her agreement.

The doctor had not taken time to eat and Jacques filled him a big old-fashioned mug full of coffee. "Thank you," the doctor said as Jacques handed him the drink.

"We must begin setting these broken bones before they become too set in the wrong position. We will need much strength tonight, you and I. I will need cloth to wrap and tie the broken limbs with and some wood to make into splints. Also there is something that I have not told Yvonne nor Olivia. Imogene and little Simone have been sexually molested. It is not a pretty sight to behold. They will have to be told."

"That animal, that poor excuse for a man. I wish I had his mangy neck in my hands right now, I would tear him apart limb by limb." His voice was so harsh the doctor was surprised, for Jacques was generally a gentle man.

"Come now," the doctor said, "we have work to do. We cannot spend our strength on a man who is nothing but a piece of garbage."

Jacques calmed down somewhat and kept himself busy helping the doctor.

The women also were occupied in helping. They kept hot water coming and the lights burning and ran about doing all the things necessary to this type of situation. The night was completely worn away when the doctor said, "We have done all that we can. The rest is up to God."

They were all exhausted. Totally spent. God had been merciful indeed to the two injured ones as they never regained consciousness during the long ritual of setting the broken bones.

The doctor threw his coat on the floor in the kitchen in front of the old wood stove and laid himself down upon it and soon was snoring. Olivia and Jacques did the same thing. The old grey tomcat opened his eyes as though amused and then he also went to sleep.

Chapter Thirty-three
Slow Recovery

Olivia and Yvonne began a life of rituals that would last many months for Yvonne and years for Olivia and Jacques.

Yvonne was a very conscientious person and took her job most seriously. From the moment that she was given the care of the child, no thought about herself entered her head. She was determined that this child would live and be whole again. As she sat at the little girl's bedside, she prayed and sang and read the Bible to her. She had the children come in every day for a visit and talk to Simone as though she were awake and could understand the conversation. The child was never left alone for even one moment. She washed her over and over again. She would take a piece of clean cloth and dip it in milk mixed with a little sugar and drip it on the child's mouth; she did the same with the homemade soup. She never dared to force solid food in the child's mouth for fear that she would choke.

Olivia was busy with Imogene in the other room. She spoke to the woman constantly. "I am mending Jacques' socks today, perhaps when you are feeling better you can help me with the mending. Your beautiful little girl is asleep in the next room. She needs you, you must get well for her sake. We all love you. You are a very special person." On and on it went, day after day. It seemed that there was never any change in their condition. Every day the doctor would come and check them out and look at Olivia and Yvonne and Jacques and he would shake his head in discouragement.

One day as Yvonne was working about the little bedroom that she shared with Simone she heard a strange noise, and as she knew that the noise did not come from her room, and she knew that it was only herself and Olivia at home with the two patients, she went into the other room and found Olivia prostrate on the floor crying hysterically.

Yvonne was shocked at the scene before her and ran over to the bed and touched Imogene's neck in search of some life signs as the doctor had showed her how to do it.

Olivia was sobbing uncontrollably. "It is no use; it is no use. They are never going to recover."

Instinctively, before she could even consider what she was doing, the nun placed a backhander across Olivia's face, and cried out in a very loud voice, "Don't you dare say that to me, don't you dare!" and she also began to sob.

There they sat, the very young nun and the middle-aged woman, with their arms about each other in the middle of the floor.

Through her tears and sobbing Yvonne said, "God told me that they would live. He did! He really told me!" and she began to cry all the more.

"Hush, hush, I believe you. After all, no one thought that they would live at all and they have made it through these two months. That alone is a good sign."

All of a sudden the nun's face turned pale as snow. "Oh," she said, "what have I done?" realizing that she had hit Olivia's left cheek. "Oh! Oh! Please, I beg of you, forgive me. I am so ashamed of myself and you are so good, too. I cannot believe that I have done such a thing."

Olivia looked at the little nun so upset and she began to laugh. She laughed so hard that Yvonne also began to laugh and neither one of them could stop. On the floor of the little bedroom they shared with each other in a way that neither one had ever shared anything in their lifetimes.

As though in one motion they both stood up and busied themselves about with the work at hand.

One day just a few short days later Yvonne was singing to the little girl and said to her, "Simone, if you can hear me, squeeze my hand."

It was just a slight tremor or twitch, but she knew that she had felt a response from the child. She ran and got Olivia. Her words were rushing out so fast and were so garbled that Olivia could not understand her at first.

"Yvonne, calm down and tell me please what is all this business about?"

"Simone! Simone! She responded when I was singing to her."

"What do you mean?" asked Olivia. "How did she respond?"

"I was singing to her and I told her, 'Simone, if you can hear me, squeeze my hand,' and she did, I tell you, she did!"

Olivia walked over to the bed and kissed Simone and spoke to her softly. "Simone, if you can hear me squeeze my hand."

There was no response whatsoever. Olivia could not have felt sorrier for the good nun. She knew how hard she had worked, and she knew that the desire of her heart was to have the child well again.

She tried to reassure her. "Perhaps, Yvonne, you want it to be so and you just thought that there was a response."

"No! No!" There was anger and agitation in Yvonne's voice. "I know what I felt and saw."

Olivia knew that there was not much sense in arguing so she decided to drop the matter and turned and walked back to her own room.

Yvonne's heart beat strongly within her and she knew that the child had responded.

The next day Yvonne went through the very same ordeal again when she tried to explain to the doctor what had happened.

He stood before her, a little portly man with a large pot belly, in his dark grey suit. His nose was the dominating feature of his face. He removed his spectacles and stood there slowly wiping them on his clean handkerchief. Without the glasses on he gave the appearance of being half asleep.

In a very low and soft voice he said, "I think, my dear sister, that what you are experiencing is wishful thinking."

Yvonne's back stiffened out and if one knew her well enough one would realize that a delicate chord had been touched.

She stood to her full height, which was about five feet two inches. Her posture was rigid and her face was flushed. "Yes, dear doctor, you are correct, having this child well and happy again is the desire of my heart. That is right, I desire it, I feel it and I believe that I need it. I want it so much I can actually taste it. I have spent many, many nights in prayer for the child and her mother. I will tell you one thing, I know that you consider me just a foolish young woman without any experience, so to speak, but I tell you I know what I felt and all of you put together cannot discourage me."

The doctor stood and looked at Olivia and just shook his head slowly. No one said a word. "I think perhaps Yvonne needs a rest," he said.

The next day the nun was putting soup in the child's mouth, a slow and tedious process indeed. She was using a very tiny baby spoon; she would make sure that the soup was tepid, and then she would fill the spoon about a third full and spill it into the child's mouth. Most of it would spill out, and she would wipe off her mouth and repeat the process all over again, in the same manner that one would feed a baby. She would keep speaking to the child about all kinds of things such as the weather, the children, God and Jesus, etc. She would tell her, 'When you are well I will teach you how to read and cipher, just as we planned." She would sing and pray.

She felt that love was a very important part of healing so she would hug and kiss the child often. On this particular day, as she had finished feeding the child, she bent over to place a soft kiss upon the little brow, and the child's eyes opened for a brief second.

It was so brief that one would hardly have noticed it. Her eyes opened and it seemed as though they were trying to focus but they had no control over themselves and quickly rolled back and closed once again as though content in their deep slumber.

Yvonne wondered to herself, *Am I so foolish that I am imagining these things? No, no. I believe that the child is beginning to respond. I am not going to tell this to anyone. I'll not be made a fool of again, but they will see, they will see. This child is going to be well again. I just know it.*

Yvonne heaved a sigh, and she began to realize just how tired she really was. She sat on the chair next to the bed to read some of her daily devotions and before she realized it she was fast asleep. She slept so deeply that she never heard Olivia enter the room.

Olivia was touched when she entered the room and saw the young nun so deep in sleep. She sat there on the old kitchen chair with her veil in disarray as her head hung to one side as though the weight of it was more than she could bear. Her hands still held fast to her little book of devotions in her lap.

We have taken advantage of this poor, dear creature, Olivia thought to herself. She was surprised when she saw a tuft of hair sticking out from under the veil and saw the lovely chestnut-colored hair.

Why, thought Olivia, *she really is nothing more than a little girl. I never realized that. She is not much older than my Marie! I never would have considered Marie capable of doing this job. At most, she is about nineteen.*

What a waste, thought Olivia. *A young woman with so much love to give should not be wasted in a convent. What is the logic, I wonder, of covering and hiding her hair like that? I guess that I am too ignorant to know about such things.*

Olivia patted her apron pocket where there was an envelope which contained a letter. She had never received a letter before and it made her feel important and at the same time it frightened her. *What does it say?* she thought. She did not want her family to know that she had never learned to read. She wanted them to look up to her. *After all,* she thought, *my family may have been poor, but they were honest and hard workers, too.* She could cipher in her head with the best of them and no one ever got the better of her when she sold her chickens or eggs, either.

The great desire of her heart had been that she would one day learn to read and to write. *I should stop this foolishness. I am too old and have too much work to do to start feeling sorry for myself now.*

I think that I shall open the window a bit and get some fresh air in here. Just as she turned back from opening the window and Simone was turned toward Olivia, Olivia thought that she saw the child's eyes open for a brief moment.

Am I imagining things? she thought. And she walked over to the bed and checked more closely. The child was lying there quietly as usual, both eyes closed. Olivia shook herself and told herself, *Enough of this nonsense, I have too much work to do to daydream.*

Later that night when all the children had been put to bed and the whole house was quiet Jacques told Olivia, "When I was in town today I saw the doctor and he told me that he brought you a letter today."

"Yes, I did get a letter today." She turned away from him as she spoke, silently praying that he would not question her further.

"Well?" he said.

She knew that he was not going to drop the matter. "Well, what?" she said rather sarcastically.

Jacques looked at his wife as she stood there in her nightdress. Something in the tone of her voice had sent forth a warning signal to him. He loved his wife and he knew her very well, and he realized that he had better be diplomatic.

"A letter," Jacques said, "is a very important thing. In all the years that we have been together this is the first one we have received."

"The letter is mine." Once again the tone of her voice was hard. "It has my name on it." She went over to where the apron hung and took the letter out of her pocket and handed it to him.

"See," she said, "it has my name on it. Read it for yourself."

Jacques was puzzled. This really was strange and unusual behavior for Olivia. *Don't tell me,* he thought, *that she is in the family way; it has been so long since we had a baby around here.*

Jacques spoke and told her, "Olivia, you know very well I cannot read."

She appeared startled and bewildered.

"Olivia," he asked, "this . . . your letter, it has not even been opened. Why not?"

He watched his wife, and there was no sound in the room except for their breathing. Her whole body began to tremble, and Jacques realized that she was crying.

"What is it?" he asked her in great concern. His concern made her cry all the more.

"Oh, Jacques," she said, "all these years I have lied to you." And as she blew her nose in his big oversized handkerchief that she had made for him herself, she lifted her head from off of his shoulder and told him, "I . . . I . . .

I can't read either," and thus saying she began to cry so hard that it not only shook her body but his also.

As Jacques stood there comforting his wife many things that had puzzled him over the years became crystal clear to him. For instance both of them had wanted their children to learn to read and write and he had thought that Olivia would teach them, but the right time never came. "I have canning to do," she would say. "I must launder" or "I must iron," and on it went.

"Shh, shh," he told her.

"But you don't understand," she told him. "I have deceived you, and now I have a letter and I am frightened to find out what it says."

"There is someone who can read your letter," Jacques told her. "Right here in this very house."

"What are you talking about?"

"Yvonne," he told her. "She will be happy to read it for you."

Yvonne was awake now because she had heard the disturbance in the other room, and she lay there upon her makeshift bed on the floor and prayed for these dear people that she had come to know and love dearly. She oftentimes imagined them to be the family that she had never had.

Yvonne was so deeply involved in her thoughts that she hardly heard the light tapping at her door.

"Yvonne! Yvonne," Jacques said, "are you awake?"

"Yes, I will be out in a moment," Yvonne replied as she scurried about for her dress in the dark.

She came out of the room very concerned. "What is the matter?"

"Yvonne, come and sit here at the table, we do not want to wake the children. We would like you to do us a favor."

"For you and Olivia I will do anything, anything at all," she replied.

In the meantime Olivia was busying herself making coffee at the big black stove.

The oil lamp set upon the table was casting eerie shadows on the walls and the ceiling as the flames flickered about. They sat, the three of them, around the big round old-fashioned table silently until the coffee was ready. Quite a photograph it would have made, too: a young nun sitting there in part of her habit. She had been so concerned about what was going on that she forgot to put on her veil. This was a big no no and if it were revealed she could be in big trouble with the convent.

The middle-aged gentleman sitting there with his beard growth of the past day had merely put his trousers on and he had no shirt on.

Yvonne had never seen a man with his shirt off, and felt fascinated by the growth of hair on his chest. She could feel herself flush and quickly turned her face away.

Last but certainly not least was the middle-aged woman, who looked every bit her age and whose hard work showed in the character of her face. Time was certainly catching up to her. She had a homemade nightgown on, made from feed bags. She did not have time to dye such a thing as a nightdress. That was for city women. She had all that she could handle with her house and children.

Finally the coffee was ready and Olivia poured three large cups of it in the big old-fashioned mugs that had been a wedding gift to them from Jacques' parents.

Yvonne knew from experience that no one rushed Jacques and Olivia. In their own good time they would reveal what this was all about.

Olivia sat at the table, then turned and looked at Jacques and he nodded his head. Olivia put her hand in her big apron pocket and took out her letter.

Slowly she handed it to Yvonne, and as Yvonne reached for it Olivia asked in a voice that she must have had as a little girl, "Please, will you read my letter to us?"

Yvonne merely nodded her head and very slowly and deliberately opened the letter, so as not to rip it.

Jacques reached over and silently took Olivia's work-worn hand into his own work-worn hand.

When the ritual of opening the envelope was over Yvonne removed the single sheet of paper from the envelope and asked them, "Are you ready?" In unison they both nodded their heads and leaned forward so as not to miss a single word.

"This letter comes from a town named Patois." As she spoke these words Olivia's whole body stiffened and she placed her hand over her heart. As neither Olivia or Jacques spoke, Yvonne continued on.

" 'Dear Olivia. This letter is from your brother George and as he can neither read nor write I am doing it for him. My name is Harland Bolivier. I am the doctor here in town. It is with great regret I inform you that your father, Marc Le Beau, died on June 12. George has eleven children and cannot take care of your mother. All of the children here have decided that your mother, Adelaide Le Beau, should come out to live with you as you are the eldest daughter and all feel that this is your responsibility. We have all given a portion of money to pay for her train fare. She will be arriving on July first. Please take your obligation seriously. She is your mother too. From your brother, George Le Beau.'"

Yvonne looked up to see the reaction on Olivia's face. "There is more," she said. "In the bottom of the letter is a postscript: 'Please return us the money if you are able.'"

Jacques patted Olivia's hand affectionately. "Our family is growing by leaps and bounds," he smiled. "And I thought that you were going to tell me that you were going to have another baby."

"What are we going to do?" said Olivia. "Our house is bursting at the seams now."

"Don't you worry your pretty head about it," Jacques told her. "We will manage as always. Come ladies, it is very late and we have a big day ahead of us. Do you realize tomorrow is July first?"

The next morning Olivia told all the children the news, and the house was filled with excitement and everyone was bustling about doing a special housecleaning preparing for the coming of their Grand-mère.

Jacques took the horse and buggy and was off to the train depot. Olivia did not go, saying she wanted to prepare a special meal, but in all reality she was a nervous wreck as she had not seen her mother since the day that she and Jacques had been married almost twenty years ago.

Jacques arrived at the train depot and inquired about the next train, which he was told would not arrive for several hours more. He busied himself around town by purchasing some nails and various other things needed about his farm.

Finally the train arrived and there was only one passenger dropped off. She was a tall woman whose face was decorated by a multitude of wrinkles and whose hands decried an age that was beyond her true age. She was obviously a woman who had worked beyond her physical capabilities.

Jacques went to the woman and said, "Are you Madame Le Beau?" She did not answer him but nodded her head in such a manner as if to say, "I am too old and tired to speak."

He took the bundle that she had in her hands and tossed it on the wagon and he took her in his arms and put her on the seat in the wagon. Silently and slowly he drove the team to his home. The woman never said a word to him all the way back.

Life seems to become more complicated all the time, he thought.

Chapter Thirty-four
A New Life

Alexandre was once again sitting by his fireside, and Genevieve sat with him. It seemed that their times together were growing shorter and shorter, as he had need of more and more rest every day.

He turned to Genevieve. "I always wanted to have the last laugh with those brats of mine and I will have it too, thanks to you," he chuckled. "Yesterday when we were talking I told you the story of how your grandmother and I met."

"Yes, Grand-père, you did tell me, and it was a fascinating story, too. Poor Grand-mère with a man like that for a father! What ever happened to him? Does anyone know?"

"Yes," the old man sighed almost involuntarily. "The next day after Yvonne found Simone and her mother he was found by some hunters deep in the woods. He had taken the coward's way out and hung himself! He died in the same manner that he lived, like a coward!" He spat the words out. "It's a darn good thing he did, too, because there were many people who would have gone and killed him if they ever got their hands on him.

"This, of course, the beating I mean, was the cause of poor Imogene's problem. She was such a tiny child, she never again entered into the real world. Her poor brain had been too badly damaged."

"I know, of course, that you went back after Grand-mère, but I would like to know the circumstances."

Alexandre looked into the fire and watched the flames leaping to and fro. The redness of the flame caught his attention briefly and he wondered how the yellow and blue tips could evolve from the same wood that made the flames red.

"My Maman and I took the train back home and neither Simone nor myself had dry eyes. I had been so fascinated on the way up and thought the trip so exciting, but I hated the train on the way back as it was taking me further and further away from my beloved.

"Maman, of course, hated Simone and would not say anything nice about her. Things came to a head one day when I told her if she did not be quiet I would move out of the house we shared with Ma Tante Jeannot. After that she kept her mouth shut because she knew that I meant what I said."

"Why didn't she like Grand-mère?" Genevieve could not understand anyone not liking Grand-mère.

"It was not just the fact that it was Simone; she would have done the same thing about any woman I was interested in.

"When we got back home I took a second job and Maman tried her darnedest to get the money away from me, but I had a goal and she was not successful. I saved every penny so I could return to Canada and bring Simone back as my wife." He again paused and looked into the fire, as if he were actually reliving the moments. "Maman could never get the best of Simone," he smiled wryly.

"Simone had told me that she would never leave without her Maman and of course I would never have expected her to do such a thing. So in order to marry Simone I had to be able to care for her Maman, too." He turned and looked at his granddaughter. "I would have done anything for Simone.

"After two years and a lot of hard work, I felt that I had enough money saved to go and get Simone and her mother. I bought myself an old car and cleaned it all and fixed it up and was ready to be on my way.

"I invited Maman to come along so she could see her mother and sister and be there at the wedding and she put up a terrible fuss, saying that I was not going to marry Simone. I told her that I was going and if she wanted to come she had better be quiet!

"I did not write to tell Simone when I was coming, as I wanted to surprise her. When we got there, we were the ones who were surprised."

"What do you mean?" She spoke softly, so as not to spoil the mood. She wanted to hear all about it.

"Well," he cleared his throat several times, "the reason that I had bought the car was that I felt it would be easier for Imogene to travel that way than in the train.

"We arrived at Olivia and Jacques' house early in the afternoon, and no one was around! Not one single, solitary soul! Not even one of the children. The house was all locked up, too.

"I suggested that Maman and Aunt Jeannot sit in the car and wait as I walked over to Simone's house. I took one look—the house had burned to the ground! There was nothing salvageable!

"My heart was broken because I knew enough about fires to know that if anyone had been in the house at the time of the fire, they would have perished.

"I was in a state of shock; had something happened to Simone? If something had happened to her, I wanted to die, too. I sat down on the ground just staring at the blackened mess that had been a house. I put my head down into my hands and began to cry. I could not help myself.

"I don't really know how long I sat there like that, but I know that it was a good long time!"

"Then I heard a soft voice. 'Alexandre, can it really be you?'

"Once again I met the woman I loved all messed up, sitting in the dirt and rubbing my eyes with my blackened hands. I was not a pretty sight at all!

" 'Simone,' I said, 'Simone.' I kept saying her name over and over, 'Simone,' and I stood to my feet and put my arms about her and we both cried.

" 'Alexandre,' she was still sobbing. 'Alexandre, it was so terrible.' And she began to cry all over again. Her body began to shake uncontrollably and I removed my jacket and put it around her shoulders.

"Simone looked at me. 'I cannot believe that you are here just when I need you the most. Alexandre, you don't realize how much I missed you!'

" 'Yes, I do; remember, I was also separated from you. Now tell me what is the matter?'

" 'Maman.' She tried valiantly to hold back her tears, but they flowed anyway.

" 'What about your Maman?' I asked her.

"'Maman is dead and so is your Grand-mère!'

"I felt as though I had been kicked by a mule. 'In the fire?'

" 'Yes,' and all of a sudden the words began to tumble out of her mouth like water over a falls.

" 'Aunt Olivia was ill and she sent for Yvonne and me. Grand-mère said for us to go and not to worry about Maman as she would watch out for her, so we hurried off. You know, Alexandre, that I very seldom allowed anyone else to care for Maman.'

" 'Yes, Simone, I know that.'

" 'Well,' she started again, 'Grand-mère had not been feeling too well herself of late and she used to fall asleep quite often as she sat in her rocking chair. And Maman seemed to be fascinated by fire lately.'

"I hugged her even more tightly. 'Go on.'

" 'The nearest anyone can figure out is that Grand-mère fell asleep on her chair and the fire probably went out and Maman tried to light it, and she caught on fire and so did the whole building!'

" 'The fire was too far gone before it was noticed and they both burned beyond recognition! It's all my fault. If I had been here like I should have been, it never would have happened!'

" 'Simone!' I shook her slightly. 'That is enough of that kind of talk, it is not your fault. Have you seen Maman and Jeannot?'

" 'Yes, I have met them. Jeannot seems like a nice person, but I can sense that your Maman does not like me.'

" 'Well,' I said, 'Maman will have to deal with her own problems, and as for us, we are going to have a wedding! Simone, I love you enough for a dozen Mamans. Were you surprised to find out I was here?' " I asked her.

" 'Yes, I was going to write tonight and tell you what had happened.'

"Two days later we were married in our special place in the pine grove. Simone wore a pale blue dress, and she let her hair hang down as I asked her to. She had made a garland of flowers to wear in her hair and it was beautiful. As I stood there I knew I was the luckiest man alive, and the proudest.

"Simone and I had talked it over and we decided to take a week and go off by ourselves. We had not told anyone else about it and when Maman found out about it, she flew into a rage and wanted to come with us!"

"She did?" Genevieve's eyes opened wide in amazement. "Did you take her?"

"Of course not. Jeannot and Yvonne and Olivia quickly put a stop to that." He smiled contentedly. "And if they hadn't I certainly would have!" he said with a twinkle in his eyes. "Yes, I certainly would have!"

Chapter Thirty-five
Alexandre and Philippe

Genevieve was walking with her grandfather into the living room. She held onto his arm, but she could feel he was getting weaker and weaker day by day.

They had asked Anna to join them, but she too knew that the time was drawing near and wanted them to have every moment possible together.

Besides, she thought to herself, *Alexandre and I have discussed all these things many times while Genevieve was away and we were the only two around.*

"You look dashing today, Grand-père," Genevieve said as she looked him over with satisfaction. He was dressed in grey trousers, a lighter grey shirt, and a dark sweater the color of his trousers, and a bright red tie.

He observed his granddaughter closely. "You look delightful yourself, my dear." They both laughed.

She had on a brown slacks suit that suited her coloring very well; her blouse was beige satin with a bow around the neck. He decided that even though he considered "pants" men's clothes, she had the knack of wearing them and still looking feminine in them.

He approved of his granddaughter; she was a well-rounded individual who had lived up to his and Simone's expectations. She was a nice person, thoughtful and generous, not given to bragging, and not many could put something over on her. She had his temper but knew when to use it and when to control it. All in all he liked her as well as loved her.

"Genevieve, I have remembered a few more things that might be of interest to you."

"What is it, Grand-père?"

"One time you asked me where we got our money. . . ." his voice trailed off.

"Yes, I remember."

"Simone and I had been married for a little more than two years. I had taken a job as a salesman to support us all. I was responsible for two households now; the house where Maman and Jeannot lived and our little household. These were not houses really, but they were two little apartments. Simone and I now had a son and another child on the way, and I hated being away from her so much, but it could not be helped; I had my responsibilities.

"I was working for a shoe manufacturer. We sold everything from baby shoes to farmers' work boots. I was on a trip into Boston when all of a sudden, in broad daylight, three men came up behind me and said, 'Come on bub!' in nasty voices.

" 'I don't have much money, but you can have what I have,' I told them.

" 'We don't want your lousy money; get in that car or else.' "

"What did you do, Grand-père?"

"I got into the car. What else could I do? They had a gun in my back.

" 'Where are you taking me?' I asked. 'And what are you going to do with me? I don't know any of you, so what can you possibly want from me?'

" 'Shut your face! You'll find out soon enough what's going on. You don't want that pretty kisser of yours messed up, do ya?'

"I decided to sit back quietly. They drove me around for about twenty minutes and then pulled up in front of a beautiful mansion with a long spiral driveway in front of it and very well-manicured lawns and flowers.

"I decided then that this must be a gangster's house, because of the way I had been brought there.

"I really thought that they were going to kill me, so I prayed for Simone; could she live through another terrible experience? Would she believe no matter what these men said that I was innocent?

" 'Stop your daydreaming and get outta that car and don't try no funny business either, if you know what's good for ya!'

"I got out of the limousine and stood as straight as I could and we all walked into the large house.

"Everything in there was absolutely gorgeous and I was amazed by it all. We stood in the foyer for a few moments until I noticed an old man being wheeled in.

"I did not realize who it was until a moment later.

" 'Okay, you guys, get the hell outta here. Now!'

" 'Yes, sir, call us if you need us.'

"The old man wheeled his chair as close to me as he could get. He stared at me for a long moment and he said, 'Well, well, if it isn't the little bastard!'

"Then I knew who it was! Only one person that I knew could be so vicious. It was my father! After all those years!

"I turned toward the door so that I could walk out.

" 'You are still a foolish little bastard, aren't you? I have guards tending the door and all over the place. I have eight dobermans keeping guard and they are trained to tear a man apart!'

"He sat back in his wheelchair and laughed nastily.

" 'What can you possibly want with me? You must know that I hate your guts.'

" 'Sure you do, and I wouldn't have it any other way either.

" 'Go up the stairs and the second door on your left is your room. Get cleaned up and come down immediately for dinner.'

" 'I don't want any of your dinner!'

" 'Suit yourself, but believe me, you shall be at the dinner table with me!'

"I did as I was told and I had to admit when I saw the feast that had been prepared I could not resist.

"As we were at dinner he looked at me very intently and said, 'Thank God you look like me and not like that mouse of a mother of yours.'

" 'I don't appreciate your speaking about my Maman in such a manner!' I retorted.

" 'You listen to me. I personally do not give a damn if you appreciate it or not! I am the king in this mansion, and whatever I say goes.' He had put a lot of emphasis on the 'I.'

"I was puzzled and at first I had decided to bide my time and not ask questions, but I found I could not take the waiting.

"My father and I were alone at the large dining room table; one servant bustled about anticipating our needs before we even knew about them. The food was excellent. I could not remember ever having better roast beef. I ate my fill and did not know if I could handle the dessert of strawberries glace, but once I got a taste of it I could not resist finishing it all.

" 'What is it that you want of me after all these years?' I hoped that I did not sound the way that I felt inside.

" 'Can't wait to find out, huh?' he sneered. 'Well, wheel me into the parlor where we can sit and talk like gentlemen and you will find out.'

"The parlor was big enough to hold a ball in. I was amazed, but the most awesome sight in that room was the massive fireplace that took up a whole wall. The fireplace that I later built for us was a replica of that one.

" 'Can you light a fire in a fireplace?'

" 'I have never done it before, but I am willing to try,' I replied to my father's request.

" 'Well what are you waiting for?' He was obviously irritated with me. He started to give curt instructions and I obeyed each order that I was given and finally there was a glowing fire in the fireplace, and the room seemed cozy rather than massive.

" 'What do you think of my house?' he asked.

" 'I think,' I said, 'that it is very impressive indeed.'

" 'What has struck you as the most impressive part?'

" 'Well,' and I stopped to think for a moment. 'At first I was struck by the spiral staircase, then I loved all the crystal chandeliers, and the very impressive bathroom and bedroom. But on second thought, I believe, it is the fireplace that impresses me the most.'

" 'Why?'

" 'Because it is warm and cozy and giving. Perhaps because I like sitting beside an open fire. Certainly, you did not bring me here to talk about how I like your house.' I smiled wryly.

"The older man looked at the younger man as though he was sizing me up. 'It isn't my house, it's your house.' He was relishing watching his son's face as he made the announcement.

"I sat there and my mouth hung open and I was speechless. My father just sat there laughing. 'Gotcha!'

" 'But,' I sputtered, 'why? Surely you are not toying with me.'

" 'Do you or don't you like the house?' he said angrily.

" 'Of course I like the house; I am not a fool!'

" 'Oh!' My father replied nastily, 'I though perhaps you had a better house than this one.'

"My own anger was beginning to rise. 'You know very well that I do not have a house!'

" 'I know everything there is to know about you! Believe me!'

" 'Then you must know for a fact that I do not want anything from you!'

" 'What a noble person. "I don't want anything from you!" ' he mimicked me. 'Well, remember this, young man, one does not always get everything one wants. Now,' he asked, 'will you do me the courtesy of listening to me for about an hour, and then you can hate my guts for the rest of your life?'

" 'I will listen.' I thought to myself, *It is only because I want to know what is going on.*

"Philippe sat in his wheelchair and carefully looked me over. *It is too late for us*, he thought. Basically, he liked what he saw. I was a handsome man and looked a lot like Philippe. I was neat and clean and took good care of myself. From all reports he had received about me, he found out that I was an honorable man.

"Philippe cleared his throat and started to speak, but before he got any words out a nurse came in and said, 'Excuse me, but it is time for your medications.' She handed him some pills and a glass of water. All the time she was not watching him but looking at me, obviously very interested.

" 'Excuse me, Rebecca, I want you to meet my son, Alexandre.'

"She walked over to where I was sitting, making her hips sway all the way, and gushed, 'I really am happy to meet you, I really am.'

"My face turned beet red and I looked the other way.

"Philippe laughed. 'There it is, Alexandre; you can have a good time while you're here. Rebecca is very willing to be friendly with you.' He laughed.

" 'No thank you,' I said huffily. 'I find comfort only in the arms of my wife and that is all I need or want.'

" 'Must be some woman!'

" 'Yes,' I said. 'She is!'

" 'Suit yourself. At your age I would never pass up an opportunity like that!'

" 'Please remember,' I said nastily, 'that I am not you!'

" 'I only have an hour so I must hurry and talk with you. After that I must retire. I know that you do not approve of me and never will. I agree that I have made many mistakes in my life, but I cannot change all that now, as it is too late.

" 'I never cared very much for my father, just as you don't like me very much. My father was a businessman and very conservative. My main thought in life was having a good time and I did, too, in my own way. I could always twist my mother around my little finger and she always came through with the money I wanted.

" 'My father disowned me, but fortunately for me he died first and left everything he had to mother, and seeing that I was her only son, she left every cent to me.'

" 'When I was a young man I loved to be around the ladies, and this is how I got mixed up with your Maman. You see, I never loved Elisabeth, but it was the challenge of the conquest that got to me. I had never slept with a virgin before, and she was so naive that she believed all the garbage that I told her.

" 'Unfortunately, she got herself in the family way and both of our fathers had a fit about it and came after me with a shotgun and forced me to marry her. She really thought that I would change and become a happily married man. Poor soul, she never had a chance.

" 'I really couldn't have cared less about the whole mess, and when you were born to me you were just her little bastard. The only one of my children that I had any feelings for was Napoleon.

" 'All these years I thought he was still alive and that I would leave everything in his name. You can believe it or not, but I cried when I found out that he was dead and you were the only one alive. You are my only living relative.

" 'I struggled with the idea, but yesterday the doctor told me that I only have two weeks left, so I have to get everything in order right away.'

"I spoke up and said, 'There are many charitable organizations around.'

" 'I am not minded to give to charity!' he spat back at me. 'My father and his father and grandfather before him worked long and hard to make all this money and it will stay in the Boisvert family, whether you like it or not.

" 'I am sorry that I did not get to know you better before this time, and I am not about to pretend that I am the doting father now! It is just that, as I said, you are my only living relative, so you get the jackpot.'

" 'I never asked . . .'

" 'You are right, you have never asked, but the matter does not hang on if you asked or not, it hinges on who I want to give it to. You're it, sonny boy, whether you like it or not.

" 'I will apologize to you about one thing, though, and that is about the method I employed to get you here. But let's face it, you would never have answered a letter or a polite phone call, would you?'

" 'You are right on that count, I never would answer anything from you.'

" 'Good,' my father said. 'Now we both know where we stand.'

"Neither man blinked an eye and neither one would give an inch to the other.

"I looked at my father and said, 'The way I figure it you are only about . . . well,' I drawled, 'mid-forties. Why should a fairly young man like you be dying?'

" 'Ah,' Philippe said, 'I thought you would never ask. I have, as is said in polite circles, a social disease, and there is no cure.' Now he laughed. 'That is something I sincerely regret!

" 'Now, Alexandre, you were brought here not to debate if you want your inheritance or not, but to receive training so you will know just what is what, and to make sure that you get every single cent that is coming to you.'

"I was puzzled. 'Training? What kind of training?'

" 'You will find out soon enough. The training begins tomorrow.'

" 'How long will it take?'

" 'Four, maybe five days, depending on how you apply yourself.'

" 'Four or five days,' I repeated. 'May I call my wife so that she will not worry?'

" 'You may call her, but only if you do not tell her where you are and what you are doing here.'

" 'I have never lied to Simone before. She will surely sense it if I do so now.'

" 'Either you do it my way or not at all!' His attitude was hateful.

" 'I will do it your way, so that I may spare Simone from worry.'

"I walked over to the French telephone and called Simone. I could hear the baby crying in the background. 'Simone, this is Alexandre, what is the matter with Samuel?'

" 'Alexandre, where are you? I have been worried about you. I tried to call you earlier today and your employer said you had not come back in.'

" 'What is the matter, Simone?'

" 'It is your Maman; she is in the hospital with pneumonia.'

" 'Calm down now and tell me what the doctor said. Is it serious?'

" 'The doctor says that she'll be all right, but you know Maman, she is screaming like a banshee for you.'

" 'Simone, listen to me. I cannot come as I have been called away for some special training and as long as Maman is not critical and is being taken care of I cannot come home for about five more days. I will call you tomorrow night. Take good care of yourself and the babies.' I paused for a moment. 'Simone?'

" 'Yes?' she said.

" 'Don't worry, everything will be fine. Don't let Maman worry you.'

"Philippe looked at me sarcastically. 'I see,' he said, 'Elisabeth is still up to her old ways.'

" 'What do you mean?' I asked him.

" 'Oh, certainly you know how she is a maneuverer of people. You know,' he said, 'I'm really surprised that she let you get married.'

" 'She had nothing to say about it,' I replied. 'I made the decision and got married.'

" 'I bet you that it is not a bed of roses for your wife! She must be a saint! I know Elisabeth would not make things easy for anyone.'

" 'Simone,' I stood up to my full height, 'is a special lady.'

" 'Look,' Philippe said, 'let's not waste time arguing about your mother, it is not my favorite subject. There is something that I want you to know before we start.'

" 'And just what is that?' I asked him.

"He looked at his son. 'I am truly amazed at how much you look like me, you must really be my kid after all.' He laughed and began to cough and could not stop and suddenly he spit up bright red blood.

"I became concerned. 'Is there anything that I can do for you?'

"Philippe shook his head, and even when the spasm was over he waited for a while before he began speaking again.

" 'Look here,' he said. 'I know that I am no prize, but I am your father and that can't be helped. Before I go to bed tonight I want to tell you that even though you cannot be proud of me you do not have to be ashamed of the money. It was all earned through honest means and a lot of sweat and tears. Not one cent was earned dishonestly, I guarantee you that!

" 'I want you to spend the next few days learning about all my property and assets so that you will know what to do and how to handle the finances.

" 'Alexandre,' his voice trailed off, 'I like you; somehow I never thought that I would, but I do like you, and I am happy that I got to see you. Don't change; be what you are, a man of honor. Your Simone is fortunate to have you, don't let your Maman tear your marriage apart.

" 'I took the liberty of buying you a new car, because your other one is falling apart. If you don't want it you can throw it away when I am gone, but for this little time I have, please indulge me.'

" 'I don't know what to say either,' I said. 'I like you, too. Somehow, you are not the monster that I pictured you to be.'

"Philippe sighed. 'There is an old saying, "better late than never." Can we let bygones be bygones? Alexandre,' he was crying now, 'would you allow me to see my grandson and daughter-in-law before I die?'

" 'Yes, I will bring them here to see you, when all this training is over. Agreed?'

" 'Agreed!' Philippe smiled. 'I am glad that I didn't surprise you with the inheritance after my death and that we will get to know each other a little.'

"I went back home after the training and got Simone and little Samuel and brought them to meet my father. He cried when he saw little Samuel and said, 'He looks just like my old man.'

"My father looked at Simone and said, 'You are even more beautiful than Alexandre described you.'

"A week to the day that we left, he passed away and I followed all his instructions and I received an inheritance so large I could hardly believe it, and it changed all of our lives, too!"

Genevieve asked her grandfather, "Whatever happened to his house?"

"Well," Alexandre said, "your grandmother and I gave it away. We gave it to the nun, Yvonne, who was so kind to your Grand-mère and she turned it into a home for homeless girls."

"Isn't that charity?" Genevieve asked him.

"Yes," he said, "it is, but remember what my father said to me. 'When it becomes yours you are free to do with it as you will,' and I did."

Chapter Thirty-six
The Last Laugh

Genevieve gave birth to a son and everyone expected his name to be Alexandre, but Genevieve said, "No. His name is going to be Harold after his father. Who knows, maybe our next son will be Alexandre."

Surprise of surprises, Anna finally consented to marry Dr. Livernois, and the wedding was held right there in the living room of the rambling old country house. Anna of course kept her "job" with Genevieve and Harold. She and the good doctor were given Alexandre's old room and Anna's room was made into a nursery for "Little Harry," as they all called him.

Genevieve knew that the time had now come for their voyage back home and the springing of surprises.

One day Genevieve and Harold went shopping and came back home with a great big motor home. She and Harold were both very excited and showed Anna and Joseph all around it.

"Look here," Harold said, "there is a shower and a toilet, there's an oven for Anna to cook on and best of all there is room to sleep twelve, so we should have enough room as there are only five of us."

"Five," Anna repeated.

Harold hugged her. "You don't think we are going without you and Joe, do you?"

Anna's eyes opened wide in wonder. "I have never been to the United States."

Genevieve went over to her and hugged her. "Well then, it is high time that you did! Anna, I need you to teach me how to be a grand lady."

Harold made a special crib for little Harry in the motor home. It was padded all around so that he would not harm himself. Then off they went.

When they arrived at their destination Genevieve went into her rich lady act, demanding this and that and the other thing, and getting it, too.

Money certainly speaks, she thought.

She wrote invitations out to all the names Grand-père had given her, to all his children and grandchildren and their spouses.

The invitations were as follows:

You are cordially invited to a memorial service in honor of Mr. Alexandre Henry Boisvert, who passed away on December eleventh of last year. These services are to be held on April twentieth at ten A.M. Father John Weyth will be officiating.

Sincerely yours,
Mr. and Mrs. Harold Cramer

Genevieve wished that she could have been there to see certain ones receive their invitations.

When the messenger came to Samuel's office in the town hall, Samuel thought that he had received an invitation to some grand party somewhere important. When he opened the envelope, his face blanched and his jaw dropped open.

"What the hell is this? Gotta be some kind of a joke."

He picked up the phone and called his brother Isaac. "Ike, you should see what I just got in the mail, I mean by private messenger. It's an invitation to the old man's funeral is what it is. I never heard of the people who sent the damn thing. You?"

"You got one, too? And all the kids? Well, I'll be."

"You gonna go?"

Isaac replied, "Of course I'm going. How else are we going to find out what is going on?"

"Yeah, you're right. Uh, oh, here comes Rachel, you can bet she got one, too! Talk to you later." He hung up the phone unceremoniously.

"Samuel!" Rachel was out of breath. "I gotta talk to you." She plunked herself down in one of the old office chairs.

"What is going on? Nobody tells me nothin'."

"Calm down, Rach, we all got the same thing."

"Well," she said curtly, "watcha going to do about it?"

"What can I do? I'm gonna go and find out what it is all about, that's what I'm gonna do, for crying out loud, it's all I can do!"

"Do you suppose that it is true?" Rachel asked.

"How am I supposed to know, for heaven's sake?" And he wiped off the top of his head with his everpresent handkerchief. Samuel had put on quite a few pounds over the years and was now the bigger of the two brothers. This weight gain caused him to always be sweating, which was a thorn in his side.

The years had taken their toll on Rachel also. She had put on a few pounds herself but seemed unaware of the fact; to herself Rachel was still in her twenties.

"Rachel," Samuel said, "I've been thinking, if the old man just died like this thing says we may be in for some kind of inheritance. For crying out loud, we're still his kinfolk aren't we? Where do you suppose the old geezer was for all those years?" he asked his sister.

"I'm sure I don't know," she said with a shake of her head.

"Isaac and I are gonna go and see what's going on."

"What about me, what am I, the black sheep or something?" she pouted.

Rachel had always had a knack for exasperating her older brother. "Look, Rachel, you wanna come, come! Just don't start your bull with me!"

"Calm down, for Pete's sake, before you have a stroke or something. You know, Samuel, you really oughta go on a diet."

"Shut up, Rachel; my weight is none of your business."

"I sure could use a raise in my trust fund, that's for sure. We can hardly make ends meet with the little pittance I get," she sighed.

"Come off of it, you dumb broad; you been living pretty good on that fifty grand a year, and not doing anything for it either." His face was turning red.

"How'd you know how much I got?" she asked him, somewhat perturbed that he knew that much about her circumstances.

"Look," he said sarcastically, "I make it my business to know these things. How would you feel if you had to work two jobs like I do?"

"Samuel, you know darn well you're making money hand over fist in that place, not only on the food but on all your illegal back room transactions. Remember, I make it my business to know what is going on with you and Isaac, too." She smiled at him triumphantly.

"Lady, if you know what's good for you ya better mind your own business!"

"You're really scaring me, Samuel," she laughed.

"Look," he said, "I'm busy. I'll pick you up at nine-thirty." He picked up some papers and acted busy so she would leave, which she did silently.

At last the big day was at hand. Genevieve prepared herself in a way that she had never before done in her lifetime. Everything about her was perfection. The dress that Grand-père had bought her for this occasion was absolutely beautiful. It was a special kind of satin imported from France.

The dress had been made by a special tailor that had been flown in and had been fitted perfectly to Genevieve's slender figure. The dress was a light blue color and the fabric was such that it hung in gentle folds caressing her body modestly. The lace around the collar and around the wrists had all been handmade and was of a slightly darker blue than the dress. There was also lace around the outline of her bodice.

She had on a necklace that really was a sapphire pendant surrounded by diamonds and the chain was made of smaller sapphires and diamonds alternating.

She had her hair done in a French twist with diamond and sapphire combs holding her hair back. Never in her lifetime, with perhaps the exception of their wedding day, had she applied makeup so carefully.

Harold walked into their bedroom and whistled. "Wow," he said, "is that really you?"

"No," she said, looking herself over in the mirror, "it is an illusion created by Grand-père."

"Don't worry, Babe, it's not for long, and remember, it's almost over with." He leaned over and kissed her lightly on the cheek.

"I guess you're right," she sighed heavily.

"Come on, Babe, think of it as fun, and if these people are like you and Grand-père claimed, it's gonna be a ball."

"Easy for you to say," she said teasingly. "All you have to do is look pretty."

Harold laughed. "I'm going to go and check on Little Harold."

Genevieve and Harold, along with Anna and Joseph, drove to the church in a limousine and arrived late purposefully. Everyone was in the church waiting and the priest went to the front of the church and made the announcement. "Excuse me ladies and gentlemen, but we must wait for a few moments as some of the guests have come from a long distance and have not yet arrived."

"Oh, no," Samuel muttered under his breath, "as if all I have to do is sit around in a church all day."

Of course the plan had been for Genevieve to arrive late so she could make her "grand entrance" and be sure everyone was looking.

When the limousine pulled up in front of the church and Harold got out and took Genevieve's hand she looked at him, "Harold, I think I'm going to be sick."

"No," he answered her, "you are not going to be sick. Pull yourself together."

Dr. Livernois came over to her. "Take a couple of deep breaths, Genevieve, and you will be all right."

Anna came over and said, "Remember we are behind you all the way."

She had thought it foolish when Grand-père wanted her to make a "grand entrance" and she had to admit she had not understood his reasoning or logic, but she soon enough found out.

She had her full-length ranch mink coat over her gown and she had left it open for effect. She took Harold's arm as they entered the church. Anna and Joseph were a few steps behind them.

She could almost hear Grand-père's voice: "You must walk slowly, and hold your head up, keep your eyes straight ahead of you."

She found that once she began, she was not nervous about it. *After all*, she thought, *I'm doing it for his sake*.

As though it had been prearranged everyone turned to see who these faraway guests were. Genevieve did not look at anyone, she kept her eyes fixed straight ahead. She heard someone say, "It's Genevieve!"

When they arrived at the front pew Harold helped Genevieve take off her mink coat and he casually tossed it on the pew beside him as if it had no more value than an old shoe. All eyes were fixed upon them.

Genevieve turned toward the priest and nodded her head in authority and he rose and began the little memorial service.

The service did not last long. There was the usual eulogy and Genevieve had added a few things to it and had the priest make special mention of the fact that over three hundred people had come forth at the funeral to pay homage to the old man because of all the help he had given them.

Samuel was livid. *The old man really must have been off his rocker! Imagine giving our inheritance to strangers.* In his heart he really meant "my inheritance." *That little witch,* he thought, *when I get done with her she'll wish she had never come back!*

Rachel's head was filled with similar thoughts. *Look at her; who does she think she is? Why, she has Maman's engagement ring on. That ring belongs to me and I'm gonna get it, too!*

Isaac sat there and was amused by the whole thing. *This must be one of Papa's pranks. Genevieve would have never thought of something like this.* He really did not care, as he had received his inheritance a long time ago and besides that he was making more money than he and Susannah could use in two lifetimes.

After the priest had read the twenty-third Psalm, he nodded toward Harold, and Harold stood up and slowly walked to the front of the church.

"My wife, Genevieve, and myself have reserved a room at the Mulberry Inn on Pinecrest Avenue. We would like for all of you to attend. There will be refreshments. There is a luncheon being served, and after that there will be a showing of the will. We thank you all for coming."

Having thus spoken he walked over to the pew and picked up Genevieve's coat and helped her put it on and escorted her out in much the same manner as they had come in. Once in the back of the church they hurried down the steps and into the limousine as quickly as they could and sped off before anyone could get to them.

Genevieve told Harold, "Let's go and see how little Harry is for a minute and give everyone a chance to get to the inn before us."

Samuel had thought that he would get a chance to talk to Genevieve before she left the church, but he wasn't swift enough. "You better believe I'm going," he told Rachel. "What kinda talk is that, showing the will? Big deal, huh? I'm gonna call Blanche and tell her to get her rear end over to the inn, she wouldn't want to miss a meal there, that's for sure."

Even though he had never been faithful to Blanche, nor she to him, there was a strange kind of bond between them.

Genevieve and Harold went to check on the baby. He was three months old now and was at that smiley cooing age and he captured everyone's heart. He was a bright, alert child, and needless to say, they were very proud of him.

Genevieve rechecked her makeup and nails and clothing to make sure that there was not a flaw anywhere.

"Let's go," Harold told her, smiling. "You've stalled long enough."

"I'm coming," and she leaned over and kissed the baby on his little cheek and his eyes lit up and he smiled at her. "Be a good boy."

Meanwhile, as the old western movies used to say, back at the inn: Everyone was waiting in anticipation, some were happy in their anticipation while others were not.

Rachel positioned herself in such a way that Genevieve could not come in and be able to avoid her. Her tenacity paid off and as Genevieve came in she stepped directly in front of her.

"Genevieve, oh, my dear, I am so happy to see you," and she sent a kiss off somewhere in Genevieve's direction. "You don't realize how much we have missed you!"

"Aunt Rachel, my husband, Harold."

Harold did not say a word, merely bowed in her direction.

Samuel came running over. "Genevieve, Genevieve, I can't believe it's really you, after all these years." He offered Genevieve his cheek and she dutifully planted a little kiss there.

"Uncle Samuel, my husband, Harold."

Harold knew about Samuel and quickly offered him his hand in greeting, which Samuel shook limply because he couldn't get out of doing so. He quickly wiped his hands on his jacket, much to Harold's delight.

Just then the call came to sit and dine, and everyone took their assigned places. Genevieve had seen to it that Uncle Isaac and Aunt Susannah were seated at their table and her cousins Henry and Nicole were to be seated next to her.

Genevieve noticed how tired and worn out Nicole looked. Nicole's face brightened when Genevieve hugged her and both of her eyes filled up with tears.

Nicole and I were best friends when we were growing up, I hope we can still keep that friendship up, she thought, looking at Nicole.

"Are you married?" she asked Nicole.

"Well," Nicole said, "I was, but I'm not anymore."

Harold noticed that Genevieve was obviously enjoying the company of those seated at her table.

The meal was excellent, comprised of spinach salad, pressed duck or poached salmon, baked potatoes and several vegetable assortments. Dessert was peach flambé.

Harold went to the front of the dining room and announced, "Those of you who have finished eating, we would appreciate it if you would make your way to the Regency room, where we are going to gather. Thank you."

Harold came and took Genevieve and Anna and Joseph to where they would view the will.

The room had been set up like a movie theater, chairs were lined up in rows, and there was a large movie screen in the front.

Everyone seemed to be chatting amiably, and all were wondering just what was going on.

All of a sudden the lights were shut off and the screen lit up, and there he was! Grand-père! Genevieve's eyes filled with tears. Everything was impeccable. He had on grey trousers with a navy blue sports coat, a snow white shirt and a red-and-gray-striped tie. Every hair was in place. He was in the living room back home, sitting in his favorite recliner. Behind his chair in full view was a lovely picture of Simone as she was before her illness.

Genevieve had had this portrait made for her grandfather because it was his favorite. Simone was smiling in the picture and gave the impression that she was approving everything Alexandre was about to do.

He smiled and said, "I want to greet all of you today. Thank you, Genevieve, for arranging this family gathering of sorts.

"Just so as to leave no doubt in anyone's mind, I am Alexandre Henry Boisvert. I am the husband of Simone Archambeault, and together we had four children, one who has long since been deceased. Our eldest child is Samuel David Boisvert; next our son Isaac Solomon was born and after that Laura, who is deceased, and last of all Rachel.

"I would like to make something clear and this is designated especially for you, Samuel and Rachel: that although I am ninety-two years past, I am of sound mind, perhaps not sound of body, but certainly sound of mind.

"I have been examined by four different psychologists, and have affidavits from them that I am indeed of sound mind. I have stood before several judges and told them of my intentions and last but not least I have engaged the world's foremost attorneys for the express purpose that this will may not and cannot ever be broken.

"So I advise you both to forget any ideas you have about future litigation. In your presence today there is a gentleman, Joseph Livernois, who had been my personal physician for twenty years.

"Much of my will doesn't concern those of you who are present today so it will not be presented here, just what concerns those of you who are present.

"All of the affidavits, that is, copies of them, will be made available to whoever would care to see them.

"Now, hereby stating that I am of sound mind, I make the following bequests.

"One. To the home for wayward girls, that once was my father's home, I leave the sum of one hundred thousand dollars immediately, and a trust fund has been set up to provide them with the sum of fifteen thousand dollars per year.

"Two. I leave the church where today's service was held the sum of ten thousand dollars.

"I would like to make it clear that these endowments are from Simone and I and Genevieve also.

"Three. To the local horticultural society of which Simone was very fond I bequeath the sum of five thousand dollars.

"Four. To the Girl Scouts and Boy Scouts of this town I bequeath five thousand dollars to each group, to be used in this town only."

And the list went on and on.

"To each of my son Isaac's children except for Nicole I leave the one time sum of ten thousand dollars."

Nicole began to cry and Genevieve went over and put her arms across her shoulders. "Nicole, the will is not over yet."

Alexandre's voice was going on. "To my granddaughter Nicole I leave the following: The deed to a new house up on Front Street, which Genevieve will give to her immediately. The house has been totally structured to be handicapped accessible. It is also completely furnished with all the medical equipment you need for your son, Russell. I pray that this little gift will help you in the care of your son. Nicole is also to receive the sum of twenty-five thousand dollars a year for the care of her son and of course herself. This is set up in a trust. By the way, Nicole, it is Genevieve who suggested these things to me and I agreed wholeheartedly.

"I must take a moment to admonish my son Isaac and his wife. How could you allow your daughter to become so destitute when you have so much money of your own? Remember, I know what you have because for the most part your Maman and I gave it to you. Shame on you both! She is in need of your help and moral support.

"My son Isaac has received all that he is going to receive from me, and he already knows that. He has made good his promise to me to keep his Maman's house in good condition. He has built himself up a business from which he derives more than an adequate income. He and Susannah have already inherited all Simone's and my worldly goods that we had in the house. Isaac has told me repeatedly that he is satisfied with this arrangement. There are several of my personal possessions that he will receive. They are of minor value but perhaps of some sentimental value to him. Genevieve will attend to this matter as she sees fit.

"Now it is my full intention to leave the balance of all my worldly possessions and all my money in any form whatsoever to my granddaughter, whom my wife and I adopted legally many years ago. This includes land, stocks and bonds, and any other investments I have made.

"This granddaughter is, of course, Genevieve Cramer, who has seen fit to take care of me and forego much of her own life to do so. I would like to say thank you to her for all of her tender care and love and kindness. It has not always been easy to care for an elderly, cantankerous man.

"Thank you, my dear," and he bowed slightly.

Genevieve's eyes were filled with tears and she realized just how much she really missed him.

"By now I believe that my son Samuel must be livid thinking that I have forgotten him and his sister Rachel. A word of caution to both of you: do not try to fight this will in any shape or form, or you will lose what you already have.

"I purposely refuse to leave anything to my son Samuel and my daughter Rachel. The reasons are as follows; both of them tried to have their Maman and I declared legally incompetent many years ago. They recognized us both as old fools and thought they had bested us on many occasions and we did not know it.

"Listen closely, Samuel and Rachel. Simone and I devised a plan many years ago that if something happened to either one of us the other would take Genevieve and move to a secret hideaway where neither one of you has been able to find us."

The more Alexandre spoke, the more glee Genevieve could detect in his eyes, although she could tell he was tiring.

"The reason we devised this plan is that we wanted to get away from our own children. We did not want Genevieve to grow up to be like any of you, and thank the good Lord she has not!

"Samuel, remember that I hold the papers on your restaurant, that is, the deed, which by now has been transferred to the hands of my son-in-law, Harold. I also know the amount of your finances and so does Genevieve. We know all about your diversion of funds to Switzerland.

"By the way, Samuel, it is seven years to the day that you had me declared legally dead and all of your so-called wheeling and dealings are now null and void."

Samuel was sweating up a blue streak now.

"Rachel, I am sure that you noticed Genevieve today in all her finery and your first thought, of course, being the selfish person that you are, was 'all these things should be mine.'

"If you had been the daughter you should have been, these things would have been left to you, but you chose not to be, therefore you also get nothing more than you are already getting if you behave yourself.

"Genevieve did not want to come here dressed like a queen, but I insisted. I wanted you to see that Alexandre Boisvert takes care of his own. My Genevieve is not a person of pretense, she is very much like Simone and I'm sure she would rather be home in her blue jeans with Harold and her son and my dear cousin Anna and my dearest friend Joseph. They are being taken care of by me.

"I want it made clear that much of the inheritance that Genevieve is receiving came from the inheritance she received when her parents died, which I wisely invested for her, and another large portion came from her worldwide concert tours.

"Isaac, I did not always approve of what you did, but I am thankful for the times we have had together the past twenty years. I thank you also that you thought enough of your Maman when she was alive to visit her every week. Those visits meant more to her than I could ever tell you.

"So in closing I leave to my son Samuel two things. One is the same little gift that each one of you here will receive as a remembrance, and the other is the watch that my father gave to me for Samuel when he was a little baby. The watch is very valuable, Samuel, and the stipulation is that upon your death the watch returns to Genevieve to give to one of her children.

"Now, in closing, to Rachel: I want you to remember, Rachel, that you are living in your sister Laura's house because of the goodness of Genevieve's heart, and you will receive your trust fund as long as you behave yourself! Should Genevieve so choose you could be left penniless, although I know about your secret accounts also. When your Maman was alive you chose to treat her like dirt and as though she were incompetent. Today I choose to treat you the same way. You shall receive all the cheap, tawdry costume jewelry that you thought was good enough for her while you wore diamonds.

"My dear children, today you have seen Alexandre Boisvert get even with you for all the pain you caused your Maman and I. I have the 'Last Laugh.' "

Alexandre began to laugh until the tears rolled down his face and before long everyone in the place was laughing.

Susannah turned to Isaac. "I love it; your brother and sister finally got what they deserve."

Samuel walked over to Rachel. "Well ya finally got yours!"

"So did you, Sammy boy!"

Samuel walked over to Genevieve and his blood pressure was up. "I suppose you think you're funny, missy?"

Genevieve looked him square in the eye. "Are you forgetting, Sammy boy, that I hold the purse strings now?"

He turned and walked abruptly away.

"Hey, Sammy," Genevieve called after him, "life will go on."

Somehow this struck her as hilarious and she began to laugh until her eyes filled with tears, and all the time she was looking up at the big screen where the image of Grand-père was. He was right; she had never had so much fun in her life.

"C'mon, Babe, let's go get little Harry so he can meet his cousins Nicole and Russell. We still have a job to do!"